About the Author

ROBBY BENSON, actor, writer, composer, and award-winning star of Broadway, film, stage, and the small screen, is now a highly esteemed professor of film studies at New York University. He also directed more than one hundred episodes of sitcoms, including *Friends* and an entire season of *Ellen*. He lives in both the Blue Ridge Mountains and New York City with his wife, singer Karla DeVito, and their two children.

Who
Stole the
Funny?

Who Stole the Funny?

A Novel of Hollywood

Robby Benson

HARPER ENTERTAINMENT

NEW YORK · LONDON · TORONTO · SYDNEY

FIRST EDITION

Designed by Nicola Ferguson

Library of Congress Cataloging-in-Publication Data is available upon
request.
ISBN: 978-0-06-124500-8
ISBN-10: 0-06-124500-3
07 08 09 10 11 ❖/RRD 10 9 8 7 6 5 4 3 2 1

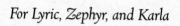

For Lyric, Zephyr, and Karla

Acknowledgments

The phrase "I would like to acknowledge" trivializes the love, life-dedication, and guidance of those who allowed me to learn from their expertise and tireless compassion, and took me safely under their wings. I'd like to start at the beginning: Jerry Segal, Ann Benson Segal, my father and mother, continue to love, teach, and find creative ways to always be there for me and for my family. My father also taught me *The Funny* at a very early age, and it seemed my job in life to try to make my sister, Shelli Segal, laugh. A laugh from Shelli, and I had purpose in life. Dad, Mom, Shelli, I love you so dearly.

I'd also "like to acknowledge" Wendalyn Nichols who has the gift of being able to jump cranial hemispheres better than anyone I've ever met; her vast knowledge of language, style, and expression inspired, guided, and challenged me throughout the writing process. Thank you so very much, Wendi.

I'd also like to thank Manie Barron, my literary agent and my friend. (Agent and friend: that's a combination that I've found rare in my decades of work in the arts.)

I must thank Maureen O'Brien from HarperCollins who became an instant friend and whose years in all territories of the arts give her a kind and caring savvy that nurtured the book—but more importantly, me and Karla. The publishing world is new terrain for me, and Maureen has gently, lovingly walked me past the land mines to a place where I feel safe and creative—and just maybe, someone will actually read my work. I also know that this book would be just another unrealized text on my shelf if it weren't for Carrie Kania's gamble on a new novelist. I must also thank Stephanie Fraser at HarperCollins who has become an indefatigable supporter and a good friend, and Jill Schwartzman, to whom I owe much gratitude for helping me rein in my desire to cram everything I wanted to say into my first novel.

My heartfelt appreciation goes out to my students and the faculty and staff at the Maurice Kanbar Institute for Film and Television at New York University's Tisch School of the Arts, especially the Chair of Film and Television, Lamar Sanders, and Dean Mary Schmidt Campbell. The patience and encouragement of my colleagues has been invaluable.

This book could not have been written without the inspiration, year after year, film after film, show after show, of the dedicated men and women on my film crews. They are my true heroes. Their artistic accomplishments are rarely noted; usually they are just referred to as a grip, a prop person, a script supervisor, a camera operator, etc. These are the people behind the scenes who never give up on *The Funny*. Most notable among them are Ray DeVally, my teacher, my friend and a helluva cowboy; Tom Doak and Pat Fisher, who are both brilliant at their jobs and true friends, but are completely underappreciated by the people who make the "big bucks"; and very specially, a director of photography Nick McLean, Sr., who has seen success and suffered tremendous tragedy, yet always made sure he was *there* for his crews, his friends.

A special thank-you goes to Burt Reynolds. Burt and I go back decades as actors together; and it was Burt who allowed me to direct him in a small film I wrote called *Modern Love* and then had the faith and the guts to hire me to direct episodes of *Evening*

Shade, which had an all-star cast. If it weren't for Burt Reynolds, I believe I would not have become a prominent director in television. Burt sticks by his friends. One can look to so many careers and find that they began with the generosity of Mr. Reynolds, whom I'm lucky to have as my friend.

Steven Arcieri, my friend and voiceover agent (another friend and agent—the math is deceiving!) for allowing me to have an income while writing this text. Jeffrey Katzenberg, Rick Nicita, Mark Sendroff, Matt Williams and Angelina Fiordellisi, accomplished artists in their own professional cosmos who obliterate all stereotypes by doing the unthinkable: they always make time to take my calls and read my work. They have given me the unquantifiable: hope; as have Cliff Bemis, Stan Brown, Sam Ellis, Valerie Silver-Ellis, Sandy Benson, Aunt Mar, Winston and Carleen Simone, the Steinbaums, the Elimelichs, the Eppleys, the Millers, the Borkowskis, the Stories, Billie, and Chet, all friends for life.

Finally, my wife and children ... Lyric and Zephyr, for constantly astonishing me with their goodness and many times reminding me to take the true path to right and beware the alleyway to wrong, no matter how tempting. My children teach me. And from a minor standpoint, also for understanding that when Dad is staring out the window, he's not daydreaming: he's working. And Karla, my best friend, partner and goddess: she has devoted 25 years to our family. She is, quite simply, *pure*. She is not my muse, she is my everything. I'd rather not wax pathetic; I don't have the language skills to explain such love, such selfless spirit. Maybe one day ... She merits the acrobatic word-play of a truly gifted writer. I'll just keep it honest: I love you, Karla.

This Book Is Rated TV-M

This is a story of a single week in Show Business, focused on Television, zoomed in to the Sitcom. The tighter the shot, the closer the picture. The closer the picture, the more obvious the flaws.

Show business has always been a safe haven for the imperfect and the needy, a home for the inadequate, a sanctuary for the defective. It is a pop culture refuge in which insanity is rewarded—oftentimes glorified.

The business of show is a singular juggernaut. It hogs the road. Delicious perversion is the fuel it guzzles. It drives by its own rules. There is long-term safety in being a passenger—a backstabbing backseat driver. Responsibility is a liability, accountability an afterthought. No one dare take the wheel.

The result? Casualties. Fresh road kill for public consumption.

This is a story of very heavy casualties.

Enjoy.

Who
Stole the
Funny?

The Phone Call

In the Beginning, there is always the Phone Call.

In show business, life-changing information is almost always delivered in the form of a phone call. The reason? No one in Hollywood has the guts to look anyone in the eye. There once was a good man who hung up his phone, smiled, went into his bedroom, and shot himself in the head. The reason? He lost his Cocoa Puffs account.

That incident later became an M.O.W.

Cocoa Snuff won an Emmy.

Every sitcom director pretends to be busy, having a wonderful life, while out of work. The truth of the matter is, unlike actors who sit and wait, staring at their phones, directors socialize, and buy cardigan sweaters and very comfy shoes. Most

> ### The Hollywood Dictionary
>
> **M.O.W.:** Movie of the Week. (No, not M.O.T.W. Don't ask.) In which the sensational stories of vulnerable people are made into entertainment for profit.

also have the annoying habit of behaving like directors in public and even at home ("Somebody get me some water, dammit!" "Yes,

Daddy"). All the while, they pretend not to be waiting for their cell phones to ring.

Jasper Jones's cell phone rang.

Jasper Jones was a middle-aged man in perfect shape who'd had multiple plastic surgeries to hide the natural aging process and was in good standing in the Directors Guild of America.

"Y'hello," he said into his phone from his place in line at Saks Fifth Avenue's men's department in Beverly Hills. A fastidious dresser, Jasper was more fashion-conscious than—conscious. Jasper had a closetful of Bruno Magli gored loafers, but now they just weren't . . . in. Especially the gored line. He needed to wear a different pair of comfortable shoes every day of the week, and since the Salvatore Ferragamo Gazette loafers were only $420 a pair, there wasn't a single reason in the world why he shouldn't do what was right for his feet, and buy seven pairs. And a new wardrobe to match.

Why the fuck do I have to wait in line? Jasper thought as he fiddled with his earpiece and his up-to-the-millisecond-model cell phone/toy. "Don't fuck up," he said (his standard greeting).

"Jasperoonie!" his directing agent answered. "It's me. Dick."

"Dick—it's Sunday. Whassup? Somebody die?"

Dick Beaglebum handled the top writers and showrunners in the television business, along with a few directors—Jasper being one of them. He loved to work on Sundays. It gave him a legitimate reason to get out of the house.

The Hollywood Dictionary

HANDLED: Made money in his sleep off his working clients.

SHOWRUNNER: Someone who literally runs a TV show on a daily basis. In keeping with the byzantine nature of Hollywood deals, a showrunner is often the show's chief writer. Usually a good politician but only a fair writer, a showrunner is great at hiring better writers. Works very hard at being eccentric.

The Beaglebum Agency sat on prime real estate in the middle of Beverly Hills. The spacious office (with bookshelves full of classics whose bindings had never been cracked) boasted a stunning 180-degree view on days when the smog (excuse me: haze) visibility was more than two-tenths of a mile. Dick had an oversized desk that he'd paid too much for because he'd been told it was made from the sea-cured oak of a sunken pirate ship, circa 1650, that was excavated from the floor of the Caribbean. Dick had bought it as a $430,000 tax write-off.

Dick leaned back in his chair and swiveled it from side to side. "Jasper," he began in his overrefined, I-swear-I'm-not-from-Hackensack-accent, "how's my wildly eccentric director?"

In Hollywood, eccentric is good. Full-blown eccentrics are even better. Eccentrics satisfy the public's appetite for showbiz buzz. And

> ### The Hollywood Dictionary
>
> **ECCENTRIC:** Affecting a style of dress, coiffure, speech, mannerisms, etc., carefully calculated to give the impression of creative credibility.

well-cultivated eccentricity gives an impression of creativity while avoiding the kinds of problems that actual creativity can cause, like the ones implied by the phrase "creative differences."

Jasper hoped Dick meant the brand of eccentric that the studios and the networks desired (required), one with eccentricities they could manipulate, influence, and regulate. The last thing Jasper wanted was to seem *too creative*.

He kept playing with his cell phone and earpiece while he had "the Help" carry his purchases to his Jag. He jumped into the car and

> ### The Hollywood Dictionary
>
> **CREATIVE DIFFERENCES:** "I don't like you! You make me mad! I'm telling!"

roared off, leaving the Help with an open hand and an open mouth. *"Son of a bitch,"* the Help mumbled, staring at the single grimy quarter in his hand.

Jasperoonie drove while rehearsing his director skills on Dick and trying to give the impression of being *very much in control.*

The ability to appear to be very much in control is an art form in itself, a survival skill everyone in Hollywood must practice until they are proficient at hiding their own shortcomings with false cleverness, pseudocompetence, and a finger trained to point at the other guy. It's the one skill a working director must have. It's more beneficial to a director than talent. As a matter of fact, talent, a rare and almost archaic quality, can get in the way of a director's function on a television sitcom.

> ### The Hollywood Dictionary
>
> **WORKING DIRECTOR:** One who has a hope of working in this town again.
>
> **CREATIVE-TYPE DIRECTOR:** One who has no hope of working in this town again.

"Look, Dick," Jasper said, hoping he sounded very much in control, "I know you love to chat, but why don't you just cut to the chase. Quicker, faster, funnier. Get to it."

Dick knew that even when Jasper was at the top of his game, he was creatively benign. In other words, he was the perfect sitcom director. Directors, even though they are considered to be somewhere near the top of the *creative* food chain, are thought of as schmucks by agents (and the showrunners and the studios and the networks). An agent who handles bipolar writers, megalomaniac showrunners, and a few schmuck directors must perfect the art of phony enthusiasm/compassion. The agent needs this talent to broker and package a sitcom that gets on the air, stays on the air, and then goes into syndication, so he can make millions upon millions of dollars off the hard work of all the schmucks. Enthusiasm/compassion gets the agent past the possible bitter negotiations or conflicts in egos to a point where everyone is excited about the Nielsen Jackpot, the Syndication Gold Mine of a hit sitcom.

Dick Beaglebum had the enthusiasm/compassion shtick down cold. He was a better actor than most of the actors on the shows he'd packaged. Dick's clients all thought he was the one person in a world of sharks who actually cared about the show and their needs. Dick was *very* enthusiastic and compassionate.

"Jasperaspercasper," he said with pitch-perfect false enthusiasm/compassion,

> ## The Hollywood Dictionary
>
> **SCHMUCK:** A hard worker. A schmuck must get up in the morning and actually show up at work: *"That schmuck did all the work."*
>
> **THE STUDIO:** A fungal, amorphous Entity made up of revolving-door executives who eventually deliver a product to the network. The studio can be owned by the network, or be an independent Entity (for now).
>
> **THE NETWORK:** A viral, amorphous Entity made up of revolving-door executives who eventually broadcast the product.
>
> **ENTITY:** *gimme, gimme, gimme!*

"I've got good news! You've been offered three more episodes of *I Love My Urban Buddies*. The Studio, the Network, everyone loves what you're doing on *Buddies*! This show is through the roof! It's become the number one show on TV—and they want you, Jasperooski! You!"

Jasper went through a red light (his directorial prerogative), almost smashing into a low-end BMW driven by an actor who couldn't afford a Jag.

"You fuck. I have the right-of-way! Take a left and drive off a cliff!" he barked like any good director, giving good strong direction.

> ### The Hollywood Dictionary
>
> **FASTER! FUNNIER!** The direction most responsible for the destruction of comedy and the rise of Reality Shows.
>
> **VISION:** Shortsightedness, as opposed to nearsightedness, which can be corrected.

"Jasperooski," Dick said, enthusiastically, "Marc and Steph Pooley *love you.* Do you know what it means when the showrunners love you? And these two don't love anyone! They don't even love each other—and they're married!"

Jasper was loved because he was a traffic-cop/yes-sir director. He had four different, very oh-so-important directions he whispered into an actor's ear: (1) *"Do it again, exactly the same."* (2) *"Do it better."* (3) *"Do it faster! And funnier!"* And finally, (4) *"Be brilliant, dammit! I thought you could act!"* Jasper would then return to the executives and showrunners with a look on his face as if he had just fixed the scene with his vision.

"Shitfuck. Dick—don't you represent the Pooleys?" The connection only now dawned on Jasper, a man whose job it was to recognize detail. An agent representing competing Entities in a creative endeavor such as a sitcom was a clear conflict of interests.

But Jasper was always happy to be paid to direct (which shouldn't be misinterpreted as being paid to *work.* Directors tell *others* to work). And, Jasper reasoned, this was the hottest show on TV. So what if there *was* a little conflict of interests? It wouldn't be the first time.

> ### The Hollywood Dictionary
>
> **CONFLICT OF INTERESTS:** Everyone wins!

Jasper looked at the new wardrobe and seven boxes of shoes in the backseat of his Jag and came to a quick and rational decision. "You know what? Just say yes. I'll

give them a helluva show.
You know," he added quickly,
"I'll give them *whatever they
want*..."

"That's my man," Dick
said, "just give 'em what
they want! Remember, that's
your job. Give 'em what they
want."

"Yes. Definitely, I'll give
'em whatever they want. I'm

> ### The Hollywood Dictionary
>
> **THE BIG BUCKS:** More money
> in one week than a firefighter
> makes in a year; more money in
> one year than a schoolteacher
> makes in a career. Not as much
> as the winner of the World Series
> of poker.

their man. I'll do it. Whatever they want."

"Great, Jasper the Master. Oh, one last thing—I couldn't get
your quote for the big bucks but I got you thirty grand an episode.
And you only have to pay me half of my commission. So it's like
thirty-three grand. You okay with that?"

"Wait a minute," Jasper said. "Explain—"

"Well, Jasper-is-faster, I *brokered* the show. I put the package
together. Without me, nobody'd have a job," Dick rambled, with
remarkable enthusiasm and compassion. Dick was in a position to
make seven figures without expertise in a craft or even breaking a
sweat. Millions, just for making a few phone calls.

"Whoa . . . now we really are talking about a conflict of interests," Jasper said. Then he turned his Jag into the driveway and
stared at the new construction on his $4 million home. "Tell 'em
Yes."

"Fan-fucking-tastic! Everything's just dandy, Jasperandy. All
good. No bad! I mean, really—*What could go wrong?*" And then
Jasper's cell phone lost its signal.

A Day of Rest or
It's Sunday. Somebody Die?

JASPER ARRIVED HOME late Sunday afternoon, with his new wardrobe for his new job, only to find that his third wife Michelle had started yet another renovation. (Jasper was referred to by divorce lawyers as an E.R.: Erase and Replace kind of guy.)

Michelle had felt abandoned ever since her marriage to Jasper, and with good cause. Basically, after the honeymoon, Jasper treated Michelle like someone on a set: he ordered her to do things and expected them to get done. Michelle hadn't counted on a relationship where she played the part of a grip or a gofer. So she began to occupy herself with design. Interior and exterior design. And with a spending fervor that forced Jasper to keep working, like the high-level schmuck he was.

Jasper hopped out of his Jaguar (the prototypical B-grade Schmuckmobile) and ordered Norma the Guatemalan maid to take his clothes into the house and press them, then hang them in his walk-in closet. Norma had an odd look of panic when Jasper directed her to do these specific chores. Jasper then gave her acting directions as well, even though Norma didn't speak English. Jasper would simply direct Norma more slowly.

"Norma—*steeeeaaam myyyy neeew cloooothes theeeen haaaang*

*theeeem uuuuup iiiiin myyyyy cloooooseeeet. Uuuuunderstaaaand?
Pronto!"*

Norma looked down, ashamed. Not her usual look of shame,
but an I-know-something-I'm-not-supposed-to-know look of
shame. If only Jasper had truly been a man of detail and understood the basics of directing, he would have been able to differen-
tiate Norma's looks of shame. Oh well.

Fuming, walking over tools and debris in the living room, Jasper stumbled through the new construction in his bedroom and
out a private automated door, beyond which he knew he would
find his wife Michelle in the hot tub he had purchased for medicinal purposes. Michelle was indeed in the hot tub—fucking the
young, muscle-bound, deck-building construction-worker-of-
the-month. Certainly, this
wasn't medicinal.

It was, however, pre-
dictable. Like many in the
television business, Jasper
made busy work for him-
self so that he rarely had to
go home at sensible domes-
tic hours. In other words,
home meant *real life*. Real
life meant interacting with

> ### The Hollywood Dictionary
>
> **MEDICINAL:** Possible to write off
> as a tax break or to have paid for
> by a union's insurance company.
> A prescription from a doctor is
> mandatory and a cinch to get.
> Those darn doctors!

real people such as a child or a wife. It was much easier to interact with a child actor or a sitcom wife. So in order to avoid his real
life, Jasper would find reasons not to come home. Schmooze over
a round of golf, cheat on his wife, whatever—anything to stay out
of the realm of reality. The women in Jasper's life had, in turn, always cheated on him.

Having caught Michelle in hot-tub flagrante (*I'll love her until
the day she drowns,* Jasper thought), Jasper silently unzipped his

pants and began to masturbate. Just as all three were about to orgasm, Michelle noticed her husband standing on the deck with his pants around his ankles and his dick in his hand.

"You sick fuck!" Michelle cried out.

"Me?!" Jasper continued to pump. "You're the one fucking the construction guy in the hot tub I paid for! You bitch . . . hold on . . . oh . . . yes, you're a bitch. Oh yes, you're a bi—"

The Hollywood Dictionary

SCHMOOZE: To schleep with asch many chicksch asch posschible. Lotsch of schex.

The construction worker jumped out of the tub and ran toward his sports bag, where he kept his eight-by-ten photo and résumé in case he ever ran into Jasper. Jasper, quivering, stepped forward to take the photo (multitasking) and accidentally stood on the compressed-air tubing of the nail gun.

Funny thing about a pneumatic nail gun: build up enough pressure in the hose, and it'll take on a life of its own. The three watched, mesmerized, as the nail gun slithered like a snake and began to rise, with Jasper as the snake charmer. It twisted, vibrated, then leapt high into the air and misfired, sending a six-inch galvanized nail into Jasper's forehead.

Jasper had finally been nailed.

The Hollywood Dictionary

INFORMANT: A bribee; everyone could use a little petty cash.

THE NETWORK FOUND out immediately that it had lost its director for the next three episodes of *I Love My Urban Buddies* because Jasper's maid, Norma, who actually spoke perfect English, was an informant.

The Studio found out an hour later that it had lost its director for the next three episodes of *I Love My Urban Buddies* because it had ties with the Los Angeles Homicide Division, courtesy of its advisory role in the studio's crime shows.

The Pooleys found out they had lost their director for the next three episodes of *I Love My Urban Buddies* because Dick Beaglebum called them. From Jasper's house. Dick had raced to the scene

> **The Hollywood Dictionary**
>
> **PERK:** Everyone could use a little petty ass.

of the accident to see if his director could direct with a six-inch nail in his head. But, alas, Jasper was stone cold.

Dick Beaglebum wasn't your Standard American Male either. He loved the perk of keeping his clients' wives satisfied. While their husbands were making television, Dick was making naughty.

Damn, Dick thought. He'd had two reasons to keep Jasper employed: he received ten percent of Jasper's paycheck and ten percent of Michelle. Now he'd lost both. He made a mental note to ask Michelle what she was going to do with Jasper's legendary shoe collection. He wore the same size.

All death aside, now there was a REAL problem: it was Sunday afternoon and all three Entities (*gimme, gimme, gimme,* ad nauseum) involved in this sitcom shenanigan—the network, the studio, and the Pooleys—needed a director to start the following morning and commit to the three episodes Jasper Jones could no longer direct. (Actually, given the present state of sitcoms, Jasper, albeit dead, still could've directed all three shows. But that's another story.)

As for Jasper Jones, he was later honored by the Directors Guild of America for his sparkling career and endless accomplishments. Jasper Jones was also given a star on the Hollywood Walk of Fame.

* * *

> ### The Hollywood Dictionary
>
> **SPARKLING CAREER:** Employment.
>
> **ENDLESS ACCOMPLISHMENTS:** Survival.
>
> **A STAR ON THE HOLLYWOOD WALK OF FAME:** A $15,000 ego trip, paid for by the recipient's public relations firm.

THE NETWORK CONFABBED at an emergency meeting of all its Presidents and Vice Presidents of Television. There were seventeen Presidents and Vice Presidents in all, so the meeting had to be taken in the large boardroom, built only for show (= status).

The Studio confabbed at an emergency meeting of all its Presidents and Vice Presidents of Television. There were twenty-three Presidents and Vice Presidents in all, so the meeting had to be taken in the corpulent boardroom, built only to intimidate (= status).

The Pooleys, the creators of *I Love My Urban Buddies* (their inspired, never-made-it-to-the-page spin-off to *I Love My Rural Buddies*, an idea the Pooleys came up with after watching a *Beverly Hillbillies* marathon one Thanksgiving), confabbed without delay in a tiny coffeehouse built only for exclusivity (= status). Their first instinct was to insist that either one or the other one of them direct the next three

> ### The Hollywood Dictionary
>
> **CONFAB:** To sound important in unusually big or small spaces.

episodes. Unfortunately, their previous direction gigs were on an animated show. As much as they wanted their Buddies to be animated, regrettably they were living, breathing humans, dammit. Their second instinct was to get high. Their third instinct kicked in while they were attempting to guzzle triple espressos: maybe they could get some mileage out of Jasper's death, with the right spin. And if they made nice-nice with the network, they might be able to get rid of Kirk

Kelly, a young James Dean look-alike they now wished they'd never cast.

The Pooleys had suddenly taken a cocaine disliking to the young actor. They were snortin' angry with him, they were! They didn't like the fact that an actor was overshadowing their

> **The Hollywood Dictionary**
>
> **LANDING:** Actually making the audience laugh. For jokes that no one finds funny except the writer, a laugh track is provided to prod the audience. Thus the term *prod-ucer.*

success. What does he do? He just walks and talks. And not well! The Pooleys were incensed that their perfectly honed jokes were not landing, and it was obviously Kirk Kelly's fault.

The Pooleys would snort a huge line in their back office, then come out with rage in their eyes and with Stephanie exclaiming, "We hate the fucking kid! We want the fucker fired! There is no doubt that the kid is doing drugs! It's obvious! Doing drugs is something we just cannot and will not copulate! I mean tolerate!"

The network, on the other hand, loved the kid. It didn't matter if he couldn't act his way out of a paper bag—he *tested* through the roof with the most valuable of demographics: 18-to–34-year-olds.

Adolescent girls from Alaska to Zimbabwe were gaga for Kirk, and he didn't threaten young male viewers, either. Yet the network and the studio knew that the Pooleys would take advantage of this stupendous tragedy, this kismet, to make their move to fire the young man.

> **The Hollywood Dictionary**
>
> **TESTED:** If Charlie Chaplin were alive and working today, he would've been *tested.* And if he'd had one bad test result (based on the opinion cards filled out by young viewers in a test audience), there would never have been a Charlie Chaplin.

The network had to maneuver and come up with a strategy that would keep Kirk Kelly on the show *and* get a director they could live with for the three weeks.

The studio executives knew the cards the network and the Pooleys were holding. They had to make love with the Pooleys and the network without spending a dime more than had already been allocated to the show's budget. Paying off contracts or shutting down the show for a week while they found a new director and maybe a new James Dean was out of the question! Unless some other Entity paid for those costs.

The Network Emergency
Conference Call

"J.T. BAKER? He's a *passionate schmuck!*" yelled Debbie, the volup-
tuous, salon-blonde, stark-naked network representative. She'd
been conferenced in from her 90210 home for the emergency
meeting, which was dominated by the Alpha Dog, the Network
President of Current Comedy, Vincent Volari (close friends called
him Vincent Volari; mistresses called him Vincent Volari). He sat
at the head of the table in the large boardroom while the rest of the
pack stood around it.

Debbie Cydnus, a wom-
an so beautiful that her exotic looks turned heads
everywhere except in the
modeling business, where
she just wasn't tall enough
("Why? Why? Why?" she
cried), became a network
executive by starting in the
mailroom and fucking her
way up to the sixth floor of Development. Her little sweet noth-
ings, whispered into executives' ears during coitus, always had a
network agenda and were laced with tongue and savvy. She finally

> ### The Hollywood Dictionary
>
> **THE PASSIONATE:** Troublemak-
> ers. Loose cannons. Delusional
> schmucks who believe they can
> elevate the quality of the show.
> *Passion* in television is bad—very
> bad!

fucked the right guy, and the exotic beauty who was born in the city of Tarsus and never grew past the height of five feet six focused her breasts in the direction of behind-the-scenes stardom. But, alas, she never lost the model mentality.

"Fat. *Too fat*," Debbie muttered as she stared at her reflection in the monitor of the 42-inch flat-screen high-definition television that hung on her wall. The only thing Deb was wearing was a wireless phone earpiece designed to match this month's hair color.

The Hollywood Dictionary

NETWORK: The Entity (*gimme, gimme, gimme*) that buys the sitcom from the studio, in a symbiotic relationship similar to that of Mother Nature and mankind. They both want what is best for *them*, but, dammit-to-hell, they still gotta live with each other. If only . . . !

"*Phat*. We're with you, Debbie. This sitcom is phat. It's da bomb!" a lone member of the pack ventured.

"Not P-H-A-T. F-A-T, you F-U-C-K!" Debbie yelled at her reflection.

The pack bayed at Debbie's moon. "We agree, Deb. Don't we, guys?"

"Well said, Deb. Brilliant!"

"You really hit the buttons that needed to be . . . pressed."

"What are you talking about, you backstabbing wieners?" Debbie snapped out of her trance and tried to switch into P.S.M. (Problem-Solving Mode, often mistaken for P.M.S.), but she just couldn't get away from reflective surfaces that drew her eyes back into the world of *Debbie Does Debauchery*: lusting after herself, loathing herself. Lust. Loathe.

The Hollywood Dictionary

BRILLIANT: Said of anything or anyone ordinary.

Lust. Loathe. Her mother. Her sister. Her mother. Her sister. She slapped herself with Jack Nicholson intensity, then struck a pose as Faye Dunaway. Debbie stared at her distorted reflection in the toaster. *That was such a good movie,* she thought.

"Now, now, Deb," Vincent Volari said soothingly. "We're just echoing your genius. We, um, get *it*. We get *you*, Deb. That's all we mean. You're on the money. Cut the fat. Lose the weight. We're right there with you."

> **The Hollywood Dictionary**
>
> **GENIUS:** *See* Brilliant.

Debbie hit the MUTE button, navigated her way to the toilet, and forced herself to vomit the seven Ho Hos she'd gorged only minutes before. She wiped her mouth, then released the button. "That's better," she managed to say.

"Good! Then we're on the same page. We're speaking the same language. Now about J.T.—"

"I think J.T. is the perfect choice for the new directing job," Debbie interrupted, with an awful taste in her mouth. "All that passion means he'll give the Pooleys hell. Like, when I was a junior exec and he was directing a show I was assigned to? Like, he spent an hour—a fucking *hour*—making leaves fall from the scaffolding. He said something about if the exterior looked more credible, the jokes would play funnier. I, like, threatened to fire him, and you know what he did? He asked for leaves with *color* because the scene was supposed to take place in the fall. He, like, drove me fucking crazy. So you know, once the Pooleys have to deal with that every day for three episodes, we'll be holding the power card, not them. Besides, even better, it's really possible that J.T. will only last the first episode. Either he will want out or the Pooleys will want *him* out, and we'll have the Pooleys and the studio eating . . ." Debbie looked at the Ho Ho remains floating in the toilet bowl. "Eating out of the palms of our hands."

"J.T. is one of those idea types," one of the dogs whined.

Vincent Volari cleared his throat. He felt it was time to focus, so he focused on the vision of what Debbie wasn't wearing. "I love the way you . . . *think,* Debbie," he said in a seductive tone. "Innovative. Out of the *box.*"

Then he seemed to remember he had an audience. His voice grew more authoritative. "Every single one of you should learn from Debbie. There's a reason she's on her way up." Suddenly his brow furrowed. "I have one reservation, Debbie," he added, to everyone's surprise. "This J.T. Baker. For some reason—I'm trying to remember why—I don't . . . *like* him. He ruined a project of ours . . ."

> ### The Hollywood Dictionary
>
> **IDEA TYPE:** Think Joseph McCarthy when he used the word *Communist.* Spoken with the same repugnant tone and disdainful connotations reserved for dictators, mass murderers, war criminals, and mimes.

"Actually, sir," Debbie said, "he, like, directed the pilot to our most successful show."

"He did?"

"Yes, sir. *Tabitha the Teenage Tallis-Girl!*"

"Really? What is his name again?"

"J.T. Baker, sir."

"Oh! Oh! I know why I don't like him! I had him confused with J.P. Brick*er.* J.P. Bricker was our gardener and ruined our topiary. That's it. Never mind. Continue."

Someone to Vincent Volari's left spoke out. "Should I take him off your list of directors we never want to hire?"

"You *think*?" Debbie lashed out. "If he does last the three weeks, at least he'll take care of our show."

Vincent Volari's memory was born again. "I know why something's bothering me. The death of the director. Whatever his name was. This could be problematic."

"I'm on the same page as you, Vincent Volari." (Think about it. Debbie's thought process, which in network terms was actually quite sane, was *on the same page* as Vincent Volari's.) "The death of our Amer-icon. The rollout of Kalamazoo P. Kardinal," she said.

The network had just spent millions of dollars in PR to bury its old icon, Minnesota B. Moose, and roll out a new corporate symbol.

"Exactly," Vincent Volari agreed. "Debbie, you are *sooo good*."

"Like, thanks. We have to make sure that the media coverage for the dead director isn't conflicting with the death of Minnesota B. Moose. We don't want anything taking away from the moose's funeral. It'll, like, really screw up the momentum we have for the introduction of Kalamazoo P. Kardinal."

"Debbie, is the cardinal red enough?"

"Yes, sir. Candy-apple red."

"I love you, Debbie."

Silence.

The underdogs in the boardroom quickly checked the reactions of their litter mates. They began to giggle and whisper.

Debbie stopped obsessing about her weight long enough to luxuriate in the words of lust that were her blow job to the top.

"I mean I love the way *you think*."

"Thank you, sir."

Click.

End of conversation. End of Network Emergency Conference Call.

The Studio
Emergency Meeting

THE STUDIO EXECUTIVES were packed in tight, even in the corpulent boardroom. There weren't enough chairs, so many of them stood.

The president of the studio had put Lance Griffin, the studio representative to *I Love My Urban Buddies,* in charge of the meeting.

Lance Griffin would stubbornly maintain to anyone unfortunate enough to be cornered by him at a cocktail party that he was a product of reverse discrimination. With all the assumption of privilege typical of the young Caucasian-American male, Lance had been certain that affirmative action quotas represented the only

The Hollywood Dictionary

THE STUDIO: The middleman Entity (*gimme, gimme, gimme*) that finds a sitcom and then tries to sell it to a network. Once the network buys the sitcom, the studio begins the practical phase of producing the shows with the showrunners from whom they purchased the sitcom. The studio and the showrunners maintain a symbiotic relationship similar to that of pharmaceutical companies and physicians. They both want what is best for *them,* but, dammit-to-hell, how can you have good medicine if the disease is cured?

possible explanation for his failure to be accepted into an Ivy League law school. Or any law school, as it turned out. In the United States. He'd believed that his GPA of 2.5 wasn't a reflection of his street smarts, just his book smarts—*and what did book smarts have to do with winning?!*

He finally earned his law degree between street-smart classes at the Inter-American School of Law in Puerto Rico and online courses taken through the Concord Law School (where he could study at his own pace . . . *"and fuck the books!"*). It was the fastest route, if not the most economical use of his parents' Internet service (dial-up, on the old system that charged by the minute), and he wanted that degree, dammit.

Lance then found his calling in entertainment law. It suited his winning nature—er, his nature to win. At any and all costs. He vowed to pay his parents' Internet bills back, and did so within the first year of "earning" his degree, by lucking out on a live-action cartoon that was being sued by the Screen Actors Guild because none of the actors portraying the action heroes were union. Lance came to the rescue of the wounded producer, set up a fake loan-out corporation, and moved the filming of the show to Vancouver, Canada, where SAG had no jurisdiction at the time. The producer rewarded Lance with a piece of the syndication rights—after profits. Instead Lance bargained for merchandising, and lo and behold, the plastic action figures became the top-selling Christmas gift that year. Lance was now an entertainment force to be reckoned with: rich and opportunistic, and he *never* played by the rules. Those qualities landed him the job as vice president of production at the studio. His job description now included being the point man on the studio's hit show *I Love My Urban Buddies.*

"Quiet, please! Let me summarize!" Lance thundered. "Jasper Jones will not be directing the next three episodes. He's dead."

"He's dead to you?" a voice quivered.

> ### The Hollywood Dictionary
>
> **TABLE READ:** The first time the script is read aloud. Often exudes the stench of death.

"No. He-is-dead. Deceased. Departed. Lifeless—like our production schedule! We begin tomorrow with a production meeting, then a table read with the cast, and then a few minutes of rehearsal with a dead director. Unfortunately, we need a *live* director. It is my—um, I think it should be *our* stance, as the studio, that the schedule *not be altered*. If we shut down to look for a live director, it will cost the studio dearly. It will also be perceived within the business that our hit show has suddenly run into troubled times. It is my recommendation that we bring in . . . J.T. Baker."

A pall fell over the room, then tripped.

"He's far too *passionate*," said someone in the back.

"He's burned every bridge in this town—at least twice!" another voice blurted out.

"He's an *idea guy*. I don't like it."

"Precisely," said Lance, who exuded so much confidence that every thought sounded like a solution. Lance had a reputation at the studio as the ultimate problem solver, though a look at his track record would reveal a brilliance at causing problems he knew he could solve.

"My strategy," Lance continued, "is that we create a big media sensation with the death of Jackson Jones—"

"*Jasper*. Jasper Jones . . . Sorry." It was a female voice. That was all Lance could tell. But he was determined to find out who had contradicted him with such a minor detail during his strategy oration.

"J-A-S-P-E-R Jones," Lance continued, truly peeved. He pontificated, "You see, if the public takes to the story, we accomplish different strata of triumph. One: more *product recognition* for our new show. We not only make headlines in the arts section *but* we milk the national headlines on the front page and the business section. Not to mention the obits. Three: we've got *product recognition* from all media sides, so our sponsors will be ecstatic!"

"Excuse me. You left out *two,*" the same female voice corrected.

"Fuck! One, two, or three! Fuck the details! Listen to my goddamn take on this mess and how I personally will spearhead the *dead stuff* and spin it to the studio's advantage! *I* am assigned to *I Love My Urban Buddies,* not whoever you are! I'm the one who was there when it was a *nothing* show. Now it's the biggest sitcom in eons."

There was no response. Lance took a deep breath. "Now," he went on, "most shows would kill for a dead guy. I say let's milk it but never lose a penny. Also, if we pitch J.P. Baker to the Pooleys, they'll shit and want to postpone a week and find a new director. This way we can say that the shutdown was their fault because we approved J.P. Baker and we'll force their production company to cover the cost of a shutdown, and we won't be out a single penny! It's kinda like the Jack Ritter thing."

"Um . . . it's *John* Ritter. And, um, his name is J.*T.* Baker, sir," the female with the detailed facts couldn't resist interjecting again, "not J.*P.* Baker."

The nerve of her to actually know any facts! Lance was seething. He glanced nervously at the president of the studio. "The fucking particulars don't matter! What matters is that the studio not pay for a week to shut down a goddamn prime-time television sitcom!"

"How do you know that J.T. Baker will accept an offer? Especially at this late date?" the president of the studio asked, finally contributing to the conversation.

Lance smiled. He was ready for this question. "J.T. Baker," he began, "has a kid on dialysis. He needs to shoot a few sitcoms a year to get his Directors Guild insurance and health plan to kick in with the hospital costs. We've got him by the balls."

"Very good," was the president's quiet response.

End of conversation. End of Studio Emergency Meeting.

The Creators and
Their Representative

STEPHANIE AND MARCUS POOLEY monopolized a tiny booth at a hip coffee shop, inhaling their coffee with a giddy Dick Beaglebum. "J.T. Baker. Ring a bell?" he asked them.

The Pooleys looked at each other. They didn't like looking at each other.

The Pooleys had had a meteoric, typical rise to fame and power as creators-showrunners in the business. They lived in Malibu. They both came from wealthy families. They'd both had stars in their eyes and wanted to be in show business, but every attempt had failed—until one day, the couple next door with five kids had a barbecue on the beach and, trying to be neighborly, invited the Pooleys.

The neighbors were a particularly dysfunctional family. The Pooleys may have lacked all creative talent but they were leeches when it came to the talent of stealing other people's lives and recording their prey's

> ### The Hollywood Dictionary
>
> **THE CREATORS/SHOWRUNNERS, THE STUDIO, AND THE NETWORK:** A perpetual ménage à trois, with each participant trying to achieve the biggest orgasm and claim the biggest genitalia in the relationship.

> ### The Hollywood Dictionary
>
> **COVERAGE:** An evaluation by an Executive who agrees to read a script. The Executive gives it to a college freshman in screenwriting school. The freshman's evaluation determines the life or death of a script. (Not to be confused with *film coverage:* "I want another close-up, dammit!")

personal problems on paper, and they saw the family next door as a possible gold mine. They began finding reasons to hang out with their neighbors, help with the kids, go on outings—all the while wearing a wire. They taped every conversation and then, verbatim, translated the transcripts into scripts without adding a single original thought. Dick Beaglebum, as a favor to a client who also lived on the same strip of beach in Malibu, said he would send the *script* out for coverage.

The coverage came back with hyperactive kudos and the sentences: "This could be the best animated show on TV. I know I'd watch it and so would all my frat brothers." The animated show about a dysfunctional family was an immediate hit. The Pooleys were immediate players.

Their next step: to get out of animation and earn credibility. That meant wearing a wire and recording a group of twentysomethings whose parents leased a house for them on the prized Malibu beachfront property to the north of the Pooleys. Other than the transfer to an urban setting, the pilot episode echoed verbatim how they all met, lived in this one house, and interacted. The coverage came back: "Totally awesome, dude! This is how it really is. I'd watch these Buddies! So would my frat brothers. And my girlfriend says her sorority sisters would too." Thus, the Pooleys became A-list players with two megahit shows, and were feared and admired by the industry.

"Who the fuck is *J.T. Baker*?" Stephanie asked, with a wicked look plastered on her Aryan, surgically altered face. She was the pit bull of the two Pooleys—not necessarily the most dangerous, she just had a bite that wouldn't let go: an important survival skill when dealing with the network and the studio.

"No offense, but you two are a little too *young* to know J.T.'s work," Dick wisely explained.

"*Young* is good," Stephanie replied, like a trained dog.

"Young *is* good," her husband repeated grudgingly.

Dick echoed the Hollywood mantra. "Yes. *Young* is *always* good." He continued, "J.T. Baker is an old client of mine."

"Old?" the Pooleys said in concert. "Old is bad," they said in unrehearsed harmony.

"He's been my client for fifteen years," Dick explained with a mischievous smile. "Every once in a while, I throw him a bone."

Dick took a sip of his coffee and began laying out his strategy with the Pooleys. "No one likes him. He's far too *dedicated*. And—get this—he's a *college professor!*" Dick said with disdain. "He lives in the mountains of Bum-fuck Someplace back East, and here's the kicker: *He used to be famous!*"

"Well then, why the fuck do we want this *old has-been?*" Marcus screamed.

"A fucking *has-been?* You represent us and you're pitching a fucking *old has-been* to direct *our baby?*" Stephanie Pooley bared her teeth.

"That's the point," Dick smirked. "Hear me out. If we go in with the M.O. that

> ### The Hollywood Dictionary
>
> **YOUNG:** Good!
>
> **OLD:** Bad! (This definition has become a mantra that cannot be repeated—or overstated, or overclarified—enough. So: Young, good! Old, bad!)

J.T. and J.T. alone is our man, the studio will have to take us seriously. They can't say we're *not* playing ball. We are! We've got a replacement! And his name is J.T. Baker, folks! Now—they've *got* to

shut down the show! They'll die when they hear his fucking name!
I mean this guy is . . . an artist! He's . . . got *vision*! Vision, for chris-
sake! He's got passion! He cares! Can you imagine the nightmare?!
Believe me, it's a foolproof plan!"

Dick was practically bouncing in his chair. "The studio will
recommend to the network that the show be shut down for the
week, you can find some other schmuck to direct, and you'll get
some rest and have your people do another pass on the eighty-
page script. That way, the studio must—they *have* to pick up the
tab for the week. Not you guys, or your production company!"

He could tell the Pooleys, with their steamy pile of ambition
and taste for delicious manipulation, liked this idea.

"Now think, guys," Dick continued. "How is the studio going
to get J.T. Baker here in time for tomorrow's production meeting? We're putting them in a no-win position! And—he lives in
Bum-fuck Someplace where there are real people and stuff that's
. . . real and stuff. In other words: he's 'rural'! They'll shit! We've
got a rural guy directing an urban show. Fuck! They'll never say
yes. Oh! And oh! Get this: Even though I represent him, I also represent you, too! So . . . I'll tell him I can't get involved in his salary
reduction! We'll offer him . . . director's scale! Odds are, he'll throw
a hissy fit and never get on a plane. It clears you guys on even another level!"

"We're not fucking actors. You don't have to explain things,"
Marcus said. "But you're sure this will work? This J.T. Baker
thing?"

"Foolproof," Dick Beaglebum beamed.

"*Brilliant*," Stephanie Pooley said.

"*Genius*," Marcus Pooley agreed.

Not the end of the conversation, but who wants to hear more?
End of Meeting.

J.T. Baker

By now, J.T. Baker's name was speeding through Hollywood like a derivative idea. Joseph Thomas Baker. It took thirty seconds at Ellis Island to chop down the Bäcker family tree and plant the seedling thereafter to be known as *Baker*. No matter; family and enemies just called him J.T.

J.T. was a straightforward guy or a hair-triggered time bomb, depending on who was talking. He had the fury of ten men—ten very self-righteous men. He believed in truth, justice, and the American way. Unfortunately, he wasn't related to Superman, nor did he live in the 1950s, and the letters *J.T.* just didn't look as good on a sky blue T-shirt as the well-known *S*. He was taught at a very young age that he could never be good enough. Therefore, J.T. grew into a tortured perfectionist (not the romantic kind; the real kind. Basically a pain in the ass to live with).

If a curious outsider were to Google J.T. Baker, they would learn that he was a Teen Star (precocious baggage), a Broadway Star (pedigree baggage), a Film Star (has-been baggage), and a Recording Almost-Star (laughingstock baggage). And then when his *time* was over and desperation set in, J.T. reinvented himself and became a Writer (cynical baggage), an Executive (imperious baggage), a Producer (my-son's-a-producer baggage, and exactly-what-does-a-producer-do? baggage), a Musician (take one-step-back-and-go-directly-to-jail baggage), and finally, for the past fifteen years, a very successful Television Sitcom Director (I'm-finally-the-big-kahuna-completely-in-control baggage). Not to mention that he sometimes sold his old wardrobe on eBay (whoa—fill-in-the-blank baggage).

Oh—and J.T. was indeed a College Professor (priggish baggage).

The job of director was the Holy Grail of Hollywood film success, but television didn't suit J.T.'s personality. A perfectionist in television is bad math: the sum of this equation is borderline insanity.

J.T.'s earnest goal was to do it all: create worthwhile television, care for his colleagues, nurture his actors, respect the craft of filmmaking, and not show contempt for the viewing public. Doing it all was in direct contradiction to the networks' standards and practices, because it cost too much. The industry tolerated J.T. when the shows he directed pulled in big Nielsen ratings and were considered hits. But when the numbers dropped and ended J.T's lucky streak, the director's devotion to his ideals became the stuff of mockery behind his back.

J.T.'s downfalls were always his own doing. His baggage-laden crusades took a heavy toll on him physically, causing him stomach ulcers and daily migraines. J.T. was ridiculously naïve for an artistic veteran, a lummox when it came to diplomacy and politicking, and alarmingly proficient in the art of self-destruction. He persisted in wearing his quixotic, utopian work ethic as a badge of honor.

The standards J. T. Baker imposed on himself were a direct product of working with adults his entire childhood. Somewhere along the way, his personal growth had been stunted and actually come to a screeching halt. He would forever be stuck with the mores of an idealistic teenager. Things were either *right* or they were *wrong*. He was a self-made man-child, programmed to be a pro, to give his all, and believe that even his best wasn't good enough. *The project* was always more important than the players. Selfishness would never be tolerated. And J.T. understood that he must always surround himself with people smarter than himself, and always gave them full credit.

While digging in deeper and deeper and becoming more and more rigid in his self-proclaimed war on mediocrity, J.T. never took a step back to analyze the scaffolding he'd erected in order to be and stay J.T. Baker. He never allowed himself a moment to realize the extreme conformity it took to be a nonconformist. To protect his freedom of creativity he became a slave to self-preservation. He no longer knew what he was fighting for, and he was exhausted.

J.T.'s standards and expectations of himself were so high that one notorious day, in the middle of directing a sitcom, he *lost direction* and began to shake. He had a meltdown that immediately became part of showbiz lore and was still legendary.

In clinical terms, J.T. suffered a nervous breakdown. What actually happened was that he'd matured within the space of a single moment. With sudden clarity, J.T. understood that he could not continue believing it was his job on the planet to make everything perfect.

With that epiphany, he no longer had purpose. And the part of him that was genetically programmed to find *the funny* in everything triggered a laughing fit as he stood, unresponsive to others, pathetically shaking in the center of a sitcom living room set. He stood on the same spot, laughing, for over an hour until his wife Natasha could be contacted and made it to the soundstage.

Natasha was the only person J.T. responded to on that fateful, fit-full day. J.T. continued to laugh at the inane, schmaltzy world he now recognized as his life. He not only had a nervous breakdown, but also found the nervous breakdown to be ironically funny. Always funny.

Natasha gently walked him to her car and drove him off the studio lot and went directly to the Santa Monica Hospital.

As they rode up the elevator in the hospital, J.T. looked at his savior and whispered, "Are you committing me?"

"You're already committed, J.T.," Natasha said with shrewd wisdom but without judgment, "to me; to our son Jeremy."

Natasha gripped J.T.'s hand and led him from the sixth-floor elevator to the maternity ward. She took J.T. to the glass window where he had stood eight years prior, when their son Jeremy was born with a life-threatening kidney ailment. Nothing more needed to be said. Together, J.T. and Natasha stood and stared through the glass at the newborn babies for hours . . . well, until a nurse realized none of the babies belonged to them and had Security escort them out of the building. But—no trips to a shrink, no vacations at a spa, not a single pill was swallowed—only now, Natasha had given J.T. perspective. From that day on, *Jeremy* became their personal code, whether they were together or not. Whenever J.T. found himself dog-paddling in a pool of dementia, Natasha would appear at his shoulder—in person or in his mind—and whisper, *Jeremy*.

SHOW BUSINESS BEGAN to leave J.T. behind.

NATASHA WAS THE one person who had absolutely no hidden agenda and whose love for J.T. was unconditional. With his trademark childlike certainty, J.T. always maintained that his wife had to be either utterly right or utterly wrong. Faithful or unfaithful. Good or bad. So J.T. came to the logical conclusion that Natasha was a goddess. During J.T.'s sole attempt at psycho-therapy, the psychiatrist had unwisely suggested that J.T. might have what he referred to as the Madonna-whore syndrome. J.T. dove at the good doctor and knocked out two of his teeth.

True story.

It was Natasha who talked him down from a roof, made him

promise that he'd never *play with sharp objects,* stopped the internal bleeding, and was the one who finally called the moving company and hauled her family out of Los Angeles, reasoning that J.T. couldn't be that self-righteous and survive in La-La Land.

They hightailed it, leaving Hollywood far behind. On the opposite coast, actually: they bought a seven-acre farm in a remote area in the foothills of the Smoky Mountains. Not that J.T. knew anything about farming. He had accepted a job as a part-time professor of film at a local university.

As Natasha had put it, "If you want future generations to understand the old-fashioned way of doing things *right,* rather than just *doing things,* you ought to *teach* future generations the right way to do things and stop complaining about it."

"You're right."

"Besides, sweetheart, the only ones who want to listen to your idealistic rants about filmmaking are college kids."

"Really?"

"'Fraid so."

"Oh."

ON THE TOP of his (admittedly smallish) mountain, J.T. found elements of life he had seen in the movies or even shot as a director. But now he was no longer a spectator. Mother Earth quickly schooled J.T., showing him that there was actually a world outside of show business. There were no hyperkinetic edits pushing the day to move faster. J.T. was so accustomed to that former existence that it took a while for him to actually believe his new pet phrase: "This is the life!" After a time, though, the rhythms of his new life became hypnotic, symphonic. He could absorb the beauty as long as he wanted to without the fear that somebody would *change his channel.* He could see . . . forever.

Damn, J.T. thought more than once, *Mother Nature would've made one helluva director. She can really bring it on! What the fuck am I saying?*

J.T. finally had a life.

"Can you smell the—who the hell is smoking?! Why would anyone smoke with all of this clean air and the mountains and the trees!?"

"J.T., sweetheart, we live in a *tobacco state*."

"Oh. Right."

J.T. learned to handle a tractor, and for Tasha's forty-fifth birthday he bush-hogged the shape of a giant heart in the cow pasture. She saw it every morning from up on the hill where their A-frame house jutted out into the clean, if a mite tobacco-y, air.

At first J.T. predicted what his neighbors might be saying behind his back. He'd write country dialogue in his head, like "That retarded liberal Hollywood Jew. He's why America's goin' to hell in a handbasket, *bless his heart*." Once he allowed himself to get to know his neighbors, though, J.T. learned that they were more substantial than any he'd ever had. Their knee-jerk kindness and generosity always caught J.T. off guard. He realized he'd had stereotypical thoughts because he'd been directing stereotypical shows for over a decade.

ON THIS SUNDAY afternoon in late summer, J.T., Natasha, and their nine-year-old son Jeremy were all midwives to Lola, a miniature Jersey cow that had become a family pet. Lola was having a rough go of it, trying to force her little calf out of her swollen body.

At first, J.T.'s mind wandered to a comic-book place, where he imagined that all of the world's troubles were inside Lola: oppression, tyranny, cruelty. All the world's problems were about to come out of a cow's vagina.

Then the cow's scream-moos finally registered. If J.T. was going to save the world, he would have to purge the pregnant cow of *the Fox Channel*!

Natasha nodded to J.T. He took a deep breath and plunged his hands into the bovine mama.

"J.T., how's she feel?" Natasha had spoken to the vet about problems that might come up with the birth, and what it would feel like if the calf were breech.

"Not nearly as good as you, but she'll do."

"Daaaad!"

"J.T.?"

He got a good grip and *pulled*. The wet calf came out so fast J.T. had to use every remnant of his athletic ability to catch it before it flew past Natasha and Jeremy. It was slippery, and lighter than he'd expected. *If I were filming this right now, I wouldn't use a filter because that would make it too sentimental,* J.T. thought as he gently laid the calf next to its mother. He fell back in the straw and laughed. Even in that moment, show business had intruded. And he was amazed all over again that there was life outside Hollywood.

"Good catch, Dad," Jeremy said.

"Thanks, big guy. Next time, you call for it." He winced as he stood up.

J.T. had bad knees. Bad ankles. A bad back. J.T. was a poster boy-man for over-the-hill jocks. All of the stunts he'd done as an actor were kicking him back. He could've really used the hazard pay now. Or the meds.

The lightbulb above the barn door started to flutter. It was connected to the phone in the house, pulsing when it rang.

"Should we run and get it?" Jeremy asked. "It could be Lola's husband, wanting to know if he's the real father."

"Funny. But if it's Lola's husband, he's calling from McDonald's," J.T replied.

"Not funny, Dad."

"Sorry . . . pain. Knee. Hurt."

"No excuse for bad jokes, Dad. You've said it a million times," Jeremy pointed out.

"You're right, big guy, one of the worst sins on this planet Earth is . . ."

"NO FUNNY," they all flatly said in sync, making it *teeny-tiny* funny.

"Funny is good," J.T. lectured for the million-and-first time as they all walked back to the house. "BAD FUNNY is bad, *ALMOST FUNNY* is okay—but *NO* FUNNY is a sin against all humanity."

The sun was starting to set behind the Smoky Mountains. They stopped and watched it disappear. "Breathtaking, huh?" J.T. whispered.

"Yeah. My asthma's kickin' in, Dad."

"*Infinitesimal* FUNNY."

"No. Dad. My asthma is kicking in."

"Oh. Shit."

Tasha ran ahead to get Jeremy's inhaler and J.T. picked his boy up, cradling him in his arms and running into the house. Jeremy recognized the funny in how pitiful he must look, but Tasha and J.T. had a hard time with that brand of funny.

Green Acres it wasn't. Lisa's trust fund had probably paid for Oliver's rural idyll. The Bakers had no such reserves. Sunsets behind mountains cost money. Cow feed cost money. Health care for Jeremy cost money. "Good times and tough times, we're a team!" J.T. would repeat. Unfortunately, somebody had to pay for the team uniforms, which put J.T. back to square one.

"Here's an ironic funny," J.T. said one day. "I can't pay the bills on my teaching salary and the only thing I've ever done in my life, the only skills I have, I left behind in Hollywood."

J.T. needed a directing gig. *Now that,* J.T. thought, *is funny.*

The Meeting of the So-called Minds

THE POOLEYS, DICK BEAGLEBUM, the Studio, and the Network all met in a very public place. Public so no one could throw a tantrum and get away with it. And public to make sure there were witnesses in case of bad behavior. It was standard protocol for savvy executives.

Each side thought this would be a tough sell and was adamant not to budge.

There was no small talk, no preliminaries. Not even a hello. Dick opened the negotiations with a story about parity and how everyone here " . . . is a partner. So there is no reason for hostilities, and whatever the outcome, the only thing that *truly matters* is *the show itself;* not the individual Entities, but the sum of the Entities," which of course was the pop culture miracle known as *I Love My Urban Buddies!*

Then, like members of a choral ensemble who'd actually practiced the composition "I know who should direct this show," Debbie, Lance, the Pooleys, and Dick each chimed in as if on cue in a perfect fugue:

"J.T. Baker."

"J.T. Baker."

"J.T. Baker."

"J.T. Baker."

There was an awkward beat—a very awkward beat—as an aging waitress set down a big plate of fries on the table. Debbie had practically inhaled the first order. She'd grabbed it from the waitress and made it very clear that these French fries were hers, dammit! This time her hand froze in mid-reach toward the second plate o' potatoes. "Wait—*what did you say?*"

"J.T. Baker," everyone repeated.

They all looked at one another. Not one of them had planned on this agreement. Not only that: no one had a backup plan.

The Hollywood Dictionary

HONCHO: Someone who passes the buck while getting the big bucks.

"Can I get you guys anything else?" the old waitress asked.

The tableful of honchos was paralyzed with indecision.

Fuck! each one of them thought. *Who can I blame for this?*

THE PHONE HAD rung at the Baker house. It was three hours past any sensible business day in Hollywood (even on a *Who-Died-Sunday*), but that was nothing new for anyone who had received *those* phone calls in the past. The answering machine in the kitchen had Dick Beaglebum's excited voice on it. Natasha was glad that Jeremy had wandered to his room before they played the message. Now she and J.T. stood, staring at each other, hearing the *voice* . . . the voice from the past. The voice that represented money for the family. Insurance for Jeremy. Suicide for J.T.

J.T. was a loving husband and lived for his family, but he was still a head case. Dick Beaglebum once told J.T. that if he gave fifty percent of himself to a show, it would still be more than one hundred percent of what others gave to the weekly process. J.T. had been so offended by the possibility of that premise that he'd curled up into a fetal position for two days. Yup, J.T. was that kind of head case.

Natasha understood all of the implications before she heard Dick's enthusiasm/compassion on the message machine—just after the message from Southern States, the farm supply store, telling them that the organic dairy feed and the 235 bales of hay were in.

"We need to talk," Natasha said as she steadily erased the messages.

J.T. began to shake.

With great enthusiasm and compassion Dick had left his phone number and a speedy message about the three episodes and how J.T. was getting a second or maybe a third life in show business. "Maybe a fourth or a fifth . . . anyway, call me, J.T. UVWYXZ!"

Then the phone rang again. It was Debbie from the network saying it was, like, great that J.T. was on board. Then the phone rang again. It was Lance. The studio couldn't be happier with the choice to have someone so experienced come in at this tragic but chaotic moment; someone to keep *the ship sailing;* someone to keep *the train on track;* someone who could keep *the ball in play.*

"Jeez. Do they actually go to Cliché School?" Natasha muttered.

The phone rang again—two voices, one male and one female. The Pooleys were so excited to be working with someone like J.T. They had heard so many old, er, great stories about him.

Where's the fucking sunset when I need it? J.T. thought. All he could see when he closed his eyes was the smog of Los Angeles and everything that represented to him.

J.T. ran to the sink and threw up. He was savvy enough to know he was being asked to step into a hornet's nest. No one in Hollywood would ever say anything positive about him and he knew that. Something was really wrong. Lance's train needed to stay on track; his ship needed a sailor; his baseball needed to be kept in play—*out of foul territory*. There definitely wasn't a *fair* territory in this game. There never had been. And speaking of has-beens . . . He threw up again.

"Now who's the cliché?" J.T. tried to say as he wiped his mouth.

Natasha put her arms around her shivering husband/director. *So fragile,* she thought. She cleaned him with a warm hand towel.

"We should've changed our phone number again. Do you think you have to go?"

"You know I have to go," was all he said as Jeremy ran into the kitchen. He wanted a snack but knew he couldn't eat or drink past eight o'clock because he was due at the hospital for blood tests, then the dialysis . . . Natasha and J.T. went silent.

"Who puked?" Jeremy asked.

"Your father was finally hit with the postpartum, cow-birthin', *Green Acres* blues," Natasha said.

J.T. tried to smile and hide his shaking from his child.

Jeremy, however, absorbed everything. From having to face daily medical traumas, he had knowledge of the world that other kids his age just didn't have. He bravely understood that without a kidney transplant, he would die. "Dad, please don't go back into the caves. Please. Please don't contaminate yourself with those people because of me. Please."

"Contaminate?" J.T. said, still trying to distract Jeremy. "I'm not sure if that's the right—well—no, come to think of it, that *is* the right word. Never mind."

The caves. That's what J.T. called the soundstages. When J.T. worked, he would usually enter the caves before the sun rose and leave the caves late into the darkness of night. The weather was a constant in the caves. Reality was warped within the caves. Millions of dollars were at stake, so in order to attain success, people allowed almost anything to go on inside the caves.

Anything.

What went on in the caves was biblical in scale: people lost all sense of priorities and moral proportion in the service of their own advancement. Temptation, power, and delusion ran rampant within the caves.

"Mom, I know. It's not my fault and could I please go to my room while you and Dad talk . . . and then Dad will pack and then . . . he'll leave. I'll go to my room. I love you." Jeremy grabbed a banana and left.

With everything J.T. and Natasha were trying to micromanage cerebrally, they also had a jolt of pride because of their son's . . . compassion. *True compassion,* J.T. thought. *He's doomed. Why couldn't he be more selfish? Why couldn't he be a good little jerk, like a regular kid? Why did he have to be so damn good?*

"I've gotta corrupt this kid, Natasha," J.T. muttered. "I've gotta turn him into an asshole. That's what he needs. He needs a good old-fashioned asshole lesson." He was trying to get Natasha to laugh. Even smile.

Jeremy was their number one priority. J.T. knew he had to go back into the caves. His Directors Guild insurance had run out and this job meant an opportunity to renew the insurance so that Jeremy could get the best health care possible. It was a no-brainer.

Natasha and J.T. sat at the kitchen table for two hours. Barely a word was spoken. After that they sat on the end of Jeremy's bed, watching him sleep. Barely a word was spoken. After that, J.T. packed a suitcase in preparation for three weeks in Los Angeles. Barely a word was spoken. They kissed.

"*Darling, reach out.* Call Asher," she said.

Before daybreak, J.T. drove two and a half hours to the nearest airport that had an early Monday morning flight to Los Angeles. If he could get on the 6 A.M. flight, he'd be in Los Angeles by 9 A.M. That would put him sitting at the production meeting in the San Fernando Valley by ten (if he was lucky), ready to *steer the boat, keep the train on the tracks,* and, most important, *protect the foul lines and make sure the ball stayed in play.*

The Red-eye

J.T. COULD NEVER sleep or watch a film on airplanes. He couldn't figure out why anyone would want to watch a movie when they could look out their window and see planet Earth from thirty-five thousand feet in the sky. The stars, the moon. *What's wrong with people?* he thought, watching them pay five dollars for a set of crappy headphones.

J.T. sat in the coach section, the studio's budget not stretching to business class, according to his trusty agent, Dick Beaglebum. At least he had a row to himself. Red-eyes from Johnson City, Tennessee, didn't exactly tend to be fully booked. He could get up and pace if he needed to, and J.T. frequently needed to.

He had no script to go over—there hadn't been time to send it. He kept thinking about the turn of events that had brought him to this point, to getting back on a plane to the place he'd sworn to leave behind forever.

Jeremy had been seven when they left Hollywood. Less than a year later, he'd collapsed one day, and when he woke up, he was in the hospital with a peritoneal dialysis catheter snaking from his abdomen and his father massaging his feet and staring at him with one eye closed.

J.T. couldn't help it. He had a habit of viewing the world with one eye closed, as if filming *the moment*. The exact provenance of this quirk had been debated at many family Thanksgivings, but the truth was that seeing the world in 35 millimeter was J.T.'s secret way of keeping disturbing realities at bay. He no longer knew if this had started only after he became a director, or if he'd taken to directing because a part of his soul responded to distancing himself through a lens.

J.T. panned to Natasha as she wiped Jeremy's clammy forehead with a cool blue washcloth. The Bakers had been briefed by doctors, nurses, and therapists about what life would now be like. They were only beginning to come to grips with the understanding that young Jeremy had a very serious illness, and that the treatments would greatly alter their lives from then on.

Jeremy was staring at a sitcom on the TV above his head. The laugh track was bugging the hell out of his parents. J.T. looked around for the remote. "Jeremy, would you like me to turn off this god-awful tripe?"

"If you'd directed it, it would be funny," Jeremy said, his throat still painfully dry.

While other fathers and sons talked sports, Jeremy and his dad would spend hours talking about "the Funny"—the noun, not the adjective. At seven, he understood the quad split. The kid just . . . *had* it.

"Wow. Um, thanks," J.T. looked away, embarrassed. "Maybe you should rest now." He found the remote attached to the nurse's call button.

"Daddy, who . . . ?" Jeremy's vocal cords had so little air to support his voice that strange harmonics were taking the place of his natural speaking voice.

Natasha urged him to drink some ice water. "Who what, sweetheart?"

The Hollywood Dictionary

THE QUAD SPLIT (TAKE ONE): A single monitor that shows four different camera angles at once.

"It's okay, Jeremy. Just close your eyes. Sleep." J.T. spoke with the helplessness of a father who could not control the situation and the authority of a television director who was used to being in control of everything.

"Daddy?"

"Yes, Jeremy. We're here."

"Who . . . who stole the . . ."

"Who stole the what, sweetheart?" J.T. asked, concerned that his son might be hallucinating from the drugs.

"No one stole anything, darling," Natasha said, her voice nurturing.

Jeremy's eyes, clear with the genius of innocence, slowly moved from the television to his father.

"Daddy—Who . . . stole the funny?"

"Who stole the funny?" J.T. repeated. He snapped his head back and looked at his wife, dumbfounded. *Brilliant. Our kid is fucking brilliant!*

Monday

J.T. WAS BARRELING along Sepulveda Avenue in a jalopy that had barely passed the California roadworthiness test eleven months before, trying to steer with one hand and talk with the other. He was on the phone with his agent, and he wasn't smiling. "You mean to tell me—"

"J.T., J.T., my main man-director-man-guy. No need to get upset over the little things," Dick Beaglebum interjected.

"Dick, I'm driving a rental car with no brakes. I can't stop the fucking thing," J.T. said in a panic.

"Why'd you rent a car with no brakes?"

"Because, Dick, when I got to the counter and gave them the reservation letters *that you faxed to me,* they informed me that they don't make reservations with *letters,* they make them with *numbers*! Numbers!"

"Well of course they do, J.T. Who confirms a reservation with letters? Really. I mean, that should've tipped you off right there."

J.T. veered to avoid a pedestrian. "Tipped me off? Dick, that was your way of telling me they weren't going to give me transportation?"

"J.T., you're gonna crash and kill yourself if you don't calm down."

"Oh, I see. If I calm down, I won't crash? Is that what you're saying?"

"Fuck you!" yelled the driver of a pickup truck.

"Listen to yourself, J.T."

"I can't hear myself over all of the honking horns! I'm going through red lights at major intersections! I just got cursed at by a redneck who's more redneck than a real redneck!"

"Huh? Just pull over, J.T."

"I can't just pull over unless I want to use a pedestrian as a brake pad!"

"Well . . . just coast until you stop."

"I'm going *downhill*!"

"Well, go *up*hill."

"I can't go *uphill* because I'm going *downhill*!"

"Of course you can go uphill, J.T. If you're going downhill, *there must be an uphill,* huh? Gotcha!"

"I'm coming to another red light. Hold on, I'm going to try the emergency brake. Damn—I'm almost fifty! This is a shitty way to die!"

"J.T.," Beaglebum quickly said, "don't tell anyone you're almost fifty! They think thirty's old. Forty's the new cutoff. You can't be funny if you're over forty. Got it?"

J.T. tossed the phone on the car seat, held his breath, and pulled up hard on the emergency brake. The rent-a-wreck skidded to a stop. He fumbled for the phone. "It worked."

"Good. Can you imagine the chatter around town if two directors died on this show?"

J.T. slumped in his seat. "Tell me I'm getting per diem. Tell me they're paying for a hotel."

"J.T.—"

"Nothing? Are you pleading poverty on the only bona fide hit show on TV?"

"Their budget is skyrocketing, Say-Hey-J-T. We have a dead guy, for chrissake!"

"We?" J.T. shouted over the honks.

"I did a little tap dance to get you this gig. You should be happy, J.T. You should be grateful. I don't hear grateful. Hello?" Dick waited a moment, then tapped the receiver on his phone. "Hello? What's that noise? You there, J.T.?"

"The car stalled." J.T. was stuck in the middle of morning rush-hour traffic with a stalled car. "Shit!"

"J.T., think of the big picture. You do three episodes which means you fulfill your Directors Guild requirements so your little boy Jack will be covered by the DGA insurance this year for his liver problem—"

"My son is named Jeremy. And it's his kidneys—"

"Kidney is a funny word, J.T. Starts with a *k*. You should try and work that into the show. Kidney. Funny."

J.T.'s voice went very low. "Dick, please *do not make reference to my son ever again*. Understand?"

"Oh, never. Never. I just wanted you to know I'm understanding and really behind you, J.T.," Dick said.

"Yes . . . behind me. I'd feel so much more comfortable if you were in front of me."

"Funny!" said Dick, thinking, *Oh man, it's already starting with this guy*. "You're funny. So," Dick continued, enthusiastically, "you'll be there for the eleven o'clock read? You know, with the car stalling and everything?"

"Have I ever *not* been there? Early? Ever? And it's the ten o'clock production meeting, then the eleven o'clock read," J.T. said pointedly.

"Hey, J.T.—*attitude*. Stay in control." Dick switched back to *compassionately*.

J.T. flipped his cell phone shut and tried again to restart the hunk-a-junk-a-burnin'-rubber. Cars were honking, men were screaming, women were yelling. Defeated, J.T. gave up trying to start the engine.

With everything he had to overcome, the one thing he wasn't ready for was culture shock. The expanse and pace of the Smoky Mountains might have seeped into J.T.'s soul and soothed his spirit, but no one in L.A. gave a damn. J.T. was a captive in road-rage limbo. Assholes to the left of him, suckas to the right, here he was, stuck in the middle of a U-turn. Stuck in the middle of a U-turn.

HALF AN HOUR later, J.T. called his agent again.

"Hello, Dick?"

"Jaysaycanyousee T! My main director-man!"

"I rented a bicycle, Dick. Will they at least pay for *that*?"

"A bicycle?"

"Yes. A bicycle." Then J.T. started to sing a pissy version of the Queen song: "I want to ride my bicycle, I want to ride my bike— will they *at least* pay for a rented bicycle?"

The young skateboarder who stood behind the counter of the Bike Emporium started singing along. J.T. held the cell phone between himself and the young employee so Dick could hear, then finished signing *business expense* on the receipt for his bike.

"A fuckin' bicycle? You're fuckin' kidding me, right? What a kidder."

J.T. shut off his cell phone, nodded to the skateboarder, and rolled the bike outside into the smog to begin his journey to the studio.

J.T. had managed to get the lemon towed back to Rent-A-Wreck, rent a bicycle at his own expense, get on the studio lot, find his parking space (which looked rather silly with a crappy bike in it), and be twenty minutes early, as usual. Of course he was drenched in sweat, but he got a shirt out of his backpack and changed in the restroom. He took out his hated cell phone again, but this time he dialed home.

"Honey?" J.T. said. There was a tremble in his voice. He tried to put up a great façade, but two hours in Hollywood had already dulled his acting ability.

"Darling, screw it all. I'll pick up Jeremy and drive to the airport right now," Natasha urged.

"Honey—don't you worry. I'll knock out these three—give 'em fifty percent, be a good boy and never be confrontational, get the insurance for Jeremy, pass GO and collect two hundred dollars," J.T. replied, making a failed attempt at *funny*.

Silence was beamed to a satellite in outer space and back down to Earth into J.T.'s phone. Finally he said, "This silence is costing us a fortune. Besides . . . Tasha . . . you can't come out here. Jeremy needs to stay in school, follow all of his medical protocols . . . I'm sorry . . . I don't know why I said that. You're the best at that."

"J.T.," Natasha paused. "J.T., when does Asher arrive? I'll feel a lot better knowing Ash is watching your back."

Asher Black was the strength, the common sense, the Zen master, the best friend that J.T. now needed when Natasha couldn't be there. Ash, a former student of J.T.'s, became a professor of film at Alabama State. He was so overqualified for that particular position that when he negotiated his contract with the university he found he was holding many bargaining chips, which translated into perks: he could take time off, with pay and expenses, if and when he went as an observer or an assistant to a director on a film or sitcom project. This meant that whenever J.T. was directing, Ash could work as his assistant and keep up with the ever-changing craft of film and video directing and production.

Asher Black was the son of black hippie parents who decided to dabble in Judaism right at the time of Asher's birth: thus the name, Asher; thus the nickname, Ash. An indication of his Southern cordiality and his uncommon decency was his gift of putting strangers at ease with his self-deprecating humor: "It's a good think my last name is Black and not *Blackwards*. It would've been tough growing up Ash Blackwards." Most people would smile and from that moment on, his name would never be an issue.

Asher was viewed (advertised) as a valuable asset to the university. He was an African-American (*Please, refer to me as black. I am a black man. I was born and raised in America. That makes me a black American. Thank you*) who could *integrate* the show business world into the orb of academia. He was the perfect recruiting tool for snagging the few liberals and blacks who were thinking of attending a college of fine arts in the deep South. Asher's forays into Hollywood, thanks to J.T.'s help, gave him real-world skills that he could then impart to his students. This was rare for a university known solely for its football team.

Being the university's poster boy grew tiring, and when Ash found work as a "punch-up" writer on a UPN sitcom, he moved to Los Angeles and began a new career as a junior writer. When work slowed, he was offered a position at UCLA teaching acting, writing, and a course appropriately titled "How to Survive in Hollywood." Most of the course was based on his firsthand knowledge of J.T. and his personal struggles in L.A. Ironically, Ash now knew more about the L.A. scene than J.T. Student became teacher, and that was fine with J.T. and Tasha.

"Asher's going to meet me on the set if he can't make the production meeting or the table read. First he's gotta teach his 'How to Survive in Hollywood' course. Maybe I should take his class while I'm here . . ." J.T.'s voice trailed off.

"I adore you," Natasha said.

"I adore you, too. Kiss Jeremy for me. Tell him . . . if I see Kobe Bryant I'll tell him he's a selfish asshole."

"You're stalling."

"Bye."

"Bye."

J.T. checked his watch: nine minutes to ten. The week was about to begin. He couldn't feel a single joint in his body as he walked toward Stage Five. If only it were about *the job*. If only it were about doing a great job of *directing* . . . if only . . . J.T. took a deep breath and disappeared into *the cave*.

J.T. OPENED THE soundproof door and entered a five-foot-square holding room, padded from floor to ceiling with old soundproofing material that had aged from white through the vanillas all the way into a stale chocolate color. It was kept in place with chicken wire stapled to beams and two-by-fours. This was the place where people stayed when the flashing red light was on signaling DO NOT ENTER because filming was in progress.

J.T. pushed a second heavy door that opened into one of the caves, also known as Stage Five. Stage Five was the home of *I Love My Urban Buddies*. A blast of icy air immediately accosted him.

"Cold is funny." That was a theory started by frightened joke writers who blamed the Southern California heat for sluggish audiences who weren't responding to their jokes. Because of that hypothesis, every soundstage was like a subzero freezer. Funny was not only cold, it was now arctic.

The experience of walking into the cave for the first time is very similar to that of a kid walking into Yankee Stadium for the first time. It's intimidating for visitors, because this is the very spot where the dramas unfold, where the heroes and villains wage war and where other metaphors are mixed. It's overwhelming. When there are no sets on a soundstage, even the smallest cave can look like an airport hangar without the 747.

As J.T. walked deeper onto Stage Five, he took a quick glance at the bleachers, which were to his left. The bleachers were just that: uncomfortable metal bench seating in stacked rows that could hold a live audience of nearly four hundred friends, family, agents, managers, and a few of the viewing public. The bleachers hadn't been cleaned since the late Friday night shoot of the previous week, and along with the litter of candy wrappers there were empty pizza boxes—never a good sign. Ordering pizza was a very cheap way of enticing an audience to stay when the shoot night was running ridiculously long—as in starting on Friday and finishing on Saturday.

Hundreds of thick black wires ran above the sets to powerful lamps, capable of creating the illusion of daylight, that were hung on metal bars and safety-wired onto grids (in case of earthquakes or lawsuits). Despite the wattage of the lamps, there always seemed to be a slight visibility problem in the caves because of the dust that perpetually floated in the air, filtering the light. Dirt had accumulated since the day the stages were built, tracked in and stirred up by generations of feet. Some caves still had asbestos hanging from the rafters that was supposed to have been removed years—decades—before.

Only in a cave could grime be glamorous. It's a magical way of seeing the world, through a filter. When you work in a cave, it's a way to develop magical allergies and come down with magical illnesses.

J.T. took a deep breath. And coughed up a loogy. After a shoot night, the caves always smelled of fear: body odor, stale beer, and distant aromatic hints of medicinal marijuana. But there was also the smell of freshly painted sets, and the moldy backdrops of what the audience would see out the characters' windows. *Same ol', same ol',* J.T. thought.

He found a corner of the set where he could get a feel for the show and quickly speed-read the overwritten episode. This was a Christmas episode with many guest stars and children. Also, every scene began with the stage direction: "This is the best ever Christmas. The *best ever* Christmas *ever* to be on film." J.T. laughed again. *How many Christmas shows have I shot,* he thought, *where everything was the best ever?*

That one phrase took the writers off the hook and put all the pressure on him, the director. Now he had to conjure up some-one's idea of the *best ever* without having a clue about what that looked like. *I guess fucking Beaglebum would want me to give them fifty percent of my best ever!*

Suddenly J.T. realized that he heard his own voice echoing through the empty soundstage. He had been ranting aloud. *That is not a good sign*, he thought, *is it? Certainly not on day one.* No one answered. Phew.

The Production Meeting

J.T. WALKED OUT of Stage Five and past two more gargantuan stages to a row of old cottages. There was no latent glamour here. He walked up the rotting wooden stairs of the first cottage, through a door that had been repainted every year for the past thirty years but never once sanded, and into the room where the production meeting was to be held.

This was a room of confrontation: a room where descriptive sentences and the actual details of filming them converged, and clashed. Thoughts. Practicalities. Left hemisphere, right hemisphere. If I were to tell you, the reader, that this room was painted a depressing gray and the walls had the pockmarks of a kid with bad skin, that although no one was allowed to smoke in it anymore the odor of stale tobacco still leached from its pores, you would have no trouble imagining it. But put that description in a script for a TV show, and at the production meeting someone from the art department would say, "What the fuck shade of gray is depressing to you? Because I find all shades of gray depressing. So? Which is it? Do you want cinder gray? Battleship gray? French gray? Hoary-haired gray? Smoke gray? Steel gray? Silver gray? Quaker gray? Gray-gray? I've gotta paint these fucking walls tomorrow unless you want to pay overtime for the depressing gray which of course would then *definitely* be a depressing gray."

A room of passive aggression.

"No, really. I want you to have that oh-so-depressing shade of gray. I'll do everything in my power to make it as depressing as possible yet still cheery and happy for a sitcom. Well, I guess you want sitcom-depressing gray! But here's the deal: how much are you willing to spend on the depressing gray? Because we have entire new sets to build."

A room of power struggles.

Then the scriptwriter would say, "You know, I've changed my mind. Strike the depressing gray. I now see the room as a thoughtful patina-green. Actually, see if you can find a Quaker green."

A room of Fuck You and You and You.

"Touché. Quaker green it is. (*Asshole.*)"

Trust me. The room is depressing and it's gray.

Which of course sends mixed signals to a director: "Oh. So now it's the room that's depressing, not necessarily the color? It also just happens to be gray? Props and Set Dressing—that should send you guys in a completely different direction. One thing's for sure it is not—Makeup, Hair, and Wardrobe, listen up!—it may be Quaker green but it is *not* a room full of Quakers."

"Oh. So what do I do with all of the oatmeal?"

It is a room where Abbott and Costello meet Vincent van Gogh. And it can be a room where unfunny comics meet a thief who forges paintings.

Now, keeping all of that in mind, add in sliding windows that don't slide and coffee stains on the one-one-hundredth-inch depressing-gray carpet.

It's a war room.

J.T. stopped just inside the door and sighed. By his count, he'd sat as director for thirty-plus other famous and forgettable shows in this very room. This would be thirty-plus, plus one.

J.T. believed that a good director had the detective skills of an experienced old cop who absorbed everything around him.

He tried to absorb the vibes of the room. *This room is empty,* he thought. *I flew almost three thousand miles to get here on time but people who live blocks away aren't here yet? What's with that?*

It was obvious that the department heads who came to the meeting only wanted to be there exactly when they had to be there. *Not a second before. Bad sign. Crap.*

The assistant director, a man named William Kay, wasn't even there. An assistant director should always show up before the others, especially before the director. An A.D. is employed for the run of the episodes to ensure continuity between rotating directors and the production itself. An assistant director is a completely different animal from the assistant *to* the director, which was Ash Black's title.

J.T. had worked with William Kay ten years earlier. He found him to be a very competent A.D., but a man who was a survivor. An A.D. should take a bullet for his (or *her*) director. But in order to survive (stay employed), this particular man had attended to his own interests first. The new directors, the old directors, the hacks, the talented ... they would all come and go, but somehow William Kay stayed employed. It didn't mean that he was a bad man or that his ethical foundation was corrupt by Hollywood stan-

> ## The Hollywood Dictionary
>
> **ASSISTANT TO THE DIRECTOR:** An assistant *to* the director has been known to *cover* the director's back.
>
> **ASSISTANT DIRECTOR:** An *assistant director* has been known to *stab* a director *in* the back.

dards. Not at all. It only meant that William Kay was looking out for William Kay.

Indeed, how could anyone in Hollywood blame a man who spread rumors, divulged secrets, and snuck up to the showrunners' office to warn them they had better keep an eye on a particular director? How could anyone in Hollywood blame a man who did it all so *sincerely*? You couldn't blame William Kay at all. These were simply the skills one needed to survive in show business. He'd have said he was just following orders.

In the *real* world he would have been left in a damp alley with a bullet in his head.

J.T. did blame William Kay.

J.T. walked up to the spread of food that was laid out, waiting to be eaten by showbiz types. Showbiz types, especially actors, loved free food. J.T., on the other hand, would never eat the studio's food. Eating *their* food meant that J.T. had bonded through protein and carbohydrates to the very people he despised. No, he was checking out the food because it was an indication of what kind of show J.T. was working on. If no one came early to eat breakfast yet the food was extravagant, there was a problem.

J.T. scoped out the food for quality. This particular two-table spread featured sections that catered to every new diet fad: a high-protein, high-fat section was carefully separated from a high-protein, low-fat section, and both were a respectable distance from a high-carb, lean-protein section. Another section was laden with fresh, out-of-season fruit, including a disproportionate number of an exotic, expensive, lumpy fruit from Thailand called noi-na. It could be used in a sentence, such as: "Are you ready?" And the sitcom answer would be: "Noi, na!" (J.T. later found out that the Pooleys liked noi-na. Because it was expensive.) There was a vegetarian section with hummus and tabouli. There was even a fast-food section for the Teamsters.

Tons of free food, J.T. thought. *No one is here. Very bad.*

The first person to arrive and stand and stare at the

The Hollywood Dictionary

TEAMSTERS: Butts of cruel, cheap jokes. Big butts . . .

food was Asher Black. Ash was nearly six feet five and towered over J.T., who noticed that Ash, at forty-one, was beginning to accumulate a roll around his belly and hips.

The two men hugged as if they were brothers who got along with each other. J.T. wasn't a fool. He knew that in many respects, Ash had surpassed him: as a human being, certainly, and maybe even as a filmmaker.

They loved each other.

When people saw the two of them together, saw all that honest affection, the rumors spread like a California wildfire:

"They're gay!"

"Did you see them hug?!"

"I saw J.T. kiss him on the cheek!"

"I always knew J.T. was gay!"

J.T. and Ash treasured the rumors. They loved fucking with everyone, and it also helped the real job at hand because it kept people off guard.

William, the assistant director, came running into the room and made straight for the food, giving J.T. a quick, *sincere,* Hollywood air kiss on the way to the lox and bagels.

"Damn you, J.T.!" William said over his shoulder. "Ten years and I've never beaten you to set. Do you know how demoralizing that is to an A.D.? During sex?"

William had the most aggravating sense of humor. He basically had one joke. He would add the words *during sex* or *after sex* to the end of almost every sentence to show how funny he could be. William never graduated from eighth-grade Funny.

He was out of breath. He still had the body of an athlete but was starting to show his bad eating habits in the form of love handles and the beginnings of a double chin.

"Hey—the more things change, the more things stay the same, huh?" J.T. said prophetically.

"During sex!" William did a spit take—all over the food.

J.T. threw a quick glance to Ash: *Never trust this guy.*

William turned around. "Oh—Flash! Brown!" he said with his mouth full. "I see you're here!"

"Yeah . . . um . . . kind of hard to miss seeing me . . ." Ash said, trying to avoid looking at the blob of cream cheese in the corner of William's mouth. "By the way," Ash continued, "I know it's been a while, but my name is A-S-H. Ash. Ash *Black*. If you actually *look at me*, it's hard to forget my last name. And my first name."

"Oh my God! Did I call you Flash? I meant Ash. I was just with my personal trainer. His name is Flash. Or is it Cash? Ah, anyway, I'm so damn sorry," William said sincerely. "But we're dope, right, my nigga?" William did his best rap pose.

J.T. spun, "Don't you dare—"

"It's okay, J.T.," Ash said calmly. "Dope?" He smiled at William.

"I ain't meanin' ta act da fool, barkin' on ya homey, dog," William said in his best urban-interact, form-a-relationship, connect-with-the-brothah lingo. He also now took the body language to a cartoon-like extreme, crossing his arms down by his groin and leaning to one side, almost losing his balance.

"I guess *you're* dope, then," Ash politely said, trying not to make the fool more of a fool.

William, happy with his urban result, went white again and turned to J.T. "I'm training for an over-thirty triathlon! Hey! What do you say to that? During sex?!" William pretend-punched J.T. in the stomach.

J.T. grabbed William's new love handles, not very playfully. "I'd say put less cream cheese on your bagel, triathlete-boy. And if you keep the *during-sex joke* going for the rest of the time I'm here, I will murder you in your sleep."

"Or during sex!"

Even though the workweek hadn't officially started, J.T. wanted to immediately remind his assistant director who the Alpha Dog was in the work equation. William's posture instantly and noticeably deflated when J.T. didn't even pretend-smile. *Mission accomplished*, J.T. thought.

"I quit smoking three weeks ago, s-so I've been substituting food for, for tobacco, but now I'm a triathloner!" William stammered, then smiled like a little kid waiting for approval from his dad.

"Wow," J.T. said, "that's great. You stopped smoking three weeks ago and now . . . you are a *triathlete*? Very impressive. When's your first race?"

"This Thursday," William answered, sincerely.

"Thursday? Thursday is camera-blocking day," J.T. said, as if talking to a mentally challenged person. "What A.D. would not be at his post on camera-blocking day?"

Camera-blocking day is the grueling day when all of the minutiae are worked out down to the millimeter. Colored pieces of tape are laid out all over the cement studio floor for the camera positions, which can number in the hundreds, and they coordinate with the hundreds of colored pieces of tape that are laid out on the set that represent each and every move an actor makes within each and every scene. It's the attention to detail on camera-blocking day that saves a show on the following shoot night. "It allows for the freedom to get back to the funny," J.T. would always say.

William raised his arm to play-punch J.T. in the shoulder, thought better of it, and scratched his head. "Hey, buddy—I knew you wouldn't mind if I was a little late on Thursday. Maybe a lot late! It means so much to me. To *my family*. Quitting smoking and all. Then becoming a triathloner. I mean, it's major! Life-changing! And I also cleared it with the Pooleys," he added, sincerely. "During sex!" William thought his bit was hysterical. Then, when J.T. once again failed to move a single facial muscle, William went back to his sincere expression.

He was so sincere J.T. just wanted to slap him, but felt Natasha on his shoulder, whispering, *Jeremy*.

"Yeah. What director needs his A.D. on camera-blocking day? And very wise of you to clear it with the showrunners before clearing it with your director."

"Now, don't make me feel guilty," William said, sincerely. He glanced nervously at Ash, who had slipped away to the drinks table and was now quietly moving closer to J.T. "I cleared it with Jasper, only he's dead now. And listen, you'll have *my* assistant. My second A.D. And she's better than I am! No shit. She really is better than me!"

"Well then, maybe she should have *your* job."

"Hey—J.T., it's me. Baby, it's me! *William.* I'm there for you, man. I've always been there for you, man. You know I'd never let you hang out to dry. After sex. Remember. It's me," William insisted . . . sincerely.

J.T. started to tremble, this time from anger. *We haven't even started and we're already behind schedule (after sex), you fucking ass,* he thought. Sabotaged by his right-hand man, his A.D.—the very first person from the show he'd made contact with. *One for one.* J.T.'s jaw muscles were steroidal in size from grinding his teeth.

Ash placed his large hand on J.T.'s shoulder. "How about a nice glass of pure, one hundred percent California orange juice, J.T.? It's *pulp-free.*"

"Pulp-free—that kinda sums it up," J.T. said, taking the juice from Ash. "Yeah, thanks. Just what the psychiatrist ordered." He drank it slowly, willing himself to calm down with every sip.

William was waiting like an eager puppy for a response. "So whattaya say, J.T.? Can I go? You're not mad, right?"

"Mad? Nah. Sure. Go. Hope you win, William," J.T. said, knowing full well that William was a long shot to even finish, let alone win. But he gave William a gentle pat on the back. He hoped it'd leave a bruise.

Ash shot J.T. a look. He was impressed. Ash had been poised for the first of the many lectures (explosions, really) to be expected from J.T. on the subject of professionalism. But no. J.T. had pledged to Natasha and Jeremy that he would stay in control. And he managed it this time. Ash grinned.

J.T., on the other hand, felt his stomach begin to make excess acid. It was no longer Natasha on his shoulder; now J.T.'s inner voice had developed Tourette's syndrome: *Jeremy. Insurance. Jeremy. Insurance. Jeremy. Insurance.*

People started to file into the room. J.T. looked down at his watch. One minute to ten. Not one of the skilled department heads went anywhere near the food. Their collective feeling of resentment was palpable as they assembled for the meeting. *A hit show—the number one show—and not a one of them wants to be here,* J.T. thought. *Not good. Again.*

They were all pros; they had done their homework. This episode had a script that they knew would probably be a page-one rewrite by the next morning. But their job descriptions told each and every one of them that they had to follow this script as if it were an authentic map rather than a harbinger of endless rewrites. (Reams upon reams of paper fed this mill, in a process that was largely responsible for the destruction of the Amazon forests.) Everyone from Props to Set Dressing to Wardrobe to Lighting knew they'd have to go through the motions of work for work's sake, following today's script, which wouldn't remotely resemble tomorrow's script.

Despite all this, when the department heads saw J.T. there were small smiles and nods. J.T. smiled knowingly back at them, giving the camera coordinator, Doc Ray Piscatori, an especially broad grin as he filed past. Most of them had worked with him before. They'd witnessed J.T.'s legendary brawls with above-the-line executives and producers, coming to the defense of his crew. They felt the respect he had for them. They knew he was one of the few directors who understood that he could never do their jobs as well as they could, who knew that it was their experience, their professionalism, their *schmuckiness* that could haul a show out of the crapper and make it worthy of broadcasting to an audience of millions.

What they didn't know was how ashamed J.T. felt about the disparity between his salary and theirs, and how determined that made him to make sure that, at least on his watch, none of the fucking millionaires who made their money off the underpaid schmucks would ever treat the schmucks like schmucks. It was J.T.'s mantra. If he'd written it down, he'd have used a fancier phrase, like "utmost respect."

They all took their seats and opened their scripts, which had marks and highlights scribbled all over the pages. They sat in a rectangular configuration, the standard arrangement for production meetings and the table reads that followed them. J.T. sat at the head of the table. William, who'd stopped to grab more food, was disconcerted to find that Ash had already sat down on J.T.'s right, the notebook he always carried at the ready. William hovered momentarily before letting out a loud, indignant breath and lowering himself into the chair to J.T.'s left as regally as could be accomplished with a plateful of bagels in one hand.

J.T. looked at his wristwatch: thirty seconds to an on-time production meeting. Not one member of the writing staff or a single producer was in the room. The showrunners, the Pooleys, were nowhere to be seen. *Not good,* J.T. mused.

William stood up and spoke, very sincerely. "Uh rugruh—" He swallowed. "'Scuse me. I regret to tell you that our last director, Jasper Jones, died tragically this weekend. It's really brutal. Awful story. Terrible. I won't take up your time now, but if anyone wants to know the details, come to me after the meeting 'cause it's really gruesome." He looked around expectantly. No one looked like they wanted to take him up on the offer. A little deflated, he continued, "Um, so, that means Jasper Jones *will not* be directing this episode. But we have in our presence the one and only J.T. Baker. He'll be with us for the next three episodes that Jasper can no longer do. Because he's dead. Now, if you all will join me in a moment of silence for Jasper."

William closed his eyes and bowed his head. Then he startled everyone by beginning to intone, sincerely, "God is great, God is good. Let us thank him for . . . uh, this production meeting . . . and the food . . ."

What a buffoon, Doc Ray thought. He rolled his eyes at Ash, who was trying to control his smirk.

J.T. took the opportunity to look around the table at the crew. His colleagues.

" . . . and for this show . . . and the food . . . and for, you know, everything. And the food. Amen." William looked up. "Thank you for sharing that moment. That was very kind of you," he said, sincerely. "Now, how about a round of applause for J.T.! During sex!"

The room was suddenly hostile. The entire crew had already come to despise William and that stupid fucking joke. Then a few looked at J.T. and smiled.

J.T. smiled back. "Well, all I can say is, William . . . that was a very moving tribute to Jasper Jones," he said.

"Are you fucking with me?" William narrowed his eyes.

"No! I must say that I am saddened to be here—"

J.T. was cut off by laughter. Everyone knew J.T. had escaped from L.A. and wouldn't be back if he didn't need the work—or the insurance.

"—um, under these unfortunate circumstances."

"Okay," William said, sincerely, "now that the tragedy is behind us, life goes on. And so does *I Love My Urban Buddies.* So allow me to begin this production meeting. Since we are waiting for the Pooleys, let's take this opportunity to go around the table and introduce ourselves to our new director, J.T. Baker! Oh! And no one has signed up for the show's softball team yet. Come on! Let's show some team spirit! During sex!"

Silence. Then, "While you sleep, William. I'll kill you while you sleep," J.T. whispered. Everyone heard him.

"Okay! Anyway, I give you—J.T. Baker!"

"Um . . ." J.T. said, standing up, "William. Allow me to do the honors. You might remember that most of these folks are *my* buddies. Let's see if I can go around the table and say hi to them. I need to gut-check my Alzheimer's. Now might be a good time to start."

"You have Alzheimer's?" William asked, sincerely incredulous.

"No, William. But if I get it this week, I'll forget that you won't be there on camera-blocking day. And if I have it now but have forgotten that I have it and don't make it through the week, don't go out and get another director. *Everyone moves up one.*"

The production meeting was off to a good start for J.T. The ones who mattered felt safe. William did not. Even *during sex.* J.T. had his A.D. firmly on the defensive, and it was only 10:04.

J.T. always took the time to walk around the table on his first day, greeting each department head. J.T. was effusive with all of his emotions, including respect for people who knew their craft, and this bubbled over as he spoke. People sat back more easily in their chairs, and even laughed, as he moved from one to the next. Then he introduced Ash.

"Everyone—or almost everyone—here will remember my assistant and fellow professor of film, Asher Black." J.T. made Ash stand up.

"Buck wild on the rilla, boss baller," William barked out, in support of his *ghetto buddy.*

"Whatever *he* says," Ash half smiled as he stood.

J.T. felt a surge of pride as the room gave Ash an earnest round of applause.

Actually, what was surging was panic. J.T. was starting to hyperventilate; his adrenaline was uncontrollable. He'd made sure that everyone in the room was back in their comfort zone, but in doing so, he'd reminded himself of how Hollywood had screwed his friends, and he was about to have a panic attack. Then, on cue, Natasha seemed to float onto J.T.'s shoulder, softly whispering, *Jeremy*.

With perfect timing, the door flew open and a showrunner walked in without saying hello to anyone. Anyone. J.T. had seen it all before. This was nothing new. All eyes were on Stephanie Pooley. She marched over to the craft service table, looked at the food, mumbled something under her breath, then poured herself a cup of coffee. She brought the coffee cup to her mouth; it was her own personal mug, with her name etched into the glass. It was like a . . . *license plate* cup. She took a sip, managed to swallow, then an extraordinary thing happened.

Stephanie actually changed—morphed—her body language to such a degree that it was cartoon-like. Seconds before, she'd been a late, angry bitch; now, backlit by the near-constant Los Angeles sun that scorched and bleached the carpet through the oversized windows, she was transformed into a Gorgon right out of Greek mythology, her hair snaking menacingly at the assembled crew. She became—Medusa! Would all who looked upon her at the production meeting be turned to stone? Or just get fired?

"The fucking coffee is cold!" were the first words from Stephanie Pooley. "Un-fucking-believable! Who is fucking responsible for this?! Who?! My drive in from Malibu was torture!"

> **The Hollywood Dictionary**
>
> **MALIBU:** Sun, sand, sea—sharks.

"Torture is a sense of anguish, an infliction of intense pain on the body or mind. What kind of car do you drive?" J.T. quipped. He thought it was funny. So did almost everyone else at the table.

Stephanie didn't.

Uh-oh, thought Ash. *He's pissed her off already*.

"Who are you?!" Stephanie demanded, trying to glower at both Ash and J.T. at the same time.

"I am J.T. Baker. I am your new director."

"*You're* J.T. Baker?" she asked, looking in the general direction of J.T. but not seeing him at all. "You're not that old."

Weird, J.T. thought.

Weird, Stephanie thought.

"Yes . . . J.T. Baker. Your new *live* director." J.T. said, trying to keep the funny from slinking sadly out of the room.

"Not for long if you keep that shit up," Ms. Pooley groused.

Is she kidding? J.T. wondered. *What shit?*

This fucker has to be kidding, Ms. Pooley thought. She said, "Now, why is it that it is only ten thirty-five and the fucking coffee is cold?"

Shit, J.T. thought, *she wasn't kidding.* He glanced at Ash, whose look said it all: *Yup, our comedy showrunner has no sense of humor.*

Maybe it's because the coffee was hot at ten o'clock when everyone else was asked to be here, J.T. thought—then realized he said.

Stephanie Pooley stared past J.T.'s left ear. "I don't like you," she said, her voice low.

J.T. glanced behind him, wondering who the hell she was looking at. No one was there. *Shit,* he thought. *She means me.*

"I *said,* I don't like you!" Now she was staring past J.T.'s right shoulder.

"Um . . ." J.T. tried to move into her line of vision so he could get her to look into his eyes, or at least at his face—any part above

The Hollywood Dictionary

COMEDY SHOWRUNNER WITH NO SENSE OF HUMOR: A penis with no balls.

the neck would've been fine—but wherever he moved, Stephanie's eyes darted away from him, as if the two of them were repelling magnets. He gave up and addressed her chin. "I was told to expect that, Ms. Pooley. But if you expect me to be here at ten o'clock to have a production meeting with you, then I expect you to be here at ten o'clock as well. It's *your* show, so if *you* would like to arrive at ten thirty-five, then I will tell my colleagues, who have been sitting around the table waiting, to arrive at ten thirty-five as well. I think that's fair."

J.T. could hear how he sounded. He could see Stephanie's face darken as he spoke. He should have held his tongue and had the gunfight at the Okeydokey Corral when it counted. But he couldn't help himself. He had the John Kerry disease. *Why can't I just learn to shut up?! What is it with me?* Now he had played his cards too early. But tardiness was a sore point with J.T.

Ms. Stephanie Pooley stewed, but then spun and spewed her venom at the craft service lady, Annie. The last craft service person had been fired. The previous Friday. J.T. did not know this fact.

"Why is the fucking coffee cold?" Ms. Pooley snarled.

Annie looked like a North Carolina possum crossing the Blue Ridge Parkway: no chance in hell. So J.T. intervened.

"That would be *my* fault, Ms. Pooley, and for that I apologize," J.T. said. He was setting protocol, which was the *right* card to play early.

"You what?" Stephanie Pooley asked, as if she'd just smelled shit. Nothing short of ripe shit.

"I put ice in the coffee. It's a southern tradition. Daniel Boone put snow in all of his men's coffee before they went on a long journey for good luck, and you know what? It always worked. So I thought I'd give it a try." He kept his face straight, and a straight face.

Silence.

"So . . . um, Stephanie, would you like me to begin the production meeting . . . after I call out for a fresh, *hot* cup of coffee?" William asked, sincerely.

"Thank you, William. Yes. I would like that very much. At least someone around here has common sense," the female half of the showrunning team said, glaring at J.T.

The door flew open again and a small, wiry man entered. His face was maroonish purple, as if he'd forgotten to breathe. His skin was oily and damp, and his tailored shirt was sticking to his body. The very expensive cotton it was made of was densely woven and looked like it would be extremely uncomfortable to wear in the heat, and even more uncomfortable since it was wet with perspiration. This wild-eyed man was caught in the storm of his own sou'wester fury.

"You fucking left the house locked and you know I don't have a set of fucking keys! What the fuck was on your mind?" the wiry man screamed at Ms. Pooley.

So, J.T. thought, *this must be the mister in the Pooley equation.*

"Not now, Marcus!" Ms. Pooley hissed. Point, set, and match. Mr. Pooley was immediately put in his place.

Well, J.T. thought, *that was fast. Now I know who wears the Armani pants in the family.* He glanced over at Ash, whose eyes said that he was thinking the same thing.

Stephanie followed J.T.'s glance and scowled. "Who is *he*? Why is that ... why is *he* here?"

"*He? That?*" J.T. answered. "*That* is Ash. Ash Black. And *he* is my assistant. And we both understand you had a *tortured* drive in from Malibu and there is no hot coffee, so we both know that when you pointed at Ash and said '*Why is* that *here?*' you were just asking a direct and simple question. Racism had nothing to do with it whatsoever."

This was another game Ash and J.T. often played. Unfortunately, once again, J.T. had started the game way too soon.

> **The Hollywood Dictionary**
>
> **MARCUS POOLEY:** A penis with no balls.
>
> **SAMMY GLICK:** A nice Marcus Pooley.

"I believe you were about to use the word *nigger*, ma'am?" Ash said, politely. Then he smiled a big white toothy smile.

"I did not! Oh!! Ah!! I would never!! Don't ever call me a . . . I can't even say it! How *dare* you!" Stephanie sputtered, already frustrated to the point of a meltdown.

"But it's okay," Ash said, showing the pink in his black lips. "We'll just say it never happened, missus."

"What? It didn't—I didn't—I never—I *would* never—ahhh!!!" She was almost in ruins. J.T. and Ash were right on target. It was fun. Dangerous, but fun.

"If you would feel more comfortable with me having a . . . *Caucasian* assistant, I think Ash would be very understanding. Isn't that right, Ash *Black*?" J.T. asked.

"Yes'm. If'n dat make de missus happy. I only needs me a airoplane ticket back home to M'ssippi. Dat's all."

Ash had never pulled this off better. J.T. and Ash were having a blast, completely defusing the nuclear reaction that Mr. and Ms. Pooley had brought into the room. The crew was fascinated.

The fun that should be associated with a sitcom just might be hidden in this room after all, J.T. thought. He rashly figured that these showrunners were no longer going to hit below the belt. He checked his watch again: 10:37. *Good one. Let's put the director back into the director.*

"What?"

J.T. turned and saw the Pooleys staring at him. He realized he must've said something out loud, but he didn't know *what*. So he just shrugged, sheepishly.

"Now," J.T. quickly turned and threw it over to William, "I believe we are all ready to start the production meeting." J.T. forced a smile at William, which he hoped communicated that, all disparities aside, he knew William was also a member of the Directors Guild. *So move it and don't let me hang here.*

"Um," William sort of took the hint, "uh, um, well, why don't we uh, keep it gangsta and, uh, all take our seats and, uh . . ."

"Begin?"

"Thank you, J.T. Yeah, um, begin, would be a good idea. *After s—*"

"Don't even think about it." J.T. glared at William as he and Ash sat back down.

"I don't think we should begin." Marcus Pooley was looking for his chair. The director's chair that had his name on the canvas back so he wouldn't forget who he was.

Stephanie stared at the standard gray metal folding chair that was placed where she normally sat as if she were going to pounce on the chair and kill it.

> **The Hollywood Dictionary**
>
> **DIRECTOR'S CHAIR**: A chair no good director has time to sit in. A chair a producer lives in.

Then her eyes went almost straight for William. "Where the fuck is my goddamn chair? The one with my name on the back of it?"

"Um, they were supposed to—" William began.

"I don't give a shit who was supposed to anything!" yelled Marcus. "My wife and I earned those fucking chairs and I'm not going back in time and sitting my ass down on these fucking metal folding chairs ever again!"

"Um, well, sir—" William stammered.

"I asked William if your chairs could be placed on the set so that you would be comfortable the moment you walked onto the stage. I'm so sorry. Really. Sorry." J.T. turned to William. "I'm really sorry, William."

"Well, next time maybe you'll listen to me. I told you they would want their chairs, J.T."

You little motherfucker. "Yes. You certainly did. From now on I will certainly listen to you. Very carefully." J.T.'s jaw muscles bulged from grinding his teeth again. Because of J.T.'s short haircut and receding hairline, it looked as if his forehead was the only part of his body on designer steroids and his eyebrows were pumping iron. It was far too revealing.

"Would you like me to send someone down for your chairs? After sex?"

"Oh, thank the Lord someone around here has a sense of humor," Marcus noted. "Yes. Please. Send someone down to get our chairs."

William turned and looked at Ash. "Ash, yo bro, could you hook a brothah up an' go downstairs—"

J.T. spun on William. "No. He can't go downstairs, *brother*."

"Hey—just keepin' it real, y'all," William said, trying to show off for the Pooleys using his communication skills with the urban types.

"It's okay, Mastah. I'za go down to da stage and fetch dem special name-chairs."

J.T. ignored Ash and looked pointedly at his A.D. "William, use your walkie-talkie and get a production assistant to bring the chairs here, please. My assistant is not your assistant. Or anyone else's. Is that clear?"

The Hollywood Dictionary

PRODUCTION ASSISTANT, a.k.a. P.A., a.k.a. THING ONE, THING TWO, etc.: Sherpa. Carries the bourgeoisie's baggage to the top of Everest but never gets credit at the summit.

William used his very expensive walkie-talkie to relay the message that the Pooleys' chairs were to be brought to the production meeting ASAP.

J.T. shifted his stare to the Pooleys, who had fallen into a silent, seething paralysis. "I think it would be wise to start while your chairs are being moved here. That is, if the two of you don't mind sitting in the same chairs as the rest of us schmucks—I mean laborers. I swear it doesn't make you a Commie. Not even a Socialist. It still means you're Grade A Capitalists, for sure."

No one knew exactly what to do. Since it is the job of a director to choose a path and move forward, J.T. did just that. "Please. Sit. Let's work. We will all sign affidavits saying that you never sat in a folding chair while you were in this room. All in favor, say aye."

The crew all chimed in. "Aye!" Lines were really being drawn.

Without eye contact or another word spoken, Stephanie yanked her chair out from under the table and flung it across the room. "All those not in favor, say aye!" She looked at her husband. The two nodded and turned back toward the table. "Aye."

J.T. rose out of his seat. "You're fucking kidding me." He immediately felt a hand gently pulling his shirt downward.

"We may be Grade A Capitalists, but be warned, director-man, this is not a Democracy. We'll begin when our chairs arrive and not a second before." Marcus sneered and looked to his wife and master: her eyes glinted in approval, and their mouths met in something that couldn't—or shouldn't—really be called a kiss.

The laborers sat awkwardly waiting. J.T. sat back down and just looked at Ash, then down at his script. He stared at a page. Its words; its ink; the tiny specks that made up the ink. The Pooleys wandered over to the food and sampled a wee bit of everything and were quite jovial with each other.

Finally, two of that young, interchangeable, and expendable breed known as production assistants came running into the production meeting room, out of breath, sweating but carrying the two director's chairs. The king watched magisterially as Thing One and Thing Two placed the chairs, then sat on his throne before his subjects and nodded. "Now, William, you may begin," Marcus Pooley I intoned.

"Wait a minute. Wait!" Stephanie was squinting at the label on the back of Marcus's chair. "You're in my chair."

"Oh!" Marcus got up quickly and moved his royal ass over to

his own chair. Stephanie then sat regally in her chair. The one with her name on it. Just in case she forgot who she was, as Marcus just had. "Now. *Now* we may begin," she said with satisfaction.

At 10:40 the production meeting began with William looking down and saying, "Yes. Um . . . okay, page one—"

"I'd just like to say, good work, everyone, last week. Ratings are in and we crushed the competish, and we're still the number one show on TV!" Marcus Pooley already felt obliged to interrupt.

"Yes. And a tragedy about Jasper Jones," Stephanie Pooley added. "At lunch if any of you would like to have a moment of silence, we will be behind you, spiritually, on that silence, one hundred percent. And so will *Entertainment Tonight* and the E! Channel. But one minor note. Actually—one *major* note: Make sure when the cameras are rolling you also pay tribute to Minnesota B. Moose. That's very important to the network."

"My wife is right. If anyone from the press asks any of you for a sound bite, you must mention the death of Minnesota B. Moose and the birth of Kalamazoo P. Kardinal. Is everyone clear?"

Mick McCoy, the director of photography, leaned back in his chair and crossed his arms. With a slight smile he asked, "What about the death of Jasper? Would you like us not to mention his death? I guess what I'm saying is, Where does it rank in the moose and cardinal universe?"

"Good question, Mike. Very good question. We don't want to appear uncaring, so what we should all do is mention Jasper's death but then use that as a really nice segue into Minnesota B. Moose's death at the network, which will lead you directly into the birth of Kalamazoo P. Kardinal!" Marcus bounced a little, pleased with his logic.

"Um . . ." William whispered for everyone to hear, "we already had a moment of silence. It was very touching."

Marcus went from zero to executioner in a whopping millisecond. "You what? You did *that* without either me or Stephanie giving you the green light? We're supposed to have our moment of silence when *Entertainment Tonight* is here, you dipshit!"

William shrank into his chair like a frightened serf. Marcus Pooley I had half risen from his throne, palms on the table, and was leaning menacingly toward William. Queen Stephanie was slightly breathless, arousal glinting in her eyes. That tableau gave J.T. the complete history, brief as it was, of the show's dynamics—as if he needed telling.

"Yes, we not only had a moment of silence, but William chose to do it before we were on the clock," J.T. interjected, reflexively sticking up for a crew member of his, even though this one had just as reflexively stabbed him in the back. "It was a mini-moment."

Stephanie Pooley would've been offended by the smirk on J.T.'s face if she'd looked at it. "Well, at least you could've waited for us," she grumbled. "That would've been the decent thing to do. Even if it was just a mini-moment."

"Would you like to have another mini-moment now, Ms. Pooley?" William asked, sincerely relieved. "I'm sure that's not against the rules of . . . What rules would that fall under?"

"You are kidding, right?" J.T. whispered to William.

"What? Oh. Of course I was kidding," William said, feeling foolish.

"Well, you shouldn't kid about death. What time is it?" Stephanie demanded.

"Almost forty-five minutes after ten, Ms. Pooley," William said. Sincerely.

"We don't have time for a mini-moment. We've got everyone coming in at eleven for the table read. So we all feel badly. That he's dead. Dead and not directing. That's what is important. That we feel bad. Now—page one. Let's go. 'The Best Ever Christmas.' Go!"

"'The Best Ever Christmas,'" William said, about to go through his very professional notes. *At least he knows his job,* J.T. thought.

"Okay, page one, page two, page three—anyone have questions so far?" William asked, sincerely.

J.T. stared at William. *Okay, so I was wrong,* he thought.

Everyone in the room was used to this. J.T. was flabbergasted. The script called for snow, explosions, and the use of a large number of children. They had just signed off on it all without discussion. *And explosions aren't funny,* J.T. thought.

The Hollywood Dictionary

CHILDREN: Underage actors who, for the most part, are paid (a lot) more than their parents.

SPECIAL EFFECTS/CHILDREN/SAFETY: *Don't see* John Landis.

"Excuse me," J.T. said before William could sincerely say "page four."

"What?" Marcus Pooley jumped up out of his precious seat.

"Don't you think we should at least have a conversation about the snow and explosions? Special effects? Children? Safety?" J.T. asked.

"What's to talk about? It says *the best ever Christmas.* It says *the best ever explosion.* What's to discuss? What is it that you find challenging to understand? What don't you get?" Marcus Pooley sat back, arms crossed, looking smug. He thought he'd trumped the director.

"Well," J.T. took a big breath and saw a vision, a mirage of Natasha in the reflection of Stephanie Pooley's glass mug of not-hot coffee.

"Yes, well," J.T. said, still gathering himself, "since I don't see a unit production manager here or a line producer—"

"We don't need those people. They are excess baggage," Stephanie explained.

"Excess baggage? I see. So should I discuss how much the best ever Christmas and the best ever explosion, *with children in the shot,* will cost with the two of you, or with Carl Hayes, who has to sign the checks? There are practicalities to discuss, don't you agree? I'm speaking to the two of you as seasoned showrunners, and we all know that a script is not a novel. Nor is it animated. I can't just go 'boom' and believe that you will have the best ever explosion. I can't have actors throwing imaginary snowballs in the snowball fight that has been written on page two."

"Are you saying you can't direct 'The Best Ever Christmas'? Is that what you're saying?" Marcus Pooley demanded.

"Because if that is what you are saying, then you are not the director for us!" Stephanie Pooley made her feelings known as loudly as she could, for the entire room's benefit.

J.T. looked at the reflection in Stephanie's cup of untouched coffee again, and saw Natasha slowly shaking her head.

"Well, as a *guest* on your set, I am not familiar with how much you are willing to spend to create your vision of *the best ever,*" J.T. said, holding his temper at bay with difficulty. He got out of his chair and lay down on the filthy carpet. He began to stretch, and then started doing sit-ups.

"We want it to look better than ... What the fuck are you doing?"

"I'm stretching my back out, Mr. Pooley."

"No you're not. You're doing sit-ups!"

"I'm strengthening my stomach muscles. It's good for the back. Now, you were saying ... You want it to look better than, what?"

"Better than *Mr. Deeds Goes to* ... um, *Miracle at Madison Square Garden* ... no, *It's Your Life!* It's your job to make it look like that. You are paid the big bucks to direct. It's our job to write it. It's that simple," Marcus insisted.

"I'd like to know *simple* things, such as how much snow you'd like to see? And I'd like to tell our wardrobe department how many extras are wearing winter clothing? I'd like to tell our location manager if you want this to be an exterior shoot or an interior?

If it's interior, the cleanup time will be an issue, so it should be a preshoot. If it's a preshoot, we will have to discuss which crew will be available. *Also,* if it's an interior, we'll have to do this without an audience, because it's against the law to have an explosion on an enclosed set with bystanders. *Also,* the children will have to be written out, if it's an interior shoot, for safety reasons—unless you want to use little stunt people."

"Little stunt people?" Stephanie laughed.

"I think he means, um, midgets," William said, trying to look important.

"Midgets? Fucking midgets? Dwarfs? Fuck—although that did just give me an idea. Midgets. Dwarfs. Hmm. It *is* the *best ever* Christmas. We will be wanting elves, will we not?!"

"You're brilliant. I had the same idea driving in this morning. But I'm glad you brought it up." Stephanie looked the teeniest bit annoyed that Marcus had in fact come up with the idea first.

"Hello? Back to pages one through three?" J.T. tried to get the focus back to practical issues. "*Also,* if it's *the best ever Christmas* and *the best ever explosion,* what does that mean *to you,* as compared to me? Because to you, the best ever Christmas could be an image, a look, or it could be the amount of presents the children are receiving. *Also,* if it's the best ever explosion, does that mean you want to visually compete with all of the high-action Armageddon films, or with the best ever explosion seen on a sitcom?" J.T. thought he'd managed to say all this without even a hint of being patronizing.

"Are you patronizing us, Mr. Film School Professor? I have a distinct feeling that you are being condescending. And that stuff just doesn't fly in the real world of filmmaking," Marcus Pooley said, very pleased with himself.

J.T. looked around the table at the members of the crew. His eyes came to a stop at his buddy Mick McCoy. Mick mouthed, *Don't—leave—us!* J.T. subtly nodded.

J.T. sighed. "No, Mr. and Ms. Pooley. I am asking serious ques-

tions that must be addressed.
But maybe the *production
meeting* is not the time or
place to discuss *production*.
You know ... why don't we
just ... move on."

> **The Hollywood Dictionary**
>
> **"MOVING ON":** *See* Ed Wood.

J.T. could see his son's brave face as he was hooked up to the dialysis machine for the first time. Jeremy always tried not to cry, but he squeezed his daddy's hand tightly whenever he was afraid or it hurt. *He's such a brave child,* J.T. thought. *He should cry. Little boys should feel that it's okay to cry ...* "It's okay to cry," he mumbled.

"How dare you?" Stephanie Pooley exclaimed in horror. "How the fuck *dare* you tell me and my husband that it's *okay to cry!*"

"I wasn't talking to you. To either of you," J.T. whispered.

"Why are you whispering?" Marcus Pooley shouted.

"Because I prefer whispering to shouting," J.T. said. Something had momentarily died behind his eyes. "Please, continue, William. You're doing great. The floor is yours."

J.T. sat back, deflated but certainly not defeated. He knew that every filmmaking skill he had ever acquired was going to be necessary—mandatory.   *I
have to make it through these
three weeks. Surely I can do
that,* he thought, again and
again

> **The Hollywood Dictionary**
>
> **PULLING A SHOW OUT OF YOUR ASS:** Buy stock in Preparation H.

The production meeting
ended a few minutes later.
Nothing from a production standpoint was discussed. It would *just happen,* according to the Pooleys. And if it didn't happen, they would throw more tantrums and blame would be ascribed and crew members would be fired, so J.T. was ready to pull *the best ever Christmas* with *the best ever explosion* out of his ass.

The Table Read

THE PRODUCTION MEETING room doubled as the table-read room, losing none of its aura of confrontation, passive aggression, power struggles—of war. The cast members trickled in and gathered round the chuck wagon—er, food—er, craft service table—each one doing the obligatory round of hugs and air kisses as they arrived. There they were—the Buddies. Their lives had forever changed because of the show's instantaneous global popularity.

If there were Tivo on Mars, these young actors would be Martian celebs. NASA astronauts were downloading shows onto their spacecraft's computer and actually screwed up their avionics with the episode about the orangutan.

J.T. watched the Buddies interact for a while, sizing them up. Betty Balz, whose big break had come in a toothpaste commercial, was just as perky-cute in person as she was on TV. Rare. Anorexic-thin, she had a perky black bob and small perky breasts with perky nipples never covered by a bra, and wore a perky shade of red on her lips—thin lips, her one feature that photographed perky on TV but in real life was less than, well, perky. Despite this flaw, she was drop-dead gorgeous—in other words, anyone involved with her would eventually drop dead. Very high-maintenance.

Devon Driver was doing shtick trying to impress her. Devon's shtick was attitudinal: he gave advice to the other Buddies, especially the hot ones—okay, mostly to Betty Balz. Betty was so perky with excitement when she spoke to Devon, her voice sounded like the piccolo trumpet on the Beatles' "Penny Lane." Just now, he was tut-tutting Betty for having signed on to promote a cosmetics company.

"But the company is offering me a million dollars for a one-day photo shoot. One million dollars. For one day!" Betty trumpeted. "Obviously they'll have the right to use the photos on buses and billboards, but why do you think *that's* such a bad idea?"

Devon really wanted to say, *Because they asked you and not me,* but he broke it down into the actor's vocabulary, putting emphasis on each *action verb*. "It's *desperate* on your part. It *belittles* you. They *coax* you with money. They *boost* your ego. They *appeal* to your vanity. I'm *astonished* you would *demean* yourself."

A putzy Woody Allen-wannabe type (ineffectually so, not least because he was six foot two, weighed about two hundred pounds, and slicked his brown hair so heavily to cover his balding spot that it photographed black), Devon was actually the Alpha Celeb off-camera, ruling the Buddy roost (and especially the Betty roost). Devon came from old money—a lot of old money. Very old money. Money so old it had Spanish conquistadors on it. His father and mother were acting teachers, so everything he did was affected, the result of bad acting classes. Devon believed, and informed everyone, that he knew more than they did about show business.

"I am . . . *hammered,*" Betty tested her acting-vocab chops.

"Good *try,* but 'hammered' connotes drunkenness. *Action verbs* should be *precise* so we, as actors, can *understand* the language immediately. So now you are *empowered* with knowledge to *instruct* your agent to *condemn* the idea and *deflect* the offer. Did I *inform* you enough to *galvanize* your position?"

"I guess," Betty *speculated.*

"To *guess* is good! Perfect! Always *remember,*" Devon said with condescension, "I *grew up* in an acting class and was *raised* in a *the-atre. Remember* that's thea-*truh*. Not thea-*terrr*."

"But what does the thea-truh have to do with *signing* a million-dollar deal with a cosmetics company?" Betty percolated.

"Real actors don't *do that*. Real actors *stay true* to themselves." Devon was getting flustered.

Helena, who just went by the name Helena, overheard Devon and snorted.

"So real actors don't *endorse* Snickers candy bars?"

"In my case," Devon said in defense of his recent promotional gig, "I had a lot *to do* with the copy and the *direction* of the ad campaign and *creating* awareness for the Peanut Allergy Foundation."

"And the direction of the paycheck? I guess you use Stanislavsky's Method acting technique when you endorse your checks?" Helena channeled Jerry Lewis in her pantomime of Devon endorsing his check, adding, "Remember, it's a C-H-E-Q-U-E! Not a C-H-E-C-K!"

"Wow," Betty swooned, "you're so community-friendly, Devon. Maybe with my cosmetics deal I could *donate* time and money—well, *time*—to people who were born with ... what's it called? Really fucked-up faces and stuff."

"I think Devon could rationalize that, couldn't you, Devon?" Helena taunted.

"It's a good thing you're a girl or else I'd—wait, you *are* a girl, right?"

"Clever, Devon. Clever." Helena was the experienced foundation of the cast—and a closet lesbian with a big walk-in closet. She had the role of the "odd" (go-to for funny) next-door neighbor. She was used to dismissing these kinds of sexual barbs. She was a gifted comedienne, an athletic, wiry woman with a shock of short red hair, who could've been a test subject for restless leg syndrome. J.T. had worked with her before and tried to catch her eye, but only managed to catch a paper napkin she'd balled up and thrown at

Rocky Brook, a young man with spiky blond hair who'd become famous for his abs from an underwear campaign.

Rocky, unlike the others, was at least holding his script, but he was shifting it from one hand to the other doing biceps curls with it. J.T. saw Rocky remove a bottle of something from the pocket of his preppy twill trousers and take a swig with his free hand. *Oh great,* J.T. thought. *Booze? Worse?* Bored with the paper-ball game, Rocky wandered over to get a better view of Janice Hairston, a blonde bombshell whose role in *Buddies* was to be flaky (every sitcom needs a flaky/dipsy/quirky blonde), and who was showing Marcus Pooley what she would look like with breast augmentation. Janice managed to be discreet enough so that everyone in the room could see.

Talented, J.T. thought.

Betty, watching with disdain, rolled her eyes, tightened her thin lips until they turned the exact shade of Dorothy's ruby slippers, and flipped her hair. Devon had now switched his attention to Janice too, and Janice, very aware of her audience, slowly licked her upper lip

> ### The Hollywood Dictionary
>
> **BLONDE BOMBSHELL:** (1) The epitome of stereotypes: an actress burdened with a beauty greater than her talent. (2) A bright, talented actress who is typecast as a dumb blonde bombshell.
>
> Janice is definition 1.

from one side to another. She wasn't a conventional bombshell: her nose and head were a little too big, the skin more Mediterranean than porcelain, even the hair bigger than had been currently fashionable until *Buddies* became a smash. But no one ever seemed to see Janice piece by piece. The overall effect of Janice Hairston was one of raw sexiness of the kind that caused blood pressure surges, adrenaline rushes, and, of course, "boners, silly."

And Kirk Kelly was there too, standing a little apart from the others; his role was as the dumb, darkly handsome, nutty roommate of Rocky Brook's character. Kirk finished off a breakfast burrito he'd brought with him and gave J.T. a shy, toothy smile. He seemed nervous.

There they were. All in one room. The Buddies. Kirk came over to say hello to J.T., which made the rest of the cast members finally notice him. The rest of the Buddies then came over and greeted their new director as if J.T. were a long-lost somebody they didn't know but should adore.

Hmm, J.T. thought. *At least I have a good cast.*

One by one the actors took their assigned seats, prompted by a sincere William. When J.T. and Ash got up to stretch, the Pooleys quickly moved their coveted chairs to the spots at the head of the table. The network babe, Debbie, whom J.T. knew from another show about twelve years earlier (when she was a secretary who still hadn't fucked the right guy yet), also sat at the head of the table next to Lance, the studio representative, who didn't bother to introduce himself to J.T.

The Hollywood Dictionary

A GOOD CAST: The factor that makes the writers, producers, and director look good.

There were no more chairs. More specifically, there wasn't a chair for the director. At the table. Where the table read took place. Where the director should sit.

J.T. did what every good-boy director should do: he went to his boss, leaned over his shoulder, and whispered, "Where would you like me to sit?" as the other people in the room began to settle.

"Jesus fucking H. Christ. You're our director and I've got to tell you where to sit?" Marcus Pooley yelled.

"Well . . ." J.T. began, very quietly. He could tell his blood pressure was over 150. "I'll just sit over here." J.T. awkwardly took a seat next to a child guest actor he hadn't been introduced to yet, then searched the room until he located Ash, who had strategically placed himself behind the writers, who looked to be barely out of their teens. If there was gossip/intelligence to be leaked, he knew it would come from this bunch. Ash nodded imperceptibly.

Marcus cleared his throat. "Stephanie and I would like to take this moment to welcome our new director, J.T. Baker."

Before anyone could acknowledge J.T., Stephanie stood up and took charge. "Marcus and I would also like to pay tribute in the form of a mini-moment to our dear friend, the former director, Jasper Jones, whose passing came as a shock to all of us," she said, trying to act sad.

"I'm sure it came as a shock to him too," one of the baby writers riffed. The other writers snorted and their shoulders bounced up and down in mock silence.

Lance stood up and straightened his jacket with a quick downward tug, then cleared his throat. "'Life does not cease to be funny when people die any more than it ceases to be serious when people laugh.' George Bernard Shaw." Lance bowed his head for a moment to let this piece of wisdom sink in, then sat back in his chair with exaggerated care.

"And don't forget the death of our mighty network icon Minnesota B. Moose and the birth of Kalamazoo P. Kardinal!" Debbie added, because she felt the network should be represented in this time of grieving.

"Okay. Mini-moment is up," Marcus announced quickly. "Now, let's read 'The Best Ever Christmas'!" He began to read the stage directions.

The director *always* reads the stage directions. This is a routine that goes back to the infancy of the sitcom form. The job of reading the stage directions was probably initiated by writers who wanted to make sure that the director took their descriptions seriously. J.T. blushed as everyone looked at him; all he could do was give a half-assed shrug.

As Marcus maintained control and read the stage directions, he emphasized the *best ever* qualities on each and every one of the pages in the script. The young man who was supposed to be an awful actor, Kirk Kelly, didn't give a very good table read. J.T. had seen that before. Wonderful actors can have trouble at table reads for many reasons.

The more J.T. studied the young man during the table read, the more he developed a theory that maybe, just maybe, Kirk Kelly had a learning disability. He had trouble reading and many times switched words around, usually in the same pattern. But more important, Kirk was giving it his best. He was very game. He was always embarrassed when he made a mistake and Marcus or Stephanie Pooley corrected him, with ugly disdain.

The baby writers laughed hysterically at every unfunny joke. *No,* J.T. thought, *nothing has changed. Who stole the funny?* That's all he could obsess about. *There's not a single honest laugh in this teleplay. Jeremy was so right. Who stole the funny? It's like: Where's Waldo? I will try and find the thief and report back to Jeremy.*

The read ended.

"Oh, we love it!"

"Great job on the script!"

"Wow! What an episode! The best ever!"

"I can smell an Emmy!"

The Hollywood Dictionary

"OH, WE LOVE IT": *This sucks!*

The actors were oozing praise.

"How do you guys do it?!"

"Remarkable. I guess that's why you guys get the—"

Yes. *The big bucks.*

William came up to J.T. and whispered in all sincerity, "What would you like to do now, boss? Usually Jasper let the cast go home and we wouldn't rehearse on Monday. During sex."

J.T. peered over his electric blue reading glasses at his A.D.

"Well, William, I'm not Jasper, and as you know, I like my actors to feel prepared. And maybe, just maybe, we might discover something funny in rehearsal. So please ask them to stay until I find out what is going to get cut based on the studio and network notes."

"Got it, boss," William said, sincerely.

The actors left the room, all with smiles, hugs, and air kisses for J.T.

Thank God. They are the only way I'm gonna get through this. We'll work hard, be funny, and make great TV, J.T. thought.

"See ya down there, J.T.," Devon Driver said with mucho charm. Damn, he was charming.

Everyone who wasn't a Pooley or an executive left the room. Only J.T. and Ash stayed behind.

"Why are *you* here? This is studio and network notes!" Marcus and Stephanie double-teamed J.T.

"Well, I've *always* been at these note sessions because it lets me know what to rehearse and what not to rehearse. It also gives me a sense as to what direction you and the studio and the network might want the episode to go in," J.T. explained.

"I'm not comfortable with you here," Stephanie said bluntly.

"Now I'm not comfortable being here, either," J.T. said. "But that's not the point. It's not about comfort or discomfort. It's about giving you the best show possible."

"Are you patronizing us again?" Marcus asked.

"If I am, it's not because I'm trying to—"

"Well, if you stay, do not

> **The Hollywood Dictionary**
>
> **NOTES:** Look how big MY dick is!

speak to the studio or the network. Not one word. We will take that as a form of betrayal. Understand?" Stephanie warned, her voice low.

The last of the writers and actors were finally gone, taking as much food with them as they could carry. The crew had left as the last word on the page was spoken.

William closed the door. "It's safe," he said, sincerely.

Safe? What is this? Marathon Man? J.T. thought as he remembered Dustin Hoffman and Sir Laurence Olivier, and the phrase of the decade: "Is it safe?"

Marcus, who was standing by the craft service table, suddenly started hurling breads, then rolls, then bagels; then, when throwing food lost its dramatic effect, he began to throw chairs around the room.

"Settle down, Marcus. It's okay. We'll take care of it," Stephanie said as if the two of them had rehearsed this moment.

"The fucking kid! I hate that fucking kid! I want that fucking kid fucking fired," Marcus Pooley fumed, slamming a hand on one of the tables. It smashed a sticky bun, one of his earlier projectiles, which completely upstaged his tirade. He stared murderously at his gloppy hand. "He's like this goddamn sticky bun!"

"I didn't think he was *that* bad," Debbie said.

"We know where the network stands on this issue, but the network doesn't have to spend endless hours on him while other things like our scripts and even our shows suffer because of so much displaced attention!" Stephanie screamed at Debbie.

J.T. stared at the Pooleys. They were either ensconced on their own planet and believed in isolationism, or they needed a fall guy for a script that was unshootable.

"We can't fire him. You guys know that. He's testing through the roof. The group of Buddies is your show. He's one of the Buddies. It wouldn't be very Buddy-like not to treat him like a ... *Buddy,*" Lance insisted.

So that's *it,* J.T. thought, smiling to himself. *The Pooleys aren't the big shots anymore, Kirk is.* It wasn't their witty banter that was testing through the roof; it was an unsuspecting kid, who happened to be the perfect television star: a little bit of talent and a whole lot of looks. That's why they hated the kid. He was indeed inextricable from the wild maze of unforeseeable idiosyncrasies that make up a hit TV show.

"Did you hear that reading?" Marcus Pooley yelled as he literally jumped up and down like a two-year-old throwing a tantrum.

"He's tanking the show! *My* fucking show!" Marcus shrieked.

"*Our* show, sweetheart. Our. Fucking. Show," Stephanie said with authority.

"He's on drugs!" Marcus carried on. "I know he's on drugs! You can tell by the way he can't read his fucking lines!"

That was as long as J.T. could last on good behavior. "*Excuse* me?" he said, leaning forward.

Everyone suddenly looked at J.T. as if they couldn't believe they hadn't bullied him out of the room. Lance and Debbie wondered just who that big, um, African-American sitting next to J.T. was. "Yes, if you don't mind my saying, accusing a young actor, with his entire career ahead of him, of being on drugs—in front of the studio and the network—just isn't . . . appropriate," J.T. said, aware of the irreparable damage a rumor like that could inflict on Kirk.

"What the fuck?" Marcus Pooley said.

"Wait," Stephanie jumped in, "did you just *say* something?"

"I guess I did. As a vested member of the Screen Actors Guild of America, I really don't want to report this verbal violation to the union. Now, if you know *for a fact* that this young man is on drugs, please, let's deal with that. Let's think of his well-being and get him some help. But if you are making an accusation based on assumption, I'm going to have to call you on it," J.T. finished, righteously.

Once again, J.T. went to bat for the oppressed, the downtrodden, the young actor who went from waiter to making forty grand a week overnight.

"They don't mean he's *on* drugs, J.T.," Debbie said quickly, "they are implying that he read *as if* he were on drugs." She smiled.

"Yes," Lance jumped in, knowing the implications of what had just transpired. "The Pooleys were implying that when he read his part, it *sounded* like a person who was on drugs. They would *never* accuse Kirk Kelly of *being* on drugs. Never. Believe me," Lance said. He looked deep into J.T.'s eyes to make a point, something he had learned at Executive School.

The Pooleys had just made a decision without having to speak to each other. They would blacklist J.T. from television. They would call all of their friends who were making television shows and nobody, from this point on, would ever hire J.T. to direct television again. Never. Ever. Again. His fate had been sealed. Less than two hours into the first day of work and he was blacklisted again. *He had spoken to the network and the studio! How dare he!?*

"I really love how this episode is going to be the *best ever* Christmas!" Debbie finally said, breaking the awkward, hateful silence.

"The *best ever!*" Lance repeated. "And I love how the explosion is going to be the *best ever*, too!"

"We're very excited about this being the *best ever* episode ... *ever*," Marcus Pooley said petulantly.

"And it will be. You know us," Stephanie added. "We never let anything go. We'll shoot this show until we have *the best ever Christmas* and *the best ever explosion*—even if it kills someone!" She slowly turned and looked pointedly at J.T.'s collar.

He smiled back politely. *Sounds like a fun week,* he thought.

"So, like, lemme make sure I understand the 'A' story of 'The Best Ever Christmas,'" Debbie said in Executive-speak harmonics (the melody being a sincere statement; the third being a condescending hint at a question—but never so obvious as to give away her own ignorance; and the fifth vibrating with a tuneful, pleasant-sounding *I'm not really sure this is what the network is looking for in this episode*).

"So," she continued, "the fact that Janice survives an explosion while shopping makes the 'A' story the *best ever* Christmas?"

Finally, J.T. thought. *Someone is taking a look at how absurd this story is.*

"I'm sorry," Debbie turned and looked at J.T. "Did you say something?"

"Oh, um, no. I was just . . . thinking."

"Anyway—am I right, you guys? Is the fact that she

> ### The Hollywood Dictionary
>
> **The "A" Story:** The "A" story is the prominent story line of an episode. Many times there isn't "a" story in the "A" story. The "B" story can be woven into the "A" story or it can be a satellite story that conveniently resolves at the end of the episode, or gives us a hint of stories to come.

survives the explosion and then makes it to the Christmas dinner scene where she gives out all her Christmas presents—is that what makes this the *best ever* Christmas?" Debbie asked with an energetic, Red Bull-plus-Starbucks smile. "And the 'B' story is all warm and fuzziness with our characters just being funny?"

"Yes," Stephanie Pooley answered in such an ugly timbre that even the musical quality of Debbie's voice couldn't blend in pitch or tone.

"I love it!" Debbie squealed.

"Love it!" Lance repeated.

Holy shit. I can feel the ghost of Rod Serling floating around the room, J.T. thought.

"It's a great story! Original and exciting and so unsitcomlike!" Debbie exclaimed while she thought, *If I don't like it at the first run-through, we'll have a page-one rewrite.*

Can we really make the best ever Christmas show ever? Stephanie Pooley thought, suddenly very excited about her show.

How much fucking money are these cokeheads going to spend on an episode that'll be mediocre at best? Lance thought as he nodded his head, smiling in a silent show of agreement.

The best ever. That's because we are *the best ever. And we'll prove it!* Marcus Pooley thought.

Damn, I'm glad I'm a teacher and not working this show, Ash thought. *Maybe it's a good thing I can't get any work nowadays.*

"Okay, the studio is slightly worried about the cost of this episode," Lance understated. "If Jasper Jones falls under the heading of *force majeure,* then, forgive me, J.T., but the truth is that the insurance will cover Jasper's death and we won't be paying two director's fees for three straight episodes. But that still doesn't cover the exorbitant expenditures to make this the *best ever* ever."

"Excuse me. First off," Marcus Pooley said, standing and posturing, "don't you want the *best ever* coming from your studio's show *I Love My Urban Buddies?*"

"Not if it's the most expensive ever, to be quite honest," Lance gently explained. "I'd settle for ... the most average ever, if the numbers were right."

"Well, fuck!" Marcus Pooley shouted. "Now I understand the state of television."

"And what's with the French? *Force mature?*" Stephanie barked. "What's with that? Speak the fucking King's English, for chrissake!"

"Actually, if you want to get technical, the King's English is not—"

"*Je m'appelle Marcus*! But what the fuck does that have to do with our show?!"

"*Force majeure*—" Lance was about to explain, but was interrupted by Stephanie Pooley.

"See? There you go again! *Oui! Bonjour!* How do *you* like it? Huh?" she said.

"It *means* ..." Lance was trying to compose himself, "in French, that if a part of a superior force ... is ... unexpected, or let's say ... an uncontrollable event should take place ..."

"Say what?" Stephanie asked, trying to make Lance feel as foolish as she felt. "Wait a minute—who's superior?"

"*Force majeure*," Lance said again, trying to keep his voice steady, "is a *legal* term, Stephanie. An insurance term. In other words—it could save everyone a lot of money."

"Well, why didn't you just say so?" both Pooleys said in concert.

"I just did," Lance said in a very Executive-like way.

"How?!" both Pooleys demanded, like dogs in heat competing for the same bitch. "How will it save us money?" The idea of saving money meant more money in their pockets, and that made this French term suddenly of value.

J.T. and Ash were aghast. Not by the machinations of the studio trying to manipulate a dead director's *destiny* into an act of God, but by the Pooleys' *density*.

Lance just didn't know when to give up. "It's a situation," he went on, "where the law casts a duty on a party—"

"Doody?" Marcus interrupted.

"Du-*tee*," Lance articulated. "Duty. The performance shall be excused, if it be rendered impossible by an act of God—"

"*God?*" Marcus asked in earnest. "Like, God-God? Or Muhammad or Buddha? We don't wanna lose our international audience by fucking offending anyone or starting another war."

"Um, it's just a phrase that means Nature, only they say God," Lance continued, wishing he could just get past all of this and let the legal department at the studio handle this matter. But no. He was forced to carry on.

"If the party—" Lance was interrupted again, this time by Stephanie.

"We don't have parties on this show. It's all work and no play. I say, 'Let everyone play on their own time, not on my dime,' that's what I say." Stephanie looked around with a self-satisfied smile that dared anyone not to like her little rhyme.

"If the *person,* let's say JASPER JONES, were to engage in an act, and that act is deemed to be his own fault and folly—"

"I'm lost," Marcus Pooley said.

"We finally agree, don't we, Poodles?" Stephanie deadpanned.

"That's my *wittle witer . . .*" and they kissed.

"*Force majeure* is something so extraordinary and unavoidable and devoid of human agency that reasonable care would not have prevented the consequences!" Lance spit it all out as fast as he could. *And this is why I went to law school?*

"Human Agency," Marcus said, warily. "Don't tell me they get ten percent, too."

"You know what?" Lance pulled out a monogrammed handkerchief, took off his glasses, and wiped sweat from his face. "Let's just say there's a lot of legal mumbo jumbo that my parents spent hundreds of thousands of dollars for me to learn so I could jump headfirst into the entertainment field, disappointing them for all eternity." Lance lied, continuing his Ivy League ruse, to the point where he even believed his pedigree.

Stephanie Pooley suspected someone else wanted a cut of their action. "What do your *mother and father* have to do with this?"

"Yeah. Why *your* mother?" Marcus asked. "Why not *our* mother?"

"Forget everything I just said. Look. There might be a way where we don't have an obligation to pay Jasper Jones's estate for the three missed episodes," Lance finally finished.

"His estate?" Marcus Pooley asked. "You mean, like his house? Why would we have to pay his fucking house?"

"His wife! His children! Whoever is left! We may have an obligation to stick to the actual document otherwise known as a contract! For the last time, we may be able to null and void said contract and save the production two directing fees!" Lance spit out.

It took more than a mini-moment, and then the Pooleys began nodding their heads in agreement.

"Well, why didn't you just fucking say that instead of ordering *escargot* and getting all French and God-worshiping and all?" Marcus Pooley said with exasperation.

"Right," Lance quickly said to appease the Pooleys.

And with that and a few other mumblings, it was over.

The notes session went swimmingly, J.T. thought. *Not a single note. Oh, I am so fucked,* he kept saying to himself. *At least I can get away from all this insanity and dive into the real work with my actors.* Then he checked himself. *"Fucked" . . . I'm starting to sound like I never left the cave. There are better words than "fuck." Use them.*

"Fuck. Er, I mean, excuse me," J.T. said. "What would you like me to work on today with the cast?" It was a perfectly legitimate question, the first one a director on a sitcom normally asked after table-read notes.

"What would we like you to *work* on?" was Marcus Pooley's reply. "How about: THE SHOW!"

"Well," J.T. asked, "which show? Considering that there's enough text for at least two shows, which scenes or sections of the teleplay would you like me to start with?"

"I'd like you to work on your attitude, buster," Stephanie hissed. "In all my years in this business, and I'm not exaggerating, I'm sure I've never seen a guest director behave the way you're doing."

"You're sure you're not exaggerating or you're sure you've never seen a director behave this way?" J.T. just had to say.

Marcus Pooley started hopping up and down. "You had better make this the best ever *fucking* Christmas and the best ever *fucking* explosion, because if you don't, the studio and the network will know that it is *your fault, completely*! Understand?"

Ja, mein Führer! J.T. thought, and turned on his heels, grabbed his stuff, and goose-stepped with Asher out of the room.

"I don't care for the way he walks," Stephanie Pooley said under her breath.

"I hate this director. How 'bout you?" Marcus Pooley asked his wife.

"Hate him."

J.T. AND ASH walked to the stage in silence, both trying to replay what had just transpired.

"Things are a bit more nasty since you were last *here*, J.T." *Here* being Hollywood. Ash was now in the awkward position of filling his boss in on the ways of Hollywood—after his boss left Hollywood because of its nastiness.

"More . . . nasty?"

"Well," Ash tried to explain, "no one even attempts faux decency. They just cut your throat and get it over with."

"Wonderful."

"Don't worry," Ash said soothingly, "I've got your back."

They were greeted by William, who was wearing his sincere, sad, puppy-dog look. "Yo, homies," he jived, sincerely.

J.T. stared at William unblinkingly. "You can stop with the Ebonics, William. Ash studied at Oxford. I'm sure he doesn't want . . . special treatment," J.T. mumbled.

"Jus' keepin' it gangsta. Gotta keep it real. Right, bro?"

Ash didn't have the heart to hit a man when he was down—or dumb, so he just smiled and said *"A'iight."*

"So," William said to J.T. brightly, "how were the notes . . . during sex?"

"Fascinating," J.T. responded as he looked around at the empty stage, slightly surprised. By its emptiness.

"I've got some bad news and some badder news," he went on. "Which would you like to hear first, boss?"

"Why don't you just tell me . . . the baddestest," J.T. sighed.

"Well," William began, "the cast thought that it was such a long script that there would be a page-one rewrite tomorrow. So they decided to go home. *After sex.*"

"Stop it!"

"Sorry."

"The cast went home? They—*decided*—to go home?" J.T. asked, smiling. He'd heard this one before and knew this was the least of his troubles on a Monday, but they did all say, *We'll see you on the set.* "Who signed the cast out? Who allowed the cast to go home, William?"

"Well, boss," William said, sincerely, "I did, sir. But I knew you'd approve because that's what we usually do on a Monday—you know, we did, before you got here. Before Jasper was dead."

"*I'm* here now, William. I'm still alive, so when you refer to what you usually do, I guess you're referring to what you *want* to do?"

"Well," William said, smiling sincerely, "I guess you caught me, boss. But I knew you'd approve."

"You knew I'd approve. So . . . William, since we worked together last, you have not only forgotten the way I work but you've become clairvoyant? How wonderful for you," J.T. said, his voice menacingly low.

Asher put his hand on J.T.'s back and suddenly, as if Ash were the connection to Natasha and Jeremy, J.T. calmed instantly.

Jeremy.

"Okay, William. Let's just say . . . you did the right thing," J.T. had to say. William had cowered like an abused toddler. "And what's the *other* bad news?"

"Well, boss," William said, sincerely nervous, "there are no sets because the studio won't approve the Christmas budget for set design."

J.T. looked up at the ceiling, hands on hips. "No cast. No sets," J.T. said. "Okeydokey."

"Even badder," William continued.

"Badder. Okay. Hit me," J.T. said.

"The kid. Kirk? He's *still here*. He wants to *work,*" William said, sincerely horrified.

"Yeah . . ." J.T. said. "That's horrible news. Appalling! An actor stayed behind! And he wants to work, no less! *And* on a Monday! I'm staggered. Galled! It's unspeakable. How could he!? How could you even manage to tell me? It's unbearable. I think I'm having an allergic reaction. Do you have a Benadryl? I've got hives popping up all over me. Work? Monday? And *the kid,* no less! The one who obviously has an attitude problem! How clear could it be?! He's a slacker! How disgusting! I'm ill, William."

Sarcasm was lost on William. "No, really! This kid is such a problem. He has such an attitude," he whispered, sincerely.

"Yeah," J.T. whispered back, "he's the only actor who just won't go home!"

"Ah, you're pulling my leg? Same ol' J.T.," William said, sincerely. "Hey, um . . . since everyone's gone and the kid is here and there are no sets, you mind if I check out for the day? I've got a lotta exercise to put in before that big triathlon. Pain makes gain. And bro, *pain is subjective!*"

"You know what, William?" J.T. said. "I think you should go. That would be very good for the show, subjectively speaking."

The Hollywood Dictionary

TO CALL IT: To have the privilege of yelling "That's a wrap!"

TO YELL "THAT'S A WRAP!": To have the privilege of yelling "We're done!"

"You are the man," William said, sincerely forgetting his Ebonics. "Wanna call it?"

"We're the only people standing on the stage, William. Why would I want to call it?"

"Tradition," William said, sincerely.

"You do the honors, William. You call it."

"Thank you, boss," William said. Then he cupped his hands into the shape of a megaphone and yelled, sincerely, into the empty cave: "That's a wrap!"

"Thank you, William. Now it's official and the time-honored tradition continues."

"Thank you, boss. And Ash, call up a couple honeys, man! Time to pop the colla an' live chilly, bro. Git down on it! Go on witcher bad self!"

"I will certainly try to accomplish all of that, William. My only hope is that I'm not arrested and beaten on the way home during my drive-by."

"I hear ya, bro! Life's tough with the lower bottom." Already packed, William was soon gone.

J.T. sat down on the cement floor of the empty stage. "I am so fucked, Ash," he said, voice barely audible.

Ash sat down beside him. "Yup. I agree. You are so fucked. Lucky for you, I'm a spiritual being and I can handle William's shit. Today. I have no clue what I'll do tomorrow, so, please—you gotta do somethin' about your A.D., director-man."

"Why? You can just add this part to your 'How to Survive in Hollywood' syllabus."

Ash gave J.T. a flat, perfectly timed stare that meant, *Do something.*

"Done," J.T. said.

They relaxed on the cold cement floor and stared up at the catwalks. Then a weak voice came from behind Asher and J.T. "Excuse me, sir? Mr. Baker?"

J.T. sat up and turned. He saw Kirk Kelly. The twenty-one-year-old *problem child*. "That's me, Kirk." J.T. waved to him.

Kirk walked forward, extending his hand. "I didn't really get a chance to say what an honor it is to meet you, sir," he said, genuine admiration in his voice. "When I heard you were going to be directing, I went online. Man, you've done a ton of stuff."

"Yeah. I wish I were proud of all of it. But it's been a great education." J.T. stood up and shook Kirk's hand.

Kirk wiped his eyes. They were red. His nose was running slightly, and it too was red. *From being rubbed, or from chemical abuse? Too early to tell*, J.T. thought. "Kirk, um, I've lost my reading glasses somehow. I'm such a boob. Really. I'm a flaky guy. I'm the only director you'll ever meet without a sense of direction. I once landed an airplane the wrong way on a runway when I was a private pilot. A little Cessna. On the wrong runway. In the wrong state. Great landing, though."

J.T. was rambling because it was his way of trying to get a fix on this young man. J.T. was tormented by detail. He studied Kirk in his detail mode. "So would you do me a favor, Kirk? I can't seem to read this call sheet. Would you read it for me? It would really help me out, since I misplaced my reading glasses and all," J.T. said.

"Um, sure," Kirk said nervously, taking the call sheet J.T. handed him. He read hesitantly, with the same rhythms and problems that had plagued him that morning during the table read.

Got it, J.T. thought. *Kirk does have a learning disability. Probably dyslexia.* "Thanks, man." he said. "Kirk, I'd like you to meet my assistant, Ash Black. He was my student when I was a professor, and now he's a professor and basically I'm *his* student. But, please, don't tell anyone."

Kirk tried to laugh. He rubbed his nose and wiped his eyes again.

"So you got a cold? Allergies?" J.T. asked Kirk.

Kirk tried to hold back his emotions the best he could. J.T. looked at this young man and wondered what his own son would be like when he was twenty-one. *Will he still be such a compassionate person?* J.T. was flooded with thoughts of his family. Kirk brought it out in him.

J.T. immediately took a liking to Kirk.

"I was . . ." Kirk faltered, then gathered himself. "I was, um . . . Stephanie and Marcus Pooley just, um . . . spoke to me. I'm just a little shook up, but I heal quickly." And with that, Kirk began to sob uncontrollably. As awkward as it was, J.T. managed to put his arms around the young actor.

"Hey . . ." J.T. gently said, "I promise I'm not hugging you for sexual satisfaction."

Kirk instantly began to laugh. He wiped his red nose and cleared the tears away from his eyes with his sleeve, irritating the skin around his eyes even more.

"So how do you like showbiz, Kirk?" J.T. asked.

"I like it, sir," Kirk said. J.T. was sure he heard a hint of Canada in Kirk's inflections.

"Professional baseball in Canada? I mean, what is wrong with this world?" J.T. said.

"I know," Kirk immediately said, his face lighting up. "Hockey in the States, eh? What's with that?" Kirk was a good kid. J.T. was now sure of it.

"So . . . um, you don't have to answer this, but is it hard being away from home? You miss your family? Your girlfriend? In . . . now don't laugh . . . this is a guess. I love to try and guess where people are from. Okay, here goes: Vancouver?" J.T. asked.

Before Kirk could answer, Ash answered.

"Toronto. Not only the wrong place but also the wrong side of the map. You're slipping," Ash said, patting his buddy on the back.

"Jesus! Toronto. How did he know? How did you know?" Kirk asked.

"Ash teaches voice. He's not only been all over the world, but he has studied with some of the best voice teachers on the planet, and he specializes in articulation and enunciation and all of that stuff that makes him so damn smart. He's teaching over at UCLA."

"Oh, stop it, boss-man. You makes me feels so red in my black face," Ash said.

Kirk looked at Ash sharply, the way people always did the first time they heard him mimicking the old stereotyped black film actors. "That's pretty cool," Kirk said. "Maybe in the next three weeks you could teach me a thing or two? Maybe I should take a class from you."

So Kirk had been crying, not doing lines of a decidedly non-theatrically-related variety. He was the only actor who hadn't gone home, the only one who wanted to work. The only person to talk to Ash and realize he could learn something. *Yeah. A real trouble-maker,* J.T. thought.

"Kirk, how can I help you?" J.T. asked.

"Well—I thought that maybe we could work. I need to . . . um, *get better*. I need to prove that I really can handle my job," Kirk said earnestly.

J.T.'s parental instincts kicked in full force. If he did nothing else on this show, he was now determined to make sure that this young actor was protected from the random, paranoid abuse of the Pooleys. "I'll tell you what I'd like you to do, Kirk," J.T. said, "I'd like you to go home and go to bed. I don't want you to think that you are making mistakes. You're not. Trust me. I want you to fall asleep thinking that there is a reason you are on this stage and not some other actor. You were the best for the part. That's why you're here. Your talent shone above all the other young men in this *wonderful* town. I'd like you—no, I *want* you to feel good about yourself. Get as much rest as you possibly can. Tomorrow is going to be the beginning of hell for all of us. You okay with that?"

"You don't want to work with me?" Kirk asked. He could not have been more defenseless.

"There's nothing to work on, Kirk. I *love* to work. I love to work as hard as I can. But right now, the writers have a lot more work to do than you. The only thing you need to work on is your rest. And when you come in tomorrow, try and be as prepared as you possibly can. You'll get a new script delivered to your house in the middle of the night. When you wake up, study it the best you can. Okay?" J.T. smiled at the kid.

"Yes, sir," Kirk said, as if all the demons that had been attacking his self-esteem had suddenly been recalled and assigned to another person.

"Oh—and even though I really appreciate your professionalism by referring to me as *sir,* how 'bout just calling me J.T.?"

"Yes, sir. J.T. Thank you. Thank you very much. Thanks."

When Kirk left the cave, J.T. and Ash sat back down on the stage floor. This time both of them lay on their backs.

"Well played, J.T.," Ash said.

"You too. I thought you'd never say Toronto. That would've been one for the record books."

"Ah, I just wanted you to squirm a little," Ash gently laughed.

"Good one," J.T. said. "Well, should we lie here for a few more minutes before we Enter Laughing into the writers' room?"

"Yeah . . . let me put my mental armor on. I shoulda worn a cup. Remember, J.T., I'm getting older. Don't throw anyone out the window. I stopped being a big, scary black man years ago."

"Got it. No one goes out a window," J.T. said distractedly. He continued to stare up at history, seeing ghosts in the rafters of the catwalks. These were good ghosts, of course. Professional ghosts.

The Writers' Room

SITCOM WRITERS GATHER to write upcoming episodes, work in teams on ideas for episodes, and on Mondays fix the script to be shot on the following Friday. Their lair is the writers' room.

The writers' room on this sitcom was down the upstairs hallway from the Pooleys' office. This was a *Pooley*. A *Pooley* was anything manipulated by the husband-and-wife team for the sole benefit of themselves. The writers' room was down the hall from Marcus and Stephanie so they could keep their eyes on the writers and be sure that work was always being done. This room also had no windows. Another Pooley. Windows would invite daydreaming.

The writers' room for *I Love My Urban Buddies* was filled with an eclectic bunch. Writers with talent; writers who were friends of the Pooleys; writers whom the network demanded be there; writers whom the studio countered with, demanding that they be there as well; and a Thing Three

> **The Hollywood Dictionary**
>
> **THE WRITERS' ROOM:** A place traditionally nicknamed with war imagery: the bunker, the foxhole, the submarine. Unfortunately, we don't live in a world where our soldiers in bunkers, foxholes, or submarines make at least thirty grand a week and order steak for breakfast.

with stars in his eyes. His name was Timothy James Jameson III. He was a recent Yale graduate and was delegated the job of typing everything the writers "wrote."

The writers used no pencils, no pens, no legal pads. They volleyed words back and forth verbally. Other people typed what they said, copied the pages, proofread them. Here, in the writers' room, the writers spoke aloud and Timothy James Jameson III typed it into a computer. The writers made jokes about everybody on the production staff who wasn't in the room. They made jokes about the actors who were tanking their jokes. Sometimes they napped. There were even times when twaddle turned into twat and they had sex; then they called their spouses to say they had to work late.

"It's fuckin' wicked," Timothy had told one of his former college roommates. "I dunno why I spent all that time and effort at Yale. Nobody writes here! They just . . . talk a lot. Shit, I can definitely do that! And the food! All the fucking food I want whenever I want it! Junk food, filet mignon, man, everything. All compliments of the studio. Or the network. Who the hell cares? No one here pays for anything! I can get clothes for free from wardrobe, cool stuff for free from props, I mean, who wouldn't want this fuckin' job?"

J.T. knocked and went into the writers' room without waiting for permission to enter. He considered it to be a good practice for a director on a sitcom to come to the writers' room after a rehearsal to report on what worked versus what could use a punch or a new angle, or should just get thrown out. He forgot, as always, that what he considered healthy—communication from the stage to the writers via the director—was hardly the norm, and in fact had become unwelcome.

J.T. noticed all of the baby faces. Some were playing darts with Kirk's picture hanging as the bull's-eye. Others were playing trash-can basketball with pages from today's script. Others were watching a monitor with—a live feed from the stage to the writers' room.

Fuck, J.T. thought when he realized he was being spied on. And all those twenty-something writers! J.T. knew that the one thing the paranoid Pooleys were most paranoid about was being exposed, and this just proved it. Having an older writer with more experience and an actual sense of funny in the writers' room would be a definite threat to the Pooleys. There wasn't a single old-timer in there.

> **The Hollywood Dictionary**
>
> **LIVE FEED:** Big Brother is watching and listening to EVERYTHING.

"What are you doing in here?!" Stephanie Pooley demanded. She was enraged that someone other than her foot soldiers was in her writers' room.

"This is where I come to report the day's work and find out what else is needed of me, ma'am," J.T. said.

"Well—report!" Stephanie said, hoping she sounded intimidating. *My God,* she thought, *what a fucking loser! And just look at him! His eyes, his nose, his neck—he probably can't afford to get his face fixed. He disgusts me!*

"Well," J.T. began to report, "the cast has left, there are no sets, and I would like to know what you want to see and hear that will give you the satisfaction that you're getting the best ever Christmas and best ever explosion."

"The best ever Christmas would be the day we don't need a director to pretend to direct our show. And the best ever explosion would be one that is strapped to your chest," Stephanie said proudly, as if everything said in the writers' room stayed in the writers' room.

"I see. Ms. Pooley, have you ever been hit by a man?" J.T. asked in a flat, nonmenacing tone.

"You're threatening me?!" Stephanie Pooley shouted. "Did everyone hear that?! He threatened me!"

"Actually, Ms. Pooley, I was merely asking a question. I don't hit women. But something tells me, from the few moments I've spent with you and your husband, that you just might be slightly punch-drunk. Just a harmless observation."

Ash began to make his way into a position where he could grab J.T. at a moment's notice.

"Speaking of bad memories, where is your husband? I have to talk to him about your young badass actor, Kirk. Kirk Kelly," J.T. said.

"Anything you say to me will be repeated to my husband," Stephanie barked at J.T.'s elbow.

"I'm sure. Well, Kirk is very game. He wants to work hard. We had a good talk and he will not be a problem at all. As a matter of fact, I believe Kirk will give you *the best ever performance*," J.T. said.

"You're doing it again. You're patronizing me!"

"No, Mrs. Pooley, not yet. I'm still making an effort to be civil. Kirk will come around."

"And what makes you think that?" Stephanie was revising her estimation of J.T. *He's not a loser. He's retarded,* she thought.

"Well . . . I'm his director, and I'm trained to observe these . . . things." *She must have some kind of mental disability,* J.T. thought. *What's so hard to understand?*

"We'll see, then, won't we?" Stephanie said smugly. "And Marcus is in Casting at the moment and cannot be disturbed, so I would appreciate you going back to the set and preparing the show like a good little director." A few chortles percolated from her baby writing staff.

"So . . . Marcus Pooley is in *Casting?* Without his director?" J.T. asked pleasantly.

"The director does not go to our casting sessions," Stephanie Pooley said with great delight.

"Maybe I'll tell that to the Directors Guild of America. You know, basically the strongest, most influential union in show business? *That* Directors Guild of America. Asher, may I have my cell phone, please?" J.T. asked.

"Um, sure. Here." Ash handed J.T. the phone, which he kept while J.T. was working so he wouldn't get interrupted.

Stephanie now looked panicked. "What the fuck are you doing?"

"I'm calling in one of a number of Guild violations that you and your husband have committed on our very first day together."
Jeremy.

"You have a 'cell phone'?" she snorted, presenting her futuristic gadget. "Everyone has a Sidekick; shit, I've got a Danger Sidekick II. A 'cell phone,'" she howled. "He's got a 'cell phone.'"

"Yes. A 'cell phone.' Then I'll use my 'cell phone' to call the Screen Actors Guild and ask them what Kirk Kelly should do. He was falsely accused of being on drugs by his showrunners in front of the studio, the network, and a director, remember?" J.T. said, dialing random numbers.

The Hollywood Dictionary

CELL PHONE: BlackBerries were now the bottom of the elitist food chain.

"Wait—" Stephanie Pooley tried to grab the cell phone. "Casting is just down the hall. And if you ever even think about whispering a word about what you see here on this show, I will personally make sure you never work in this business again!" *I will,* she thought. *I've done it before to animators and voice talent and I'll do it again.*

"So I take that as a threat, and everyone in this room heard you." *Crap,* J.T. thought. *It's only Monday and I'm already being banned from the business again. What is it about me that brings this out in people?*

Asher gently pulled J.T. from the writers' room. *Only Monday. Shit. What's gonna go down on Tuesday?* he thought.

Look at those two, Steph thought. *I wonder which one is the hus-band and which one's the wife.*

Asher closed the door behind them. They began to walk down the hall.

J.T. felt Natasha's spirit sitting on his shoulder and began to sing softly, "Now if you feel that you can't go on . . ."

"Can't go on!" Ash echoed.

"Because all of your hope is gone!" J.T. sang.

"And your life is filled with much confusion," Ash sang, much better than J.T.

"Until happiness is just an illusion . . ."

"And your world around you is crumbling down . . ."

"Darlin', *reach out*!" J.T. said.

"Reach out for me!" Ash sang. And then together, as they walked down the hall, they spun into their choreography.

"I'll be there, with a love that will shelter you! I'll be there with a love that will see you through . . ."

And they danced like two of the Four Tops, trying to forget what they were up against, as they entered the bizarre world of casting.

Casting

As Ash and J.T. danced down the hallway toward Casting, J.T.'s cell phone rang. J.T. was certain that it was Natasha calling from the farm back East, *reaching out* to him. And he would be proud to say, "I haven't knocked anyone out yet, doll-face. Came close, though. *Jeremy.*"

Asher answered the phone, and after a few words handed the phone to J.T. *Beaglebum. For you*, he mouthed.

J.T. accepted the phone with resignation. "Hello?"

"Hey, J.T.-*orama*. The J-T-ball man! How goes it?!" Dick asked, enthusiastically.

"I already have a nickname, Dick. It's *J.T.* Just J.T." Getting a phone call from his agent moments after leaving the writers' room was not good. Predictable, but not good.

"J.T., don't be so serious! Have fun! Here's a good joke: What-taya call someone who is just a little bit dyslexic?"

"I dunno, Dick. Syd Lexic?"

"Funny—you're funny. Kirk! That's who."

"Really. And how would you know this information, Dick?"

"Hey—I got eyes an' ears everywhere, and J.T.? There's no room for all of your self-righteousness in the eye-ear-nose-and-throat of E.N.T.V.," Dick said . . . compassionately. "Haven't you learned that yet?"

"Yeah. It's a pandemic and I just haven't been infected yet."

"There ain't no antibody for what's comin' atchya, J.T."

"Oh, I've seen lots of anti-bodies," J.T. managed to say. "Let's skip the checkup and go straight to my diagnosis: you're my agent. You are the Pooleys' agent. So lemme guess what this phone call is about," J.T. said.

"Look, word's out that you already *care too much*. You're *shot-happy*. You're going overboard on the technical stuff, but what everyone wants is your expertise with actors," Dick explained, enthusiastically.

"Is that it?"

"Uh, no. They also are complaining that you are trying to *elevate the quality of their show*."

"Did I hear you correctly, Dr. Beaglebum? Say that last part again, because maybe it's not an E.N.T. I need, it's more like a—" J.T.'s bewilderment was cut off.

"I said, people are complaining that you are trying to *elevate the quality of their show*," Dick repeated.

"And?" J.T. waited. "And that's a *bad thing*?"

"J.T., you're really causing problems. I can't fix *these* kinds of problems for you," Dick explained.

"I didn't rehearse today, Dick. The actors were let go before I could even say hello to them on the stage. As for *shot-happy* and *caring too much about the technical stuff*, I don't even have access to camera and won't until Wednesday or Thursday, depending on what the Pooleys—your *clients*—will allow me to block or what they will allow me to preshoot. And as far as my expertise with actors, I nursed a twenty-one-year-old actor out of a sobbing seizure because your other clients had abused him. And as far as being accused of elevating the quality of the show, all I can say is . . . *Thank you*," J.T. finished, a little too quietly.

"Now, now, now, I'm sure everyone's overreacting. Even the kid. He's an actor, for chrissake. He's paid to overreact. But listen, J.T.—this is very important. Very. I can't get in the middle of things because I represent both you and the Pooleys. But I have to tell you something off the record—?"

"Hit me," J.T. said.

The Hollywood Dictionary

OFF THE RECORD: Recorded by every possible means.

"If you don't start behaving on this show, the Pooleys are prepared to make sure you never work again—and we both know what that means. Especially with your son on chemo and you needing the insurance and all," Dick pointed out.

"My son is on dialysis. And are you threatening me on their behalf? I just need to know where you stand, considering that you're my *friend* and you can't get *involved*," J.T. said.

"Well, theoretically, since it's a conflict of interests, I gotta watch *their* backs, too. I mean, you're just directing three episodes but they're the showrunners on a sitcom that could run for years and years. You catch my drift?"

"I'm catchin' somethin'. Your drift's startin' to smell like bullshit."

"Hold on now, J.T., I'm trying to help you."

"You're trying to help me by explaining that elevating the quality of a show is the wrong thing to do? You're speaking a language I don't understand, Dick."

"Well, tell me if you understand this: *They hate you.* I don't want to see your career ruined just one day back on the job."

J.T. couldn't think, let alone think of something else to say. He just slumped down the wall and sat in the middle of the corridor on the way to Casting. Asher eased down and sat next to J.T. They looked at each other.

"Oh, and one last minor thing," Dick continued.

"Don't tell me. Let me guess. Um, they've hired someone to

whack me and you get ten percent of the hit man's money, too," J.T. said.

"Funny. Very funny. No. That's not it," Dick said, as if it could possibly be *it*. "Here's the deal, J.T. The show is not titled *I Love J.T. Baker;* it's called *I Love My Urban Buddies.* If you defend yourself against the Pooleys by going to your union, you will be in a war of attrition with lawyer's fees that'll eat up your kid's hospital fund. You hear me, J.T.? No union. Do not involve the Directors Guild, Screen Actors Guild, or any guild that you think you can go to. If you do, you're toast."

"Toast. My boy. Union. Defend myself, all *baaaaad.* Gotcha. Thanks. Since you're my *dear friend,* I'll make sure never to forget this confidential little chat—by the way, you don't mind the fact that I've been tape-recording this conversation, do you, dear friend?"

"What!?"

J.T. flipped the cell phone shut and handed it back to Ash.

"Anything I should know, J.T.?" Ash asked.

"Use your imagination."

They got up and walked down the hall to Casting.

As they entered the casting area, which consisted of a series of seats where actors sit and wait nervously to be called into *the room*, J.T. and Ash saw that all the seats were occupied by gorgeous model-type dyed blondes with major cleavage. *Interesting,* they both thought.

A Pooley.

The two men made their way to the casting office, knocked once just to be polite, then opened the door. There, in the middle of the room, stood a beautiful young actor taking off her bra in front of Marcus Pooley and a mortified casting assistant named Teri.

"What the fuck are you two doing in here? This is Casting!"

Marcus Pooley yelled like a kid caught in the woodshed making naughty with his cousin's fipple flute. Oh, and his cousin, too.

"Let me see. Casting. Well, I had to educate your wife, so I may as well educate you. According to the Directors Guild of America bylaws, the director is supposed to be a part of the casting sessions," J.T. said.

"DGA bylaws? What? Are you going official on me? This is a casting session for *my* show! Not *your* show!"

"Look, Marcus, Mr. Pooley, I'm not here to be your adversary. I'm not here to take your show away from you. I'm not here to do anything but *help*," J.T. tried to explain.

"You director types. What makes you think I need your help?" *Need his help,* Marcus thought. *He could help by going back to Fuck-me-in-the-bum or wherever it was Dick said he was from. Yeah. That would help. Maybe I'll tell him that. No. Maybe I should have Stephanie tell him that.*

"Marcus—I don't want to get into a war of words with you. It's only Monday, and for some reason we've gotten off to a bad start. Let's try and begin anew. What do you say?" *My God. It's still only Monday?*

"I'll think about it," Marcus said.

"So while you're thinking about it, may I ask why this young actor is taking off her bra?" J.T. inquired, handing the young bombshell (also definition 1) her blouse as he waited for an answer.

Marcus rolled his eyes, exasperated. "If we're going to have the best ever *Christmas,* I'm going to need the best ever *Santa's helpers,* you retard. Jesus Christ. Isn't it obvious?"

"Well, to me, keeping in mind that I'm a *retard,* it seems like you're looking for the best ever Christmas *present*—not to be confused with past or future. Now, where in the script, at any point or on any page, is there an indication that we need a sex-crazed Santa? And if there is, where are the big fat Santa *men* waiting to audition?" J.T. asked.

"I'm the writer, and if I suddenly say I need a Santa's helper, I've got to go through *the process* of finding a Santa's helper! Oh—I forgot," Marcus sneered, "Chanukah doesn't *have* a fucking Santa!"

"I was under the impression that this was not a cable production. *I Love My Urban Buddies* is an eight o'clock show on a major network," J.T. said, trying not to rise to the bait.

"Wowy! You're so informed."

"So, considering that fact, and respecting your job as the writer and showrunner, why would you have a young lady take off her bra? I can't shoot her naked. And you can't broadcast a show with her naked."

"Well," Marcus Pooley said with a superior air, "here's where you don't know shit about running a show. I dress Santa's helper in something skintight. Then, on shoot night, I turn the air-conditioning up as high as we can and she gets cold and her nipples stick out and bingo—November sweeps! We get big ratings! Numbers! It's a numbers game, man!" Marcus sat back, triumphant.

"But even if that were the case, it's very warm in this office. Were you planning on blowing cold air on this young lady's breasts? Maybe massaging her nipples with an ice cube?"

"You are clueless, aren't you? I need to know that she isn't *deformed*," Marcus Pooley said, defending his reasoning with a continuous shaking of his head.

"Deformed?" J.T. asked.

"Yeah! Like . . . three nipples or cancer or something," Marcus explained.

J.T. looked at Teri, the casting assistant. Her eyes went straight to the floor. J.T. turned around and locked eyes with Ash. They exchanged a look that said, *Do you believe this?*

J.T. turned to the very embarrassed topless woman. "Excuse me, miss," he asked, looking only in her eyes, never below her chin, "are you deformed? Do you have three nipples? Forgive me for asking you this."

"No, I have two nipples, see?" the actress said proudly.

"There you go, Mr. Pooley, sir. The actor isn't deformed and has two bona fide nipples," J.T. stated with his hands on his hips. "Anything else you want to ask this young lady that could possibly indict you in a sexual harassment suit?"

"Don't go all lawyer on me, mister. And don't tell me you *believe* her?! She's a fuckin' actress, for shit's sake!" Marcus Pooley said. "She could've had surgery, and just for your information, I've seen women with three nipples! I've seen women who were men! How do I know that she is not a man? Huh? Tell me that!"

"Are you a man, miss?" J.T. asked the actor.

"Oh no! I'm a woman. I can prove it," she said as she began to pull up her skirt.

"Yes!" "No!" Marcus and J.T. said simultaneously.

"She's . . . an . . . actress!" Marcus Pooley spit out. "She'll say anything to get the job! I need proof!"

"Please get dressed, ma'am," J.T. said to the woman, handing her the rest of her garments.

"Look," Pooley said, his Irish temper starting to bring out his freckles, "I'm an artist. This is show business. Seeing her tits is my artistic job. If I lived back in the . . . *whatever* days, I'd paint her naked and my masterpiece would hang in a museum. And if I were a doctor, you wouldn't even take a second to question my fucking motives."

"Yes, you have a point," J.T. said calmly, not giving ground, "but *you are not a doctor*! I won't characterize my perception of you as an artist but I'll hang you in a museum of your choice! Back to the point: it is my job to be involved in casting, even if it's not the norm in the sitcom world anymore. I do know that having young women strip for your nipple approval has nothing to do with network television. Shall I continue, go back, or would you like to take a walk out to the parking lot with me?"

Ash took his hands out of his pocket and stood in his *ready* position. *Oh man. Here we go.*

"It's a fucking good thing your black bodyguard is here for you. I'd like nothing more than to wipe your ass all over this lot," Pooley spat, then grabbed his jacket and stormed out of the casting room.

J.T. and Ash released their muscles from a fight-or-flight clench to a thank-God-it's-over couch-potato-laxation.

"I'm so glad you guys came in here. This is ... disgusting. I didn't know what to do! He would've had me fired for sure if I didn't have this casting session," Teri said, trembling.

"Maybe, since they are *co*-showrunners, you ought to report the session to Stephanie Pooley. Tell her who Marcus thought had the best nipples," J.T. suggested.

"Does that mean I didn't get the part of Santa's Best Ever Helper?" the young actress asked.

"Um ... forgive me for saying this, but—you're a grown woman. What the hell are you doing taking off your top for a part on a prime-time network show? Shit! Do whatever you want, but ... shit, every time someone like you allows this to happen, you're just ruining it for a lot of other young ladies." J.T. caught Ash's warning look, and quickly said, "I'm sorry. I have no right to lecture, but ... I'm sorry. I'm a teacher. That's my real job and ... I just can't help myself. I'm sorry. Forgive me, but get your clothes on and get out of here."

"So does that mean I still *didn't* get the part?" she asked, completely oblivious.

Jesus Christ! J.T. thought.

Jesus Christ! Ash thought.

Jesus fucking Christ! the blonde babe thought.

"Yes. That means you did not get the part," J.T. said, looking at her, shaking his head.

The blonde gathered her things dejectedly, making sure her picture and résumé stayed behind in the room as she left. J.T. was absolutely expressionless.

"Hey, helluva Monday, huh?"

The two men stared out the casting office window and saw a Chinese restaurant, off the lot, across the street: *Hunan Delight. Eat In or Go Home.*

"See?" J.T. said quietly. "That's funny . . ."

"Wanna grab a bite?" Ash asked.

"Nah. I think I'll *Go Home* and stew," J.T. said.

"Well, you're one step ahead of me. I think I'll go home and marinate. What a first day," Ash said as the two men began to leave.

"Yeah . . ."

"Where are you parked?" Ash asked.

"Um, I rented a . . . bicycle. How 'bout you?"

"Shit, J.T. You want me to take you . . . where? What hotel?"

"I'm staying with my old friend Oliver."

"Oliver. Oh yeah. Give him my best."

"Will do."

"Um . . . my apartment is in Westwood. If you ever need to 'get away,' maybe go look at the ocean—" Ash was reaching.

"Ahh. Actually it's all good. I could use some more humility. Anyway, a refreshing bike ride might just get a little angst out of my system."

J.T. and Ash each went their different ways. They always had completely separate night lives from each other when they were working on a job away from home. Out of friendship and respect, neither ever asked what the other did unless one of them offered a story. Ash was able to go out and have a little fun, or make notes for his upcoming classes based on the day's work. J.T. usually collapsed at Oliver's and did his own homework for the following day's grind.

Oliver Clift was a gifted actor J.T. and Natasha had met in the early eighties. Now, they were like family. Oliver's place was close to the studio, an enormous stroke of good luck for J.T. now that his transportation was a rented three-speed Schwinn bicycle. On this particular night, Oliver and J.T. would bitch about the state of the business, and then bitch about the business again. And then again. Of course there was a phone call home somewhere in the midst of all the bitching and laughing. J.T. was horrible on the phone when he was in his warrior mode. The only thing that calling home did for J.T. was give him an irrepressible, irresponsible urge to go to LAX and hop a plane back home. He also hated to complain. So he kept the calls home loving but short.

After he hung up, J.T. would close his eyes and imagine himself back home. His cinematic memory would visualize *his movie* where Natasha and Jeremy's faces were lit by the energy of trillions of pulsating stars combined with the warm light of random rhythmic fireflies appearing, then disappearing, covering and hovering above the wild grass.

Jeremy, he'd hear Natasha whisper, her strength calming him and sending J.T. into an unexpected sleep.

ASH YELPED WHEN his "cell phone" began to vibrate in his pocket. Instinctively he looked around to see if he might disturb someone, even though he was outdoors and the sidewalk was nearly deserted. Despite the time-zone change he wasn't sleepy, so he thought he'd challenge the song and *Walk* in L.A.

"Ash. Dammit, Ash? Asher, are you there?"

"Tasha?"

"Ash. Oh—I've been trying to reach you—hold on a sec— Jeremy, could you turn down *The Daily Show*? I can't hear—and close your eyes."

"But Ma, I can't sleep! And he's FUNNY," Ash heard Jeremy say.

"All right. I've just got to talk to Ash, then I'll come tuck you in. Asher? Still there?"

"Yeah. Still here."

"Well—spit it out. How's he doing? Is he gonna make it? Really. Ash, if you're not honest—crap, you're always honest—if you're not forthcoming, I'll hop a plane and bring him back myself."

"Well, it's not unusual that a Monday is a Mayday, but as messed up as everything is, I think he's taking the high road."

"Ash—truthfully, how bad is this one?"

"Bad. But on a scale of one to ten, ten being, you know, the China Syndrome, I'd say this is a . . . five and a half. Maybe a six. Nothing he can't handle."

"Is he eating?"

"Only when I shove something at him."

"Does he have a decent car?"

"Um . . ."

"Um, what?"

"Tasha? He um . . ."

"What?"

"He . . . is riding a bicycle."

"Good. Just a test, Ash. Sorry to do that to you, but I've gotta see who's being real with me."

"I'd never lie to—"

"I never said that you would, Ash. Not telling me something I need to know and lying are two very different things. Just wanna make sure neither of those two very different things crosses paths with us. I'm gonna go tuck Jeremy in. Thanks."

"Same ol', same ol'. We'll have a great Tuesday."

"Love ya, Ash. Thank you for being there. We'll talk."

"We'll talk."

What an understatement, they both thought.

Tuesday

EVERY TUESDAY THAT found J.T. in Los Angeles alone and working for insurance money, he would follow a pattern he'd established for the benefit of his family life. He would awaken at 4 A.M. so that he could catch Jeremy and Natasha just before they left for school, Eastern time. This morning was no different. J.T. dialed home. Jeremy answered. *His voice is changing,* J.T. thought.

"Hey, Dad."

"How's my J-man?"

"Good. How's work?"

"Good."

"Cool. By the way, you're a really bad liar, Dad. But it's cool. Love you. Here's Mom."

"J.T.?"

It was a new day; new attitudes, new . . . It was, well—new.

AFTER HE'D CHECKED in with the family, J.T. tapped a code to open the new black metal anti-identity-theft mailbox at Oliver's house and pulled out a yellow manila envelope which contained the day's *new* script. It was addressed to G.T. Baker. *I'm sure it was an honest mistake,* he thought. *New! New everything!* Then he thought again.

Who the fuck am I kidding? Why do these nutcases hate me so much?
He opened the envelope.

The color of the script was green, the usual Tuesday color.
But as J.T. walked back to the house, he noticed that the weight
of the script wasn't usual. It was heavy. Like a feature. He pulled
the script all the way out, turned to the last page, and saw the
number 78. Seventy-eight pages for a twenty-two-minute sitcom? And today, the seventy-eight pages *meant* something. He
had to rehearse and block all seventy-eight pages before the
producers' run-through, which was usually scheduled for four
o'clock. *Well,* J.T. thought,
*it's a pisser, but nothing I
haven't done before.*

J.T. tossed the envelope
on the kitchen table, made a
cup of tea, and then sat
down to study the rewrites.
With two hours to go before
daybreak, he was ready to do
his homework. Even though
seventy-eight pages was just
a stupid size for a sitcom
script, he wasn't nervous

The Hollywood Dictionary

BLOCK: Choreograph the actors
to squeeze out every drop of
funny from the teleplay. *See:* The
Likelihood of Keeping Everyone
Happy.

**THE LIKELIHOOD OF KEEPING
EVERYONE HAPPY:** *See:* Famous
Jewish Hockey Players.

---

about it. This was a mountain J.T. knew he could climb. He enjoyed the challenge. And he knew he would enjoy the accolades the
network and the studio would shower upon their savior, because
they too would receive this seventy-eight-page script and wonder
how it would ever be up on its feet by the time of the run-
through.

Then J.T. looked at the cover page. He was ready to curl up into
a fetal position when he saw, typed out in big, confrontational letters, DIRECTOR'S NOTES.

"*Director's Notes*"? he thought. *I haven't directed anything yet. How could I possibly get director's notes?* He began to read:

1. Do NOT have the family in the family room.

   Interesting concept . . . but . . . okay.
   He read on:

2. Do NOT use any form of explosives for *the Best* Ever *Explosion.*

   How am I supposed to make it the best ever explosion without explosives? I know, they want to do it in post. They'll animate it or CGI the explosion.

3. There will be NO postproduction animation or computer-generated imagery for the explosion.

   "Maybe," J.T. said out loud, "I'll just make my cheeks really big and go BOOM!" Then he caught himself: it was still dark outside, and Oliver was asleep. *Shut up*, J.T. told himself. He could feel his heart racing as he read on.

4. Do NOT use *snow* of *any kind* for *the Best* Ever *Christmas.*

   Well . . . maybe it's supposed to be Christmas at the equator. J.T.'s mind was flooded with angry sarcasm. He was livid.

5. Producers' run-thru will be at *noon*.

6. New "B" story. "B" for Les "B" ian. Features Helena, of course. Trying to "bring her out of the fucking closet" in next few episodes with subtlety. Make sure it's subtle. We want to be subtle here. Subtle is the key word.

Subtle? J.T. thought, skimming the newest script until he found a page that mentioned Helena—Helen, in the script; Devon's character was called Derek, and Janice's was Jill:

This is how WE want it: *"Thanks,"* Devon's character says, prac-tically salivating. *"It's not for you, idiot,"* Janice's character says. *"It's for* her," *and Janice hands Helena the naked blow-up doll. Go to Commercial.*

The GIFT is a FEMALE blow-up DOLL.

                    DEREK: (Practically salivating)
Thanks.

                         JILL:
It's not for you, idiot. (Looks at Helen) It's
for *her.* (She hands Helen the naked blow-up doll)
                                        C.U. on Helen's Reaction.
                                        Go to Commercial.

Subtle. About as subtle as food poisoning, J.T. thought.

J.T.'s eyes bounced back to number 5 in the notes: Producers' run-thru will be at *noon.*

Noon? This was the most outrageous of all. Seventy-eight pages of staging and rehearsing that began with a 10 A.M. call for the actors to show up, and they wanted to see a run-through at noon? *Two hours later? Seventy-eight pages? It's almost impossible,* J.T. thought. But just possible enough to make J.T. look incompetent. Well . . . here we are. Tuesday.

He could see the future and it didn't include any heroics. Bummer.

J.T. RODE HIS bike up to the studio gate before the sun rose.

"License, please," said the studio security guard. He was wear-ing mirrored sunglasses although the sun had barely risen.

J.T. shifted his backpack to one side, got his license out of his wallet, and handed it to the guard, who disappeared inside the small guardhouse. A good five minutes later, the security guard emerged and said, "I'm sorry, sir. There is no pass for you here at the gate."

"That can't be right," J.T. objected, stuffing his license back in his wallet. "I'm directing *I Love My Urban Buddies*. I'm here all week."

"Well, sir, I don't know what to tell you," the security guard replied, doing his job well. "If you want, you can call the production office—when they open up. I'm sure someone will be there in about three hours or so."

"Now looky here, friend," J.T. said patiently, "I'm here to do *work*. I need to get to that stage and start mapping out blocking because I only have two hours with my cast before there is a producers' run-through."

The security guard gave J.T. a hard looky. He took out a packet of gum. He slowly opened it, unwrapped a single piece, placed it in his mouth, disposed of the wrapper, opened another piece, placed it in his mouth, and disposed of the wrapper before turning his attention back to J.T. "I'm sorry, sir, but if there is no pass in my computer, then I cannot allow you onto the lot. These are still difficult times."

"Screw difficult times! I have a producers' run-through at noon and I haven't even seen my sets!"

The security guard had a way of chewing that placed the gum perfectly between his teeth, creating sealed bubbles that would pop over and over again.

"What if you were a terrorist, sir?" *Pop.* "What if you were al Qaeda?" *Pop.* "What if you wanted to blow up the stage?"

The guard was actually serious. "Look at me," J.T. said, trying to compose himself. "Do I *look* like a terrorist?"

"Dunno. Never met one," the guard said flatly, chewing his

gum in an annoyingly slow rhythm. J.T. straddled the boy's bar between the seat and the handlebars as if that would make him more believable.

"Do you have to meet one to know what a terrorist looks like?"

"To be quite honest, sir, I hope never to meet one." *Pop*.

"Well, your wish is coming true, because you still haven't met one!"

"*Yet*. You see what I mean?"

"No!"

"How can I be sure?"

"Okay. Good question. Consider this: Why would I be here early to work if I weren't a diligent director?" J.T. tried to reason.

"No director gets here early. Especially this early. That makes you *very* suspicious to me."

"Strangely, *that* I can understand."

"And if you really were the director, you would have a pass. *And a car*. Not a bicycle."

"That's absurd. This is a perfectly nice bicycle."

"How many speeds it got?"

"Three."

"If you were a director with a bicycle, you'd have a ten-speed."

"That's not necessarily true."

"And wear better clothes. No offense."

"None taken. Look, I can understand where you're coming from," J.T. said. "But since I *am* a director, and these *are* my clothes, this is a perfectly good example of why stereotypes are . . . stereotypes," he finished lamely.

"And your backpack looks very suspicious."

"Suspicious? Why? Because it's red? Schoolkids carry backpacks!"

"That's my point. Schoolkids carry backpacks. Directors don't."

"That logic is corrupt!"

"Corrupt? What are you getting at?"

"Bogus!" J.T. was getting angry. So angry that he began to dismount his bicycle. "Look—"

"Get back on your ve-hi-cle, sir."

J.T. understood that tone. He got back on his bike.

"Why don't you turn your *ve-hi-cle* around, sir," the guard said firmly.

"I respect you," J.T. began, "I respect your job and I respect how difficult it must be during these trying times—"

"Yeah. Everybody respects me until it's them I gotta turn away. I'm always the bad guy. It's a shitty job and shitty times, so I won't even try and be nice anymore. Turn your crappy bike around or I'll call the cops. Do we have an agreement of understanding?"

"Yes. To recapitulate the redundant, we have an agreement of understanding."

"Don't be an asshole. Just go. Now!"

J.T. turned his bike around and headed for a small 24/7 coffee shop he used to eat at, more than twenty years earlier, when he had a three-year deal at the same studio to write screenplays. *Now, I can't even get onto the lot*, he thought. *How pathetic. And twenty years ago, I rode a bike to work because I wanted to. Could this be my all-time low?* He considered a moment. *No. If I didn't have the job, that would be an all-time low.*

"Perspective, perspective," J.T. kept muttering. "Think of Jeremy. Think of *Jeremy* . . . where's Natasha on my shoulder? Where is she?!"

J.T. continued to mutter as he pedaled. How could he not have a pass? *Even if they hated me, what purpose would it accomplish to not allow me to get onto the lot, into the stage to do my homework? What kind of twisted minds am I dealing with?*

Even inside the restaurant, J.T. kept mumbling as he drew blocking configurations like a madman. What would make the almighty words of the Pooleys funnier? What blocking would complement this so-called joke? What would play in concert with this bit? What wouldn't take away from these words? "Who stole the funny? I thought this was supposed to be funny!" J.T. shouted.

The patrons in the restaurant stopped for a moment, stared at J.T., then went back to their isolated, behind-a-wall, Los Angeles preoccupations.

He fumed. His plate of egg whites arrived, and he started shaking Tabasco sauce on it. *Funny isn't rocket science. It's harder.*

He took a bite of his eggs, sputtered, and reached for his water. *Maybe it can't be fixed.*

J.T. was incapable of indifference about anything. He was trained like a thoroughbred to be a winner. It was instinct, not altruism. It was genetic, not sympathetic. The only thing time had taught J.T. was that his hot-blooded passion was a W.M.D., and to be very careful not to blow sky-high over something as trivial as a *parking pass*. Nevertheless, he continued stewing as he sat in the restaurant. He simply couldn't calm down.

By the time J.T. finished his notes and his spicy egg-white omelet, he had made himself nauseated with his inner monologue. *Subtle! A naked blow-up doll.* He took out his cell phone and called the production office, just on the off chance that someone might actually show up for work on time. *At least the "A" story is the same. Not that surviving an explosion makes a great "A" story in a sitcom, but at least we have something to hold on to. Just chill. You can handle this*, J.T. thought.

A guy at the next booth, his eyes red and his nose bulbous and even redder, laughed, "You think you can handle it. But you can't. It'll get you in the end. It gets everybody."

"I'm sorry," J.T. said, trying to harness politeness from somewhere in his anger. "I didn't actually mean to say that out loud."

"That's the first stage of losing it, pal. You work in TV, right?"

"Yes . . ." J.T. was suddenly pulled into this man's world.

"I'd wish you good luck, but fuck—I'd just be wasting words."

The man with the bloodshot eyes and the Rudolph nose got up and left. *Whoa*, J.T. thought, making sure it remained only a thought. Then a sound came from his cell phone and brought him out of one man's nightmare and back into his own.

"Y'ello?" a bored, I-work-in-sitcoms-and-you-don't voice said.

A Valley girl. Great. "Yes," J.T. began, "I am J.T. Baker."

"And that means . . . what?"

"And that means, I'm directing your show and there was no pass for me at the gate this morning," J.T. said, trying to hold it together.

"What time did you get here, J.T. Baker?" the I-think-I'll-humor-him voice asked.

J.T. tried to keep his voice level. "It should not matter what time I get anywhere. The stage should be made available to a director around the clock so that the director can get the show shot by Friday!"

"Oooh, aren't we, like, a teensy bit full of ourselves?"

"*We?* What is your name?" J.T. demanded.

"My name is Julia Pooley. I'm, like, the niece of the cousin of the creator of the show you're supposedly directing," the I'm-so-important-and-you're-so-not voice said. "What is *your* name again?"

J.T. took a cleansing breath. "I am coming back to the lot and will be at the gate in five minutes. If there isn't a pass for me to come onto the lot and do my work after I have had this conversation with you, Julia Pooley, I will consider that my services are no longer needed and I will go home. And home is not in the San Fernando Valley. Home is five hours away. By plane. Please, I beg of you—do the wrong thing and let me go home." He hung up.

He gathered his notes, paid his bill, and left to face the day's adventure. He was already exhausted.

* * *

J.T. PEDALED UP to the security gate again and stopped in front of his new guard-friend. "Remember me?" he said brightly.

"No, sir. I do not." *Pop*. New gum, no doubt.

"You're just saying that! You're messin' with me!"

"My job isn't to mess with you. My job—"

J.T. dropped his act. "I know what your job is! Shit! Is there a pass for J.T. Baker in your computer now?"

"I'll check. What did you say your name was, sir?"

"Oh, give me a break. J-T-B-A-K-E-R!"

The guard went inside his little guardhouse and closed his guardhouse door. J.T. saw him look at his computer screen. The guard reacted as the intermittent glow of the screen flickered on his face. He opened the guardhouse door and leaned out of the guard gate.

"I'm sorry, sir. I have a pass here for a J.T. Baker. But not for a J.T. B-A-K-E-R."

"Very funny. Very good. You should be a comedy writer. You should be a shoe salesman. You should be anything but a studio guard!"

"What's up, Joe?" A Los Angeles police officer got out of his vehicle, which J.T. only now noticed had been parked to the left of the security gate. "This gentleman seems to be a bit agitated."

"Want some gum, Larry?"

"Gum sounds good. What kind ya got there, Joe?"

The police officer walked past J.T. and over to Joe, the security guard.

"This is that new kind that ya use when ya can't brush your teeth. Makes 'em white and fresh-feelin'. Minty fresh."

"Yeah. I've seen commercials for that. Lemme give it a try."

Joe slowly unwrapped a piece of gum for Larry. Larry folded the gum into fourths before he put it into his mouth. For some reason Larry felt it necessary to gaze upward while coming to a taste conclusion.

"Yup," Larry said, "minty fresh. Feels good. Tastes good."

"Either arrest me or give me a piece of gum!"

Both faux cop and show cop turned and stared at J.T. without blinking.

"He's been giving me trouble since early this morning."

"I thought you said you didn't remember me!"

"Calm down, sir," said the cop. "This really is good gum, Joe."

"I told ya."

"Does he have a pass, Joe?"

"If he can show me ID that he's J.T. Baker, he's got a pass."

Larry turned and straightened his belt. The one with the standard-issue, real live, this-could-make-you-dead gun on it.

"Where is your ID, sir?"

"Finally. Some sanity. It's in my wallet, which is in my backpack."

"Step away from the vehicle and let me search your backpack, please, sir."

"If I step away from the vehicle, the vehicle will fall over. The vehicle doesn't have a kickstand."

"That is your problem, sir. Not mine. Next time you might want to save up and get yourself a kickstand. Now—step away from the vehicle and hand me your backpack."

J.T. got off of his bike and gently let it go. The vehicle-bike, of course, fell over.

"There. Satisfied?"

"No, sir. Please give me your backpack."

"Ray-dee-oo." J.T. took his heavy backpack off and held it out for the police officer to take. And held it out. Eventually it was too heavy to continue holding, and J.T. just—let go.

As the backpack hit the ground, most of its contents came out onto the ground too. His papers, his cell phone, his wallet.

At that moment, J.T.'s cell phone rang.

"Dive for cover!!! His cell phone rang!!! It could trigger a bomb!"

Everyone in the vicinity—passersby, studio workers, a cyclist—all bolted. The studio guard hid in his guardhouse with his fingers in his ears, praying. The cop dove, going airborne for a very unspectacular distance of two feet. Everyone froze. The cell phone rang. And rang.

"This is a terrible misunderstanding. I can ex—"

"Nobody move. No real director uses a cell phone anymore—a Razr, maybe. Everyone stay down." The cop slowly rose to his feet and gently, oh-so-carefully, opened the cell phone. He could hear a voice. He slowly put the phone to his ear, keeping his weapon and his eyes trained on J.T.

"Hello?" the officer said.

Everyone's eyes went from the cop to J.T. Back and forth. No one dared move any part of their body other than their eyes. This cop looked scared and a bit trigger-happy.

The cop walked over to J.T. His weapon was still pointing at him.

"It's for you."

J.T. slowly took the phone. "You might wanna consider holstering your weapon, officer."

The cop handed J.T. the phone, then put both hands around his weapon and aimed it between J.T.'s eyeballs.

"Or maybe not."

J.T. slowly put the phone to his ear. "No funny business. See? I'm just talking on the phone. Please don't shoot me for that."

The cop didn't move.

"Hello?"

"Hey, boss," William said, sincerely. "What's goin' on out there?"

"William, where are you? You can see what's happening here?"

"Stage door. See? I'm waving. During sex!"

J.T. thought about looking, then thought better of it. Only his lips and eyebrows moved as he spoke on the cell phone. All other body parts were rigid. "Listen, William, I'm not messin' around. As your director, I want you to tell these ... *nice gentlemen* that I belong here," he said. "They think my cell phone is some kind of bomb trigger-thingy."

"Okay, boss, here's the dilemma: I don't wanna get fired or blown up. Survival, boss. That's what it's all about. Survival."

"I'll survive your ass—"

"After sex?"

J.T. began to breathe deeply, imagining all the creative and barbaric ways he would torture William if he ever made it back to the cave.

"Where's Ash? Putting money down on some bling-bling?"

"William, this may come as a shock to you, but you're a fucking racist."

"No way. I love black people. Not crazy for Hispanics and Chinks, but I really like black people. They play good basketball."

"Forget it, William—do the right thing; here and now. Okay?"

"What would you do if you were me, boss?"

"I'd join the circus."

"Funny you would say that, because ever since I was a ki—"

"William, tell them *on the phone*. Now!" J.T. looked at the cop. "Okay if a clown posing as my assistant director IDs me?"

Jeremy.

J.T. WHEELED HIS bike cautiously over to the director's parking space, half expecting the cop to follow him. Since the bike had no kickstand, he propped it against the studio wall. *It looks silly,* J.T. thought. *Aw, what the hell.*

He walked into the cave, and even though a man of his experience shouldn't have been shocked by anything, especially after the morning he'd had, J.T. was shocked.

The stage was completely empty.

No sets. No construction. No painters. Just food.

J.T. stood there shocked for a little longer, just for good measure. Then he noticed William, who was trying to run the audience stairs—presumably for cardio strength. William was sweating and breathing heavily, and was having trouble getting up the one tier.

"Hey, boss!" William yelled out, sincerely gasping for air. "Glad to see you made it in okay. Were you serious about the circus thing?"

J.T. stared hard at his A.D. "No. I was serious about the racist thing." J.T. took a moment to look at the cave. "William, why isn't there . . . Why is the stage empty?"

William came sprinting over to J.T. but tripped on an electrical cable and hit the ground hard, face-first.

"I think I broke my fucking nose," William said, sincerely in pain.

William looked up at J.T. His nose was bleeding but it didn't look broken. A huge egg was beginning to swell on his forehead.

"How's it look?" William asked, sincerely.

"Well, you look . . . Hispanic. Actually, with the swelling around your eyes, a little Chinese. After sex."

"I broke my fucking nose, didn't I?" William said, starting to panic.

"I don't think your nose is broken, but I do think you should get some ice on that forehead. You've got an egg the size of . . . an egg. Chicken egg. No—wait—now it's more like a baby dinosaur egg. You could possibly give birth to another forehead in a matter of minutes if you don't get some ice on that . . . embryo."

"Thanks, boss. I'll just go get some ice. We've gotta talk. I've got some bad news and some even badder news," William said, sincerely nasal in tone.

"Look, it's Tuesday. I refuse to panic any more today."

"Oh yeah? Just wait till you get a load of this news," William said, sincerely, walking away with his head bent low.

Great. More bad news, and my A.D. is walking like Quasimodo.

J.T. heard footsteps echoing in the large, empty set. It was Ash.

Asher, usually an even-tempered man, looked very upset. He looked—furious. J.T. had never seen him look furious.

"They wouldn't let me on the lot. Said I looked like al Qaeda. And I called in our passes *twice* yesterday," Ash fumed.

"I hope you didn't say you were working with me."

"Yeah. As a matter of fact, I did."

"They thought I was al Qaeda, too," J.T. said, trying not to laugh. "By the way, you just missed our *best ever* stunt. William took a header while he was running to tell me more bad news. It really wasn't funny—but—actually it was hilarious. Look at me: I've turned into *them*!"

"Is he okay?" Ash asked. He was always concerned. About everyone. Honestly concerned. "Should I call First Aid?"

"Naw, he's all right. A bloody nose and a big bump on his forehead. What time have you got?" J.T. asked.

"Ten of ten," Ash said, looking at his watch.

J.T. knew when he was in time trouble. And when all others thought they were in time trouble, J.T. knew when they were out of harm's way. It was a skill that had taken years to hone, just as a jockey knows twelve-second furlongs on every mount.

"We're fucked," J.T. said.

William came loping back to J.T. in an odd serpentine pattern, holding an ice pack to his head and with white tissue paper stuffed in both nostrils. The new weight on his forehead had apparently affected his equilibrium.

"Boss, I'm fine!"

"Okay. So what's the rest of the bad news?"

"I don't get it."

"That's because you hit your head."

"Oh." William was sincerely confused. "Um, so you want the bad news, or the badder news, or the really bad—"

"Just tell me what's going on!"

"Okay, one: every actor has called and said that they would be a little late this morning. After s—"

"Stop! How can I get a producers' run-through ready in two hours if I don't have my actors? Or even two honest-to-God hours to get the work done?!"

"I know, boss. That's bad. Now, the badder news is the studio still hasn't approved a budget for the show so the designers can't even submit blueprints so they can't start to build a set."

"Today is Tuesday. How are we going to preshoot the best ever explosion that can't have any form of explosives *tomorrow* if we don't have a set today?" J.T. asked. He was smiling by now. He knew this was going to be one of those weeks. So why fight it? *Just think on your feet,* he kept thinking.

"But the really bad news is Helena, you know, the dy—the *gay* one who plays the next-door neighbor? She's in her trailer refusing to *come out*. Hey—I made a joke!" William laughed sincerely.

J.T. fixed a stern stare on William. "Why won't she *come out*?" he asked.

"She's having girlfriend—I mean, *partner*—problems. And she thinks the script isn't gay-friendly. She said she's tired of being *the butt* of all the jokes. Hey, that was kinda funny, too!" William's bloody tissues popped out of his nostrils when he laughed.

"Okay, Mr. Funny Man, is there any more *badder* news?" J.T. asked.

"Isn't that enough?" William said, sincerely. And this time, his sincerity matched the words that came from his bloody lips.

"Where's her trailer? I'll go talk to Helena."

"It's out that back door, near the *men's room*!" William almost fell on the floor with laughter. J.T. gave Ash a nod and started walking toward the back door.

BACK IN THE writers' room, there was a phone call for Marcus or Stephanie Pooley. Neither was there. Neither had awakened in their oceanfront home in Malibu. Thing One, who hadn't lost his job yet because the Pooleys hadn't yet arrived, was told to call them on their cell phones and find them. The person making this demand was the studio representative, Lance.

"Whattaya want?" a groggy female voice answered.

"Ms. Pooley, I have Lance Griffin on the line for you," Thing One said.

"Fuck . . . Stephanie groaned. She rolled over and saw that Marcus was out on the balcony flying his remote-control miniature airplane.

"Marcus! Goddammit! Marcus! The network is on the phone."

"Can't you see I'm busy?! I'm really bugging that surfer dude out there. Ya gotta come see this."

Stephanie got out of bed and marched over to Marcus. He was flashing ass to a surfer who was waiting for a wave about two hundred yards out in the tide of the Pacific. He held the controller to a remote airplane that was buzzing the surfer.

"Gimme that," Stephanie said, grabbing the controller. "Don't show him your bum or buzz him—dive-bomb the loser." And Stephanie hit the surfer dude in the back with kamikaze accuracy, knocking him off the board. "Did you see that? The dumb fuck's underwater."

"Good one," Marcus snickered. "Hey—I don't see him . . . do you?"

Only the surfboard popped back up out of the ocean. It wasn't attached to any dude of any dude-kind. The Pooleys looked at the open dude-less ocean, then at each other.

"Want M&M pancakes for breakfast?"

"Okay," Marcus said.

"Ramona!" Stephanie shouted. "Pan *cakies con* M&Ms *pronto.*"

"Who's on the fucking phone?" Marcus asked, hearing a voice coming from the receiver.

"It's me, Marcus. *Lance.* Good morning."

"Yeah. Well, it may be a good morning for you, but I'm dyin' *here,*" Marcus said.

"Here? *Here* is . . . *where?*" Lance asked.

Without missing a beat, Marcus yelled, "I haven't left the lot! I'm trying to give you a show that is the *best ever* and I've got nothin' but naysayers tellin' me what I can and can't do. So I had to . . . get out. I'm clearing my head. Taking a walk around the studio lot usually does that for me." Marcus looked around for his pajama bottoms.

"M&M pancakes for you, Mr. Marcus?" Ramona asked, popping her head into the bedroom.

"Who's that?" Lance asked.

"Illegal aliens selling M&Ms for a Girl Scout trip to . . . Cambodia."

"It sounds like the illegal alien is near the ocean."

"She's just . . . waving the M&M bags and it sounds like the ocean."

"Right," Lance sighed. "Look, we *must* meet on the budget. We're supposed to be shooting the explosion tomorrow and I need to know how many carolers you want to blow up. This stunt is costing us on both ends, the effects *and* the stunts, let alone the special set that hasn't been built yet."

"Of course it's been built!" Marcus shouted.

"Now, Marcus, don't try and bully me, please. Let's be civil. No set has been built. I am standing right now in the middle of a stage that has not been built. The stage is *empty*, Marcus." Lance moved his $300 sunglasses to the top of his head just to satisfy himself that he was right. "Empty."

"The set was built and it looked . . . *ordinary*. So I told them to tear it down and build me the best ever set . . . *ever*! I mean, that's bullshit, what you're saying or what they've told you—*it wasn't built?* Really? I want that lying son of a bitch fired!"

Lance put his sunglasses back on. "'Everyone thinks of changing the world, but no one thinks of changing himself.' Leo Tolstoy."

"Whatever," Marcus said. "Hey! I'll take the gummy bears. I hope you take dollars 'cause gringo ain't got no pesos," he added for that touch of reality.

Lance caught himself beginning to believe that Marcus actually was on the lot, not in Malibu. That the set really had been built and that Marcus hadn't liked it and had had the set torn down. Simple as sunshine. Pure as day. *Man*, Lance thought, *this guy is good. A real snake. Ya gotta admire that.*

"Marcus, how quickly can you *return from your walk* and get to my office?"

"I can be there in . . . about an hour," Marcus said.

"An hour! Goodness. I never realized what a large lot we were on," Lance said.

"I'm clearing my fucking head! Okay?! You don't want to meet until . . ." Marcus looked out at the ocean. The surfboard was floating toward shore, and there was still no sign of a surfer. "He's disappeared. He could be drowned for all I know."

"Who would that be, Marcus?"

Marcus recovered quickly. "J.T. Baker. That piece of work who calls himself a director is drowning under the pressure."

"So J.T.'s not been working out for you, Marcus?" Lance said slowly, trying to mask his glee. This was Lance's opportunity to get the showrunners to take a stand to fire the director, which meant a shutdown to fix all the problems that were blossoming by the hour, which meant that Lance and the studio would not be responsible for the downtime moneys: the showrunners would have to cover that expense. It seemed like a great opportunity for Lance to maintain some control of the sitcom that was number one in the Nielsens but number two in the crapper.

"Not working out? This guy walks around in a beret holding a fucking riding crop! When I was down on the set, everyone was lollygagging and he was . . . *playing actor games.* My God! We have a run-through at noon. You'd think this joker would get his act together and put the fucking show up on its feet," Marcus said, squinting for any sign of life near the surfboard. "I'll see ya in about an hour or two." He pressed the off button on the cordless phone. "Where's my M&M pancakes?"

Lance looked at the still-swelling face of William, who was standing near him on the empty stage, pretending not to eavesdrop. *Just another chess move,* Lance thought. *Ah, why dignify it? Just another checkers move.* Thank God he'd hired the fall-guy schmuck director.

"Where is J.T.?" Lance asked William.

"He's in with Helena. She's very upset with the script and she has personal problems. She didn't seem to be in the mood to . . . um, work," William explained, sincerely.

Lance looked at the stage. There were no sets on his show. There were no painters or construction workers going home; there were no actors showing up except for Helena, who was upset and unwilling to work. *How do I get around this?* he wondered. Then it hit him. He opened his cell phone and speed-dialed Dick Beaglebum.

"Mr. Beaglebum's office," a young female voice said.

"This is Lance Griffin with the studio. I'd like to speak with Dick. Dick Beaglebum," Lance said impatiently.

"Let me see if he is here," the young voice answered back.

"Don't fuck with me! I know where you sit and I know where he sits and I know where you two fuck. It's a small office and—"

"Lance. Lance-a-roonie! How goes it?" Dick said enthusiastically, fumbling with the phone.

"We've got a huge problem, Beaglebum," Lance said. "This J.T. so-and-so that you brought in here from Lord knows where is destroying the show!" Lance alleged.

"Whattaya mean?" Dick asked. "It's Tuesday morning! How could he fuck up already?"

"Well, he has. The show has never been in such disarray! And I can't get two words out of the Pooleys, they're so angry."

"They're always angry . . ."

"That's not the point. The point is, everything has come to a fucking standstill because of this quack. Where the hell did you get the impression he could direct a half-hour network show?"

"The guy used to be—"

"Used to be. Has been. Is no longer! Not a single thing is happening. He's . . . taking over! He doesn't approve anything and so no work has been done and we have an explosion to shoot tomorrow!" Lance dropped his voice to a whisper. "I'm afraid you've really fucked up on this one, big guy."

"Why are you whispering?" Dick asked.

"I don't like to hurt people's feelings, okay?! My job is hard enough. Now, I'm afraid you're going to have to share some of this burden. I'll have Legal call you and we can renegotiate some of your syndication fees."

Lance flipped the phone shut before Dick could get a word out. With any luck, he could not only salvage this mess but actually rearrange the profit-sharing. Lance looked at William.

"You never heard a word of this. It never happened. Understand?" Lance told William.

"Understand. I mean, understood!" William said, sincerely. He was excited. William loved the intrigue!

"Good. Play your cards right and everyone moves up one. That means, guess who will be calling 'Action!' around here? Understand?"

"Oh my God! Yes, *sir*. I understand. Thank you!" William's smile was so large that his just-forming scabs started bleeding again. But he didn't care. His boss, the Big Boss, Lance Griffin from the Studio, had just told him that if he played his cards right, he'd be directing. No more A.D. shit for him! After sex, during sex, before sex! *This is too good to be true,* William thought as he watched Lance stroll off the stage and head back toward his office in the administration building.

Ash heard everything. He had stealthily positioned himself under the risers, still in good form as J.T.'s eyes and ears. But unfortunately for J.T., not even Ash could follow William into his office, to see and hear what he did in there.

Like most A.D.s, William had his own small, windowless office where he could hang out during breaks and do his paperwork. Like most such offices, William's was on the stage against a wall, strategically placed next to an exit so he could go get his stars from their trailers and bring them back to the set.

William closed his door. He giddily dialed a studio phone number on the standard-issue ivory push-button phone.

"Hello? Marcus?" William's smile drooped. "I'm sorry. I meant, Mr. Pooley?" His smile returned. "I have some info you should have. Our new director just went into Helena's trailer to discuss *artistic content*!"

"Get me that fucking asshole director. Call him on his cell phone. Do it—*now*!" Dick shouted as he was humping his secretary. "Now . . . now . . . oh yes . . . now . . ."

J.T.'s cell phone began to ring as he sat with Helena in her Winnebago. He'd forgotten to leave it with Ash.

"Aren't you going to answer that?" Helena asked J.T.

"Nah. I know it isn't my family, and I'm here to work, so who-ever it is doesn't really matter at this moment. Anyway, go on. Tell me. What bothers you about the script?" J.T. spoke in a clear, gen-tle, but firm voice.

"Well, okay. Everyone knows I'm a lesbian. In real life. *Everyone* knows. Why all the Chanukah *bush* references from *my* character? And 'Brokeback Christmas'?"

"I understand . . . It's a new 'B' story that should be okayed by you—at least it should be finessed by you. How can I help?"

Helena took a beat. She got up and began pacing as much as her Winnebago would allow. She looked at J.T., trying to decide whether to trust him. After all, he was the director. Basically he just wanted her on the set. *Aw, fuck it,* she thought, and began to speak.

"I'm being . . . pressured by the lesbian community to be their *spokesbian.*"

J.T. gave her a nod of understanding.

"The newspapers have been writing snide, biting articles about me," she went on. "Last week, I fought back. I wrote a letter to the editor of the *Los Angeles Times,* basically telling them to leave me the fuck alone. It felt so good to get it out of my system. When I saw it in print, it felt even better. But since then, every day, there's been another follow-up article or editorial. All I want it to do is stop!"

"Helena, I'm not the wisest person, but I can tell you this: *Never, ever get into a war of words with an enemy who purchases ink by the ton,*" J.T. said—from experience.

"But there's more, J.T. My partner . . . everyone . . . they're giv-ing me deadlines. They're telling me if I don't openly *come out,* they'll do it for me. They're treating me like I'm the one and only person who can make the lesbian issue palatable to the average American. Hell, they want me to speak for *all* homosexuals!"

"How do you feel about that?"

"Look at this script! What am I supposed to do? I'm truly at odds. I know it may be good for 'the movement,' but I don't know if it will backfire and really screw up my career. I'm a comedienne. I'm not the poster-child type. Now, I don't have a choice," Helena said, waving the rewrites.

There was a moment when neither Helena nor J.T. knew what to do or say next.

"Well," J.T. finally said, "this has to be a very personal decision, and unfortunately, only you can make it. I don't envy you, but *we must work now*. Like you said, you're a *comedienne*. No matter what, all of us are here for one purpose, and one purpose only, and that's to get this show shot. So I beg of you—don't sit in your trailer and smolder over this. Come out and work on the show. Do what you do best. Make people laugh. You have a gift. You will figure everything else out in time. But now, to be quite honest, Helena, we have no time. So whattaya say?"

"J.T.—you're not gay, are you?" Helena asked.

"No, but some of my best friends . . ." and they shared a false and predictable laugh.

"I'll be out in a few minutes. Let me just gather my thoughts and stop crying. I'm sorry. I'm really sorry."

"I understand. Take your time. But not too much," J.T. said, smiling.

Who would ever believe that I am somehow influencing gay history? J.T. thought.

Who's he kidding? Helena thought. *Of course he's gay.*

BACK ON THE set, Ash immediately filled J.T. in on the conversation he'd overheard, and the two swore that one day they would write a book about the insanity of it all. All of the actors had arrived but were eating or reading the paper or the trades. Highly unprofessional. *What else is new?* J.T. thought.

J.T. gathered his actors and was very precise about how the next two hours would proceed. Since he barely knew anything about the sets, he would make assumptions; those assumptions would be based on making the words or the actors funnier. "Or," J.T. said, "if you or your words are in danger of falling flat, the blocking is going to tap-dance. That means it's gonna take the viewer's attention to something other than the actor with egg on their face or the writing that isn't working."

> **The Hollywood Dictionary**
>
> **THE TRADES:** Insider tabloids fronting as credible sources of showbiz information. *See* Spin.

And then J.T. gave a quick speech, one that he had given before. It was based on protection. He told the actors—the regulars—that the staff and crew would come and go, but if the show were to stay such a superhit, they would have to learn how to stick together as a group and always take care of one another. J.T. gave this particular speech because he had been given a similar speech when he was a young actor by a director he still had the utmost respect for.

"This director, whatever his name is," Devon whispered to Betty, "sucks the big one."

"Whattaya doin' tonight?" Betty whispered back.

"My girlfriend's pregnant and she's pretty upset. Says it makes her look fat. She doesn't feel sexy."

Betty smiled and nudged him playfully. "Wanna do somethin' with me?"

"Lemme think about it."

Rocky Brook took the bottle out of his pocket, which turned

out to contain liquid Vicodin, and downed a quaalude with a quick swig. Kirk watched.

"What?" Rocky asked defensively. Like, about to go to war defensively. "What?"

Kirk wasn't sure how to respond. "Can you act taking all that stuff?"

"I act better." Then Rocky's tone jerked into an about-face, and he got all chummy with Kirk. "I won a People's Choice Award when I was mixing Vicodin and Oxycontin but I felt sluggish—in a bad way. Now, *this* combo relaxes me—in a good way. You can try it if ya want." Rocky's speech was beginning to slur.

Again, Kirk wasn't sure how to respond. "Yeah. Maybe sometime I'll give it a try. Not now, though."

"Nah' now though," Rocky mocked. "Wha'? What? What?! You don' fuckin' think it'll help?!" He was ready to go to war again.

"Hello?" J.T. raised his voice. "Anyone actually listening to my great speech?"

The cast just mumbled.

"Great!"

After which J.T. took a deep breath and began to work. He did *his thing.* For two hours he barely took a breather, moving portable chairs, assuming that *this* would be *there*, asking for things that would make the actors more comfortable and getting the full seventy-eight pages out of their mouths, with movement that made sense to the scenes as well as their characters.

All was going well, except for the fact that the show's not-so-ditzy-in-real-life vixen, Janice, had taken a liking to J.T. (She took a liking to most directors. She had a father-figure complex.) Every chance she had, she would make sexual jokes or ask for a banana in the scene as a prop and swallow it whole. Every chance J.T. had, he let it be known that he was all business and was very happily married, and made comments: "Janice, you really don't want to

see that in reruns twenty years from now, do you?" And it seemed
to work.

J.T. had been the object of advances from actresses on many
shows. It never had to do with J.T.'s personality or even a remote
physical attraction: sex was an easy route to the intimacy and trust
that all actors needed to feel between themselves and the director.
Fortunately for J.T., he knew the routine, and one way to break the
tension was just to break for lunch.

The entire cast was meant to be having a rolling lunch, which
meant that a table filled with four hundred dollars' worth of Japanese food was set up in the corner of the cave so they could eat as
they supposedly worked, because their day would be a long, grueling, two and a half hours. J.T. actually let them take ten minutes
on their own.

"Hey, where's the wasabi?" Devon complained in his whiny
New York way. "I ordered extra fuckin' wasabi, man. Dude, what
does it take to get wasabi?"

"I know," Betty sympathized. "At least they remembered the
ginger." She nuzzled up to Devon, the Alpha Buddy. "So whattaya
think of this new director?"

"He sucks," Devon blurted. "I want some goddamn wasabi!"

Kirk reached for some chicken teriyaki but Rocky Brook
grabbed the bowl and dumped the whole thing on his plate first.

"Sorry, chump," Rocky slurred, pulling out his Vicodin for another swig.

"No problem," Kirk whispered. He went for the vegetable tem-
pura instead.

"Speak up! Shit! You think you're on mic?" Rocky snapped back
at Kirk. Obviously that Vicodin swig hadn't been big enough.

Helena was on a hunt for chopsticks. "Please don't tell me they
forgot the chopsticks again. Please. William?"

William came running.

"Yes, Helena, my favorite of all favorites."

"Funny," Devon snorted. "You're so funny, William, maybe you should be . . . I dunno, an *A.D.*? Leave the funny to the funny people. Clear?"

"Don't tell me," William said, sincerely, "they forgot the wasabi again."

"This better be the last fucking time this happens," Devon shot over his shoulder as he wandered to the end of the food line—where there was a mountainous pile of green Japanese mustard: wasabi by the pound. "Never-fucking-mind," Devon belted out "from the diaphram," and took a big swipe of wasabi with his fingers.

Janice was not about to be derailed from her purpose by eating. She thought she'd test her *trust issues* with J.T. After spending a couple of minutes hovering near the food table, she wandered back to the imaginary set where J.T. stood in concentration, imagining the real set that was supposed to be there.

"I don't like where I'm sitting in the 'A' scene," Janice said sweetly, knowing all too well that those words were catastrophic for J.T.—for the production. They meant a complete reblock of the scene in those five minutes that were left before the run-through. Five minutes before all the producers, showrunners, and studio and network reps arrived.

"Janice," J.T. said sternly but with a hint of give in his voice, "why don't you like that particular seat?"

"Because . . ." and then Janice began to weep. She tilted her head slightly north, so that the light caught her tears and magnified the moisture. "I can cry on cue. Whattaya think of that?"

"I'm not sure that's a skill you'll be needing in a sitcom. Now, what is it about that particular seat that makes it . . . unsittable?"

Janice wiped away her tears and answered flatly, "Look, J.T., I'm the highest-paid actor here," she said too loudly, "and if I don't want to sit in a certain spot, I have every right to sit *elsewhere*." Janice smiled to herself, obviously enjoying this little power play.

J.T. tried to ignore the murmuring her comments immediately

provoked from the other actors back at the food extravaganza. "Janice, I thought this through. I put you there so I could see your reactions on camera, not the back of your head—which is lovely, might I add. But there is a purpose behind what you may perceive as blocking madness on my part. I want to take care of you and your character. And it is five—no, *four* minutes before run-through, and I refuse to give the powers that be a sloppy run-through. That is my job requirement. And I don't care if you despise me for it. I'm the boss on the floor. And I've gotten used to being hated." J.T. stayed calm, but his tone was urgent.

"Sorry. No go." Janice smiled and walked away from the set.

J.T. tried to take a deep breath. William smiled at him, sincerely. Ash was ready to act, waiting for the cue he figured was about to come from J.T. The friends had been through similar routines before.

"Okay. William, round up all my actors for Scene A," J.T. said loudly. "We'll re-block in the four minutes we've got. Please tell Janice she isn't needed since we only see the back of her head and she has her shit together and knows exactly where she wants to sit. Kirk, I think you deserve to be taken care of in this scene," he said even louder.

Of course! Ash smiled. *Perfect play!*

"What the fuck?" Devon bellowed.

Betty complained, "Jesus, Janice, I need my ten minutes. I want my ten minutes. The director gave me ten minutes."

"Eat me, cunt," Janice spat. "J.T.," she protested to the director, "you know I've been nominated for two Golden Globes and four People's Choice Awards, don't you?"

"I don't believe in awards for television, so forgive my ignorance," J.T. said.

"Well, the point is, the *people* love me. That's what counts. People. *Ordinary people.* They just *love me.*"

"I get it. People love you."

"Look, J.T., I didn't mean to make your life harder, I just feel more comfortable sitting in the other chair."

"Can you give me a reason, Janice? Is it a power move, or is there a purpose behind this?"

"My *left* side," Janice said, as if it were code that J.T. should've understood immediately.

"Janice, you mean to tell me that you want to move to a different chair because—"

"Yes. My left side is *my best side*. I refuse to be photographed from the right."

"Janice, do you want me to block this entire episode based on the fact that you never want the right side of your face photographed?"

"What's the big deal?"

"Well, Janice, the big deal is that a show should be blocked and shot for what is best for the show, not what is best for the left or right side of your face. This is not a photo shoot, nor is it a feature film. There are any number of other decisions that have to be made about camera angles, on top of which, Janice, do you realize that this is a FOUR-camera show? Four cameras shoot the show simultaneously from different angles. If one camera is shooting your left side, another camera is shooting your right side so that the scene can be cut together. So what you're asking me to do is not only selfish and vain and honestly beyond my comprehension, but Janice, don't you get it? It's also mathematically impossible!"

"That's not what Jasper said last week."

"Janice, I could tell you, just like Jasper probably did, that I will only shoot the left side of your face, and you'll feel satisfied and that would be the end of the story. But I'd be lying to you, as Jasper obviously did. I can't lie to you. It's absurd."

"Okay then, it's very clear that you're not going to take care of your actors like Jasper did. Did everyone hear that? J.T. doesn't give a crap about his actors. He's not an actor's director. He's a techie, camera director. So, everyone," she went on, gesturing widely with her arm, "spread the news: We'll just have to take care of ourselves. I am sitting in the other chair. No discussion. End of story."

Devon leaned over to Betty. "Told ya he sucks."

"You're so . . . savvy. You can feel these things instinctively," Betty said adoringly.

"Yeah, well, I've been around awhile. This is my third sitcom."

J.T. turned to Ash and just smiled. "Okay! You've got it. Now, please get ready for run-through. I have to reblock the scene and put Kirk in the good seat. Excuse me."

"Why Kirk?" Rocky asked, now in a paranoid state. "Is he your favorite? Is it because he gets the most fan mail?"

"I didn't know that. I get a ton of fan mail," Devon said, suddenly feeling hollow. "I'll bet I get more hits to my Web site."

"Excuse me!" J.T. abruptly stopped the lunacy. "I'm putting Kirk in the chair because it makes sense for the scene."

"Says who?" Rocky volleyed.

"Says the director," J.T. returned.

"So that's how it's gonna be, huh? We're supposed to do what the director says? I mean, grow up."

"Rocky, I am a grown-up. I'm also your director. Please behave with the courtesy that is deserving of that relationship."

"Huh?" Rocky took out his bottle of Vicodin and took another hit. Then he grabbed a quaalude from his pocket, popped it in his mouth, and chewed on it.

Kirk whispered to Rocky, "How are you even standing, dude?"

"Don't force me to treat you like a child," J.T. warned. "Allow me to treat you—all of you, like artists I respect."

"Oh. Well . . . okay then." The quaalude hit that fast. And Rocky and the other cast members started to get into their positions for the top of the scene, with Kirk sitting in Janice's chair.

J.T. had his eyes glued on Ash, both knowing this particular part of the routine. And on cue:

"Wait," Janice said. "J.T., you know I have all the respect in the world for directors. As a matter of fact, on any set that I'm on, the director is king!"

"Perfect. Then, as king, Janice, I proclaim: YOU SIT IN THAT SEAT! Are we clear?"

"We're clear," Janice seethed. "We're very clear."

"Janice, if you want to storm off, storm off quickly. Run-through is in three minutes," J.T. said. "Everyone else, last chance to hit the boys' and girls' room. Let's set for run-through!"

Ash and J.T. caught each other's eyes. William came running up to J.T. "Boss, should I set for run-through?" he asked, oh so sincerely.

"We should've already been set," J.T. said, his voice flat.

"Well, seeing how Janice—"

"William, have I ever, in all the years we've worked together, ever been late with my cast for a run-through?" J.T. asked bluntly.

"Never, sir," William said, disappointed. He would've liked nothing more than for this to be the first time.

"Set for run-through, please," J.T. repeated, and walked to the men's room. His only chance to relieve himself. He made it a point never to call a five-minute break on his own behalf.

"Man, this director just sucks," Devon said, not even trying to keep his voice down.

As soon as the break was called, Helena had headed back to her trailer. In her peripheral vision, she caught sight of Marcus Pooley jogging (a jog he had been working on to match the jogging style of Tom Cruise) over to her.

"Helena?"

"Hello, Marcus."

"A wittle biwdy told me you weren't happy? Marcus is here to make all things better again!" Marcus took out a small Altoids tin. Slowly, mischievously, he opened the tin and revealed a fine white powder. "Mommy says it's nice to share."

"Step inside my trailer, little boy."

WHEN J.T. RETURNED to the set (from the men's room used by any and all on the lot, not the one in his office, because he hadn't been given an office—another DGA violation), he saw an entire audience of 18-to-34-year-olds (killer demographics!) being seated in the bleachers. *This can't be,* J.T. thought. *This is a run-through. Our first run-through. Without sets. How could there be an audience? The actors will be holding their scripts. They've barely had two hours with the material. They should be nurtured at this point in the week, not judged.*

J.T. ran over to William. "What the hell is going on?"

"I'm setting for run-through, boss."

"The audience. Why is there an *audience* here?"

"Oh! What is, *The Pooleys want to see if their jokes are landing*?"

"Wrong, William. The Final Jeopardy! answer is: What is, *That's absurd!*? We haven't worked on the jokes yet. We haven't finessed anything! How insecure are they? Do the Pooleys understand what an accomplishment it is for everyone involved to even give shape to this many pages in this little time? Do I win for losing, William?"

"Huh? Hey, man," William said, sincerely, "I think I know what you mean. It's really tough on you."

"Not me, William! The cast! They'll tank if they don't get any feedback. This is the time when we should be building confidence for the week."

"Man, J.T., that's why you get the big bucks. You about ready for run-through?"

Over the next few minutes before the run-through, J.T. watched the reactions of the cast members as they each realized in turn that they would be playing their first cold run-through to an audience. To J.T.'s surprise, they weren't angry. They were excited like schoolkids peeking out from behind the curtain in the auditorium.

The Pooleys entered the stage like royalty, pretending to know people in the audience and waving to them in three different Miss America styles of waving.

THE RUN-THROUGH CAME and went—without a single laugh or giggle from the audience. It was a tornado of action and words—individual actors' trademark bits, laughs from the writers who were trying to protect their territorial jokes, awkward moments of silence.

They had pulled it off, in J.T.'s world. In his world, just making it from page one to page seventy-eight was a victory. In the actors' world (on this set, anyway), getting from page one to page seventy-eight meant they should have the rest of the week off until it was time to shoot.

J.T. congratulated his cast on the effort, and then it was over. J.T. could finally take his first healthy deep breath and look around. No sets, less than two hours for rehearsal, and every single actor had come through. Especially Kirk Kelly. Kirk had done a tremendous job. Obviously he had memorized his lines. No reading. Nothing could have proved his willingness to try and work hard more than that.

J.T. felt a gentle tap on his shoulder from behind. He turned. Standing there was Kirk.

"I, um"—Kirk looked down, then forced his eyes back up—"wanted to thank you and Ash."

"You really don't have to—"

"Yeah, I do." Kirk twisted his head twice, then stepped forward with his left foot once. *Obsessive-compulsive, too?* J.T. thought. *Poor kid. How come I didn't see that before?*

"I just had to say thanks. It's not like I don't know what you did for me—*are doing* for me."

"Well, Kirk," J.T. said as he watched Kirk go through his head and foot movements again, "not only is it my job, but I want you to succeed. You're a wonderful young man, and . . ."

Kirk quickly took a small pill from his pocket and placed it under his tongue.

" . . . Um, I was saying, you're gonna be great."

"Please thank Ash for me. I know they want all the actors to get lost so they can give notes and everything they do, so—again, thanks, man."

Before he left, Kirk twisted his head twice, stepped forward with his left foot once, and then started to walk away, but suddenly turned back and touched the spot on the floor with his right foot, then started to leave again.

Notes were about to begin. J.T. was steeling himself for the usual barrage of comments the titled elite felt they needed to make to justify their attendance at Notes ("Why did Devon touch his face during the joke?" "I saw that, too!"). He didn't see Kirk stop to tie his shoelaces, which were already tied. But Ash, sitting alone in the bleachers, noticed that Kirk continued to tie and untie his shoes.

J.T. gathered with the Pooleys, the gaggle of executive producers/coproducers/ producer-writing staffers—anyone who had a title—and set for Notes in the middle of the empty stage. Not a one acknowledged J.T.'s presence.

William whispered loudly to Marcus and Stephanie, "It's safe!"

"Not one fucking laugh!" Marcus Pooley smoldered.

"Who are you addressing, sir? Because your cast did an exemplary job," J.T. said immediately.

Marcus spun on J.T. "This script is funny. Are you telling me the cast did a great job?"

"Yes, I am," J.T. repeated. "I have faith in the process. It worked, and it also failed miserably. That is what run-throughs are for. The show is exactly where it should be on a Tuesday."

This was high treason. In the world of the Pooleys Rule the Universe, no one spoke to a Pooley like that, and everyone there knew that.

"No one laughed and my script is funny," Marcus Pooley repeated.

"*Our* script, Poodles," Stephanie reminded him. "*Our* script is funny."

"If you believe that, so be it," J.T. said, standing his ground.

"Then it must be your direction that sucks, because nothing was fucking funny! Did you hear one laugh from that audience?" Marcus screamed.

Ash decided that now was the time to share. "If you will excuse my impertinence . . ." he interjected. Necks cracked as heads whipped round to see who had the balls to speak up in this *high-level* argument.

William thought he could avert a confrontation. "Yo, bro, ya got mad game, but—" Before J.T. could say it, Marcus snapped, "Shut up, William." *Finally,* J.T. thought, *we agree on something.*

"Zippin' it!" William quickly said, making the zipped-mouth move—but had to add, "After sex."

Marcus Pooley was on fire. At any moment he could've set off the sprinkler system. He turned to Stephanie, the only one who truly understood the depths of his outrage at Ash's lack of understanding of how the totem pole worked. "That . . . that *accomplice* of J.T.'s keeps undermining me! He keeps sneaking in places and then *talking*! I cannot have him talking! Make him stop!"

Before Stephanie could intervene, however, J.T. said, "Please, Ash, go ahead."

"They enjoyed the show very much," Ash said with a pleasant look on his gentle face.

"And you know this because . . . you have special fucking powers?" Marcus shouted into the bleachers. "You mind-read? Okay! Mind-read me, Mr. Special Powers. What am I thinking now, M. Butterfly?"

"Hold on a moment," J.T. said, coming to his friend's defense.

"No! You hold on a fucking moment! How dare this . . . this . . . this . . ."

"Man?" J.T. said.

"Man! How dare this . . . this . . . agh! This *man* tell me that this audience enjoyed the show? How the fuck could he know?"

"Because, Mr. Pooley," Ash said in his calm baritone, "their tour guide told me."

Marcus Pooley froze in mid-rant. "*Tour guide?*"

"Mr. Pooley," Ash continued for all the group to hear, "your audience was a group of beekeepers from Bosnia and Herzegovina. They are touring the States to get tips on pollination, which of course, I'm sure you know, is one of the first steps in creating an independent and thriving food source for their country."

"Bees? Fucking bees? So?! They still should've laughed, you dumb fuck."

"There's no need for personal attacks, Pooley," J.T. said with a different tone in his voice.

"But bees? Did you hear him? He's saying they didn't laugh because of pollen?! Holy shit! I've heard excuses, but that one takes the fucking honey!"

All the writers laughed. Not a single laugh was genuine. J.T. walked over to Ash to show support and, as the maestro, allow Ash to have the next solo.

"I believe you are missing the point, Mr. Pooley," Ash gamely continued.

"*And the point would be*? They are African killer bees? Bumble-bees?"

The writing staffers laughed like a group of dentists playing with the nitrous oxide tanks after business hours. Ash waited for the cackling to subside. "No, Mr. Pooley," he said slowly, "not a single one of them *spoke English*."

Silence fell with a silent thud. The writers tried not to move, but they were all checking each other out with quick eye movements. Lance, who'd had no reason up to that point to throw his weight around, blew his chameleon-like cover by trying to stifle a laugh. Instead, snot came out of his nose. He quickly grabbed his silk handkerchief, but he couldn't stop laughing.

Lance was, in fact, very impressed. Not so much with the script as with the efficiency of the run-through. Lance actually knew what J.T. had just pulled off. From the cover of his handkerchief he smiled at J.T., who acknowledged the gesture with a quick, non-committal grin.

The Pooleys looked daggers at Lance, then sheathed them to look at each other. In that symbiotic moment, Marcus was appointed spokes-screamer.

"Who's responsible for this?!" he bellowed. "We had an audience that *didn't speak a word of English*?! I want to know who is responsible for this group from Bosnia and the other group from Hertze-go-renta-car-ia!"

"Herzegovina," Ash corrected Marcus, respectfully. Ash then continued as only Ash could; and J.T. loved it.

"It's a country formed by two very distinct territories: Bosnia takes it name from the Bosnia River. Herzegovina gets its name from the German noble title *Herzog,* which, interestingly enough, means 'duke.'"

"Interesting? This is interesting to you? 'Duke'? Did I ask for a fucking lacrosse game?! I asked for a fucking *audience*! Who's responsible for all those fucking dukes being here?!"

A small female voice, tentative in its unaccustomed humility, squeaked from behind the writers. "Um, it was such late notice that this was the only group I could get."

J.T. recognized this voice, only now it wasn't arrogant and bitchy or safe because she was talking into a telephone.

"Who the fuck are you?" Marcus yapped.

"Marcus, it's me. Me. Julia. Julia . . . Pooley? Your cousin Tommy's niece? So I'm, like, your cousin too."

"You're fucking fired, that's who you are! I want you off the lot by the time I get back to the office. Fuck. An audience that doesn't speak English! I told you this script is funny!" But now, Marcus was very insecure. "Am I right? Am I right?"

"Of course you're right," came a Doppler-like response from the writers.

So J.T. took out his script and a pen, and was ready for notes.

As Marcus's cousin's niece fled the room in tears, Marcus Pooley spotted Kirk Kelly in the shadows, still tying his shoes. He ran to Kirk with scenery-chewing dramatics, hugging him and lathering him with spittle and praise.

"I'm so damn proud of you, kid! What the fuck are you doing onstage? You should be resting. *Why isn't he resting, William?*"

"That's what I was trying to tell you, boss. It's not safe."

"Well, kiddo, Kirk, my boy, get outta here! Get a massage! You deserve it!"

"Yes, sir. Thank you, sir," said a stunned Kirk, who did a contained version of his obsessive-compulsive movement and then jogged off the stage.

As soon as Kirk left, Marcus turned to William. "Is it safe now?" he asked, looking around him. "Are all the fucking actors gone?"

"It's very safe now, boss," William said, the pencil he'd been puffing on in place of a cigarette bobbing in the corner of his mouth.

"Okay." Marcus Pooley sighed and looked at Lance. "I don't know what the fuck to do with that Kirk Kelly kid. He's tanking the show! I want him gone."

"Well . . ." Lance said, "I thought he did . . . a much better job than at the table read. It's obvious that *someone* has been working with him." Lance looked at J.T. again, smiling and nodding his approval.

Weasel, thought J.T. He knew from Ash that Lance had him in his sights. He was being set up, but Lance didn't want anyone to know which gun the bullet was coming from. Lance's mistake was to think he'd fooled J.T. into believing he was the good guy.

In the meantime, the praising of J.T. had its intended effect of infuriating the Pooleys.

"I don't like the chair Janice sits on in the 'A' scene!" Stephanie, the Style Führer, barked.

"Um . . . it's a *folding* chair," J.T. said.

"Um . . . Ex-fucking-actly!" She mimicked J.T.'s tone with surprising accuracy.

She's not a bad actor, he thought. What he said out loud was, "What I mean is . . . we have no sets; no set dressing for that scene. So I grabbed the first chair I could find in order to give you a noon run-through."

"Excuses. Blame! I don't want to hear a fucking word about *why*! I just want to see results! No fucking folding chairs on my show!" Stephanie yelled, gesticulating at a taupe metal folding chair instead of at J.T.

How odd, J.T. thought. "I'll make sure that note gets to set dressing," he said, jotting in his notebook. He took another deep breath. "I think, if you don't mind my saying"—he chose his words carefully—"we should discuss the best ever explosion that, according to the director's notes I received, should have"—and then he read straight from the notes—"*no form of explosives* in the best ever explosion."

"What's to discuss?" Marcus Pooley said bluntly. "I want to see the best ever explosion and I don't want to use explosives. What's not to get?"

"Wow. Well, where do I begin?" J.T. shook his head.

"Are you being condescending to me, Baker?" Marcus Pooley threatened.

"I'm at a complete loss as to how you'd like me to accomplish this feat. You know, the best ever explosion with no explosives, no animation, no computer generation; how does one do this?" J.T. honestly wanted to know. "Do you want compressed air to blow the fake snow we don't have a budget for and add a *kaboom* in the postproduction mix?"

"One does this if they are a skilled dire*ctor*. Making film is nothing more than an illusion. If you cannot find a way to give me the illusion of the best ever explosion without explosives, then you are not a dire*ctor*. You are merely taking the production's money." Marcus Pooley glanced at Lance to see if he'd appreciated the reference to the budget.

> **The Hollywood Dictionary**
>
> **THE "A" SCENE:** Not to be confused with the "A" story. All the scenes are alphabetized. When edited together, they should tell both the "A" story and the "B" story by the final credits. (Jeez! Look how many credits there are!)

"Okay—*an illusion*. You've got it. So—the purpose of this best ever explosion is that Janice survives, being one of the carolers? And that is the 'A' story that makes this the best ever Christmas?"

"Duh," Stephanie expectorated.

"D-U-H," J.T. said, writing it down verbatim into his script, "I just want to make sure I'm clear with you. *D-U-H. Duh.* Gotcha. *Duh.* Good note. Done!"

William found this funny. So funny that he inhaled the rubber eraser on the end of the pencil he was smoking. He began to choke. He pointed to his throat.

"He's just pulling another one of his stupid jokes," Marcus said as he continued to look through his script for more director's notes.

"Um, I don't think he's kidding." Ash tried to address the crowd. Not a single person listened except for J.T. The two men stared at William for a beat. William kept grabbing his throat and looking more and more desperate. His face was bulging to comic proportions and even his hands were turning red.

"Yo, bro—HELP—" was all William could muster. Then he began to lose consciousness.

"What's wrong with you people?!" J.T. yelled. "Someone call 911!"

J.T. and Ash stepped into action to save William and do the Heimlich. Ash was stronger than J.T., so he went behind William and put his arms around his chest, just below the V in his rib cage. J.T.'s contribution was to keep yelling. "Did anyone hear me? Someone call for help!"

Just before Ash was about to squeeze William and hopefully dislodge the rubber eraser, William opened his mouth and smiled a goofy smile, with the little eraser sitting on the end of his tongue.

"Gotcha! Gotcha good! Both of you! Ha! That was a good one, huh, bro? Fo'shizzle my nizzle, my main man," William said to Ash.

Ash took in a large breath. "What the fuck are you talking about? Really?"

"Really, really?" William asked, sincerely.

J.T. immediately took over before the man who was meant to be his calming influence actually lost it. "William," he said through a clenched jaw, "how's 'bout I put a cap in yo ass if ya keep on muggin' da language of the black man. Get it? Can-I-state-it-any-clearer?"

"Cool, bro." William shrank back, but not before giving some Chicano gang sign with his left hand.

Ash and J.T. looked at each other, then at William, then back at each other. The last look said it all: *What a nut.* As they returned silently to their seats, William pleaded like a little boy, "C'mon, don't be mad. It was only a joke! I thought you guys would appreciate a good joke. C'mon!"

Just as they'd settled back into their chairs and the sniggering from the producer-writers had quieted into white noise, Marcus's mouth twisted into an inhuman contortion. This meant he was furious, but had to hide it for some reason behind a smile. J.T. looked around for the source of the latest affront.

Marcus was tracking someone with his eyes. He'd asked if it was *safe and now that lesbian actress was walking near his notes session!* Another minute and she might've heard one of the carpet-muncher jokes. That was definitely unfair. He glared at William.

William mouthed, *Sorry, boss,* very sincerely. He was feeling a tad nervous. In a matter of seconds he had pissed off both the director and the showrunner. He slowly shrank into a corner.

"Oh, Helena!" J.T. called her over.

"What the fuck are you doing?! Are you out of your mind?!" Marcus Pooley hissed to J.T. Then he turned and intercepted Helena, hugging her in his simian way. "Oh, Helena, what would this show be without you?"

"I agree," Stephanie Pooley chimed in. "You're . . . brilliant!"

"Brilliant is the phrase!" Lance repeated.

J.T. tried to get to the point. "Helena and I spoke earlier and—"

"You . . . SPOKE . . . with Helena?" Marcus Pooley was feigning apoplexy. Or maybe he wasn't faking it.

"Yes, we *spoke.* That's what directors and actors do when there is a place in the text that the actor is wrestling with. She was having trouble connecting the words and the character. We spoke. Communicated," J.T. said. Something was wrong. Marcus wasn't actually angry—he wasn't as good an actor as his wife.

"You had to use the word *wrestling* in front of a lesbian?" Stephanie now stepped in with diversionary tactics. "I mean, is that a stereotype or what? Just because her sexual preference isn't what you Bible Belters think is okay, you don't have to be evil and ignorant and judgmental! How dare you!" Stephanie was glowering at J.T.'s shirt pocket.

"I didn't mean to—wait, *wrestling* isn't a male or female term, I just meant that your actor—"

"And you're calling our actress an *actor*?" Marcus Pooley jumped in.

J.T. made the mistake of getting defensive. "I call all of my actors *actors*. *Actress* is not a term I usually use, for reasons I don't feel it necessary to get into now."

"*My* actors? When did they become *your* actors?" Marcus Pooley immediately snapped back into being genuinely furious. Marcus was in cocaine withdrawal. He hadn't had his chemicals in over an hour.

J.T. felt exhausted. Not *that* again. He had to get back on track. "I think," he ventured, "that Helena has a few issues about all of the Chanukah *bush* jokes, and I agree with her."

"*You agree with her?*" Marcus Pooley's eyes could not have squinted more. It was a squint one usually associates with the grunt that accompanies childbirth.

"You . . . *agree* . . . with her?" Stephanie asked with a huge smile plastered on the most visible of her two faces.

Something was definitely wrong.

"Yes. That's what I said. I *agree* with her," J.T. repeated, standing his ground.

"Oh no—I *don't* have a problem, J.T.," Helena said brightly, leaving J.T. hanging out to dry.

J.T. whipped around so quickly he felt a spasm in his back. He stared at Helena. "You . . . don't?" he asked, confused. "Wait . . . you said—"

"I said that I loved these jokes. I think the writing is brilliant. Winning! Refreshing. You must have misunderstood me, J.T.," Helena said.

"How can you say that with a straight face?" J.T. asked, his shoulders slumping. Even though this sort of thing had happened to him too many times before, he couldn't hide the fact that he was hurt. He looked at Ash, who just shook his head.

Steph continued the attack. "There you go again! A *straight* face! Another lesbian reference! She *killed* on those jokes," she howled, now staring at J.T.'s left hand. "Killed!"

"Really. I've never laughed harder," Marcus Pooley chimed in. "What the fuck world do you live in? What planet are you from?"

Hearing that line from a guy who looked like a chimpanzee pulled J.T. out of himself. "Okay . . ." he managed to say. He was starting to get a good lay of the land: he had to be wary of his actors, too. *How sad,* he thought.

"Sorry, my bad," J.T. said quietly.

"*You're bad* is quite the understatement," Marcus Pooley chortled.

"If notes are over, I'd like to go devise a way that I can give you the illusion that I'm a director," J.T. said.

"Sarcasm is the last fucking thing we need this week, mister," Stephanie Pooley snapped at J.T.'s shoes.

"I have one question for you, Ms. Pooley," J.T. said calmly.

"Only one? And you call yourself a director!"

"When you say all of these awful and cruel things to people, do you ever look them in the eye?"

No one moved. Stephanie finally exhaled like a frustrated child—in the direction of J.T.'s left shoulder.

"Just wondering." J.T. merely smiled, turned, and walked away. Ash met up with him at the stage door.

"I hate that director fuck," Marcus Pooley took aim at Lance after J.T. left.

"I agree, I agree. I'm working on it," Lance said.

"You see how he thinks it's *his* show? *His* actors! *His* sets! I mean, who does he think he is? I look people in the eye!" Stephanie Pooley snarled at Lance's briefcase.

"Gimme time. I'll make you two very happy. Just give me time," Lance said.

Alone in his corner, William had the same smile as the Cheshire cat.

J.T. WAS NUMB all over. As he and Ash passed into the small holding area between the stage door and the door to the lot, he thought it was a little strange that his brain could notice that he could not feel his body parts.

"You hangin' in?" Ash asked.

"I think I'm gonna quit, Ash."

"What? You can't quit."

"I know. I'm a coward. I think about Jeremy and I know he'd want me to *do the right thing.* The right thing is to walk out of here. I can't *do the right thing.*"

"Whoa, J.T." Ash gently put his hands on J.T.'s shoulders. "Look me in the eye, buddy. Now—let's get a grasp on the situation. Yes, these people are scum. But because of these scumbags, your son is going to get the best treatment possible. You wouldn't have it any other way. If you believe that Jeremy would want you to leave, then that's his youthful idealism. You can't afford to be idealistic. That would endanger your family. So think about picking blueberries with Tasha and Jeremy next summer every time you start to drown in the scum. Promise me."

"You're right. Blueberries," J.T. mumbled.

William popped his head through the door. "You wanna do the honors, boss?"

It took J.T. a beat to figure out what William meant and who was boss. "No, William, I want you to do it. It'll be good training for you since you are so close to moving up to director."

William immediately started hyperventilating. "What? I'm an A.D. You're the director. I don't wanna be a director. Who told you I wanna be the director?"

"William, just call it." J.T. was tired of the games.

"Gotcha, boss." William escaped back onto the floor of the cave. J.T. and Ash heard him yell, "That's a wrap! Good work, everybody. All of the actors: That's a wrap! After sex!"

There wasn't a single actor left on the stage, but William savored the words. *Pretty soon, I'll be the director calling "That's a wrap!"* he thought. *After sex.*

J.T. and Ash headed for the production office to find an empty office.

J.T. HAD QUIETLY summoned as many of his department heads as he could; even Carl from accounting was asked to be there.

"Ms. Smart," J.T. said to the production designer, "I have an idea. It seems the Pooleys want me to direct the best ever explosion without explosives and with two carolers, children, and no snow. That is all the information I have been given. So I'll try and responsibly take those instructions and give them the best ever *fucking* explosion that we are capable of producing under these dysfunctional conditions." As J.T. started to get involved in his ideas he had a habit of losing track of time and place. In this case, he had a large cup full of ice and was not only chewing on the ice, which was annoying as hell, but his tongue became numb and his speech became . . . muddy.

"Let's show them what we are all cabable of doing, eben though we're blaying right into their hands." Crunch. Crunch. "It doesn't matter. It's our . . . duty to be as cleber as we can. I'm going to need the helb of all of you. Any and all thoughts are belcome. I want to tell you my idea and then you tell me what you hab to do to make this work by tomorrow morning when we shoot *the best eber exblosion!*"

Everyone was riveted in the worst way. Finally Ash raised his hand.

"Es, Ass? Go ahea."

"Thank you, J.T. I think I speak for all of us here when I say, WHA?" Ash couldn't help himself. He started laughing, and as soon as he did, the others started in as well, including J.T. The tension of the day was released, gloriously released. Just what a comedy needed: laughter.

"Eberyone take fibe," J.T. said. "My tongue is brozen. Sorry."

After J.T. had a hot cup of tea and the door was safely closed, all of his defenses dropped and he was ready to proceed.

"Okay—now my tongue isn't numb, but I'm highly caffeinated. So if I speed-talk, just tell me to slow down." J.T. took another sip of his tea. "Carl, how much money is in the budget for this best ever explosion?" he asked the accountant.

"One cup of tea makes you highly caffeinated?"

"Two cups. I had one at the table read. Anyway, I don't drink coffee and I stay away from cola, so, yeah, a couple of cups of tea and it's to the moon, Alice."

"It takes me three espresso shots to even get a slight buzz."

"Carl, now I know what to get you for *your* best ever

The Hollywood Dictionary

GAG: (1) A bit. (2) A stunt. (3) In this case, gag means gag.

Christmas. But I really need to know how much is in the budget for the best ever explosion."

"I'm not really at liberty—" Carl began.

"Carl. Carl, if we are going to be proud of our work, we have to throw protocol out the window. Now, let's do this the old-fashioned way—let's actually *try*. How much money is in the budget to do this gag?" J.T. asked firmly.

"Ten thousand," Carl answered.

J.T. gagged.

Then he swallowed and said, "We'll do it for half. That's how we'll take care of you, Carl. Thank you. Next. Ms. Smart, how long and how much to get two panes of candy glass put into an ND set with windows?"

"I liked the meeting before when we couldn't understand you. Any chance we could go back to the Ice Age?"

"I'm afraid you're in the Ice Age on this sitcom."

"Yeah. Well," she leaned back up against the wall and accidentally turned the lights off. "Shit. I hope that wasn't an omen." She flicked

> ### The Hollywood Dictionary
>
> **AN ND SET:** A nondescript set. Almost any wall will do.
>
> **CANDY GLASS:** (1) Fake glass spun from real sugar that won't injure anyone when it breaks. (2) "Put that down! It doesn't mean you can eat it! *Actors* . . ."

the switch back on and started calculating the process. "I could probably put two nondescript walls together from stuff we have lying around and throw some candy glass in the windows by late tonight. If we buy sheets of candy glass in standard sizes, I'll just have construction build a nonworking window frame, if you're okay with that. We'll just cut the window frame to the size of the candy glass."

"Very good. What do you think your total cost on that and that alone will be?"

"Pennies compared to what is in the budget now," she said, accidentally revealing the truth. J.T. realized that in getting his crew excited about doing something the old-fashioned way, about trying to do it well and be proud of it, he would also get someone to slip up and reveal the actual cost of the stunt as it now stood in the budget.

J.T. understood the importance of knowing the real numbers. The budget was crucial. It was his main weapon of mass construction in order to bargain with the executives in order to get the best ever explosion done properly, and *without* explosives.

"Okay, Mr. McCoy," J.T. asked his director of photography, "can you get me a Steadicam rig with a variable-speed motor? I'm going to want to hide some of our own poverty and then take advantage of what we know we can pull off, and do it so well that it will look expensive and slick. So I'll need at least a ten-to-one lens on that sucker. We'll be sharp on what's working for us and the rest will drop off into mush. Forget 24P for this stunt. Let's go nuts: high-octane, sixteen-millimeter. Possible?" J.T. asked with a laugh, knowing this was fun for Mick.

> **The Hollywood Dictionary**
>
> **24P:** A video hybrid that is cheaper than film. Think tofu hot dogs.

"For you, boss, I'd go and steal it. It'll be there," Mick said as he opened the window to get some air into the room.

"How much, Mr. McCoy?"

"I'll get the rig as a favor. The lens rental is thirty-five bucks a day." It was the perfect answer because it was so contagious. Ash stood in the corner and just watched the body language of everyone in the room as they all became excited about being a part of something they could be proud of again.

"And," Mick continued, "I'll get you the best Steadicam operator I know. He's also become expert with the variable-speed motor."

"Thanks, Mick. Okay—who can answer this next question: *How many of our seventeen producers can I trust?* In other words, is there anyone on the producers' staff who would understand how to do the poor man's version of this explosion yet make it look stylized and better than what they'd normally get? Is there any one of them we can get on board?" J.T. already knew the answer to this one, too.

J.T.'s eyes scanned the room. "That's what I thought," J.T. said. "All right then, Rod, I'm going to ask you to overstep your bounds as head property master. Are you comfortable with that?"

Rod shrugged, a twinkle in his eye. "Matters what you want me to do. I feel comfortable taking out one of the Pooleys, but if you have me whacking both of 'em, I'd have to think about it. Okay—I thought about it. I'll do it." he said, getting a huge laugh.

"I need for you to go into the studio's film library and find any and all public-domain footage of explosions," J.T. said.

"But they'll all look like shit," Rod answered.

Suddenly pride was an issue. *Good,* thought J.T.

"We are going to get away with murder on this one. Billy," J.T. asked the head of the transportation department, "can you get Janice's picture car on the set first thing tomorrow so we can place it before any of the execs get on the lot? As soon as

> ### The Hollywood Dictionary
>
> **PICTURE CAR:** The actual vehicle that will be photographed; fire regulations state that, if placed on a soundstage, it must have an empty gas tank. Sometimes it has no engine. And often when the scene is over, the cars *with* engines are delivered to the producer's garage.

they see the automobile, the set, the lights . . . the game's over. We've gotta be ready to roll the second we're on the clock. Possible?"

"You got it, boss," Billy answered without thinking twice.

"Perfect," J.T. said.

Maybe this wasn't going to be a bad week after all. For J.T., these kinds of creative efforts were why he kept coming back to direct, despite the suits and the Poodles.

"Okay, so here's my plan. *We can only do this once.* No second takes. So we'll rehearse the shit out of it: we have the carolers, as many as they will allow us to have, so we can get the feeling that this is the *best ever* Christmas," J.T. said. He smirked back at the smirkers and raised his voice above the grunts. "Then I'll find a purpose for Janice to walk to her car. On a cue, we'll go high-speed as she leans into the car, we'll rack focus to just beyond the windshield, and we'll have the public-domain shitty explosion projected onto the front windshield of her picture car, but it'll be soft and Janice will be sharp so all we'll see is a fuzzy impact and the viewer's brain will fill in the blanks. Boom, impact, explosion, flames, in the reflection of the front windshield as we personalize this and go with Janice. She'll take the force of the reflected explosion. As she falls backward, we'll shatter the candy glass in the ND windows. We'll have E-fans blowing debris and fuller's earth onto the set along with a little smoke. Janice will finally get up when the smoke clears. Our heroine will have survived the best ever explosion, thus making this the best ever Christmas. In postproduction we'll give the explosion and the aftermath a helluva sonic symphony, and bingo, the *cheapest* best ever explosion in the *cheapest* best ever Christmas, and when this airs on TV we can all look each other in the eye. Whatta you guys say?" J.T. was a little breathless. So were the crew members, to be honest.

The Hollywood Dictionary

PUBLIC DOMAIN: *Freeeeeee!*

From the half nods and mumbly murmurs, J.T. sensed a some-what positive consensus. He had a team. Maybe not the most rah-rah of teams, but a team nonetheless. It was as if the *biggest ever* weight of the world were lifted off his aging, aching shoulders.

"Now, at any time of the day or night, I want questions. Ideas. I need thoughts. Brainstorms. Anything you guys think of is more than welcome: it's mandatory," J.T. said.

The suits and Poodles had set up a *Them* versus *Us* atmo-sphere. Now, finally, the *Them* could fight back, creatively. Maybe even neuter a Pooley "Poodle."

As the crew members began to leave the room and go on their missions, J.T. made one last request: "Everyone, please, don't let the negativity of this particular show stop you in your quest to do this bit as well as it can be done. And if you guys don't mind, the ear-lier we all arrive tomorrow on the set, the quicker we can get this in place and work out the kinks without the pessimists there to tell us we're fucking up. If we can show them a mock rehearsal as they walk onto the set, we just might pull this off. Everyone cool with that?"

Everyone was. Or at least no one said no.

"Well," J.T. said, "this oughta be interesting."

"Don't you think it's going to work?" Ash asked.

"Oh, it will definitely work. That's not the point. The interest-ing thing will be to see if we're *allowed* to pull it off. Somehow it'll leak, before tomorrow morning. I'll have to get out of here and be *unreachable.* When the Pooleys find out, they'll think it'll be hokey. Far from the best ever. They also won't understand the power of not actually seeing the explosion. In actuality," J.T. said, as if teach-ing class, "with the limitations that they've put on us, the reflection of the explosion will have more visceral clout than a gas tanker truck in an action movie going up in flames. And the candy glass windows shattering along with the E-fans and the debris flying in at a hundred and twenty frames per second, well, it'll kick ass. Yeah . . . I know this crew can pull it off."

J.T. and Ash exited the building into a starless night. It was about a ten-minute walk to their modes of transportation. The two men stopped at Asher's car, which was parked next to J.T.'s bicycle. "Nice wheels," Ash said flatly.

> **The Hollywood Dictionary**
>
> **THEATER IN L.A.:** Baseball in Canada.

J.T. seemed startled for a second, as if he'd forgotten Ash was even there. He tried to brighten up. "What are you doin' tonight, Ash? Any plans? You okay?"

"I'm seeing a show for my Theater 101 class," Ash answered. "It's the perfect object lesson on what not to do."

"What kind of masochist are you?! You're seeing *theater in L.A.?*"

"Yeah," Ash said, laughing, "so basically, I'm not doing anything."

"Wow. You've got more guts than I do. From sitcom to theater—in Los Angeles. Wow. Ouch. What did you do in a previous life, Ash?"

"Maybe I was a *Pooley*."

"Let's kick ass tomorrow, Ash. Let's make some good TV. Whattaya say?"

"Yeah. Let's kick ass," Ash agreed.

J.T. started to wheel away. Suddenly an automobile revved its engine very close to the men, its tires wailing as they spun on the cement. Halogen lights lit up the parking lot, picking out J.T. like an actor in a spotlight. Like a target.

A fully loaded Humvee with a V–8 engine and oversized tires was bearing down on J.T.

"J.T.?" Ash said, his arm trying to reach out for his buddy. "Either call 'CUT!' or look the fuck out!!"

J.T. looked the fuck out to see the military vehicle coming straight for him, gaining speed with every tire rotation. He froze, stunned, just standing there squinting to see who was trying to run him over.

It was Janice. He couldn't be sure until the Humvee was only five yards away from killing him. Ash dove in front of the vehicle and tackled J.T., taking him and his rented bicycle out of the path of the killer B actor. Or in this case, actress.

Ash and J.T. landed safely in a heap. Janice had not swerved, even at the last minute. This was an insane woman, used to getting her way, who was outraged to the point of murder. It was only thanks to Ash that J.T. wasn't dead, with his name in the *DGA Magazine* obits next to Jasper Jones's.

The Humvee came to an awkward stop. Ash and J.T. disentangled themselves as quickly as they could, watching for the white reverse lights that would mean it was coming back to get them. But the red brake lights stayed on.

"You wanna be king?" Janice screamed out of her window. "Well, the King Must Die!"

J.T. jumped to his feet. *This is it,* Ash thought. *The man's going to chase the bitch down. I'd better call the police.*

Instead J.T. simply smiled. Very quietly, but just loudly enough, he called out after the car, "Get some rest, Janice. You have a big day tomorrow."

That's all he said. In her fury and lack of satisfaction, Janice roared off and scraped her newly purchased vehicle on the side of the stucco studio offices. It was over as quickly as it had started.

"Impressive," J.T. whispered.

"Impressive? She almost ran you over, J.T." Ash said, still shaking.

"No, impressive that she quoted Mary Renault, *The King Must Die,* rather than Stephen King or Michael Crichton."

"She was going to kill you, man," Ash said, an octave too high.

"She's got three more days . . ." J.T. looked at Ash. "The fun just never stops!"

Wednesday

WEDNESDAY BEGAN—WHETHER J.T. liked it or not. On this particular shoot day (actually a *pre*shoot day), with all of its intangibles, there would be an additional, very tangible factor to contend with: children.

J.T. pedaled off to work in the early morning smog/haze. The consequences of being on a bike in traffic were not measured so much in time as in the relative chances of being hit by the road-enraged driver of an SUV. Or a Mini Cooper. L.A. might be one of the only places where road rage could swell in the driver of a hybrid.

The Hollywood Dictionary

PRESHOOT: (1) When scenes are shot that cannot be accomplished in front of an audience on Friday night because of expense, time, danger, or fear. (2) The easing of the workload for Friday night. (3) Less to memorize for Friday night.

J.T. thought about the children who were going to be on the set. He thought about being a child actor on a set. He thought about being a child actor once the sets were gone.

Fucking kid actors! Has-beens before graduating from high school. Fuck, they're all doomed. They might never come close to the happiness they felt when they were ten fucking years old. A fifteen-year-old shouldn't experience the panic of a midlife crisis.

J.T. was stopped at a red light next to a black Lincoln Navigator. The driver startled him: "You talkin' to me?"

"Wha?" J.T. still hadn't realized that his habit of thinking out loud was becoming a danger to him rather than a mere nuisance.

"I *said*, you talkin' to me?" the man asked again.

"Um, no, Mr. DeNiro. I was just thinking—*Wow, I am such a fan . . . !*"

The light turned green and Robert DeNiro and all the other drivers surged forward into the Hollywood morning, leaving behind the director, who was pedaling as fast as he could.

J.T. GOT ON the lot. Not without a long look for his pass in the security computer, of course, and not without a body search.

Once in the production office, J.T. said to no one in particular, "I'm going down to the set school to talk to the kids. Get 'em ready for today's shoot, just in case anybody needs me."

"Why would anybody need you?" asked the voice of Thing Five.

I wonder where Robert DeNiro was going, and why couldn't he take me with him.

J.T. knew he would find the child actors in the set schoolroom, which was a satellite dressing room—basically a small double-wide with air-conditioning pumped into the ovenlike tin box. He knocked on the schoolroom door, and thought he just might have heard a nervous voice tell him to come in.

When he opened the door, J.T. saw all of the kids for this episode at different desks doing their work. Their highlighted scripts were next to their math and science books. A few looked up; one or two recognized him, and soon the room was buzzing: *What's the director doing in here?*

"Good morning!" J.T. said to them. "Mr. Thacker, right?" he asked the balding, fiftyish man at the corner desk who was apparently the on-set teacher. "Okay if I run through the program for the day with my actors?"

Leo Thacker nodded, so J.T. launched into the briefing. As he spoke, Mr. Thacker was very fidgety. He kept getting up, pacing the side of the room, and peeking out of the schoolroom window. He had a sheen of sweat on his forehead. His underarms were already completely wet, and the collar of his buttoned shirt was soaked. His chest was pushing his old-fashioned vest back and forth in a pumping motion—hyperventilating, J.T. suspected.

"Excuse me, sir?" J.T. addressed the set schoolteacher, who seemed unusually troubled. J.T. could not have directed Leo Thacker to play *desperation* and *fear* better than he was playing it in real life. Something was wrong.

The Hollywood Dictionary

ON-SET TEACHER: Often little more than a highly paid babysitter.

"Mr. Thacker?" J.T. tried again.

"Hum?" Leo Thacker said, startled.

"Are you feeling ill?"

"Me? Ill? No. I'm fine. Just fine," Mr. Thacker lied.

J.T. made a mental note: *Not a good liar.* He watched as Leo Thacker used his forefingers to nervously scrape his thumbs. Both thumbs were raw—bleeding, in fact.

"Okay, kids," J.T. said, keeping his voice low and calm, "you're needed on the set. Follow me, please."

If Mr. Thacker registered that it was a little strange for the children to be called this early, he didn't show it. He allowed J.T. to escort the children to the set, where J.T. left them in the charge of one of his grips. Then he quickly headed back to the production office. He started at a quick walk that turned into a jog, and then, as his mind went to places only a writer-director would go, he started sprinting.

At the production office, J.T. was greeted as if he had leprosy. "Um, hello? The director is in the office," he called out in a sing-songy tone. But he was pointedly ignored.

"God-fucking-dammit-what-does-a-director-have-to-do-to-get-some-attention-around-here?!"

That got the attention of the particularly beautiful Thing Six. "May I help you?" she asked.

After a cleansing breath, J.T. responded, "Yes. Please. My name is J.T. Baker."

Now he could be ignored for a reason. "J.T. Baker" meant the same thing to this beautiful young lady as it did to everyone else in the office: *Do not engage this director in any conversation whatsoever.*

"I'm directing your show," J.T. said.

She took the bait. "Oh, it's not *my* show! It's the Pooleys' show," she said.

Very well trained, J.T. thought. "Yes . . . um, I need to ask some-one about the schoolteacher. The schoolteacher, Leo Thacker, who is taking care of the minors on the show?"

Thing Six looked around in a silent plea for someone, anyone, to help her out. But the one thing the staff members were good at was ignoring people.

She was saved by Billy, the transportation captain, who was just coming out of an office.

"J.T.? What's up?"

J.T. motioned Billy to come closer. "I don't know," he said qui-etly. "That schoolteacher, Leo Thacker—something's not right. I can . . . sense it." J.T. felt slightly foolish admitting it.

"Funny you should mention that skinny fuck," Billy said, never one to be subtle. "Someone called this morning and asked if he was on the lot. They didn't leave a name, wouldn't say who they was or nuthin'. It was just about an hour ago."

At that precise moment, the world of art merged into the world of reality with a wily, natural absence of sophistication. If it had been a ten o'clock one-hour TV drama, it would've been handled with more flair or it would've been canceled. As it was, J.T. only noticed how unremarkably it began once it had begun to unfold. It was all so . . . ordinary.

A man dressed in a blue suit with pant legs that were cuffed an inch too short, revealing white socks and well-worn shoes, came into the production office. *Someone get this man to Wardrobe,* J.T. thought.

"Who's in charge here?" the man asked. No one spoke up.

"Well," J.T. finally said, "I'm the director, so that definitely would *not* be me."

"Oh. Sitcom, huh?" he said.

"You got it," J.T. said, immediately liking this man who had a sense of irony.

J.T. looked out the production office windows and saw four black sedans speeding past the office on their way to the stage . . . past the stage . . . to the schoolroom.

"FBI," the man stated, showing his badge.

Marcus Pooley chose that moment to come bounding down the stairs. "What's with all the tension?" he asked eagerly.

He was in early. *Must've been kicked out of the house by Stephanie,* J.T. thought. *What a fucking buffoon.*

"Who are *you*?" the man with the badge asked Marcus.

"Who the fuck are *you*?" Marcus Pooley replied.

"He's such a fuckin' jerk," Billy whispered into J.T.'s ear.

"I'm FBI Agent Tiffy," the man with the highwaters said. "Now I'll ask again: who are you?"

"I'm Marcus Pooley, the Creator and Showrunner of the number-one sitcom—excuse me—the number one *show* on television, *I Love My Urban Buddies*. And you are in *my* production office. What the hell do you want? Wait—did you say your name is FBI Agent . . . Tiffy?" Marcus began to giggle.

"Do you have a man working for you by the name of Leo Thacker?" the federal agent asked.

"Oh no—not again," Marcus Pooley blurted.

Now J.T. was truly alarmed. "What is going on? That man was just with the children!"

Marcus's face darkened. "Oh, don't go getting all heroic and gallant on me. Jesus, gimme a fucking break! I can't believe this. Leo gave me his word!"

"Can someone explain?" J.T. asked in what he hoped was a controlled voice.

"Leo Thacker has prior convictions for selling child pornography on the Internet. We have information that his operation has grown from distribution to the actual production of child pornography. And we also know someone tipped him off and he knows we're right on his . . . butt."

"Wait—no—wait—" J.T. kept looking from the FBI agent to Marcus Pooley and back.

Marcus threw up his hands, all innocence. "Hey, don't blame me. All the mothers signed off on it. They knew Leo's past. They understand that in America we give people a second chance."

J.T. stared at him. "A child pornographer . . . is the on-set schoolroom teacher? Is that what you're telling me?" he demanded.

"I don't have to tell you shit, J.T. You're just the fucking guest people-mover," Marcus Pooley laughed.

"These are *my* kids," J.T. said.

"What is it with you? Why do you think that everything is *you, you, yours*?"

"Because, whether I'm a hack, a people-mover, or fucking Fellini, I'm the *director*, and in matters like this, the buck stops somewhere. And that somewhere is me. Someone has to take responsibility. And that is my job when I come in to work. No one under me gets hurt, and that includes *being taught by a child por-*

nographer!" It was official. J.T. was finally losing his infamous temper.

"Oh, fuck you, J.T.," Marcus said, as if that settled it.

J.T. wouldn't let that go unchallenged. But he filed it away because he didn't want to waste another second on Marcus Pooley's playground tactics. *This one,* J.T. thought, *will come back to haunt the pig.* How, where, and in what form would later be determined. But he would *get his.*

"Follow me. I'll take you to where Leo Thacker is," J.T. said to the agent.

"Oh, fuck all of you!" Marcus yelled as the two men, followed by Billy, started out of the production office. "You're overreacting! This is ridiculous!" He kept yelling even after the men had left the office. "Stupid, stupid, stupid. That's what this is. Dumb!" He looked around to see Thing Six, Thing Five, and the other office staffers staring at him.

"What? So I saved a few bucks by hiring this guy. Think of it as good karma. I gave the perv a second chance."

No one said a word.

"Okay then." Marcus tried a new tactic. "Think of it as more money in the till and better holiday gifts for all of you. Maybe an *I Love My Urban Buddies* sweatshirt. Huh? How's that sound?"

This seemed to be a reasonable proposition. The office workers went back to their jobs. Satisfied, Marcus Pooley ran out to catch up with the others, who had nearly reached the little schoolroom.

IT NOW DID look to J.T. like something out of a movie. A bad movie. A dozen or so FBI agents had surrounded the double-wide. They were trying to be as unobtrusive as possible, which as far as J.T. could tell meant wearing identical blue suits and sunglasses. No one was actually trying to stay out of sight.

Note to self, J.T. thought: *If ever shooting a scene where FBI agents surround a building, don't make it look like this.* To J.T., who was always seeing life through a movie camera, it looked phony. *But fuck, it's not.*

"He's in there," an agent said, running up to Agent Tiffy, reporting everything he knew.

"Is he alone?" Agent Tiffy asked his clone.

"Yes."

Agent Tiffy gestured to the other agents, silently waving them forward. J.T. wasn't sure whether that meant him, too. "Um, are we in the way? Is there something we should do?" he asked.

"No! Just shut up and stay where you are!" Tiffy paused. "Have you got insurance?"

"Funny you should ask that, because—"

"Come on, guys!" Marcus Pooley's voice arrived, followed shortly by the man himself. He was running down the studio's exterior mock-up of a New York street, yelling all the way. "He's just an old perv! Don't you think you're making a lot out of nothing? I mean, why the big production number?"

"Keep your voice *down*!" J.T. ordered him reflexively.

"Yeah!" Tiffy agreed.

"He's got a gun!" an agent stage-whispered to Agent Tiffy. "A sawed-off shotgun!"

"He's got a fucking gun?" Marcus Pooley squealed, suddenly giddy. A pleased, opportunistic look took control of his sour features. "He's got a gun, J.T.!" he said, bouncing with excitement.

"I heard," J.T. responded to his boss without looking at him.

"Are you thinking what I'm thinking?" Marcus asked.

"I don't think that is *ever* the case," J.T. said.

Marcus tugged on J.T.'s arm. "J.T.—go to the stage and grab a camera. This is going to be priceless footage!" he said. "The Best Ever . . . *Easter.* No! A Reality Show! *Pervs!*" I dunno. Something! We can work it into something! Just go grab a camera! Hey, did

I ever tell you my idea: "Going to War with the Stars? Can you imagine? Celebrities on the front line? Whattaya think?" Marcus babbled. "Come on—grab a fucking camera!"

"*No,*" J.T. said firmly, pulling his arm away.

"Look. I'll make you a partner on whatever comes of the footage. Sixty-forty."

"Quiet."

"All right, fifty-five–forty-five. I'm not going any lower. I hired the perv and this is my equipment we're gonna use. Deal?"

"Fuck off."

"Well, fuck off to you too. I'll go grab one of the guys and I'll get this on film and it'll be mine. All *mine.*"

J.T. finally looked Marcus in the eye, which made the showrunner take a step back. "You don't use film, Mr. Showrunner, Executive Producer, Creator of All That Is *the Best Ever,*" J.T. hissed. "You shoot on *tape!* At least learn your own fucking format. And by the way, there is a man in that schoolroom with a *sawed-off shotgun.* This *isn't* a Reality Show. What is the *matter* with you?"

"Oh, Goody Two-shoes. Like you didn't think of filming it, too," Marcus shot back, and he turned and ran toward the stage to fetch a camera and a cameraman.

J.T. stared at Marcus's retreating back, his gut like lead. He *had* thought of filming it. J.T. thought of filming everything. But now he felt mortified as hell about it. He had actually had the same thought as Marcus Pooley. Jeremy was right. He felt contaminated.

"Leo Thacker, this is Agent Tiffy with the FBI," Tiffy called out. "I would like to ask you a few questions. Drop your weapon and come outside."

"Go to hell!" said the voice from inside the schoolroom.

"Leo Thacker, we have this schoolroom surrounded. Please don't make a scene," Agent Tiffy said, appropriately.

"Make a scene! Make a scene! Please, oh, make a scene!" Marcus Pooley hollered as he came running back in front of a hand-held 24P camera that was tethered to a cable snaking out from the stage door. "Hurry up! Get closer! Hurry!" he yelled at the camera operator.

"I'm *working* on it!" The young camera operator was struggling with the tangled cables and the delicate, expensive camera he had been taught to respect and treat with great care.

"Don't *work* on it—fucking *do it*!"

Inside the schoolroom, Leo Thacker paced slowly back and forth. He hated who he was. He couldn't control his urges, his instincts. He had asked for help, but no one ever cared, not really. And now this. Tempting him with a job where he was surrounded by little children twelve hours a day. *My father was right. I'm diseased. I have no business being on this planet.*

Leo took the sawed-off shotgun and placed the barrel in his mouth.

A gasp erupted just outside. One of the agents had made it to the window and was peeking in. "Shit!" he burped. "He just put the shotgun in his mouth!"

"You mean he can fit the entire barrel in there? Yes! We got ourselves a degenerate Deep Throat!" Marcus Pooley exclaimed. "Give me that fucking camera!"

"No, put the camera away! Let me speak to Leo," J.T. yelled out.

J.T. ran past Agent Tiffy and up the few stairs, and was opening the little schoolroom's door before anyone could stop him.

"Sir!—Come back!—DO NOT GO IN THERE!" Agent Tiffy shouted.

"Are we rolling? Are we rolling or what?" Marcus Pooley shrieked at the camera operator.

"We don't have enough cable, Mr. Pooley," the young man mumbled as he fumbled with the cable that had reached its limit.

"We WHAT?! Are you shitting me?! You're the cameraman, for fuck's sake! Make the camera work!"

"Well, sir, it doesn't happen to work that way . . . Also, if I knew we were going to be—"

"If you knew that a perv was going to blow his brains out, you would've had more cable? You're fucking fired!"

"Thank you," the young man said. "Thank you so damn much."

"What are you waiting for? Get the fuck out of here. Drop my fucking camera and get the fuck off this lot!"

"Anything you say, sir."

The young cameraman dropped the $100,000 camera—which, to Marcus's surprise, did not break.

Marcus ran to the camera and tried to pull it closer to the little schoolroom, but the cable was stretched to its limit. He looked at the cable, did a quick analysis of the situation, and unhooked the camera from the cable, leaving the camera free to go wherever he went.

"Done! Ha! See, you moron?! All you had to do was unhook this shit!"

"Jesus! Why didn't I think of that?" the young man yelled back as he kept walking farther and farther away.

J.T. eased into the schoolroom and gently closed the door behind him.

"Don't come any closer or I'll pull the trigger," Leo mumbled with his mouth full of metal.

J.T. stayed where he was. "Leo," he said, "it doesn't have to be like this. No one is accusing you of anything."

Leo pulled the gun out far enough to say, "I know what I've done. What I'm doing. They'll put me away forever. And do you know what they do to guys like me in prison?"

Note to self, J.T. thought: *They really do say that in real life.* "Leo, think about all of the options open to you if you'll just put that gun down."

"I'm sick. I know I'm sick."

"I'm sure Agent Tiffy can get you help."

Tears poured from Leo's eyes. "I'm a criminal. I've broken laws. I've done . . . unthinkable things, and . . ."

"I'm getting all of this, J.T.," Marcus Pooley whispered from an open window, pointing the camera at the action. "Get closer! J.T., this shot is too wide. Get in closer!"

Leo jerked straight. "Stay where you are. I'm warning you!" He shoved the gun back in his mouth.

"This is good! This is good!" Marcus bleated.

Leo's sad eyes moved slowly to J.T. Without saying a word, he was asking for forgiveness. At the same time, the back door to the stage—the door no one thought of covering with an FBI agent— slowly opened. Standing in the doorway was six-year-old Angelina, who played the guest part of Amy on the "Buddies, Best Ever Christmas" episode. She was holding a crayon and a photocopied worksheet of leaves falling from a tree that she had colored.

"Mr. Thacker? Wanna see what I just colored?" And then she looked up—and froze. So did Leo. So did J.T.

"Perfect," Marcus Pooley directed. "Great stuff!"

J.T. ran for the young girl—but it was too late.

BOOM!

Everyone on the scene processed the bang with confusion. It hadn't come from the schoolroom, but from another direction. Leo was still standing; there was no blood.

Oh!

The players who surrounded the double-wide suddenly felt a great deal of tension leave their bodies. The sound had come from an exterior big-budget Spielberg movie that was shooting on the lot. Distant bells and applause from the crew were heard signaling that the take was over on the movie set and that the explosion had gone well.

"Oh, thank you, Mr. Spielberg. Thank you, God," J.T. murmured as he reached Angelina and held her in his arms, shielding her with his body; protecting her from the possibility of violence and potential nightmares. But not to worry, Leo had not pulled the trigger.

POP.

Leo pulled the trigger and his head was no more.

Skull and brains splattered the wall behind him, looking like a school art project. His headless body recoiled, stayed upright for a count of three, and then just collapsed.

"I got it!" Pooley yelled. "I got it all!"

Little Angelina, covered in blood and chunks of skull and brain, screamed a continuous, high-pitched, shrill sound of terror that J.T. knew would stay with her for the rest of her life. He held her tightly while the FBI agents poured into the schoolroom.

"Excellent!" Marcus Pooley said to himself. "Cut, print— *mooooving* on!"

J.T. removed Angelina from the scene. He carried the little girl, who was clearly in shock, to her mother.

Mom was sitting outside the stage door on the other side of the lot, having a cigarette. As J.T. walked toward her, his brain couldn't shut off. *The sound. The sound from the movie set was far more . . . authentic . . . than the real sound of the gun. Gotta remember that. Shit—I hate myself.*

"Good morning, Mr. Baker," Angelina's mom said, caught off guard. "We worked on our lines all of last night. Didn't we, Angie? She's not having trouble with the 'K' scene, is she? We worked especially hard on that one, didn't we, Angelina?" The child's mother continued to prattle as she took Angelina's limp body from J.T. "Angelina! What—why are we so messy? Did we finger-paint? Remember what I told you, I don't know how many times? Mommy told you we should never finger-paint in our wardrobe! Now look what we've done! We're a mess!"

J.T. tried to interject, but the mother was performing for

the benefit of the director and out of fear that her child might lose such a coveted job, not to mention the financial bonanza of guesting on *I Love My Urban Buddies* that was mailed to her P.O. box.

"Mrs.... I'm sorry, I'm still learning names," J.T. said, not knowing what else to say. "Your daughter's very likely in shock—"

"*Miss*—I'm divorced," Angelina's mom said, turning on the charm. "Miss Jacobi. But you can call me Wilma," she said, not paying a bit of attention to the fact that her daughter was motionless. "If Angelina is tired, it's because we worked on that 'K' scene until well past midnight. But we know our lines and our business. Don't we, Angie?"

Angie didn't respond. J.T. shepherded the mother and child back onto the stage and gathered all of the children. "William!" he shouted for his A.D.

"Here, ready, and waiting, boss!" William responded, sincerely.

"William, what is the situation with . . . how much does everyone know about . . . what just happened?"

"I'd say everyone knows everything, sir," William reported, sincerely. "Mr. Pooley is trying to play back the footage as we speak. After sex."

"How can you make a joke when—please inform the studio legal department immediately. Find out what kind of trauma treatment they have in place, and send all of the children home."

"*Send all of the children home?*" William asked, sincerely confused.

"*Send all of the fucking children home?*" Marcus Pooley shouted from across the stage. "Are you kidding? You have no authority to do that! We have scenes to shoot!"

"All of the children *will* go home. Immediately. And I will walk them to their cars if you insist on giving me any trouble. And . . . I'll have each and every one of my colleagues here"—J.T. gestured to all of the grips and electricians—"hold you down as the children leave the premises. Have it your way—or my way. You tell me."

Silently, deliberately, the crew members stopped what they were doing and stared at Marcus. "You think you are such hot shit!" he sputtered. "So you have the schmucks on your side. Well, you don't have the people who can green-light an eight o'clock Thursday night blockbuster hit: *Pervs!* And you could've been a partner on it. Fine. Send the children home." Then he spun on the crew. "And as for all of you, if any of you side with this trouble-maker, I'll not only have you fired, but I will personally see to it that each and every one of you never works for me or this network or this studio ever again!"

To a man, to a woman, the crew formed a group behind J.T. Except William. He just waffled back and forth, never committing his body language to one side or the other.

"Oh, oh, oh, you are all going to resent—I mean, *regret* this moment!" Marcus Pooley seethed. "Now, somebody show me why I'm not getting any playback on the footage I shot!"

"You didn't shoot any footage, Pooley," J.T. quietly said. "You unhooked the cable. It's not a home video camera . . . *sir*."

For once, Marcus Pooley was speechless.

J.T. WALKED THE children out of the oppressive atmosphere of the cave and into the bright Southern California sunshine. Today of all days, the haze had cleared and the sky was impossibly blue.

"Take care," he said to the parents. "I really am unqualified to give advice, but I'm sure the studio will have trained personnel that the children can talk to. Go home. We'll call you and tell you what is going on . . . At the moment, I'm as unsure as anyone." He kept listening out for the EMTs. Surely the FBI had called them. Surely they'd be here any minute now to examine Angelina.

"Mr. Baker?" a small voice asked tentatively. "Mr. Director?"

"Yes, sweetheart?"

Angelina looked confused. *Definitely still in shock,* J.T. thought. "Do you have a question?" he prompted.

"Yes . . . Do I still have to do my homework?"

J.T. was ready for abstract questions from these young co-workers. But answering an honest, very sensible query was beyond his current abilities. Before he could come up with anything that would make sense to a child after she had witnessed her teacher blow his brains out, Angelina's mother quickly answered.

"Of course you still have to do your homework. There'll be another teacher here tomorrow and you'll want to show that teacher just how smart you really are. And Mr. Baker, don't you have one bit of worry. She'll show up tomorrow ready for work, lines memorized, and her attitude will be professional. I can't speak for the other moms and"—she looked around at the other parents—"stepmoms, but *my* kid will never use the 'incident' this morning as an *excuse*. No excuses, right, Angelina?"

"Right, Mommy. No excuses," Angelina whispered.

"Just go home and love each other . . ." J.T. said, then turned so the children couldn't see him as he burst into tears.

"What the hell did you do, child?!" Angelina's mother said as they rounded the corner and headed to the parking structure. "And now look! You made the director cry!"

Wednesday . . . and they weren't even on the clock yet.

"WHAT A PUSSY! He just broke down and started crying." Marcus Pooley was back in his office, leaning over his speakerphone. He spoke into it the same way trained actors use microphones when they accept an Academy Award: as if they had never used one before. He was powwow-wowing with Lance from the studio and Debbie from the network. It was eight-thirty. Marcus had had

Thing Three, who'd been promoted to be his new assistant, track both of them down.

"Hey, guys, hold on one sec." Marcus accepted a fresh cup of hot cocoa from the puppy-like Thing, who was trying to do everything in his power to please. Marcus stepped away from the speakerphone and whispered, "You're fired. Now. Go. Scoot."

"But . . . why . . ."

"It doesn't matter why. But since you asked, I don't like Swiss Miss hot cocoa. I like Nestlé's."

The assistant cocked his head in confusion. "This *is* Nestlé's."

"Oh." Marcus took a sip of his cocoa. "You're right. You're fired anyway."

The space between the assistant's bottom lip and his chin suddenly became concave. "You . . . *bastard*! You're a pig! A donkey! A—"

"Here—go to the zoo on me." Marcus threw a twenty-dollar bill at Thing Three, who stormed out of the room without taking the money.

"He, like, cried?" Debbie asked. Her sultry voice (not an acquired affectation, but the real result of her constant vomit-fests) filled the mid-range equalization of the speaker.

"Can you believe it? The fucking director? Yeah! He cried!" Marcus giggled.

Thing Three returned, grabbed the twenty off of the floor, then disappeared again.

"I think that's cute that he cried," Debbie said, purring. It was more of a sexual response than a fully developed, compassionate reaction.

"We have to get back to the subject," Lance said. "How do we spin this to our advantage?"

"I'm worried that his stupid death will, like, conflict with our death of Minnesota B. Moose and the birth of Kalamazoo P. Kardinal. That's a very real concern for the network," Debbie made clear in her adult voice.

"Debbie—a pedophile was our schoolteacher!" Lance reiterated. "He was under investigation for selling kiddie porn over the Net! We're fucked!"

"I know!" Marcus Pooley jumped in. "We'll write an episode, okay? Stay with me here . . . We'll write an episode that deals with our kids. And how the kids blindly trust a next-door neighbor! And before anything can happen, one of the Buddies will come to the rescue! Just like we would in real life!" He was jumping up and down as he was concocting the story.

"But . . . none of us have any kids in real life," Lance countered.

"So? What the fuck does real life have to do with anything?" Marcus shot back.

"I, like, like it," Debbie said.

"The moral of the story will be: Don't trust anyone!"

"Hey—yeah, what's to sweat?" Lance said, finally catching on. "It's like Marcus said, none of us need to have families to make family television. That's our *family*." He put his feet up on his desk. "You know," he said, "it's like George Bernard Shaw once said . . . um . . ." He sat back up and grabbed the book of quotations he kept in the top drawer. He frantically flipped to a dog-eared page and gulped before he read, "'If you cannot get rid of the family skeleton, you may as well make it dance.'"

"I love it!" Marcus said. Then, "Wait. Huh? Yeah! Dance! Damn you, Lance. How do you do that? You're like a fountain of knowledge!"

"Hey, man, somebody's gotta know his shit around here."

"Guys," Debbie interrupted, "stop, like, patting each other on the butt and sum this up for me. And what about Kalamazoo P. Kardinal?"

"Debbie, we'll feature the new icon in some PR stunt this week," Lance smoothly assuaged. "You cool with that?"

"Like . . . like, okay."

Marcus wasn't finished. He was on a roll. "What I'm saying is: You don't need to be dead to write about death. No one on my writing staff has any kids and this is a family show with kids. So the way I look at it, we're doing our viewers a favor. We're helping them with real-life family problems. We're helping them solve family questions. Catch my drift? We're giving them a family on television that they can relate to, so they can say, 'Maybe we oughta try and be more like them. They love each other. They love their Urban Buddies.' I think we're performing a great civic service. That is, unless you wanna go back to my pitch about the eight o'clock Thursday shoo-in blockbuster, *Pervs!*"

Lance had long since forgotten to be cautious about what he said in his own office, even though he taped the conversations. He said in a rush, "We're not only right, Debbie, but we are going to be proactive about this! Marcus'll write an episode about 'The Pedophile Next Door,' but in this case, our 'A' story will have a happy ending. We've gotta move fast on this so we're all saying the same thing to the media. There are helicopters hovering over the studio right now."

"There are?" Marcus got up and ran to his window, looking up. "Cool."

"Okay. I guess, like, whatever," Debbie finally agreed.

"Great. Just backdate the title page on the episode so that no one thinks we're covering our asses," Lance told Marcus.

"Will do," Marcus Pooley said. "It'll read like I wrote it a month ago."

"Okay," Lance said quickly. "I think we're done. We handled this well. Agreed?"

"Agreed," agreed Debbie. "I think I'm gonna lose my sig—"

"Agreed," agreed Marcus.

"Um, Marcus, I believe Debbie has lost her signal . . . Marcus?"

Marcus was already on his way out of the production office,

feeling swell. Problem solved! Now all he had to do was to make sure that the suicide of the schoolteacher didn't delay today's filming. They had the best ever explosion to shoot! He jumped into his private MARCUS POOLEY ONLY golf cart and headed back to the stage.

ON THE STAGE, J.T. had composed himself and was setting the shot for the best ever explosion with his crew and Mick McCoy. They went through the steps slowly, a beat at a time, so everyone knew their cues and responsibilities. Mick knew that J.T. had been badly rattled by what he had just witnessed. He hoped that by keeping J.T. busy, he could keep him sane for the time being. So they worked.

J.T. called out for the stand-in for Janice to walk back over to the car to fetch her purse on the front seat. He began the litany of cues he would call out, speaking louder than necessary for the benefit of "Mr. Kite." Even when J.T. would single someone out by gesturing or looking in their direction, he would yell loudly enough for everyone to hear—and be hoarse by the end of the day.

> ### The Hollywood Dictionary
>
> **MR. KITE:** The person who ought to be listening to the directions but who might not be, who ought to know what he should be doing but might forget to do something as simple as plug an element into an electrical socket.
>
> Mr. Kite, a television set's Mr. Anybody, represents the variable that could cause failure.

J.T. pointed to Charley, the projectionist, and hollered, "The projection of the explosion from the public-domain footage *should* begin to roll as soon as Janice's head is inside the car." Then he put his hand on Kevin, the assistant camera operator—who flinched slightly. Kevin was a Vietnam veteran, and a little jumpy.

"Then we'll rack focus to Janice so the projected explosion footage is soft in the frame but the fiery detonation looks very powerful in the reflection of the front windshield of the car. Then there will be a cue to shatter the candy glass. It'll sound something like this: SHATTER THE CANDY GLASS!"

Mick guffawed, but the others just looked confused. J.T. sighed ruefully, and continued to walk the rehearsal. " . . . And then and *only* then will I cue the E-fans to blow debris onto the set, which will sound something like this: E-FANS! E-FANS! E-FANS!" This time, Kevin laughed. The big vet thought that was funny.

"And . . ." J.T. was beginning to fade. His voice had less volume with every direction. "And . . . a simultaneous cue will be given to Skip to go hi-speed/slo-mo and push in on the Steadicam toward Janice, to give the feeling of chaos and the concussion of a large explosion."

> ### The Hollywood Dictionary
>
> **E-FANS:** Quiet electric fans that can give the impression of wind, can help smoke dissipate for an illusion of depth and diffused light, and are never, ever quiet— thus their nickname, *F-fans*.

"I'm there for ya," Skip waved, not looking up from his how-to-build-your-dream-log-cabin book.

"Finally, if we're lucky, when the explosion and the debris die down, the camera speed will ramp back down to normal and Janice will brilliantly convey the realization that she is *the luckiest ever woman,* and it was not her *time,* thus making this—everyone say it with me—*the Best Ever Christmas!*" Mick, Skip, and Kevin joined in. Not exactly everyone, but it was progress.

This is so fucked, J.T. thought. It didn't really matter that the crew members, and particularly Mick, seemed impressed. Theory was always an easy sell for enthusiastic creative types like him, but it didn't mean he'd sold himself. J.T. feared that his scheme wouldn't look as good on film as it did in his mind. No matter. There was nothing left to do except execute this plan with conviction.

J.T. and the crew orchestrated the scene and rehearsed it over and over for timing, reflections, and basically Murphy's Law until they were all satisfied that it would not only work, but actually look spectacular. They even felt proud and pleased—sensations that had become increasingly unfamiliar to them of late.

"Great job. I mean it. Take a break," J.T. said. *What more could anyone ask from their crew?* he thought as he looked around at them. *They really pulled this one out of their asses.*

Then Marcus Pooley walked onto the stage. He looked at the jerry-rigged setup and demanded, "What the hell is this?"

"This is your best ever explosion, Mr. Pooley," J.T. explained quickly, immediately deflated.

"This looks like amateur time in Dixie! We're in Hollywood! Where's the special effects man? Where are the stunt guys? What's with this set?!" Marcus was working himself into another tantrum. He actually began to stomp his feet.

J.T., already emotionally spent, made the mistake of sighing. "Look, if you'll let me explain—and we'll run this step by step for you, and you can look through the lens of the camera—you'll understand what we're trying to accomplish."

"So you feel like you have to run it *step by step* for me? Because what—I'm stupid?"

"I didn't mean it *that* way—it's just easier to explain what's going on visually, that's all," J.T. said. *Breathe, breathe.* "I'm just trying to help you."

"Help me." Marcus began to limp around the set. "Oh, Tiny Timmy Marcus needs help. Will you help me please?" he held out his hands as if he were begging for alms.

J.T. tried one more time. "Marcus, my intention is only to be of service."

Mick looked away. Kevin whispered into Skip's ear, "I'm gonna knock the shit outta that punk. He keeps messin' with J.T., you mark my words, I'll take him out."

"Calm down," Skip said, still engrossed in his log cabin magazine.

Marcus limped up to J.T. "Oh, will you service me, Great and Powerful Director?"

J.T. put his hands to his head. "Let's get one thing straight—"

"Oh, straighten me, Great One."

"That's it!" J.T. threw up his hands. "You will no longer treat me, or anyone on this set for that matter, like you're a bored millionaire and we are here to entertain you. Enough. Do you get it? Enough."

"You tell him, J.T.," Kevin added, and stood up, all six feet six of him, to emphasize his point.

Marcus was unbowed. "So here we are. What to do?" he sneered. "No stunt people and no special effects man? This is what you give me when I write *the best ever explosion*? That is how you *help* me? *Service* me?"

"Sir, you are the showrunner. You are the executive producer—"

"You finally got something right!"

"What I was getting at, Mr. Pooley, is that *you* and *only you*—forgive me—or your wife—can *approve* stunt people and a special effects person. You did *not*. You even went so far as to instruct me *not* to use explo*sives* for the explo*sion*. So our burden is to tell your story while staying within the limitations you have placed upon us all. Sir—I believe that we are about to accomplish what you have requested *and* more."

J.T. was trying not to sigh again. He'd known he was going to have to go through this dog and pony show to sell how they shot the scene to the Pooleys, but like a woman who forgets how much childbirth hurts and has another kid, he'd forgotten how draining it would be—more exhausting than actually shooting the scene.

"Mr. Pooley," he went on, "I have learned a few valuable lessons over the years that I can apply to your scene in order to give you the best ever explosion. I have learned that if you don't have the money to blow something sky-high, don't film the event, film *the result* of the event and how it impacts the characters. Sometimes, doing it that way can be more powerful, more effective than seeing the usual big kaboom we're all used to. We can add sounds in postproduction to make what we shoot today into an extremely chilling moment."

"Blah, blah, blah, blah, blah," Marcus mocked.

"Indulge me," J.T. said, trying to control his temper. "One . . . once upon a time, on a warm and balmy summer night in Saugatuck, Michigan, when I was just a kid—"

"Oh, spare me. What's next, home movies?"

J.T. kept his cool by constantly looking down at the marks on the set floor, which reminded him of the abundance of work yet to come.

"As I was saying: when I was a kid and sitting out on our porch, on a very dark night—no streetlamps on this road . . ." J.T. closed his eyes for a beat and traveled back in time. "Now, I remember this vividly. A cop pulled a couple over and I couldn't see anything except the blue and red flashing lights from the police car through the limbs of a tall pecan tree. When the couple was asked to get out of their car, the husband became belligerent."

Marcus spun in a bad Michael Jackson move. "Ooooh, big word for such a wittle kid."

"Are you gonna hear me out? Because there is a great filmic lesson to be learned."

"Teach me, O Great Orson Welles of Sitcom!" Marcus wandered over to a cart of goodies and grabbed a cookie. "Do continue. I love bedtime stories."

Even my darling Natasha would rearrange your face, J.T. thought. He tried to wet his lips, but either the caffeine from the tea he'd been drinking all day, or the Excedrin from the bottle he was downing with the tea, or the stress that made him drink too much caffeine and down Excedrin had dried out his mouth.

"I'd like to hear the story, J.T.," Kevin said with genuine interest.

"Okay. So there I was, alone on the porch late at night, the night sky absorbing—no, *sucking* the flashing lights of the cop car into the black hole of infinity. And the trees . . . the trees took on different shapes every time the strobing police lights revealed new limbs that looked wicked, foreboding."

"Damn, you're a good storyteller, J.T." Kevin walked closer.

Marcus let out a precious exhalation. "Please, spare me. You stick to your day job. Let the writers write."

"I'm almost finished."

"Yes. You are."

"Let him finish," Kevin said in a menacing baritone.

"Right," J.T. said, batting his eyes. "Then the husband bolted from the car and he started to run. Mind you, I couldn't *see* anything—I just *heard* his shoes as he ran on the gravel road. I *heard* the wife scream, 'Please, honey—don't run!' I *heard* the cop yell, 'Stop or I'll shoot!' "

"Then what happened?" Kevin asked, leaning in closer to J.T.

"Then, Kevin, I *heard* a bang."

"A bang? Like a gun bang?" Kevin asked.

"No, not like a real gun bang . . . like a gun bang in a *Scorsese movie*."

"Oh. Small-caliber, or—"

"Just finish the fucking story!" Marcus grabbed a tin of Altoids from the cart and emptied several into his mouth. He started crunching loudly and his eyes started to tear from the menthol. "Now look what you made me do. I'm gonna OD on Altoids I'm so bored."

Kevin was wiggling his hands like an excited kid. "So there was a bang but we don't know the kind of gun, but I'd suspect it was a standard-issue—"

Even Skip was getting restless. He tore his eyes away from the centerfold of his magazine—a full-color shot of his dream cabin—and pleaded, "Kevin, let J.T. finish."

"Right, Skip. Sorry, J.T."

"No prob, Kev. Okay. Then, *after* the bang, I heard a kind of animal sound. Then I realized that this horrible wailing, this frightening howl was coming from the wife. Those sounds . . . they were noises I didn't think could come from a human. I never actually saw a single image other than a pecan tree and bushes lit with random primary colors from a police car. But to this day, I swear I saw it. All of it. My mind filled in every terrifying detail. Those phantom graphic visuals that were inspired by what I *didn't* see have stayed with me for over forty years. In other words," J.T. turned and looked into Marcus's eyes, *"the mystery is sometimes more powerful than in-your-face storytelling."*

"Blah, blah, blah, blah, blah. Very sweet story. You're a kid. You've got a porch. Pecan tree. Limbs, lights, dead guy. Bingo: wife howls. Try an' pitch that to Warner Brothers. Shit, you could put a roomful of ADD kids to sleep with that one." Marcus rooted around on the cart for something to ease his mint problem and found a supersized pack of Tango Mango gum. He ripped it open and shoved two pieces in his mouth. "What next? Family vacation slideshow with a Ken Burns effect?" He yawned.

"Well, I liked that story, J.T.," Kevin said. "Got any more?"

"No!" Marcus interjected. Unfortunately, so did Skip.

Marcus wandered back onto the set. "Lose the 'Once upon a time' and just tell me what's gonna happen."

J.T. inhaled and began: "As soon as Janice is out of makeup, we'll run it as a dry rehearsal once, and you can watch on the monitor if you wish, and then we'll do it. And the beauty of it is that we can't dick around. It has to work on take one."

"Take one! You're not giving me choices?" Marcus Pooley stomped again.

J.T stabbed his script with his index finger. "Mr. Pooley, *you* actually gave us no choices. You are very lucky that you have a crew who can pull this off and make it look like a real stunt without paying for stunts or effects," he spewed. "You're one *fortunate* mother. You fired the best cameraman working in sitcoms this morning, but Mick managed to get you the best camerawoman to take his place."

"You did what?! A woman? A woman cameraman? I've heard of women stunt coordinators. They call them cuntordinators. What the fuck do they call a woman cameraman?"

"Your worst fucking nightmare, if you don't can it, buddy." Sheila, the camerawoman in question, stepped from behind her camera and leveled a searing glare at Marcus. This time he did cower slightly.

J.T. looked at the two of them and said, "Well, I'll skip the introductions. Now, back to shooting this in one take—"

"I don't like that," Marcus said petulantly.

"I don't care. I'm doing you a favor, even if you're too—"

"If I don't like what you shoot, *I'll* direct take two," Marcus stated recklessly. "I can aim four cameras on the action and get just as good of footage as you. None of that 'one camera' shit. That way, I'll have leeway to cut the scene the way I see it!"

Kevin was picking up J.T.'s body language. He left his post next to the Panavision camera and moved to J.T.'s side like a comrade-in-arms, ready to come to his defense. "You okay, buddy?"

J.T. gestured that he was okay. He then tried very hard to continue to state his case without letting his family down and getting fired on the spot, which meant using his *very calm voice*. "When the credit reads 'Directed by J.T. Baker,' that is precisely what it is going to mean," he said.

That was the one speaking line that calm got. It knew what was coming next, and got the hell off the stage. Ash knew too, and followed.

"And P. fucking S.: If you point all four cameras at the same thing, then basically you're just shooting one camera and one take! In other words, they're all going to give you the same shot, four times, during the same performance! What the fuck good is that?" J.T. was furious. Obviously.

Ash came out of nowhere and brought J.T. another cup of tea. "Hot tea, big guy. Two sugars. Just the way you and *Natasha* like it," he said.

J.T. inhaled the aroma of the tea and it immediately worked as sense memory: it was as if he were at home with Natasha. It was an ingenious move on Asher's part. J.T. took a sip, then leveled his gaze at Marcus. "I am your fucking director. This is how I choose to shoot your ridiculous *best ever* explosion. End of conversation."

Crap! Ash thought. The tea bit didn't work.

Then a magical thing happened. One crew member started clapping, then another, and then more until J.T. was surrounded by applause and thoroughly embarrassed. *Note to self,* J.T. thought: *This hand-clapping one by one is corny. Figure out another way to show group camaraderie.*

Marcus Pooley, of course, was incensed. He marched straight up to J.T. until they were inches apart, his eyes narrowed, his body rigid and shaking. "You're gonna be gone soon. Take my word on that! Make plane reservations for next week, because I'll be goddamned if a twerp *has-been* fucking *ex*-pinup boy like you will tell me how to shoot my own creation!"

Calm suddenly returned to J.T., but not the calm that had fled. He took a step forward, forcing Marcus to back away. "Do what you've got to do, my friend. Do what you've got to do."

Ash was scared. Again.

Marcus planted his feet in his new, safer spot and sputtered, "I'm not your friend, and I most certainly will not do what I've got to do! I mean—I will do what I *want* to do!"

It struck J.T. that all that was missing was the Daffy Duck costume, which is what saved him from continuing to stalk Marcus around the stage. "In the meantime," he said, "as soon as Janice is ready, we will shoot Marcus Pooley's great creation: *the best ever explosion.*" Then he walked away to cool off.

"Where are you going? What are you doing?!" Marcus screamed at J.T.'s back.

"I'm picking blueberries, Mr. Pooley. Just pickin' blueberries."

ASH FOLLOWED J.T. outside the cave and walked with him stride for stride. "Just some info that may make you wanna wear your flak jacket: Marcus has been snorting more cocaine in the last hour alone than I've seen in my entire lifetime."

"Man, how do you find these things out?" J.T. just stopped and stared at his friend.

Ash shrugged. "Hey, man, I got your back," he said.

The two men hugged—a little too long, just to fuck with anyone who might be watching.

Ash pulled away and scratched his forehead. "J.T., it's amazing. Maybe it's even revealing. I seem to have absolutely no stage presence. I don't lurk in the shadows—I don't have to. People just have a way of . . . not seeing me."

J.T. smiled. "Whatever you've always done, please, keep it up."

"Wouldn't have it any other way. And speaking of having no stage presence, you didn't notice, by chance, that I was late this morning, did you?"

"Ah, you didn't miss much. Just a pedophile blowing his brains out."

Ash looked sharply at J.T., who had a peculiar look on his face.

Kind of like the first time someone who doesn't like art sees Michelangelo's *David*.

"Are you okay, man?"

J.T. squinted and looked upward. "Wow. It's still daytime," he said deliriously.

CONRAD CUTLER, THE senior vice president of Broadcast Standards and Practices, was waiting when J.T. and Ash got back onto the set. His suit was clearly tailor-made and his rimless glasses expensive, but he wore them almost apologetically, as if he'd rather be in khakis like J.T. He walked over to the men and asked Thing Seven to go find Marcus and tell him to join them.

"Hello, J.T. Good to see you back in the saddle," Conrad said.

"Hey, Conrad. I think I just fell off my high horse," J.T. responded. He'd known Conrad since the executive was a bit actor, at the time when J.T. was transitioning from acting to writing with directing gigs in between. He'd even had the opportunity to direct Conrad. Their history made for familiar but sometimes awkward chemistry, now that they were no longer teammates fighting on the same side against random network rules.

Conrad patted J.T. on the shoulder, then looked at Ash and said, "I see you brought your secret service with you. How have you been, Asher?"

Ash liked Conrad. Conrad had always been very reasonable in the past. Conrad remembered his name.

"How have I been?" Ash grinned. "Well, would you care for an honest answer, or the standard one?"

"Standard will do."

"I've been great!"

"Glad to hear it."

Conrad was also not one to waste time. The niceties out of the way, he clapped his hands and said, "J.T., I want you to hang in there."

Oh fuck. What now? J.T. thought. "Hang in there, J.T." was not a phrase that preceded anything he wanted to hear.

"Now, I'm going to make life slightly more difficult for you, but don't take offense," Conrad went on, checking to see if Marcus was in earshot. "I've had my ear to the ground and know what you're trying to accomplish in the long run, and I'll stay out of your way. I just have to do my job."

"No problem." J.T. shifted his weight but remained very cordial. "Understood. Completely."

Marcus Pooley came over and sullenly joined the others as if he had been asked to move to a ghetto. "What? Get this over with quickly. What?!"

Conrad looked at the showrunner with obvious distaste. "We're going to have to bargain a little here, Marcus," he said, taking out a slim notepad from his inside suit pocket.

"Like what? What?!" Marcus said, hyper from the cocaine high that was quickly wearing off. He tried to peek at Conrad's notes.

"Well—this being an eight o'clock show"—and then Conrad began reading off his pad— "the network cannot have more than two carolers at the time of the explosion. And if the candy glass shatters, we can see *no* blood," he explained, looking up to see how the showrunner was taking the compromises.

"Not a problem," J.T. quickly answered, believing that the faster someone signed off on the notes the less unpleasant matters would become. Wrong.

Marcus got in J.T.'s face the way an angry baseball manager does just before the umpire tosses him out of the game. "Where the fuck do you get off telling this man that *it is not a problem*? This is not *your* show!" he yelled.

Why, oh why can't this be baseball? J.T. thought, turning his head away from the menthol-mango-chemical stench of Marcus's breath.

Then Marcus spun on Conrad. "If I want blood, then I'll get blood!" he snarled. "Even if I have to call the man over your head, or even the network president! How would you like that, Mr. No-Blood?"

"We don't need blood, Marcus," J.T. said, shaking his head. "It would look out of place. We're stylizing everything. Putting in an element of cold reality will send visually mixed messages. Not to mention that it would expose our flimsy production values and wreck the clever illusion we have all worked so hard to create. It would look silly and classless. As it is, if it works, it will be a very hip way of telling the story of a main character surviving the best ever explosion."

"Don't talk down to me, Mr. College Professor! I want blood!" Marcus Pooley declared. "You two can go off and live together in the land of *Let's Never Offend Anyone*! What—did the perv schoolteacher blowing his naughty little head off give you a phobia about *all* things red and chunky, or just blood? Is Manhattan clam chowder off the menu in the studio restaurant permanently? Are you wimping out on me, Mr. Big Shot Director? Are you gonna cry again?"

Marcus Pooley is going to get knocked out someday, J.T. thought. But after the morning suicide, he had lost his taste for a fight, so he just turned to Ash, who forced a smile. J.T. got the message quiet and clear, and followed suit with his own forced smile. Once J.T. managed to make his lip curl upward, Ash shook Conrad's hand and excused himself.

"I'll be seeing you," Ash said.

Conrad nodded, "I know you will."

J.T. looked to see where his best friend was heading, but Ash was gone. *Shit! The guy really is invisible. Amazing,* he thought.

Conrad was all business. "I'm sorry to say I *do* have the authority on this. If you use blood, we will never air this scene. It's that simple."

J.T. chimed in softly, conserving his energy but still dogged. "We're not using blood. I have been hired, at least for the moment, to be the director. No blood. Period. *My call.*" J.T. was really over-stepping his boundaries, but he knew if he did it with enough confidence, Marcus might not realize it.

It worked—just. Marcus remained belligerent. "If I want blood, I'll put it in . . . in post. That's what I'll do!" He started to walk away, then turned back. "But the final decision is certainly not J.T.'s, and it is by far not for some low-level, power-mad guy in a suit from the network to say. It is the Creator's! Mine! Understand?!"

Conrad and J.T. watched him storm off. "Shit, J.T.," Conrad asked, "why on earth do you do this?"

"DGA insurance. My kid . . . needs it."

"Oh God. I'm really sorry. Hang in there. And listen, J.T.? So, off the record, whatever you do, don't hit this Pooley guy or his cockeyed harpy of a wife. They're the network's cash cow. As long as they're in the top ten, the Pooleys could be speaking in tongues and spewing pea soup, and the big boys would still turn a blind eye. And this Marcus Pooley character seems like the type who would sue you for everything you're worth," Conrad advised. Then he lowered his voice. "J.T., listen," he said.

"Yeah?"

"I did a little snooping around. Make sure the Christmas bag of gifts that Janice holds in the scene doesn't say *Saks Fifth Avenue.*"

"Will do," J.T. said. "Trust the Pooleys to try and sneak in a product endorsement for some extra cash." Then he smiled. "It's good to see someone who still does their homework."

"Yeah—people hate me for that," Conrad said.

"I know the feeling," J.T. answered. "Okay, I'll make sure we Greek out any brand names. We only have one shot at this bit. I'd hate to have to lose the scene."

* * *

J.T. Went Back to the set and went over the details of the shot with everyone—stand-ins, extras, carolers, Skip, Kevin, and the sound crew—to make sure they were all still on the same page. J.T. would call out the cues one by one, and if all went correctly, they would have the shot.

"William," J.T. called out, not knowing where William was but hoping he was where he was supposed to be: on the set. Ready to work.

"Here!" William called back from a place he wasn't supposed to be: in the prop room playing with gadgets, singing a lyric to a kids'

> ### The Hollywood Dictionary
>
> **TO GREEK OUT:** To hide or change brand names of products so that companies don't sue the production. "I saw a fucking beauty shot of a Tylenol bottle, and Excedrin is one of our sponsors! Lose the scene!"

song. William threw down a $400 antique Zephyr model train and came a-runnin'.

"Please notify all the *Powers That Be* and get them down to the stage so that they can see the shot," J.T. said without even looking in William's direction. Notifying the Powers That Be was protocol. Debbie from the network wanted to be there; so did Lance from the studio. William nodded, sincerely, and then went and made all the calls.

J.T. went over to where Mick and Skip were standing. "You guys ready for this?" he asked, rubbing his hands together.

"I was less ready for marriage," Skip said flatly.

Kevin was blowing compressed air into the gearbox. "I'm ready too, J.T."

"You're the man, Kev."

J.T. mumbled, "Now, if I can only get Janice out of the makeup chair, we can shoot this puppy."

"Please, put the puppy out of its misery," Skip added.

JANICE HAD BEEN sitting in the makeup chair for over two hours. She was a gorgeous woman to begin with, and J.T. knew that this was her way of getting attention from the director. He took the cue and headed for the makeup room.

J.T. knocked gently and was greeted with "Go away!"

"Sorry," J.T. said, opening the door, "can't do that."

"What do you want?" Janice demanded.

"Oh, you know—one of those obnoxious director thingies—like, 'When will you be ready?'"

"I'll be ready when I'm ready," Janice said. Then she pointed to her jaw. "I see a shiny spot right there, Marta," she told the makeup lady.

Marta, long-practiced in putting up with stars, shrugged slightly at J.T. and powdered the imagined spot. She knew that a television star's anger could burn as hot and as quickly as their career, so she protected herself with silence.

J.T. motioned Marta to step back, then stood in front of Janice. "Janice, we are ready for you. This shot has to be done in the next thirty minutes. You will be on the set in five minutes, or I will pull you from this chair. Don't make me throw my authority around, please," he warned.

The Hollywood Dictionary

TO BE PULLED FROM A CHAIR: To be *pulled* from a chair.

Janice looked up at him petulantly. "I'll be there. Just get out."

"Will do."

Janice watched J.T. close the makeup door behind him, then said to Marta, "Why do all the good ones have to be happily married?"

Marta, still-employed Marta, just smiled. *You heifer,* she thought.

As J.T. HEADED back to the set, Marcus Pooley came toward him with a swift, odd gait, cantering on his toes. *Is he in pain, or is that just the way he moves?* J.T. wondered.

"What the fuck is taking so fucking long?" Marcus demanded.

"For a man of words, you certainly are a man of few good ones," J.T. commented.

"What the fuck?"

"Janice was exploring some character choices, and I think she's onto something."

"*What,* for fuck's sake?"

"It's matte, perky, unprepossessing."

"Say what?"

J.T. shrugged. "In layman's terms? Basically, she's powdering her nose."

"Well, why didn't you just fucking say so?"

"I guess," J.T. smiled genuinely, "I guess I just like to hear you say 'fuck.'"

"Say fuck?"

"Yeah. You're really good at it. It's nice to be good at something."

J.T. patted Marcus on the shoulder and went to make himself another cup of hot, sweet caffeine water.

By THE TIME Janice made it to the set, Debbie and Lance had arrived. So had the other half of the Pooleys, along with the gaggle of baby-writer-producers. They all stuck together in the corner. On the other side of the set was the quad split.

J.T. was going over the scene with the crew yet one more *last time* when Stephanie Pooley suddenly started yelling. She hadn't been heard from yet this morning, so it was no surprise for J.T. that she would make a big to-do right before the scene was to be shot.

"What kind of bag is Janice carrying?!" Stephanie barked out, running onto the set as if she were running to rescue a baby from a burning building.

"We can't have this! *Fifth Avenue*? Where's the *Saks*? It's *Saks* Fifth Avenue! How dumb are you people?!" Stephanie was spinning around, not knowing who to yell at.

J.T. stepped forward. "Ms. Pooley, we had to Greek out the label according to network standards and practices. It's very common."

"No! My Urban character that Janice is portraying— beautifully, might I add— comes into the city, and shops at *Saks*! It's a character trait. Saks! *Saks*, goddammit!"

> **The Hollywood Dictionary**
>
> **THE QUAD SPLIT (TAKE TWO):** Knowing how to watch a quad split properly is a rare skill. Very few executives, let alone show-runners, have this skill. There are a few, though. Those show-runners, however, are getting old. Like . . . thirty-five.

So now there was a stoppage over the bag Janice was carrying. It was a convenient excuse for Stephanie to make a scene; she didn't appreciate that she'd missed all the fun of the suicide and had generally been left out of the loop all day. And, of course, Stephanie *did* have an arrangement with Saks. In return for product recognition, Stephanie had been promised . . . products.

J.T. tried to explain for Janice's benefit. "Conrad from the network told us to Greek out the product association. Saks is very recognizable, and we do not want any conflict with your show's sponsors who may be competing with Saks. In other words, the Saks truck will not be backing up to your garage leaving you all kinds of goodies for promoting their brand."

Janice looked from J.T. to Stephanie. "You know, if Saks wasn't going to be part of my character, someone should have told me."

"Saks might not want to be associated with the best ever explosion, Janice," J.T. said. He turned to Stephanie. "Ms. Pooley," he said, enjoying himself, "I sincerely hope you and Janice don't have some kind of backdoor product-placement deal with Saks to get freebies."

Stephanie's face became so taut that the stitch marks under her earlobes looked vulnerable to the laws of physics. "Fuck it," she spat, "just shoot the goddamn scene. But next time I want things like this to be cleared through me! Everyone understand?!"

> **The Hollywood Dictionary**
>
> **PRODUCT PLACEMENT:** "Back the truck up to my garage. Look kids! Daddy's got hundreds of cases of Pepsi and Nike shoes for everyone . . . on the block!"

The crew members looked at one another, not really knowing which one of them she was targeting. J.T. figured it was probably better that way. Now they could shoot.

"I still don't get the whole Greek thang," said Janice. "What happened to English?"

No one was listening.

"ROLL CAMERA!" William yelled. Then he mumbled, "After sex."

"Speed!" Larry from Sound called out; Sound was ready.

Darla, the camera utility clapper, shouted, "Pickup, Scene K, 'The Best Ever Christmas,' *I Love My Urban Buddies,* take one! One camera, Super 16, variable-speed!" and then she clapped the board in front of the lens so that the sound could be synchronized with the picture in editing, and all was ready.

J.T. was so into the filmmaking that he didn't realize that he was biting his lower lip, which started to bleed. "Action!" he yelled. "Cue Janice." Janice walked to her spot, listened to the (two) carolers, and then remembered to go back to the car to get her *Fifth Avenue* bag.

"Cue projection!" J.T. yelled. The projection on the windshield of the public-domain explosion footage was reflected perfectly on the glass of the car.

"Look up, Janice! Rack focus, Skip! Cue the candy-glass detonation!" J.T. walked behind the Steadicam, popping up and down and screaming out the cues over the roar of the variable-speed motor.

The shot was working perfectly. The candy glass shattered on cue as if the concussive power of the phantom-reflected explosion had blown out the surrounding windows.

"Ramp up to a hundred and twenty frames per second, Kevin!" J.T. yelled, jumping again. The motor revved to increase the uptake of film. "Start the E-fans! E-fans! E-fans! And cue the debris!" The fans hummed and pieces of the "explosion" began to fly. "Smoke!" J.T. screamed over the din. "And Janice, look up—LOOK UP—you can't believe you're safe! "LOOK TO YOUR LEFT! YOUR *OTHER* LEFT! GOOD! LOOK STRAIGHT OUT, INTO THE LIGHT OF THE PROJECTOR! GOOD!"

Janice took the direction perfectly. Through the lens, which was all that really mattered, it looked like Janice was looking through the windshield at the huge explosion that was being projected onto it. You could see the flicker of the action in her glassy eyes. Everything was smooth. The shot had actually worked. "And ... end sticks, Darla! Ramp back down to twenty-four frames; CUT!" J.T. yelled.

As soon as the shot was over, J.T. released an immense breath.

It made his body go limp in a good way. What had been keeping him upright, apparently, was pure stress. He suddenly felt giddily proud of his cast and crew. He jumped straight up and kept patting Skip on the back. "Beautiful job! *Everyone*. Well done!" He shook hands with Kevin and hugged Mick. Then he walked through the candy glass debris and thanked the (two) carolers. Then he stuck his hand out to Janice.

"Well done, Janice."

"Your lip. Your lip is bleeding, J.T."

"Ah, no complaints. You'll be proud of your work and this shot. Thank you."

He left Janice and her befuddled stare to go around shaking hands, beaming at his crew members, who were actually . . . smiling. The pride was back. *What a great feeling*, he thought.

J.T. was flushed with pure adrenaline. "Call down the . . . whatever and . . . Good work, everyone!"

All the while, he'd been wiping his bloody lip on the shoulder of his shirt every few seconds. He was completely unaware of how potent, and how ambiguous, that visual of him was. If you thought of J.T. as humble and proud of his crew, then the visual was one of a warrior wounded for the good of the cause. If, however, you perceived him as a megalomaniac, control-freak director, the visual then became one of a mad scientist. The wide eyes, the frenzied gesticulations, the agitation in the lip-biting, the bloody spittle, the crimson-stained shirt—let's just say that a sane person would not want to get him pissed off.

"EVERYONE STOP WHERE YOU ARE!" Stephanie Pooley yelled, storming onto the set with Marcus right behind her. Everyone stopped. "It wasn't *on TV*," she declared flatly.

J.T. froze mid-celebration. "Huh?" he asked, truly thrown.

"It was *not on the television!*" Marcus Pooley repeated for his wife.

J.T. wiped his lip again and tried to process what he was being told. He was still breathing a little heavily. "I don't really understand what you two are saying. Honestly. I'm not being disingenuous— or anything else that might offend you both. I just don't understand what you mean when you say it's not on TV."

"What the fuck is there *not to understand*? The shot! The scene! *The best ever explosion!* It was not on the TV!" Marcus Pooley said as condescendingly as possible.

"Oh—you mean—you didn't see it on the quad split?" J.T. asked.

"That's exactly what we mean!" Stephanie Pooley barked, looking at a birthmark on J.T.'s neck.

"Are you sure you were watching the correct camera on the quad split? Because we were only using one camera, and the others were just aimed off of the set, to be out of the way. It could be as simple as that," J.T. said, unwilling, for the moment, to let them get to him.

"*It wasn't on TV!*" Marcus Pooley said again, stamping his feet as if he liked to repeat words over and over.

"Look, maybe the feed to the monitor was disconnected, or the wrong camera was punched up on your monitor, but I guarantee you it was *on TV*," J.T. said, now defending the shot that just seconds earlier he'd been celebrating.

"How do you know you've got the shot if it wasn't on the monitor?" Stephanie Pooley challenged.

The moment was over. J.T.'s blood pressure began rising as fast as the decibels of his voice. "Because, you see that camera operator over there? His name is Skip. He was the fucking camera operator on a little movie you might've seen called *Raging fucking Bull*! Martin Scorsese wanted Skip! Michael Chapman wanted Skip! What do you think people did before there were video feeds that went back to gawking producers and executives on a goddamn monitor? They trusted the skills and respected the word of their fucking camera operator! And now, because the business is so fucking cruel to its own, an artist like Skip is forced to shoot shit like your sitcom! You see, Skip is the *best ever* fucking camera operator! And Kevin is the *best ever* fucking assistant camera operator. So if Skip says that *he has it* and Kevin says *it was in focus,* then we'll do this the old-fashioned way and wait for dailies!"

"Dailies?" the Pooleys repeated simultaneously.

J.T. was now officially angry, the mad-scientist visual in petrifying, full-frame close-up. He knew that his crew—and even Janice—had done something worth kudos, yet these Pooley assholes were pissing all over their efforts. They didn't deserve anything as good as what they'd just been given. J.T. was ready to fight at any cost—to his reputation (again), to his bank account (again), and even to his ability to get insurance (he wasn't thinking. Again). He'd lost all sense of where he was, of right and wrong. All he saw was the two-headed Pooley enemy, and it was going to go *down.* "Hey—I know! Let's play a game!" he said, spitting more blood.

> **The Hollywood Dictionary**
>
> **DAILIES:** (1) In the feature film world, film is sent to the lab, developed, and viewed the following day. When asked if the dailies were any good, an old, cynical producer once said, "Have you ever heard of bad dailies?" (2) "Look at how wonderful the film looks! I look! You look! We all look!"

The flickering spirit of Natasha on J.T.'s shoulder whispering *Jeremy* to calm him down and give him the strength to take the high road was no match for the intense, muscular, life-force fury J.T. was conjuring. Suddenly Ash appeared and saw J.T.'s naked ire.

"I know the dollar amount you two make on this show to pretend you know what you're doing," J.T. raged. "How about we bet . . . let's say, one hundred thousand dollars that the shot was ON fucking TV!"

Oh crap! thought Ash. *What am I going to tell Tasha?! He's gonna kill somebody!* Ash hadn't seen him this mad since the time he threatened to throw an executive from the USA Network out of a window.

"One hundred thousand dollars? What, are you crazy?" Marcus Pooley asked.

"*Two* hundred fucking thousand dollars that the shot was ON TV!"

Conrad, who'd stayed to watch the take, moved forward. *Please don't hit them, please don't hit them,* he willed J.T.

Debbie and Lance watched with fascinated horror as the director nobody wanted saved the Pooleys the trouble of inventing a reason to fire him.

J.T. was now up in Marcus Pooley's face and was discharging bloody dribble on him every time he upped the ante. "Was it ON TV, Skip?" J.T. asked his camera operator without taking his unblinking stare away from Marcus.

Skip smiled mischievously. "It was *on TV,* J.T.," he said with pleasure.

"Was it ON TV, Kevin?" J.T. asked his assistant cameraman, whose PTSD was beginning to manifest itself in the form of twitches and tics.

"It was *on TV,* boss," Kevin said in his deep, powerful voice. Those who worked with him frequently knew that he was only a twitch away from going nuclear and having a Vietnam flashback.

"It's cool, Kev. It's cool. Calm down," Skip whispered to Kevin.

"Kevin—send that shit to the lab early. Are you okay with that, Mr. McCoy?" J.T. asked, still not taking his eyes off the Pooleys.

"Yes, sir, J.T.," Mick said, "you've got it. Off to the lab."

"You're going to owe me two hundred fucking thousand dollars," J.T. said vengefully, "so you'd better get your fucking checkbooks out." By now J.T. sounded like a little kid on a playground: *How 'bout that? I can "fuck" just as well as you. Fuck!*

Ash finally pulled J.T. away and walked him out of the cave and into the light of day where J.T. could *walk it off*.

"Man, I guess I'll have to say it again: Sorry I wasn't there sooner. This time I had to go to the bathroom . . ." Ash said. "But I did hear you all the way from there. You were very . . . loud. And forceful. And—"

"I behaved like an ass, didn't I?" J.T. whispered to Ash.

"Yup," Ash replied.

"Fuck!"

They took a stroll past the crime scene from earlier in the morning. The police were finally allowing the coroner to take Leo Thacker's body and what was left of his head away to the morgue.

"But," Ash said, "if the shot works as well as I think it will, you've had a very productive morning." He smiled.

The body bag was lifted out of the schoolroom and heaved into the van marked CORONER/MORGUE. "Yeah . . . productive morning . . ." J.T. repeated as he watched the remains of the child pornographer being loaded into the van. The doors closed and the vehicle drove away, off the magical studio lot where today, nothing was an illusion.

The Llllaker Girrrrrls!

JUST BEFORE J.T. and Ash returned to the cave, Dick Beaglebum came running toward them from the direction of the parking lot, waving his hands and out of breath. He was really sweating. "J.T.! J.T., wait!"

J.T. tried to remember the last time he had really looked at Dick Beaglebum. He'd forgotten how small and roly-poly Dick was; on the phone, he always sounded smooth, enthusiastically slick. J.T. closed one eye and tracked the man as he approached. *I wouldn't cast the part of Dick Beaglebum with this schlub,* he thought. What he called out was, "Dick? Dick Beaglebum—is that . . . you?" like an actor in a straight-to-video movie.

"J.T.," Dick gasped out as he arrived. Then he doubled over, trying to catch his breath. "I came down as soon as I heard."

"Heard what?" J.T. asked.

"Heard on the news about the suicide. The degenerapearoonie! The Perv-Griffin." Dick's verbal intercourse could turn lexical right-to-lifers into etymological abortionists.

"Yes . . . It was . . . awful," J.T. said.

"It's *fantastic*. It's all over town! It's *national* now. CNN, Fox, MSNBC! And they've been saying your name in some of the print releases!" Dick said with glee. "I couldn't've bought you this kinda PR!

J.T. threw a worried glance at Ash. "My name? Why?"

"Baby! J.T., don't go all right and wrong on me, babe. This is very good for you. It's one thing for the industry to know you're shooting the number one sitcom. It's quite another for the general public to know. It's free publicity and any publicity is good publicivious, babe," Dick said, finally standing upright and almost breathing normally.

"It's a *tragedy*," J.T. protested.

"Not if you ask me—or maybe the rest of the country. One less child predatoreador on the planet the better!"

"Well . . . I really don't want to talk about it, okay?" J.T. said.

"Fine. But I guess the guy really *lost his head*, huh?" Beaglebum giggled.

"Not funny," J.T. said. "Funnier than anything in this sitcom, but not funny."

"He kinda *went head over heels*, huh?" Dick laughed, looking around for a more sympathetic audience and finding only Ash, who was standing with his arms crossed and a stony expression on his face.

"Enough," J.T. said.

"I guess his *perv-ormance* is over! Hear the one about the perv who gave *good head*?" By now Dick was doubled over again, this time in hysterics.

"Look—if you want to make dead man jokes, go and stand with the producer-writers who are on the stage right now, just snickering with pleasure that a man died today. Their jejune joke sessions have perked up since the suicide."

"Hey—no need to get all fuckityuppitybum, J.T.," Dick said. "Look, I actually wanted to *kill two pervs with one stone*. I've got something for you, J.T. And you too, um . . ."

"Ash," Ash said.

"Ash! Yes of course. Sorry." Dick Beaglebum stopped and stared at Ash. "You're black?" he noticed.

"I *am* Ash Black. Unless you are referring to the color of my skin. In that case, I am still Ash Black. Correct, J.T.?" Ash asked.

"Yup. Still Black-black," J.T. said.

"Well, anyway," Dick said, "I want *both* of you to have these." And he took out a huge stack of basketball tickets from his pocket.

J.T. stared at the purple and gold lettering. "Laker tickets?" he asked, confused.

"Oh, I get it," Ash said. "Because I'm black, you think *I'll* really enjoy the *basketball* game, don't you?"

"No—don't be silly. My son David is having his bar mitzvah on Saturday. At the Staples Center! I want you two to be there. Even though you're black and all. Sammy Davis Jr. was a black Jew, ya know."

"So am I," Ash said, facetiously.

"No shit! Is this a weird world or what? Anyway, it just wouldn't be the same if you two weren't there. Here are your tickets." And Dick handed the two perplexed men printed tickets from the Staples Center that had the time of day and *David's Bar Mitzvah* printed where the team's logo usually appeared.

"I . . . don't know what to say . . ." J.T. mumbled.

"Whattaya mean? It'll be the best fucking bar mitzvah this town has ever seen! First off I have a rabbi who has not only worked large crowds before, but he's also a pro at theater-in-the-round. Did a bar mitzvah in St. Louis at the Muni! And he's known as *the rabbi to the stars*. He's also an agent at William Morris. Talk about range! Your multitasking! Also—also, get this—I've got THE LLL-LAKER GIRLS!"

J.T. realized his mouth was agape when he went to speak and found it was there ahead of him. "The Laker Girls? For your son's bar mitzvah? Why?"

"Why?" Beaglebum laughed. "Why not?!"

"I thought it was a religious ceremony," Ash said.

"It is! 'Today I am a man' and all that stuff. What better way to be a man than to have the LLLLaker Girls?!" Beaglebum's chest was puffing with pride.

"Well . . ." J.T. was lost for words. A lot of words *were* in fact going through his head, but he resisted the temptation to organize them into speech.

"And," Beaglebum motored on, "you'll never guess what happens after the reading of the Torah! Come on—guess!"

"I have no clue. You bought your son a ticket on the Space Shuttle?" J.T. guessed.

"My son, David, will play Kobe Bryant, one on one, in a game of Bar Mitzvah Ball! Kobe Bryant! Can you believe it?! Kobe fucking Bryant is going to play my son one on one after David reads from the Torah! I got the prop department on another show to make me basketballs that look exactly like matzo balls!" Dick was so excited that there was a distinct possibility he would keel over. His breathing was still labored.

"Well, it certainly beats my bar mitzvah. My bar mitzvah was actually boring by comparison. I mean, all I got was *spirituality*," J.T. said.

"My God, Dick," Ash said, "how much is this setting you back?"

"Over a half a mil. But—I did some creative accounting and I think I'm actually gonna make tons o' dough off of this. Not only that, but I packaged *Can You Top This Bar Mitzvah?* as a reality show on Spike TV. This bar mitzvah is the prototype—the pilot. I'm parlaying the exotics into major cash. Some putz father rented out the Kodak Theatre where they do the Oscars and held an Oscar-themed bar mitzvah. Pfff! Do you know how good my bar mitzvah's gonna be compared to his? Everything included, it cost them a little over four hundred thou. His kid read the Torah like a bad acceptance speech: 'You love me! You really *ba-ruch ah-tah a-do-nuy, eh-lo-hay-nu* love me! I'd like to thank my father—' Oy! But now I'm the big cheese. And I pulled a fast one. Not only is it more expensive, but I'll recoup, baby! Recoup, exec produce, and syndication here we come, *V'-HI-GI-AH-NOO LAZ-MAN HA-ZEH!* For you black-jews, *Ash:* 'and enabled us to reach the joyous occasion of our son's bar mitzvah!'"

J.T.'s brain just didn't work like Dick's. "Exec produce your son's bar mitzvah? Recoup?" he asked. "How are you going to make money, at the Staples Center, with Kobe Bryant, matzo basketballs, and the Laker Girls?"

"Okay, get this," Dick said mischievously. "I also hooked up with Phat Azz's manager and we went over the numbers. It seems his biggest demographic is young white boys, and that demo is so important to his record label that Phat Azz is willing to share the bill and the gate with me as long as I fill the seats with young white record-buying Jewish boys! And Phat wants to be the host of *Can You Top This Bar Mitzvah?*"

J.T. shook his head. "My father used to use an old Yiddish expression, *Mensch trachts, Gott lachts.* It means, 'Man plans, God laughs,'" he said.

Dick ignored him. "I'm even sharin' merchandising! Do you know what that means?"

"Yes. Unfortunately, I think I know what that means. Your thirteen-year-old son has a very good chance of being a very fucked-up man. Forgive me, but my sensibilities have been tested today and I'm afraid I'm failing every test," J.T. said, and just turned and walked back to work.

"Well . . . I'm sure it will be . . . very *pious* entertainment, Mr. Beaglebum," Ash said, trying for a decent transition to make up for J.T.'s abrupt departure.

"It already is!" Dick took the tickets back from Ash, looked at the seats, then returned them. "Look, you seem like a nice big black guy," he said with his quintessential agent-élan.

"Um, thank you."

"If you want to sit closer, just let me know. I can't get you on the floor but I can seat you with the B-list celebs and players."

"I'll think about it."

"I'm going inside to give out some more tickets. The more famous people I give comps to, the more the kids will wanna pay to
get in. I may even have a deal with the E! Channel. A&E turned me
down, but take away the A and whattaya got? E! And E! is talkin'
some mighty big numbers. Then: fuck Spike TV! Just gotta clear it
with Phat Azz's Posse. See you in there!" Dick had his breath back
completely by now. With a little skip in his walk, he went into the
cave, shouting "The LLLLaker Girls!"

"EVERYONE WHO WANTS to go to Las Vegas with me on our private
jet, be out front in ten minutes," Stephanie Pooley announced. "I
hope the cast is on that plane. I know how hard you boys and girls
have been working and it would be good for you and very good
for the show if you let off some steam in Vegas. Remember," she
added, "what happens in Vegas . . . may be in next week's episode."
The boys and girls giggled conspiratorially.

"Vegas!" Devon said, imitating the Vegas voice-over voice.

"I wanna go!" Betty made sure everyone heard her. She hated
being left out of anything fun.

"Excuse me? Whoa—I mean—really? I don't mean to pop anyone's balloon," J.T. said as he moved forward, blocking Stephanie's
way. "The cast has only worked . . . actually a total of *less* than two
hours. Tomorrow is camera-blocking and they don't really have
their blocking *or* their lines down. I'd like to use the rest of today as
a cleanup rehearsal so Thursday and Friday will go smoothly."

"I told ya he sucked. He doesn't want us to unwind." Devon had
already started gathering the cast. As the Alpha Actor, he wanted to
make sure no one stayed behind.

Stephanie stared with a mixture of anger and amusement at
J.T.'s shirt collar.

"Listen," he said quickly. "I want to give you a good show. I need the actors. Two hours of rehearsal—please, look me in the eye and let's get on the same page about this. Please."

"I like it when you grovel," Stephanie laughed. "My actors are under a great deal of daily stress. You can't imagine that because you were never in a number one show."

"She's right," Rocky managed to say, swigging his Vicodin. "I'm under a lot of stress. I just auditioned for that big Oliver Stone movie."

Devon's ears pricked. "So did I."

"My audition went, well, as my agent put it, I knocked his—"

"—socks off," they both said in sync.

"Who's your agent?" Devon demanded.

"I'm at Quad."

"I know that, Rocky. So am I. Who represents you at Quad?" Devon demanded again.

"Veronica. Veronica Goliath," Rocky said. His eyes were actually looking in different directions thanks to the narcotics.

"She's my agent, too," Devon said, pissed at this news. "When did you hop agents?"

"Last week."

"She . . ." When Devon got really pissed off, his way of trying not to show it was to take long pauses. "She . . . told me . . . she would never . . . handle another . . . *Buddy*."

"I know," Rocky revealed. "She lies."

"She . . . lies?"

"Yeah. The other day when I caught her in a lie, she said, 'Oh, don't tell me you've never been lied to before, Rocky.' She's a great liar. Really, really good at it."

"Yeah. I suppose ya want a good liar for an agent," Devon conceded, calmer now.

"No shit. And Veronica Goliath is the best."

The actors had wandered away from Stephanie and J.T. during this exchange. Meanwhile, Stephanie pressed her advantage. "So let me explain," she overenunciated. "One can't quantify the stress an actor goes through with the number of hours worked! These actors work in their private lives. They're famous. They always have to be 'on.' They need a release. I can sense it. In other words, end of conver-say-see-on!"

That was all the cast needed to hear. Like a bunch of little kids who hear the recess bell, they practically ran out the stage door, where vans were waiting to whisk them to the Burbank Airport, on their way to a fun and stress-free evening in Las Vegas.

"See ya," Janice flaunted her bulging breasts, twisting her torso as she brushed past J.T. and left the cave.

"*Vegaaaaaaas!*" Devon said, this time doing his best Nicolas Cage.

J.T. was, once again, absolutely in a pucker. Baffled.

"Can I, like, come, too?" Debbie asked.

"It wouldn't be the same without you, Deb," Stephanie replied immediately. She understood that this would be a chit she could hold over the network babe in any future dealings.

"I'm, um, going to stay and get some paperwork done," Marcus Pooley said petulantly.

"You do that, Marcus," Stephanie dismissed him. "We need a strong leader here at home, keeping an eye on this dipshit so-called director."

Steph pecked Marcus and practically danced off to join the others.

J.T. watched her go, then looked at his hardworking crew. "Well," he started to say, and burst out laughing. Most of the crew laughed as well. "Thank you for a good day's work, and if I win the two hundred grand from the Pooleys, we'll share it evenly. Until then—it's a wrap. Be ready for hell tomorrow."

When the stage had emptied, J.T. and Ash walked out the back door of the cave and took five minutes to sit on the step and just soak up the sun that they never saw when they worked normal hours. They sat. Completely still. Contemplating what the fuck had just happened.

They closed their eyes and pointed their chins up to the sun and smog—and the flight path of the Buddies' chariot—the Pooleys' private jet—from the Burbank Airport.

"Mr. Baker?" Kirk Kelly said, startling the hell out of J.T.

"Yes? Oh! Kirk. How come you're not flying to Vegas to 'de-stress'?"

"I just wanna work. I was wondering if you would help me with a couple of scenes. I'd love to get a handle on them so I can find some bits with you and maybe we could make them a little funnier," Kirk said.

He wants to work?! When do the meteors hit? J.T. thought.

J.T., ASH, AND Kirk went into the cave and began working, line by line, move by move, slowly getting through most of the scenes. Ash played all the other parts as Kirk opened up. He started coming up with ideas for bits; when he did, J.T. would brainstorm with him and then they'd take the bit to a ridiculous extreme, pull it back a drop, and tinker some more until they were satisfied they had something that was funny.

"It's all rhythm, music. Think of comic timing in terms of music," J.T. explained, as he often did to his actors. "Hard work and preparation makes a good actor malleable and unafraid of change. You'll embrace the changes and immediately

> ### The Hollywood Dictionary
>
> **COMIC TIMING:** (1) A gift from the comedy gods. If it has to be taught, it can be taught with music as the template. Unfortunately, if it has to be taught, it probably doesn't exist in the student. (2) The essence of *the funny*.

start thinking—*Funny!*" Most actors understood. Kirk caught on beautifully.

J.T. began to feel excited again about directing; about teaching; about nurturing and being there for his cast—well, for one actor. One actor was all it took to put a spring back in his step. He wanted to shake the other actors and yell, *See this? This is what it's all about. It doesn't matter if you want to work on a studio lot or in the basement of your uncle's house. This is the process that makes it all worthwhile.*

J.T. had to finish with Kirk, but Kirk wanted to stay and work by himself. "I really want to be comfortable and nail it this week," he said.

What can you say to that? J.T. thought. He smiled, "Carry on. I'm going to the production office if you need anything else or want to ask any questions."

"Thanks, J.T., Ash—I mean it," Kirk said, then bent his head back to the script.

"You know you've saved that kid's career," Ash said to J.T. as they headed toward the production office. "Whatever else happens this week, I hope you remember that."

J.T. didn't know what to say to that, so he sidestepped it. "I'd rather be teaching a pack of freshmen than checking in with Marcus right now." But no matter how he felt about Marcus Pooley, it was professional to check in at the production office to see if there was anything more he could accomplish on this . . . day.

"Allow me," Ash said, opening the door to the office.

J.T. stepped inside. "Excuse me," he asked a sweet-faced Thing Eight, "can you tell me where I can find Marcus Pooley?"

"Marcus Pooley? I'm new. I've only been here for about twenty minutes. But isn't he the creator of the show?" she asked.

"Yes, that would be the Marcus Pooley I'm inquiring about," J.T. smiled.

"Well—he asked not to be disturbed. He's casting."

"Casting?"

"Who are you?"

"I'm J.T. Baker."

"J.T. Baker," she said, looking for a pen. "Can I take a message? Are you here in reference to a job?"

"I, um, am the director," J.T. said, trying to keep the smile on his face.

"Oh. *The director.* I was told about you—you're not going to yell at me, are you?" she asked, honestly.

"No. Why would I yell at you?"

She lowered her voice. "I was told that you were . . . I'm sorry . . ."

"Go ahead. Tell me what you were told. Please. I'd love to hear it," J.T. pried.

The young Thing began to recite the warning she'd received—presumably as soon as she'd stashed her purse in a drawer—as if she were being tested. "Well, you prey on weaker beings than yourself. You are a bully and you have a terrible time with authority."

"Is that it?" J.T. asked.

"No. You're . . ." she stopped.

"Please, it's okay. Continue. I might as well know who I am," J.T. coaxed.

"You are an asshole," she went on, counting off each offense on her fingers. "A prim Donna. You think being a director in sitcoms is like being a director on a feature film. You care way too much about things that don't matter, and you're a homosexual who hides behind a wife and family but you have your boyfriend on the set with you when you are away from home," she finished.

J.T. did a stage turn to Ash, who blew him a kiss.

"Anything else?" J.T. asked pleasantly.

"Yes." The young production assistant was far too honest. She hadn't learned a thing about show business.

"What?" J.T. asked. "What is the last thing?"

"Um . . . you are being fired. A replacement has already been made for next week—I'm so sorry. Was I not supposed to tell you any of that?"

"You did a superb job. You retained an enormous amount of sh—*information* in the twenty minutes in which you've been employed. Good for you. You'll do well in this business. Just make sure you never repeat any-thing you said to me to either of the Pooleys or you will be looking for a job next week, too. Thank you."

She looked worried. "Yes . . . you're very welcome."

Once the office door had shut behind them, J.T. turned to Ash. "Ash, do me a favor and go back to the set—keep working with Kirk."

> ### The Hollywood Dictionary
>
> **"YOU'RE FIRED":** A phrase uttered in Hollywood with more frequency than "I love you." Not "I love ya, babe." Just "I love you."

"But—"

"Ash, you're as good if not better than I am. Please. Go back to the set."

"If you do anything stu—"

"I'll reach out. Don't worry."

Ash did what J.T. asked.

J.T. kept seeing visions of Natasha and Jeremy in everything, so he began to sing very quietly to himself as he walked down the hall to Casting, *"Now if you feel that you can't go on, Because all of your hope is gone, And your life is filled with much confusion, Until happiness is just an illusion, And your world is crumbling down, Darlin', reach out. Reach out . . ."*

J.T. reached out and put his hand on the knob of the makeshift casting office. Whatever lay behind that door, he had better handle it right. Now that he knew he was going to be fired, it was more important than ever for him to keep his temper in check and not give anyone a valid reason for calling him incompetent. He was pay-or-play for all three episodes, which meant he could get his payment and his DGA insurance if he was fired.

He also had to forgo the satisfaction and self-indulgence of quitting, because in order to get his insurance, he had to either stick out the whole three weeks or be officially fired.

So J.T. sang a few bars of "Reach Out, I'll be There" again, then opened the door and looked around at the actors waiting to audition.

They were all Kirk Kelly look-alikes.

J.T.'s legs started to buckle. His blood pressure bypassed its familiar, steady, climb and rose meteorically. He became light-headed and had to hold on to the doorknob to make sure he wouldn't pass out.

The Kirk clones glanced up, decided J.T. wasn't a Somebody, and went back to their private preaudition rituals. J.T. went over to a watercooler, drank a couple of cups, and tried to look unobtrusive until his pulse subsided. Then he went over to the door to the inner office and walked into Casting unannounced, interrupting a young man who was reading from the very scene J.T. had been coming to discuss with Marcus Pooley.

"What the fuck are *you* doing here?" Marcus stood abruptly, confused and angry.

"Excuse me for barging in, Marcus," J.T. said as he barged in. "I, being a member of the Directors Guild of America, not to mention being a registered Democrat and a card-carrying member of the YMCA, wanted to be in the casting sessions so that I could be of more help to you in the next two days of work. I want to know what is on your mind; how I can make better choices and give you ... *what you want*." J.T. tried to say it without it sounding like a bald-faced lie.

"*Really?*" Marcus Pooley was momentarily thrown: *a Demo-*

crat and a member of the Y? *What did that mean? What was the crackpot getting at?* "Really?" Marcus repeated.

"Yes. As *really* as *really* gets. I see you are auditioning young gentlemen for Kirk Kelly's part."

"Yes. I got the okay from the network to make the change. Actually—I didn't get it *from* Debbie. She's on a plane with Steph right now on their way to Vegas. So I asked the second-in-command over at the network. He said he didn't know what I was talking about but he was sure that since it was my show and I felt passionate about this situation I should make the decision that would be best for the show. I called Lance from the studio but it seems he was unreachable, and since we have a time crunch, I took the network's advice and am doing what is best for the show." Marcus finished by pulling his wallet from his back pocket and removing his Producers Guild of America card. "Bet you don't have one of these."

J.T. took out his own wallet and held up another card: "Automobile Club of America!"

"Academy of *Television* Arts and Scientists!" Marcus countered, showing his card.

"That would be *Sciences,* not *Scientists.* And if you need proof, take a gander at this: Academy of *Motion Picture* Arts and *Sciences,*" J.T. smiled as he produced his card.

"Well—American Federation of Television and Radio Artists!"

"Ditto!" J.T. countered. "Local Musicians Union 802!"

"Screen Actors Guild *Producers* Health Plan!"

"Ditto and I'll raise you one DGA *Producers* Health Plan!"

"American Express Rewards Club!"

"Staples Business Rewards Club!"

"I have season tickets to the Los Angeles Dodgers!"

"I know when I'm beaten," J.T. said, putting his wallet back in its holster.

J.T. looked at the casting assistant, hoping to find someone else who shared his outrage at this stealth casting session. The assistant's eyes were focused on the caftan-draped middle-aged woman who was chewing loudly on ice while trying to settle all of her three-hundred-odd pounds comfortably on a standard-issue studio couch. "Can I get another Super Gulp Diet Pepsi here?" she asked the assistant. "It's an oral thing. Diet. I need to keep my mouth occupied so I sip on a Super Gulp all day. It's diet so no calories! Bingo!"

"I'm sorry," J.T. said, holding out his hand to her, "I don't think we have met."

"Hello. Forgive me for not getting up, but I'm Loretta Nady. Kirk Kelly's manager."

"I see. And, excuse my ignorance, but ... by any chance are those Kirk Kelly look-alikes out in the waiting room, who are learning Kirk's lines, 'your' clients as well?" J.T. asked.

"Of course!" Loretta cheerfully admitted.

"Interesting, Marcus," J.T. said pointedly.

Marcus heard the accusation in J.T.'s tone. "Changing out a lead in a show is hard. No one likes it. But Kirk has proven that he just can't cut it," he quickly explained. "And replacing him would be very expensive if Loretta wasn't on board to help us defer the costs. It's called show *business*, J.T. It's not called *nice business*, but we all must do our best to make it civil."

"I was actually ... just coming over to tell you how wonderful Kirk was doing. Both you and Loretta should know that he has a *learning disability*, and now that he has memorized his lines, he is doing marvelous work. He was even willing to stay today to work all by himself. He not only has the part nailed but is helping me with blocking, considering that tomorrow is camera-blocking day and the cast is now at the Bellagio 'de-stressing' with your wife."

"A learning disability," Loretta said with a laugh. "Don't tell me you fell for that one!" Loretta tried to sit forward. She turned and looked nervously at Marcus but then, pro that she was, made a quick recovery.

"Ms. Nady, I thought you represented the best interests of your client, who at this moment is unaware of his new unemployed status. The young man is working

> **The Hollywood Dictionary**
>
> **SHOW BUSINESS:** (1) One-tenth "show," eight-tenths "business," and nine-tenths bullshit. (2) *See* Yogi Berra.

his heart out to *please* everyone," J.T. said, staring at Loretta without blinking once.

"Oh, give me a break," Loretta said, shifting her buttocks, "we all know what this is about. You want to be the hero. You want to show that Kirk can do the work. Well, here's a Morse code to J.T. Baker: *The kid is talentless and we're going to stop the bleeding before his hemophilia hurts the show.*"

"Loretta, what do you get out of all of this? I mean, you're going to screw Kirk on his way out and screw one of these young men on the way in—but what do *you* get? A producer's credit?"

"That is none of your fucking business, J.T.," Marcus Pooley said, hoping Loretta would take the hint.

"You think I would settle for *just* a producer's credit?" Loretta let her ego get the best of her. "A producer's credit *and* twenty-five grand a week. I might as well be a writer on the show. I'm a part of the *creative process* now, so I'm being compensated for my efforts."

"Okay. Fine. I just needed to ask a question," J.T. said, "but all of this changes things. So I'll just be on my way." J.T. started for the door.

"J.T.," Marcus called out, "don't you dare go back to the set and tell Kirk what is going on! Do you hear me? You have no right. And—besides—if I do not find a better actor, I will be forced to stay with Kirk. So if you tell him and then I decide that he stays,

> ### The Hollywood Dictionary
>
> **PRODUCER'S CREDIT:** In Hollywood, producer's credits are handed out on Halloween instead of candy.

you will have done irreparable damage to my show. Do you understand?"

"Yes ..." J.T. said over his shoulder, "I understand, completely."

"Also," Marcus continued, "you should keep blocking with him. That could help you. Use him like a chess piece, and then tomorrow when Kirk's replacement shows up for work, you'll just have to show him the blocking you did today with Kirk. You know, you won't be starting from scratch, only the new Kirk will be starting from scratch. Get it?"

"Gotcha."

J.T. shut the door. He walked down the hallway and looked into the eyes of every young man who was up for Kirk's part. This was not the first time, by any means, that J.T. had been *asked* to keep a secret from an actor that would have a dire impact on the actor's career. This was not the first time J.T. was told to keep working with a fired actor, using the actor as a meaningless piece of flesh while the executives found another piece of flesh to take over. So J.T. did what he had done in the past.

J.T. burst through the door and onto the stage, and strode purposefully over to Kirk.

"What is it?" Kirk asked. "What's the matter, J.T.?"

"Do you own a cell phone, Kirk?" J.T. asked.

"Uh, no. I have a Sidekick III from T-Mobile with real Web browsing, a built-in camera, an organizer with PC sync, photo ID, AOL instant messaging, text messaging, and a six-megabyte e-mail account." Kirk proudly produced the gadget.

"I didn't ask you to do a commercial—I asked you if—can that NASA-thingy make a fucking phone call?!"

Ash looked at J.T. and slowly closed his eyes. He knew exactly what was going on. He had been there before when J.T. had asked if an actor owned a cell phone.

"Yes. Here it is," Kirk said, puzzled, handing it to J.T. "It makes *phone calls*."

"Don't give it to me, I don't know how to make the fucking thing work. Look, please," J.T. asked him, "please call your manager. What's her name? Loretta? Loretta Nady?"

"Yes! That's my manager. Why?" Kirk asked.

"Just give her a call on that thing, that's all. See if anything is . . . *up*."

Kirk dialed Loretta's number. He waited. *Answering her phone must be a major ordeal,* J.T. thought, imagining the large woman trying to do anything remotely physical. There was a short neuron flash of Loretta making love and then J.T. begged his brain to make the visual (the director's cut with bonus footage) go away!

Finally Loretta answered. "Loretta?" Kirk asked.

"Hello?" Ash and J.T. could hear Loretta's breathless voice amplified through Kirk's small cell phone.

J.T. mimed a shrug, then a thumbs-up sign. "Um . . . anything *up*?" Kirk asked.

"No! Nothing! Why would you ask that?" Loretta wheezed.

J.T. whispered, "Ask her where she is. Ask-her-where-she-is!"

"Um . . . where are you, Loretta?" Kirk asked. Ash couldn't help shaking his head. Kirk suddenly looked so very vulnerable.

"I'm out . . . at a meeting!" Loretta big-gulped.

"Gimme that fucking 'crackberry' thingamajiggy, Kirk." J.T. grabbed it before Kirk could even respond.

"Loretta, you filthy liar. You are in a casting session not fifty yards from here, auditioning your own clients, trying to replace Kirk. So—now everything is on the up-and-up and you can get your twenty-five grand a week and your producer's credit and Kirk can fire your fat ass for betraying him, and this young man can no longer be tortured by the Pooleys or by you and he can go home and reevaluate his fucking life!" J.T. kept hitting random buttons until the Sidekick III finally shut off.

Kirk had tears in his eyes and was motionless.

"Go home, kid," J.T. said. "You've just had your first real-life showbiz stab-in-the-back. You're a good, very good actor. You have great heart and great instincts. I hope you stay in the business. If you do—learn from this. Don't let it affect your soul—just let what you know now be a part of future equations. You are not the only one to have been fucked today in the sport of show business. It's happening all around you. It'll hurt like hell, but do me a favor and *don't quit*. You're too good and you want it for all the right reasons."

Kirk still said nothing. J.T.'s reaction was to do what he always did: talk through a problem aloud. Kirk's situation was focusing him, defragging his mind—and making his Robin Hood syndrome kick in. It was a tangible problem J.T. could finally fight on his own terms and on his own pious turf. And whether he won this fight or not, it was the perfect way to cleanse his soul and tell himself he was not one of *them*. He would never see it as a self-serving left hook to Marcus Pooley's chin triggered by emotion. He would feel redeemed if he could manage to take care of this young actor.

"Listen," he said, putting a hand on Kirk's shoulder, "there is a good chance that they won't find anyone as talented as you—or even a greater chance that the network executive who thinks you're cute and good for the show will go berserk when she finds out later this evening—I'll call her. And when—well, *if*, I should say—they want you back on the show, here is the name and number of a lawyer." J.T. tore a sheet from his notepad and scribbled a number on it. A memorized number, Ash noted.

"I'll brief the lawyer before you call. I want you to hold out for an enormous amount of cash. I want you to fuck them in the very same showbiz way they are fucking you: doggy style. Only better. You may win out. So cry—but when you're done crying, make every move with great thought. And that thought should be: *They tried to destroy me. How can I destroy them?*"

J.T. was now steering Kirk in the direction of the stage door. "Actually—don't do that. Let this lawyer do it for you. You try and keep your spirit clean. But stay by the phone. I think I can help make this work in your favor. Now, go home! And don't pick up your phone, no matter what, unless you hear my voice on the answering machine or it's this lawyer calling you. *Do not speak with the Pooleys, Loretta Nady, the studio, or the network.* I think . . . I really think I can help you in a big way on this one, Kirk. Now go. Go home. Screen your calls. Go!"

Kirk went.

J.T. watched him go, feeling the adrenaline rush of solving Kirk's problems and rearranging his fate and generally acting as a grand seigneur on a mission to aid the oppressed. There was nothing ambiguous about this fight, and that fact alone was liberating to J.T.

"Amazing . . ." Ash said.

"We're in with a pretty scummy lot of people this time. Not as bad as some others, but pretty scummy just the same. Oh, and they're firing me, too," J.T. said, softly.

"Duh," Ash said. "Everyone could figure that one out, big guy."

"Well," J.T. said as he put his arm around Ash, "everyone also thinks we're lovers. So, dear Ash, it's been a great Wednesday! I love you, and let's see what Thursday brings," J.T. said. He turned to the empty stage and *did the honors:* "That's a wrap!"

J.T. PEDALED HOME, managed his anger, and didn't kill himself biking to Oliver's house. He just couldn't focus on the traffic. He was in the world of getting Kirk's job back. He grabbed the phone the second he entered his buddy's house. He placed an urgent call to

Debbie, who *didn't want to be disturbed because she was on a very important business trip,* but J.T. managed to get past her assistants and finally through to her anyway.

J.T. explained the situation with Kirk in such a way as to make Debbie feel that things were happening behind her back. In Debbie's fury, she swore that Kirk would not be replaced. J.T. gave Debbie the number of the lawyer who was now representing Kirk, hung up the phone, and knew precisely what was going to take place during the rest of the night. He could sleep with a clean conscience.

THE LAWYER NEGOTIATED a new salary for Kirk, doubling his old one. The lawyer also put a provision into the agreement that because his manager, Loretta Nady, was now employed by the Pooleys and working on the sitcom in a creative capacity and for personal gain, which was certainly in a conflict with her client's interests, she was denied, per Screen Actors Guild regulations, any of her managerial ten percent that was to come off the top of Kirk's salary.

"T . . . TASHA? UM, I'm at Oliver's and . . ."

"J.T., Ash already called and told me everything."

"I failed our son."

"Nonsense. J.T.—get past yourself."

"Um, would you still love me if I murdered someone because they weren't funny?"

"Let's see," Natasha played along. "Not funny is a crime. I don't think it's punishable by death, but it could involve some serious jail time."

"I was a real asshole today. I completely lost it."

"How are you now?"

"I didn't quit . . ."

"Then you didn't fail anyone."

"I became the Sergeant at Arms of the Moral Police," J.T. whispered.

"You gave yourself a promotion!"

"I deserved it."

"Of course you did, sweetheart." There was a brief silence. "I think I saw a home video of a Moral Policeman pummeling an unfunny man on an episode of *Ethical Cops Gone Wild*. Cable. I couldn't sleep."

"'Nuff said. You're right." And just like that, Natasha was back on J.T.'s shoulder. "I love you."

"J.T., you call me if you need me. Any time of the night."

J.T. could barely whisper, but he tried. "I will. 'Night. Love you."

"Love you, too."

"For all eternity."

As J.T. hung up the phone, he thought, *How do people with big fingers use those tiny phones? What am I thinking? What is wrong with me?*

Thursday

THE DREADED CAMERA-BLOCKING day had come. The camera and sound crews were in early, setting up their equipment, ready for a nine o'clock on-camera/everyone-ready call. J.T., still employed, was there. Ash was there. Kirk Kelly was there, looking newly confident. William, the first assistant director who was essential on camera-blocking day, was not there.

"With any luck," Ash said, "maybe the swim part of the triathlon was in shark-infested waters."

J.T. sighed as a squat, Nordic-looking person with a full head of golden hair and a body like a discus thrower approached them.

"Who's he?" J.T. asked Ash.

"*He* is a *she*," Ash corrected him. "Second assistant director. Her name is Thor."

"No."

"Yeah. Remember? She's William's second, stepping up while your pal competes in his triathalon."

"No."

"Oh yeah."

They both looked at Thor.

"Father wanted a boy, huh?" J.T. deadpanned. The *cruel* was spreading to J.T.

"Shut up."

Thor strode up to shake hands with J.T. "Pleased to meet you," she boomed. "I take it you are the director. J.T.?"

"Yes. And you are . . . ?"

"Your first A.D. for the day, Thor."

J.T. had to hear it from her mouth.

"Listen," Thor began, "before we get started, I'd like to clear the air: I have a lower intestinal problem that I'm gonna have fixed sometime over hiatus. Spasmodic colon. I pass gas a lot. I might as well excuse myself now for all the times I will pass gas today, rather than pretend it's not me."

J.T. started to crack a joke, realized she was serious, and coughed. Ash pretended to have something in his eye.

At least she's honest, J.T. thought. Then it dawned on him that he'd be enveloped in a bubble of gas-fog all day long. As if on cue, Thor cut her first slice o' cheese. As promised, she didn't apologize. In turn, J.T. didn't apologize for holding his nose, either. "Where are the scripts, Thor?" he asked nasally.

"They haven't arrived from the production office yet," Thor said, zipping another one off.

"Well . . . Thor, isn't that slightly odd?" J.T. managed to get out. "I mean, today is camera-blocking day. I did not receive a script in my mailbox and we have no scripts available to us on the set? I mean, doesn't someone in the production office realize that we cannot camera-block a scene if we don't have pages for the scene?"

"That is correct, sir," Thor said in a military manner. "I'll look into that at once!"

"Um, Thor?" J.T. stopped his A.D. before she could get away. "Thor, where are the actors? We begin, supposedly, according to the call sheet, *in five minutes.* Where are all the actors?"

"The actors, sir," Thor said solemnly, "are on a plane which is scheduled to arrive at the Burbank Airport at niner-fifteen, runway one-zero-eight. They will be escorted immediately from the airport to the soundstage by transportation, sir!"

Zip-a-dee-doo-dah. *Oh dear Lord,* J.T. thought as he inhaled a smell exactly like that of a combined paper mill and sardine cannery.

"Their ETA is approximately ten-oh-five, sir!"

"Well, that blows," J.T. said.

"Yes, sir. That does blow. I'm going to the production office to reconnoiter with the production assistants in order to gain the information as to why we don't have our scripts, sir!" And Thor was off, leaving a foul odor in her wake.

The camera crew and everyone else who had to spend the day on the stage floor (rather than in a booth—or, say, on the beach) were *very* unhappy that William was not present. It seemed that the entire crew knew of Thor's problem, and even though they felt for her, they did not like the idea of spending an entire day holding their breath as she moved around the stage. And what she'd told J.T. wasn't true: whenever her problem became severe, she actually would try to make it seem like it was someone else by standing within a group of grips or gaffers. The crew really hated that. But at least it gave them something to talk about all day other than the Pooleys.

Kirk Kelly took the opportunity to come up to J.T. "I, um, J.T., I don't really know how to say thank you enough for what you did for me," he said—at a low volume, in case the wrong people were listening. *"They also renegotiated my contract."*

"Hey, man, you did your work; you were blindsided. You would've done the same for me," J.T. said.

"I would've?" Kirk said, caught off guard.

This moment of unadulterated truth has been brought to you by the new regime of actors and executives in show business, J.T. thought. Everyone J.T. knew from the old school would certainly have done the same thing for J.T. But this kid ... Kirk Kelly was honest enough—or dense enough—to actually wonder if he would've taken a bullet for J.T. had the situation been switched.

"Kirk," J.T. smiled.

"Yeah?"

"Kirk, this woman walking toward us—the smaller, heftier woman, not one of the babes—is Thor, our first A.D. for today. I'd like you to follow her around and get a taste of what she has to go through. It's always good for an actor to have invaluable knowledge of the other skilled personnel who help to make a show *be* a show. It's a respect 'thang.'"

"Um, okay."

Thor came marching back onto the set with two more gorgeous new Things—Ten and Eleven?—who must have been hired first thing this morning. J.T. saw that they were carrying boxes of scripts.

"Merry Christmas," Thor said in her deep voice.

"What's this?" J.T. asked.

"This—these—are today's rewrites," Thor said as she and the two stunning Things plopped the heavy boxes of scripts down on a foldout table. Every camera operator, soundman, electrician, and grip could not take his (or her) eyes off the new production assistants. J.T. just grabbed a script and quickly leafed through it, looking for asterisks. An asterisk was used to indicate that a line had been changed.

There wasn't a single line that did *not* have its own private asterisk.

J.T. was aghast. A page-one rewrite on camera-blocking day? He looked at the goldenrod pages and saw in the "Director's Notes":

The *best ever explosion* has been cut.

"What?!" J.T. said, but it came out of his mouth as an odd animal sound. Suddenly J.T. had new pages, no cast, and the clock was ticking on a day when the plug would be pulled twelve hours from the production call—which had been 7 A.M. for the crew.

With a ridiculously long, *new* script, everyone on both sides of the camera would be learning new information at the same time with only twenty-four hours before the show was to be performed in front of a live audience. How could J.T. be expected to orchestrate this miracle of all miracles with a brand-new script (new "A" story!) that even he hadn't read and a cast that wasn't on the ground yet and a crew that was taking direction from a lame-duck guest director?

J.T. was flabbergasted. He walked over to Mick Mc-Coy. "Mick," he said, "I don't want to sound desperate, but—"

"J.T., they did this last week, too. They have no clue. And the worst part is that everyone will eventually come through and they'll get their show in the can, and then they'll think they can get away with this bullshit *every week*. We're screwed. It's happening on every show. All over town. Every lot."

> ### The Hollywood Dictionary
>
> **GOLDENROD SCRIPTS:** A new color is used for every rewrite day of the week. When delivered on camera-blocking day as a page-one rewrite, a goldenrod script is equivalent to a golden shower.

"Mick—what about that ridiculous explosion that we shot and took seriously and also spent half the day on? What was the word back from the lab? Was it at least a good piece of work?" J.T. suddenly felt very vulnerable talking to his old buddy; way too vulnerable for a good director.

"J.T., look, you and I go way back—these fuckers wouldn't allow the lab to process the film. They must've known they didn't want to use it, so they thought they were saving money by just telling the lab not to process it. I'm sorry. As stupid as the concept was—it was a damn good piece of film. I'm sorry, man. Really." Mick kept apologizing. J.T. could think of nothing to do, so . . . he hugged Mick.

J.T. took the new script out into the sunlight and began to force his eyes to speed through it. There was a new story line. The best ever Christmas had to do with the Buddies' compassion in bringing in the lesbian next-door neighbor, who was a stand-up comedienne (and who couldn't get a gig), into their home for a big Christmas dinner scene. *A new "A" story about inviting a stand-up comic to Christmas dinner makes this the best ever Christmas? I don't know what to think anymore,* he thought.

J.T. wrote quick little notes and diagrams next to the dialogue on each page. But as he speed-read, he noticed something very disturbing. The episode had the lesbian comic doing nothing but old Borscht Belt comedy, tarted up with gay themes. The only jokes in this very unfunny episode were by the lesbian comedienne who lived next door. And those jokes were old and stolen. Not one original thought was on pages one through sixty-five.

Stunned, J.T. paused. Then he started reading the old, stolen jokes out loud—one, it seemed, for practically every page.

"I was so ugly—How ugly were you?—I was so ugly when I was born, my doctor slapped my mother. I was so ugly that once when I was making out with a girl and I asked her if she was going to hate herself in the morning, she said, I hate myself now! I was so ugly, I met the surgeon general and he offered me a cigarette. I was so ugly that my girlfriend asked me to join her bridge club. Then she begged me to jump off.

J.T. stopped reading. He couldn't believe that there were absolutely no funny situations in this situation comedy, but also it was now full of jokes that had seen more days on this earth than most of the writers' ages, *combined*. And they had a powerful and talented comedienne in Helena. Why would they put her in the position of busting her own comedy chops with Borscht Belt oldies?

"J.T. Baker, sir!" Thor said, startling the shit out of J.T.

"Yes, Thor?"

"I have some difficult news to report, sir," Thor said.

"Go ahead. I'm ready for anything."

"Well, sir, the plane has not left Las Vegas yet and Helena is in her trailer and is refusing to come out, sir!"

J.T. didn't even bother to say thank you. He walked at a quick pace toward Helena's trailer. *Here we go again.*

"Is Marcus Pooley in the office yet?" J.T. asked as he was walking away from Thor. Thor passed gas, ran her fingers through her Thor-like hair, and said, "Marcus Pooley is in. Stephanie is with the others in Las Vegas, but available by phone."

"Please ask Marcus Pooley to meet me at Helena's trailer," J.T. said.

"Yes, sir! Will do, sir!"

J.T. KNOCKED ON Helena's trailer door.

"Go the fuck away!"

J.T. knocked again. The door flew open.

"May I come in?" he asked.

Helena's face was swollen from crying. Her pale skin was blotchy and had patches of hives breaking out, even down her neck. She wore an old-fashioned man's undershirt—the kind that was sometimes referred to as a *wife beater,* but J.T. hated that expression, so he just thought of it as something his Russian grandfather might have worn under his newly pressed suit.

"Have you seen this crap?!" Helena spat. "Have you seen what they've given me to say?! *One time I went to a hotel. I asked the bellman to handle my bag. He felt up my girlfriend!* Can you believe this?!"

Helena was furious. She didn't know whether to cry or to break something. So she cried and then she broke something.

"Helena, I really don't know what to say at the moment. You and I are probably neck and neck in the reading process. I just got this a few minutes ago. I'm as . . . astonished as you are," J.T. said, trying to calm Helena down with his demeanor.

"*My girlfriend was never nice. After our last date I asked if I could give her a kiss on the cheek—she bent over!* What the fuck?! Am I playing the Catskills? J.T., what is happening here?"

J.T. tried to say something, but Helena kept turning the pages and reading her lines like a madwoman.

"*The Christmas season makes me think about suicide. So my psychiatrist wants me to pay in advance! Hello?! All I've ever known my entire life was rejection. You know how it feels to be the only lesbian in third grade? Even my yo-yo refused to come back!* Shoot me now!" Helena dropped the new script and buckled onto her trailer couch. "J.T., this is the 'A' story. My character is pathetic to such an extent they invite me over for the *best ever* Christmas dinner. This isn't about a few quick fixes. I'm fucked!"

"Helena," J.T. said very softly, "my dad was a comedy writer from the late fifties into the seventies. He was a big deal. Decades of work. Remarkably talented. Every single one of these jokes lives in my subconscious somewhere. They were good jokes at the time. As a matter of fact, I wouldn't be surprised if my dad wrote a few that are now in the script. That really isn't the point. The point is, who is your character? I thought she was a very hip stand-up comic. Not Henny Youngman or Rodney Dangerfield. I don't understand these bits, either. And I'm guessing from your . . . distaste for the material, you don't understand why your character is saying this stuff, either."

"*Once I caught a Peeping Tom booing me?* J.T., the last sitcom I did, I made over a quarter of a million dollars an episode. Now, this?!"

"Why didn't you go to Vegas with the rest of the lemmings?" J.T. asked.

"You've got to be kidding me. I *play* Vegas. Why on earth would I ever go to that hellhole unless I was being paid a fortune to perform there?"

Helena was finally in the world of the sane. She had actually calmed down. Until, of course, Marcus Pooley knocked at the door and let himself into the trailer.

"Hello, girls," Marcus said as he let himself in.

"What do you want?" Helena asked.

"I heard that you were slightly upset at the new draft of the 'Best Ever Christmas' episode and I wanted to let you know why we wrote the things that we wrote. I figure, once you understand what we are trying to do with the episode, the show, and your character, you'll be on board completely."

"How can you make her a hip comedienne in year one and then turn her into a Borscht Belt has-been in year two?" J.T. asked with great loyalty to his actor.

"That's the beauty of comedy! That's the beauty of sitcoms! And that is the beauty of your character! From week to week, we can do whatever we need to do." Marcus turned to Helena and smiled his wittle-boy smile. *"Altoid?"* he said as he took out a tin from his pocket and mischievously handed it to Helena.

"Yeah, I could use an *Altoid*." Helena took the tin and went to the back of her trailer, behind a small partition.

"If you two will excuse me for a few, I need to freshen up."

"Helena, snorting coke won't make the episode better," J.T. protested.

"Excuse me, Marcus, but the story is abysmal. All *the funny* comes from recycled jokes," J.T. ranted in a hushed whisper. "The jokes are funny; they've always been funny, ever since I first heard them when I was . . . say, *five years old*."

"How dare you! I'll have you know that my writing staff spent all of last night here on this lot, rewriting this episode and coming up with jokes that would make Helena's character sympathetic and sad so that when she is taken in by her Urban Buddies, it makes for *the best ever Christmas!*"

Marcus is either in denial, J.T. thought, *or he's just really, honest-to-God ignorant as hell. Retarded, maybe.*

"What the fuck did you say?" Marcus seethed.

"Um," J.T. tried to cover, "Marcus, you and I have had a very bizarre relationship since I arrived here on your show, and I must tell you—I only want what is best for you and for your show. That's why you hired me," J.T. started to say.

"We *hired* you because our other director took a nail gun to the head. Plain and simple. Not because of your talent but because we could get you at cost. And we thought the studio and the network wouldn't touch you and your holier-than-thou reputation. We didn't want to shoot this week! We wanted to shut down! Your agent manipulated everyone by recommending you because he thought nobody would touch you, either. But it seems that the network and the studio also thought of you because they thought *we* would never touch you, either. So . . . here you are. Sorry to burst your bubble," Marcus Pooley said in an evil tone.

There was a joke after all, J.T. thought. *The joke is on me.*

"So? What's the point you were going to make, J.T. Director-Man?" Marcus Pooley sniggered.

"These jokes," J.T. managed to say.

"I told you! My writing staff was up all night putting this new script together!" Marcus exploded.

"Marcus, if staying up and working all night was equivalent to good writing, we wouldn't be having this discussion. It only means that your writing staff is probably very sleepy today."

"How the fuck dare you!"

J.T. started reading randomly from the script. "*My mother never breast-fed me. She told me she only liked me as a friend.* Rim shot. *I could tell my parents hated me. My bath toys were a radio and a toaster . . .*"

Marcus was laughing. "They're hysterical!" He grabbed the script. "Hey—here's a good one! Okay. How about, *The last time I was in a woman . . . was at the Statue of Liberty.* How's that?"

"What do you mean, *How's that?*" J.T. said with a look of horror. "That, Marcus, is *Woody Allen's joke*. From *Crimes and Misde-meanors*. That . . . that's plagiarism. And not all that logical for a lesbian to say, either."

"Boys . . . boys . . ." Helena returned, looking . . . rejuvenated. "I'll say the jokes. I *get it* now." She rubbed her nose.

"Do you hear that, Marcus? You're a good drug dealer. A lousy writer and a horrible showrunner. But you can always make it on the street. Your actor will now say whatever is on the page because she's coked up, when what the two of you should be doing is con-versing like adults about what each of you are trying to accom-plish. Now—it's just one-sided. Exactly the way you want it to be. And this, from a talent who earned a quarter of a million dollars an episode on her last sitcom!"

"No, J.T. It's okay. I'm fine. All is well." Helena was trying to end the conversation as quickly as she could.

"A quarter of a mil an episode?" Marcus howled. "I wish she were making that little here. She's robbing the till. You'd faint if I told you what she was taking home per episode, you fool."

J.T., indignant, slowly turned and looked at Helena; so many unasked questions in his eyes.

"Look—it doesn't matter what I make. I love the script. Every-thing is good with the world."

"Hear that, Mr. Troublemaker? Satisfied?" Marcus, beaming, gave his coked-up lesbian star a quick peck on the cheek. He made a silly hand-wiping gesture. "Thank you! I'm on my way to put out other fires. Adieu!"

J.T. was still staring at Helena, who refused to look at him. "My girlfriend broke up with me this morning. She was moving out when I left for the studio," she said flatly, as if this fact would make everything okay.

"Sorry about your love life," J.T. said, slamming the trailer door behind him.

Outside, he leaned against the trailer, marveling that he'd fallen for Helena's act twice. He had no idea why he was passionate about anything having to do with his job. He felt foolish. He was fighting for the right to say he made the cesspool less smelly.

Thor came up to him and immediately passed gas.

"Sorry. Hurts like hell and smells like the dickens," she said. "I have an update, sir," she went on, as if reporting in to her general.

"What is it, Private Thor?" J.T. said reflexively.

"That's not funny. Are you making fun of me?" Thor narrowed her eyes at him.

J.T. looked at Thor in turn and realized she could probably kick his ass. "I'm sorry, Thor," he immediately said. "I'm ... just not used to someone who is on the ball as much as you are, that's ... all." It was time to inform the Center for the Prevention of the Spread of Cruel Humor. J.T. realized he was now officially *cruel-infected*.

"Oh. Okay. Anyway ... here is the update: the airplane from Las Vegas will touch down at the Burbank Airport, runway one-niner-zero, at eleven thirty-three. I would say by the time the cast arrives here and has eaten lunch it will be one o'clock, sir." Thor let a fat one go that sounded like a lowrider's muffler and smelled like New Jersey. "Yowee. That one hurt."

"Where's Kirk?" J.T. asked.

"He's working on his new lines."

J.T. WENT BACK into the cave and gathered the crew members, who kept shifting en masse as Thor tried to join them.

"Ladies and gentlemen, we have a very peculiar situation; I'd like to break you now and ask that you return, having eaten lunch, by one o'clock. You can run errands, take a long lunch, and if any of you can, please take a script from the boxes that are over on the foldout table and read this week's brand-spankin'-new episode. It's a page-one rewrite. I figure the more we all understand this week's script, the faster we can reach the goal of getting this puppy camera-blocked and shot by tomorrow night. I won't be able to do this without your help. So it's only a request, but if you feel up to it, please grab a script and give it a read. Thank you. I'll see you all back here at one o'clock."

J.T. grabbed another script. So did Ash. The two men went to the fake park outdoor set where many films had been shot that needed a park, sat on the fake park bench which, if you sit on it, suddenly doesn't make it fake anymore, and began to study the new rewrite.

"Ash?"

"Yeah?"

"You got the cell phone? I need to call Beaglebum."

Ash pressed the button that speed-dialed through to Dick's office.

A sweet female voice began, "Beaglebu—"

"This is J.T. Baker. Please connect me with Dick. You don't have to see if he is in. Whether he is shaking his head no or nodding yes. Just put him on! Now!" J.T. said, completely sick and tired of the Hollywood bullshit. J.T. waited. Looked at the fake park and wondered if the live squirrel knew it was in a fake park. Or cared.

"J.T., my man! How are you?!" Dick said, very enthusiastically.

"You tell me. You know I'm being fired, don't you?" J.T. stated more than asked.

"J.T.—really. I can't get into that."

"Dick, you certainly can get into that. You're my agent!"

"Yes, but I'm the Pooleys' agent, too. I'm caught in a very difficult position."

"Correct. *You're* caught! *Your* position is difficult?! *I'm* the one who is being blindsided. I'm the one who is being fired. I'm the one who needs representation," J.T. said as he tried to keep his anger in check by concentrating on the squirrel in the fake park, scampering up a fake tree.

"Look, J.T., you're my friend and that makes matters even worse. The Pooleys are my friends. They hate you. They both said that you would never direct next week's show or any other show unless it was over their dead bodies."

"Is that an option?"

"J.T.—you need a lawyer, pal," Dick said.

"I can't afford a lawyer! I came to town to do three shows. I need the money from these three shows! I need the insurance, Dick!"

"What can I say? You must've really pissed the two of them off, because they'll let you finish this week but they said there is no way you are starting work on their show next Monday." Dick somehow made it sound harmless.

"Dick, I don't know how to say this—but I must have these three paychecks from them and the insurance from my union. I'm not going to give you a sob story—but this is it! I'm pay-or-play, correct?"

"Yes, you are. But ... *Marcus is willing to negotiate*," Dick quickly said.

"Negotiate? How much?

> ### The Hollywood Dictionary
>
> **PAY-OR-PLAY:** A director is paid in full for all contracted episodes either for completing the work or if officially fired. Directors like pay-or-play not just because it alliterates, but because getting officially fired from a lengthy contract gets them a paid vacation.

And if you're willing to tell me this information, then you *are* representing *someone*. I mean, just telling me he's willing to negotiate means you're willing to represent him!" J.T. said, thinking aloud. "Are you somehow representing me, too?"

"Look, I'm just trying to help both parties. Now—Marcus said he is willing to give you this week's salary and one more half salary, but nothing more and definitely not all three. It's a take-it-or-leave-it deal. Whattaya say?"

"Well, Dick, it doesn't seem fair. Does that mean I'm officially fired? Or am I being baited to quit, which would annul the pay-or-play aspect of my deal?"

"No," Beaglebum said, "he won't say you're fired—*officially*."

"That's . . . weird. Um, listen. I'm not good at this sort of thing . . . See if he'll give me two salaries; considering that I'm promised all three, see if that'll work, the motherfucker," J.T. said, confused.

"I never figured you'd negotiate. I'll look into it immediately. See ya!" Beaglebum had hung up, and somewhere in deep space, the connection was terminated.

"Whassup?" Ash asked.

"They won't fire me officially and they're willing to negotiate—but my contract is pay-or-play."

"Are you gonna negotiate?"

"I don't know—I do know I'll need the dough and benefits from all three shows to be eligible for guild insurance. Shit."

"Are they allowed to negotiate a 'pay-or-play' contract?" Ash wisely asked.

"I dunno," J.T. ignorantly responded. "But at this point, anything is better than nothing."

The two men stared at the fake park. The squirrel ate a fake acorn, choked, fell out of a fake tree, onto the fake sidewalk, hobbled, then really died on the fake grass. The two men were sure that the squirrel wasn't faking. Nope.

"Sir, the cast is here in the greenroom eating lunch and they've asked to see you immediately on your return," Thor said in a plodding monotone.

"They're here?" J.T. asked, surprised.

"Yes, sir. In the greenroom, sir. Awaiting your presence, sir!" Thor said.

"Very well. That'll be all, soldier," J.T. said. Thor's face dropped and she looked at the dead squirrel.

"It was a . . . bad joke. I'm sorry."

They headed back to the stage, but along the way, J.T. and Ash maneuvered out of Thor's wing-tip turbulence and quickly headed for the cleaner air of the greenroom, where the cast awaited J.T.'s arrival.

J.T. OPENED THE door to the greenroom and witnessed all of the regular cast members, the Buddies in *I Love My Urban Buddies*, raising their hands as if in some kind of vote. Devon was leading the poll.

Janice turned and saw J.T., who nearly fell to his knees.

"Janice—your hair—it's no longer . . . blonde. You're a brunette."

"So? I was hired for my talent, not my looks."

"Janice? Did you clear this with . . . the studio? The network? The Pooleys?"

"Why?"

"Why? Because you play the sexy *blonde* in the show," J.T. said.

"I think that if anyone has a problem with what I've done, then I will call the Screen Actors Guild and complain of discrimination. Maybe even sexual harassment," Janice said.

"Sexual harassment? Who sexually harassed you?"

"Marcus," Janice said.

"I thought you were sleeping with Marcus," Rocky said.

"I wouldn't fuck Marcus Pooley with somebody else's dick," Betty ding-donged in.

"Oh fuck!" Devon howled, falling to the floor in hysterics. "That was *sooo* righteous."

"Fuck you," Janice said as she slapped playfully at Devon, who was still rolling around on the floor.

Helena rose. Suddenly the other actors were quiet. She had an extremely powerful presence. "Can we get on with this?"

When no one responded, Helena walked past J.T. without looking at him and left the room.

J.T. ignored Helena's exit. "Janice. This is none of my business and I'm nothing more than a guest director, but if we had hired you . . . let's say it was me . . . let's say I hired you as an actor because of something that I had in my mind, and one of those things was blonde hair. Wouldn't you have to agree that being an actor, a skilled, trained professional, that if I didn't think you could interpret the part as well with brown hair, I might ask you to wear a blonde wig? Do you understand what I'm getting at? Your hair? Your wardrobe? Your shoes? You are an actor? You embody a character? Or do you simply love making trouble?"

"That's not fair, J.T. I like my new hair."

"So do I," Devon Driver said from the floor (making sure the words began in his diaphragm).

"Fuck the hair!" Rocky yelled at his compatriots, then took a swig of liquid Vicodin. Then chewed a handful of Oxycontin. "Fuck! Let's get it on!"

The five cast members still in the room agreed, and converged on J.T. like killer bees beginning to swarm around an unsuspecting picnicker.

"We all have something to say to you, J.T.," Betty said. Then she looked around for help.

"You know that speech you gave us on the first day of rehearsal?" Janice asked J.T.

"You mean, way back on . . . Tuesday? Two whole days ago? Basically, the last time I saw any of you, except for Kirk?"

Kirk gave J.T. the thumbs-up. *What the hell does that mean?* J.T. thought.

Rocky now looked insanely furious and ready to kill—literally psychotic. Rocky had a checkered past, all obsessively recorded in the media. He had a history of coming in and out of rehab facilities so often that there were jokes about his using the Betty Ford Clinic as his mailing address. Rocky had all the symptoms of what J.T. called *Post-Depart-em Depression*. The illness always flared up after a celebrity *departed* from a high-profile show. It was triggered by being in the public spotlight on a daily basis (and loving it; yet saying you *despised* it!) and then suddenly becoming yesterday's news. Once the magazines, the talk shows, and the tabloids stopped giving the celebrity publicity, the celebrity would go through a horrible bout of depression, longing for the attention they used to at-

> **The Hollywood Dictionary**
>
> **POST-DEPART-EM DEPRESSION:** (1) See security footage at Hollywood 7-Elevens. (2) Read the tabloids. On any day. (3) Or don't. Please . . .

tract, then do whatever it took to get back in the spotlight and keep the publicity machine rolling: doing drugs, getting a DUI, holding up a 7-Eleven, shoplifting, becoming hunger-striker anorexic, even attempting suicide.

"Look, motherfucker," Rocky Brook said, his body trembling like a junkie's, "we don't like to be told *what to do*. Get it? We know our characters. We know how they think. We know how they move. We don't need some has-been director coming in here telling us, 'Move here,' or 'This is funny if you try this'—we don't *need* you, man! We don't want you here! We'll sit on the fucking couches and we'll move when the fuck we want to move! Do you get that? Do I have to spell it out to you?!" Rocky was now out of control—even for a drug addict. He began to punch things like an amateur boxer; taking wild roundhouse swings at empty soda cans, small lamps— things that wouldn't hurt.

Kirk stepped in front of Rocky. "Whoa, man," he said. "This guy is on our side. He goes to bat for the actors, man. Be cool."

The cast went quiet. *Wow,* J.T. thought. *That was really nice. How do I say thank you?* J.T. was thinking out loud, yet again.

"You don't have to say thank you, J.T.," Kirk said softly. "You've really saved my butt. I should be saying thank you to you."

If only there'd been time for J.T. to make something of this momentous change of pace.

A small knock came from the door, followed by Thor sticking her cropped-blonde head into the greenroom.

"Excuse me, sir, but we're back from lunch and—"

"Well, *we're* not back from fucking lunch, okay?!" Rocky shouted, and threw a magazine at the door.

Thor closed the door to protect herself, then reopened it slightly to give J.T. one last bit of information. "And sir," she tried to speak as quickly as she could, "Helena has gone home. She said she was emotionally distraught."

"'Emotionally distraught'?!" J.T. finally lost his temper.

"Sir—I'm just the messenger. Please don't kill me," Thor said, looking oddly defenseless. The insanity of it all was starting to overwhelm J.T.

"Sir," she said, "and this isn't for 'publication,' but her girlfriend is moving out. She went home, crying hysterically, trying to stop her. I mean—I wasn't trying to stop her, sir. She was going home, trying to stop her girlfriend. From moving out. Sir. Just wanted you to know, sir," Thor said.

"Thank you, Thor. Now I know."

"We'll all be waiting out here for you and the cast to get started. We're slightly behind, you know—"

Thor was cut off as J.T. lost control. "'Slightly behind'?! We shoot this fucking show tomorrow and we have a page-one rewrite which I'm sure no one in this room has read and you're telling me we're slightly behind? We're fucking *four days* behind!"

"Just the messenger, sir," Thor said, and closed the door.

J.T. turned around and looked at the cast of *I Love My Urban Buddies*. He looked at each of their faces. He tried to decipher any hint of normalcy; humanity; benevolence. He couldn't find any emotion or personality trait that he recognized, except on Kirk's face.

"J.T.," Janice spoke up, "we all took a vote and we've decided not to come out to rehearsal until the network renegotiates our contract." And all of the other Buddies nodded and made gestures or noises of approval.

"Um," J.T. was trying to formulate a sentence, "don't you think that's a little premature? This is only your second year . . ." J.T. was lost. Again.

"It wasn't *a little premature* for Kirk!" Rocky said with resentment.

"Fuckin' A," Devon added.

"Take a look at this!" Janice said as she thrust a *TV Guide* into J.T.'s face.

The cast of *I Love My Urban Buddies* was on the cover. Smiling. The caption: "The Only Hit in a Dismal Season. Again."

"It's a fucking advanced copy! Only our second season but our third *TV Guide* cover!" Rocky Brook said, still shaking. He found his backpack and took out a brand-new bottle of liquid Vicodin, didn't even bother to turn his back, and chugged.

"We're household names. See our faces? Why should everyone make money off of our faces and we get left behind in the dirt?" Betty asked indignantly.

"Betty," J.T. began, "how much do you make a week?"

There was silence. Everyone was afraid to tell anyone else what they made, even though in theory they were all supposed to be making the same—what they call "Favored Nations" in Hollywood.

"Do you make forty, fifty grand a week?" J.T. asked.

"What does that matter?

> ### The Hollywood Dictionary
>
> **FAVORED NATIONS:** "I get what you get—only a lot more, but don't tell."

We're still all underpaid," Devon Driver finally got off the floor
and protested.

"You are underpaid?" J.T. asked with a straight face. "I see. By
whose standards? I mean I have neighbors who don't make in a
year what you guys make in a week. And you don't even work all
week. You put in a few hours of rehearsal and go to Las Vegas and
return whenever the fuck you want and with whatever hair color
you wish and then you hold everyone hostage because *TV Guide*
puts your faces on the cover? Does anyone see the insanity in all of
this? Am I the only one?"

The Buddies erupted in protest, giving their reasons why they
were underpaid and underappreciated. J.T. zoned out. He looked
at them, stared at them, but all he could do was think about the remarkable pros he had worked with over his forty-year career, and
he couldn't help but wonder what they might think of this ridiculous mutiny.

George Burns. What a man, J.T. thought. *What a work ethic.
This would've killed him if he hadn't already been dead.* J.T. kept
thinking. *Paul Newman. Joanne Woodward. Hal Holbrook. Ossie
Davis. Why is Ossie Davis dead? Mel Gibson. Why can't he be dead?*
A stream of names flooded J.T.'s consciousness: people he was so
proud to have worked with, directed, been directed by, shared the
stage with. And what would all the young actors J.T. had worked
with—how would they feel as spectators of this greed-fest? All of
them, like . . . well, like . . . J.T.'s sentimental journey into righteousness came to a quick end. He could only think of the old pros. Not
a single name of an actor under the age of fifty came to mind. *Rod
Steiger—dead. Why?! Okay—how 'bout Morgan Freeman, Gene
Hackman, Burt Reynolds, Danny Glover, Maximilian Schell.* J.T.
started to feel the aches and pains of being old and sitting in an
awkward position, pretending to listen. *Jack Lemmon is dead,* he
thought. *Crap! How come he's dead and these* Buddies *aren't? Crap,
crap, crap!*

"Crap? You think it's crap?" Rocky, now slightly subdued by his Vicodin and not so rocky, finally got J.T.'s attention. "So that's why we're striking. We're household names and we want our due. We want the money that should be coming to us. We want what is *fair*! We want it now; we've got 'em over a barrel!" He started getting woozy, and had to sit himself down.

"We want, we want, we want—" J.T. said, then stopped. He looked at these young brats and knew they were holding all of the cards . . . at this particular moment. There was nothing J.T. could do except go to the Pooleys and explain why they weren't working today. *Maybe, just maybe, by tomorrow everyone will get what they want and what is owed to them and they can actually put in an honest day's work,* he thought.

J.T. got up and left the room. Just before he closed the door behind him, he heard Devon Driver say, "See? I told you it would work!" J.T. opened the door again, stuck his head inside the greenroom, and smiled. "You're a punk," he told Devon. "I feel for you. I feel for all of you." Then he closed the door and walked away.

J.T. didn't really know where to go first. He had to tell the Pooleys but he also had to make sure that his crew wasn't dismissed and paid for only half a day, so he headed onto the floor of the set. Everyone was staring at him. Some just shook their heads.

"What?" J.T. asked. "Did I miss something?"

Larry, from Sound, walked over to J.T. and patted him on the back. Doc came up to J.T. and hugged him. J.T. had no idea what was going on.

"We heard everything," Larry finally said.

"What do you mean, you heard everything?" J.T. asked.

"Well," Larry said with a shit-eating grin, "I put a wireless mic on Kirk this morning when we were all waiting around. I wanted to see how much interference I'd get out on the *Urban Exterior Street*. The kid helped me out and we went and tested it. Only problem . . . *I forgot* to take it off the kid and the kid forgot he was wearing it. Everything in the greenroom was piped out here. I mean, once I started hearing how much shit they were giving you; I thought the crew oughta know what you go through. Then, when they launched into the pay-us-more-money thingamajiggy and you called 'em on it with that line sayin' that they make more in a week than your neighbors make all year, well, that was classic. I recorded the whole thing," Larry said. "It'll be all over the Web tonight. Even if they get what they want, it's good to know who you're workin' with, ya know?" And Larry extended his hand and shook the hand of J.T.

"Well," J.T. said, "I've got to go and tell the Powers That Be what we're dealing with. Make sure none of you sign out until I get the okay that you've been here for a full day's pay. Who knows what *they'll* try and pull."

The Hollywood Dictionary

WIRELESS MIC: (1) A wireless microphone. (2) "Oops! I didn't say that."

Doc Ray Piscatori, the camera coordinator and weekend cowboy (he team-penned cows—a rodeo sport—and rode his horse as far from civilization and showbiz as possible every weekend), came up to J.T.

"J.T., I have a favor to ask of you, buddy."

"Sure," J.T. said, scarcely listening.

"I've got . . . Shit, man—I don't want anyone to know." Doc Ray shuffled his feet, then looked J.T. straight in the eye. "I, um, have cancer." Doc Ray lifted his shirt up to reveal a portable chemo pump hung in a sling that was hidden under Doc's baggy shirt.

He had J.T.'s attention. "I'm—"

"J.T., look—do you think I could take this hour or so to run to St. Joe's Hospital and get my radiation. It takes barely a half an hour round-trip if I book it. Then I'll be back to work. I'll even bring the new script—"

"Go, man. And don't worry when you get back. I'll cover. And get something to eat."

"You kinda lose your appetite, but . . . thanks, man. I'll be right back, ready to work."

J.T. watched Doc Ray try to run-jog and make sure his portable chemo pump stayed in place under his shirt. *Holy shit,* he thought.

"I second that," Ash said—meaning J.T. was thinking aloud yet again.

J.T. AND ASH walked over to the production office to explain to the Pooleys the latest of the absurdities that had become commonplace in the television world. On the way, J.T. called Dick Beaglebum again.

"Dick Beaglebum's office," a new sexy young female voice answered.

"This is J.T. Baker and let's pretend you know that Dick Beaglebum is sitting five feet from you and he's not shaking his head no. Please put him on the phone."

"J.T., the man! How is the director of all directors?" Dick said, enthusiastically.

"Am I officially fired?"

"J.T., as much as the Pooleys hate you, they refuse to say you are *officially* fired."

"If that's the case, please tell them to get me a pass for Monday's table read and production meeting," J.T. said calmly.

"What? Now, wait. What do you mean?"

"I mean," J.T. continued, "I want you to tell them that I'll be at the gate early on Monday, as usual, and *ready for work*. I have a contract to work on three episodes and *I will honor my contract*."

"I don't know if that is so smart, J.T."

"For whom? Of course it is. They want to beat me out of my

money and I want to work. They either say I'm *officially fired* and they pay me, or they have to supply their director, which would be me, with a new script, blueprints of sets, and a pass to get on the lot first thing Monday. I'm in a working mood, Dick! Why don't you give them a call and see what they think? I'll wait for your answer. By the way, I assume Marcus Pooley said no to the two weeks' negotiation of my salary?"

Dick considered compassion for a nanosecond and decided to stick with enthusiasm. "He said over his dead body; absolutely not!"

"Good."

"What are you implying, J.T.?"

"Do I have to imply? I'm here on a three-week *pay-or-play* job and now I know I'm being fired."

"J.T., you need a lawyer, my friend. I told you that."

"And I told you that I cannot afford to be in a war of attrition with rich fucks while my salary goes to some law firm. I need my agent to get me paid or to let me know I'm fired. I don't live *down the block*. I can't just *go home*. If I were to go home, if I were to get on an airplane, that would nullify my pay-or-play contract and that would give the impression that I'm quitting. Well, *I'm not quitting*, which means I must be officially fired. I'm ready and willing to go to war—er, *work*. And I will be at work, no matter how embarrassing it is, every single day, even if there is another director and the cast and crew get direction in stereo, unless someone plays fair and pays me what I'm owed and tells me I'm officially fired! Now—since my offer to negotiate my salary with the Pooleys has been turned down, then my offer is off the fucking table! I want—Dick, you bastard—I *need* these paychecks. I need the insurance that goes with these three paychecks. You let them know I'm here for the next two episodes after this one whether they like it or not—or, until they fire me."

There was no response from Beaglebum. "Goddammit, Dick,

have the decency to at least tell them what I'm telling you. The money we're talking about is peanuts to you; birdseed to them. They could amortize their losses over the course of twelve episodes and it would barely cover the bagels and cream cheese at the table read!"

Still there was absolutely no response from Beaglebum. "For God's sake, if you can't stick up for me, if you can't or won't go to bat for me, at least have the decency to see through the crap and acknowledge that this is a pissing match to Marcus Pooley and it is real life to my family!" J.T. heard silence. "Crap!" J.T. slammed the cell phone shut. "He wasn't even on the phone for all of that. How pathetic is this getting?"

"Shit, man, I'm really sorry," Ash said as he took the cell phone.

"Don't worry . . . As bad as I am at playing these little games, I know the basic rules. Rule number one: D*on't quit*. Make them *fire you*. Rule number two: D*on't quit*. Make them *fire you*. Rule number three: Have no shame. When it comes to getting this insurance for my boy's treatments, well, they may have ego on their side, but I used to be an actor. I literally have no shame. Now, let's see how they're going to take the fact that their entire cast of regular Buddies are threatening to strike if they don't get a pay raise. Then we'll worry about getting the show shot, somehow, by tomorrow evening."

The two men walked into the production office, past the two newest Things (Twelve and Thirteen), and straight into Marcus Pooley's private office. He was on the phone.

"Over my dead . . ." Marcus looked up and saw J.T. "I'll call you back," he said, obviously to Dick Beaglebum.

"Steph? Stephanie Pooley, my darling wife? Will you join us in my office, please?" Marcus called out.

Stephanie emerged grudgingly from her own office, preoccupied with the new draft of the "Best Ever Christmas" script. "This better be fucking important!" she yelled, then stopped for a beat when she came into Marcus's office and saw J.T. standing there. She looked pointedly past J.T. and accidentally looked at her husband.

"You know," Stephanie said to Marcus as she read one of the lines in the new script, "I love these new jokes. *I decided to play it cool with my girlfriend so I let her make the first move. She packed and went to Florida!* That is so clever! Who wrote these jokes?"

"Um," J.T. interrupted, "Adam so-and-so and his partner Eve."

"I assume you don't have the ability to recognize a good joke from a bad one," Stephanie said to a fur-trimmed mirror on the wall behind J.T.

"No, I don't have that malady. Unfortunately, I've been infected with *Those Jokes Are Not Original Syndrome,* known more commonly as T.J.A.N.O.S. Congratulations, you are the ten thousandth person to have stolen those jokes! What do you win? Why, you win a slot on prime-time TV! News flash: Just because your words are being heard by fifteen million people, it doesn't mean they'd even make a decent postcard."

"Postcard?" Stephanie blurted. "Haven't you ever heard of the *Internet?* Hello? *E-cards?*"

J.T. shook his head in disbelief. "I think you're missing the point."

"Here's *the point:* What is it you want, and why aren't you on the floor working?" Marcus Pooley asked with contempt.

"Well," J.T. began, "your lesbian next-door neighbor has gone home because she is emotionally distraught, and your Urban Buddies have gotten together and are behaving like a pack of wild animals on National Geographic, and they're demanding a pay raise. Oh—and your bubbly blonde bombshell is now a brunette."

"We know everything and we are working on it," Stephanie barked.

"You know . . . everything?" J.T. asked, surprised.

"I spoke with Helena and told her to go home. We need to take care of our delicate flowers," Stephanie Pooley said.

"Your delicate flowers?" J.T. asked, outraged. "You know . . . A man who works for you named Doc Ray Piscatori went to the hospital and is having his delicate-flowered ass radiated at lunch and wears a chemotherapy machine under his shirt. He's dedicated and refused to let *his* problems be *your* problems. Were you aware of that?"

"Who?" Stephanie asked with disgust. She did not want to hear about any illness that was too icky to visualize. "I don't want some schmuck not up to full speed on my crew. What did you say his name was? We need a healthy crew. This show is hard enough as it is."

Marcus settled into an even tone. "We are aware that our cast of Urban Buddies wants more money. We are aware that they are sticking together as a group. We are aware of that because whatever is piped through audio onto the set is also piped through audio and video into our monitors here in the production office," Marcus Pooley said.

"And," Stephanie added, still looking sour at the thought of that ickiness on her set, "I am aware that Janice colored her hair because we were both together in Las Vegas when that happened. We were . . . slightly drunk." She looked awkwardly toward, but definitely not at, her husband. "She'll have blonde hair by the time we shoot tomorrow night," she said quickly, which was as close to apologetic as it appeared she would get.

"She—*you what?*" Marcus Pooley aimed his hate at his wife.

"It's taken care of. I have a hairdresser coming in from off the lot to work with Janice this afternoon." Stephanie didn't like being confronted—nor did she like being confronted in front of J.T. and Ash by her annoying husband.

"Excuse me," J.T. said, "but how am I to deal with the cast of *Urban Buddies*, who want a pay raise because they saw their pic-

ture for the third time on the front of a *TV Guide* and are refusing to work?"

"I said: *We are aware of the problem with the cast of Urban Buddies and are dealing with it as we speak.* They will be ready to work first thing tomorrow morning." Marcus Pooley had the tone of a chess player who knows he's in control of the board.

"Well, first thing tomorrow morning is *noon*," J.T. reminded them. "Tomorrow is shoot night so we only get the cast for ten hours plus dinner. We shoot at seven in front of a live audience. We have a page-one rewrite that none of them have looked at. Oh— and they refuse to be directed. They said, verbatim, 'We will sit on the couch and move when we feel like it.'"

> **The Hollywood Dictionary**
>
> **"FIRST THING TOMORROW MORNING":** A phrase uttered in Hollywood more than "I love you" or "You're fired."

"Well, isn't that too bad for you?" Stephanie Pooley said with delight.

"You have your work cut out for you, unless you are too incompetent to fix this situation, and therefore incompetent to do your job. Therefore, too incompetent to fulfill your duties; and to be paid." Marcus Pooley felt like he was one move away from checkmate.

"How on this earth do you make any connection between their poor professional behavior and my competence to do my job?" J.T. fired back. "Ash, please make a note of this."

Ash quickly took out his university notebook and wrote down everything that was happening—as if it mattered. *At least it makes J.T. feel better,* Ash thought.

"Well, you are the one who empowered them with the concept of sticking together and taking care of each other," Marcus went on, throwing a deliberate curveball. "I think your words were, 'There will be lots of directors, lots of executives who come and go, but you as actors are vulnerable, and to be strong you must always take care of each other and watch each other's back. Especially since you are a hit show.' And you are the one who not only went against me, your boss, but in doing that, got Kirk Kelly a raise. Of course the others want a raise, too." He smirked. "You've really fucked up. Mr. J.T. Big-Director-Man."

"I see. You think that what I said helped fuel this backlash? This refusal to work? Their demands for a pay raise?" J.T. was now worried he might actually be held responsible for this breakdown in the sitcom week—a frightening and sobering thought, even if it wasn't true. He could never get into a legal battle with the likes of the network, the studio, or the Pooleys. Not on these trumped-up, bogus, but somehow convincing charges.

J.T. ran his hand over his hair, a sure sign to Ash that he was about to backpedal. "I only meant to strengthen their backbone and give them confidence," J.T. said in what he hoped was a reasonable tone. "I was trying to get them to feel comfortable before the Tuesday run-through and to stop backstabbing one another during the scenes. They had a tendency not to *play* the scenes but wanted to *win* the scenes. The speech I give is to encourage a working relationship that breeds nurturing and teamwork rather than selfish star mentalities. It's always worked before in the past on pilots I've directed that have gone on to be hit shows."

"Goody-goody for you. All I know is that I have six regular characters that *play* our Urban Buddies and they all want a pay raise in year two!" Marcus Pooley shouted.

"Look, I can realize how . . . distressed you may be, but the television flame burns hot and fast. These young people realized that they were on the cover of next week's *TV Guide* and they're being called the only sure hit of the season and we've created money monsters in this business. There's no way to get away from the past few years and the kind of money that's being thrown at actors on hit shows. These kids probably know they've hit the lottery. They want to milk it for all it's worth. I can't completely blame them because I know what you and the rest of the *above-the-liners* are making off of a hit show."

Oops, thought Ash. J.T. had been doing okay until that point.

"Here's what *I* have learned, J.T. Baker," Marcus Pooley said, toxic from mixing stimulants and downers (and who knew what else), "I expect you to shoot a show tomorrow that is worthy of *I Love My Urban Buddies* being on the cover of *TV Guide* three times in two years. I expect that. I expect nothing less. I expect it with absolutely no excuses. I have been patient, and up until now—"

Yeah, you're about as patient as a rattlesnake, J.T. thought.

"What did you say to me?"

"I said that out loud?" J.T. asked.

"Are you really that stupid?" Marcus looked at J.T. like he was getting the greatest idea of all time. "Yes! A Reality Show. We'll call it *Are You Really That Stupid?!* You can be the pilot episode. Just you. Steph, hand me my little video camera. We'll start shooting right now."

Stephanie actually did grab the small home video camera (which Marcus had brought in just in case anyone else decided to blow their brains out), and she aimed it at J.T. and began shooting. The whole scene had shifted from the absurd to the surreal, so that J.T. suddenly imagined himself a character in a Fellini film.

Controlling every action so that he didn't shift from outraged to violent, J.T. gently put his hand on the video camera and pushed it down. He did notice, though, that while she was shooting, it was the only time Ms. Pooley ever actually looked directly at him.

"I know you and your wife have a problem with me—"

Stephanie Pooley threw the video camera to the floor, where it broke in two. "A 'problem with you'? That's the understatement of a lifetime. We hate you, you fuck." Yes. She really said that.

"You broke my camera, Steph," Marcus hissed angrily under his bad breath.

"Later," Stephanie warned her mate.

"You know . . ." J.T. said, "if I weren't a gentleman, I would clean your clock, lady. I would go after you first because I have come to realize that you are a tougher rival than your husband, who I think would scream like a schoolgirl. I don't want trouble, but if you ever treat me this poorly again, I will change your life. So I urge you both: Let's keep this as civil as we can." J.T. stared both of them down.

Stephanie and Marcus most certainly wanted to get J.T. into a position where they could let him go because of his temper; that was and had been their plan from the moment they decided they didn't like him. But they never figured on being alone with J.T. when he finally snapped, so they suddenly became very cautious. So did Ash. He watched J.T.'s feet to see if they were heading toward the Pooleys. That would be his cue to step in and not let J.T. self-destruct with infantile behavior, no matter how satisfying it would be for him at that moment.

"I need to know: Are you threatening us? Physically?" Marcus Pooley asked.

"I need to know," J.T. countered: "Are you firing me, *metaphysically*? Are you threatening to fire me? I've heard from Dick Beaglebum that the two of you are going to make sure that I *never work in this town again*. Is that a threat, a fact, or are you so unoriginal that you can't come up with your own invectives? What kind of game are we playing? How real are the odds? I've been doing this all my life—I'm willing to play with you. Are you willing to play with me?"

There was something in J.T.'s tone that was slightly insane, a menace that made even Ash uncomfortable. He started pulling J.T., who was so focused on his enemies that even he had forgotten about the sitcom itself, toward the door. "J.T.," he said, "let's get back to the set and get ready, the best we can, for tomorrow."

* * *

J.T. AND ASH left. Marcus Pooley and Stephanie Pooley looked at each other like they'd both just realized that they needed diapers. J.T. had made quite an impact that only strengthened his *passionate* reputation.

"He's fucking insane!" Marcus trembled.

"We needed a witness. We had him. We could let him go based on his temper alone," Stephanie agreed. Then she brightened. "Do you think we could pay the black guy to be our witness? He probably wants to direct. Maybe we could offer him some deal in year ten."

"Not a bad idea," Marcus seethed, "but we wouldn't have had to pay anybody if you hadn't broken my fuckin' video camera!" His sentence was a crescendo building into a scream.

"Later," was all Steph had to say to get Marcus to shut up.

As J.T. AND ASH walked back to the set, Asher was assessing the week and wondering how the hell this show would ever get shot by the next night, with a live audience, no less.

"That's part of this awful game," J.T. said, as if he could hear Ash's thoughts. "There is always a way. And the network believes that. No matter how awful the week, these people always get their shows done. Now it is my job to be clever enough to figure out how to direct a bunch of actors who don't want to be directed—how to get them to memorize sixty-five pages even though they will never be able to memorize sixty-five pages by the shoot— to figure out how to shoot this puppy with camera people who don't know where the actors are going to move and still be proud of the episode once it is finished."

"It sounds impossible," Ash said.

"This is a very easy business if you really break it down," J.T. said to Ash, for a moment his professor again. "Believe me—I'll sit on the set for a half an hour or all night but—I'll figure it out. Let's bet on it. Five bucks. Whattaya say? It'll give me an incentive." J.T. smiled.

Ash returned the smile. "It may be the easiest five bucks I'll ever make."

"In all of the years that I've shot sitcoms, I have never had a Friday night go down in flames. Believe me, the odds are with me, not you, my friend."

And the two men disappeared inside the cave of Stage Five. J.T. knew all eyes from every crew member were watching his every move. They all were interpreting how the next few hours would go, how tomorrow would go, just based on J.T.'s body language.

J.T. sat down on the couch, relaxed, and spread out. He looked up at the crew and smiled. He was in the mode of *However long it takes me, I'm going to get it done, so no use in complaining.*

"You may all go home," J.T. announced. "Tomorrow's going to be one helluva day and night. Thor can tell you what time your calls are, but I'm pretty sure we meet at noon. *We're going to shoot a show.* The best show we possibly can. I just haven't figured out exactly how we're going to accomplish this task, but make no bones about it: *We're going to get it done and we're going to feel proud of our work once we're finished.* So . . . my advice? Get a really good night's sleep. You're going to need it." J.T. finished by just melting into the couch on the set. He sat there and thought, *How can I pull this off? How . . . ?*

J.T. watched everyone pack up for the day. He sat on the couch where all of the Urban Buddies had become famous. As he sat there, he smelled the microwave popcorn, the sign that the electricians would be there working on lights for a few hours. And he could smell the special cappuccino maker, which also made hot chocolate, a comfort "food" for him. He loved having hot chocolate with his son Jeremy. Jeremy. *Yes,* J.T. thought, *I will shoot this fucking show.*

"So," Ash said, handing J.T. an unexpected cup of hot chocolate, "what's on your mind?"

"I think . . ." J.T. began, but his eyes were caught somewhere between the land of the fake park and the dead squirrel. "I'll make you a deal, Ash. Get me about fifty white sheets of foam core—you can get them from Mick McCoy—and then I'll need two rolls of gaffer's tape and six magic markers—all different colors, they have those in the prop department—and oh, you've gotta catch them before they leave, and make sure there is a ladder that can stay out for me all night—if you can do all of that in the next five minutes, then you can go home and get a good night's sleep. And owe me five bucks."

The Hollywood Dictionary

FOAM CORE: White cardboard used by directors of photography to bounce hard light off the white surface and fill the actor's face with soft, attractive, movie-star light.

J.T. was onto something and Ash could tell that he was beginning to get excited about his oversized order of office supplies. As a matter of fact, J.T. was starting to get a little goofy with disobedience by habit. Ash knew that some of it was sheer cussedness: J.T. wouldn't go down without a fight, and was prepared to stay up all night and come up with a magical solution. Most of it, though, was obviously simple exhaustion.

J.T. wrote CAMERA TEST on a script and angled it at the camera that was sending the live signal to the Pooleys' offices. Then, in front of the camera, he cupped his right hand to Ash's ear and whispered—making sure that the Pooleys (because he knew they'd be watching) knew he was whispering. Something about being secretive made J.T. feel silly and triumphant. He knew the Pooleys wanted to know everything. Now he was showing them that there was something on his mind—and they didn't know what it was. It was a kindergarten power play, but hey, *know your opponent*, J.T. thought.

"Ash—" J.T. whispered, "the brats don't want to be directed but they're not good enough yet to direct themselves. They also don't know their lines. *All I have to do is treat the episode like a giant puzzle.* Okay—if I color-coordinate each character's dialogue and write it out on cue cards, place the cue cards on each individual set in such a way that the actors *have to get up and walk to a certain spot to see and read their lines,* then, in fact, *I have actually directed them.* I've made them move *and* know their lines. And I'll coordinate the shooting scripts for each camera operator so they will know where the actor is going in each and every scene, for each and every line! It's going to work, Ash." J.T. was hopping up and down with excitement, painfully gulping the very hot hot chocolate.

Ash laughed. "That's . . . fucking *brilliant,*" he said with true admiration.

"Ash—grab Mick before he leaves. Tell him I need to see him ASAP. And see if Kirk is still on the lot. If he is, tell him to come see me on the stage."

"Will do," Ash said, and ran off to catch Mick and Kirk before they left. J.T. happened to look up and saw that he was on the live feed. He just smiled.

BACK IN THEIR offices, Marcus and Stephanie had each been staring at their flat-screen LCD monitors.

"He's smiling. If I fuckin' had a gun, I'd kill him," Marcus spat.

"You do have a gun, you twerp," Stephanie spat back. She'd come back to Marcus's office and overheard him. He hated it when she did that.

"I mean here. On the lot. Not at home."

"You want mine? It's in my purse."

Marcus looked at his wife as if he'd never actually seen her before.

"What?"

"Steph, you have a gun? I mean . . . you carry a gun?"

"What of it?"

"Go shoot him!" Marcus demanded.

"Fuck that. I'm not gonna end up in some HBO movie about a showrunner who shot her director. You go shoot him. You're the one who said if you had a gun you'd kill him. Here. Here's my gun." Stephanie pulled a small handgun out of her purse.

"Wow. You could shoot . . . me?"

Stephanie put the gun back in her purse. "I wouldn't dwell on it, Poodles. But I wouldn't forget it, either."

ASH DELIVERED EVERYTHING J.T. had asked for, including Mick and Kirk. He was also thrilled with the notion that J.T. was happy and had a theory . . . but it was only a theory. He said as much to J.T. "And," he continued, "it's going to take you forever. I mean all night. You won't be done until . . . shit; it's a massive job. I've got to stay and help you."

"No," J.T. wouldn't hear of it. "It's very important that tomorrow one of us is rested. Besides . . ." J.T. stared off at the set, part of his mind preoccupied with his brainstorming, "I don't have time to talk or be nice . . . you get that. I've got to act out each character in the scene and know exactly where I can hang these cue cards so that they are never in the shots but also it doesn't look like our actors are reading them because I've taped the cue cards in the wrong eyeline. I might end up acting like an ass tonight—you know, get pissy 'cause I'm already tired—and I don't want you on the receiving end of that. It's best I do this alone. But I think this'll work, Ash." J.T. mugged for the monitor again. "I'll have plenty of time to rest this weekend. Go get some sleep, my friend. Oh, and one last favor you could do me: Can you go by Oliver's and get my suit, and bring it tomorrow?"

"Suit. You got it." Ash knew when it was pointless to protest. He gave his brother-from-another-life a hug and, against his better judgment, followed J.T.'s wishes and left the cave for the night.

Mick and Kirk had been waiting just out of the sight lines of the monitor where Ash had asked them to stand. Kirk hung back, but Mick now started toward J.T. "You wanted to see me, J.T.?"

J.T. met him and pulled him off to the side so that the live feed couldn't see the two of them conspiring.

"Mick," J.T. whispered, "I want to ask a . . . delicate favor. It puts you on the line and I don't want any political harm to ever come to you, so say no if this is too much."

"What, J.T.?"

"You know the film that is at the lab and never was developed? The shot that 'wasn't on TV'?"

"I'm on it," Mick smiled.

"Can you get it digitized by tomorrow evening so I can use it as a playback on the monitors for the audience without it going through the Pooleys or the editor?"

"Say no more. It's as good as done." Mick had a contagious smile. He marched with new purpose out of the cave to make the single phone call to his "man at the lab" that would ensure the footage would be there by morning.

Then J.T. went over to Kirk, who by this time was

> ### The Hollywood Dictionary
>
> **DIGITIZING:** (1) The process of converting analog film into digital video information so it can be played back as video footage. (2) One take means that an editor doesn't have to be involved in the digital playback. (3) A huge gamble.

beginning to step a little back and forth in nervous excitement. "Kirk, I'm going to trust you. I'm also going to need your help."

"You name it, J.T."

"I don't understand your . . . reading disability. Can you help me?"

"How?"

"Well, Kirk, I'm going to write cue cards out for you and I need to know that you'll be able to read them. In case I alter a line, here or there."

"Oh," Kirk said quietly.

"Tell me. I want to make this work for you."

"Well," Kirk began. Nervous was getting the better of excited, and his physical tics became more pronounced. He moved backward two steps, then forward two steps, twisting his head from one side to the other and touching the boom stand in between each move. "It's not that simple . . ." he finally said.

"How can I make it simple?"

"Can you fax me my lines? I can learn my lines one sentence at a time."

J.T. looked around the set and picked up a page of yesterday's rewrites that was discarded on the cave floor. "Write down your fax number," he said, giving Kirk the page and a pen. "What else?"

"Well—"

"I'm planning on writing all the Buddies' lines on cue cards in different colors."

"Shit, J.T. Colors really fuck me up. Can my lines be in black?"

"Black! They'll be in black."

"But you'll still have to fax me. I, I, I, can't do it—I, I, I, can't do it—"

J.T. put his steady hands on Kirk's shoulders. "Kirk, I will do anything, everything, to make this work for you. I'll fax you your lines and I'll write your cues in black. But just know that you have to do something for me."

"What?"

"When you hear that fax machine ring, that's the start of your day. This isn't going to be like any other shoot day. Get up, study, and show these fucks what you can do."

"Okay. Okay." Kirk was now in a tornado of compulsive behavior.

"Kirk, is there anything else? Tell me. Tell me and I'll do it for you."

"Um, well, um, if I get the pages early enough, I can have my girlfriend read them into my computer. My computer can talk. Isn't that cool?"

"Yeah, that's pretty cool," J.T. said, suddenly reminded that he was talking to a bona fide *person*. "You'll get them before daybreak."

"And whenever my girlfriend's not around, I can type 'em into my computer and I can have the computer read them back to me, over and over again. It's just so cool."

"Looks like you're finding ways to handle your . . . so what else?"

"Well, um, maybe for *the best ever Christmas* words, if I have to say them, you could draw a Santa face?"

"A Santa face equals the best ever Christmas?"

"Is that stupid?"

"Will it help you?"

"A lot."

"Then it certainly isn't stupid. Tell me more. Teach me—what else?"

"Well, um, if you could keep the sentences short. That would help a lot."

"You got it."

J.T. could see how frightened Kirk still was. "Listen to me, Kirk. You will be more prepared than anyone else. Also, tomorrow, if there is anything, anything at all, that is bothering you or that makes you feel like you can't pull this off, come to me and we'll fix it. I swear to God, Kirk, I will take care of you. That is my job. I will not let you down. Okay?"

Kirk wanted to believe J.T., but still wasn't used to anyone in show business looking out for his best interests. "I guess we'll, um, see, um, what happens."

"The worst thing that can happen is that I call 'Cut!' and pretend we have technical problems and you and I will go behind the set and figure everything out. I am there for you, Kirk."

"Okay. Fax! Don't forget to fax!"

"I'm there for you."

J.T. gave Kirk a genuine hug. Kirk left the cave still dealing with his demons.

J.T. WAS VERY pleased with himself. Finally alone on the stage, he sat back on the couch and started to look for secret places to hide all of the cue cards that would have to be numbered and would need to synchronize with each script he had to make up for each individual cameraperson. But first J.T. went over to the camera that was sending the live feed up to the production office and pointed it at the EXIT sign.

MARCUS WAS NOW alone. "That fuck," he muttered. Then he yelled at the monitor, "Good thing my wife took the gun, or else you'd be a fuckin' dead director walkin' . . . directing . . . you'd be dead! Dead!"

J.T. BEGAN. ON and on he went, writing out cue cards, walking through each scene as each character, walking through each scene as each individual camera, trying to make sure that no camera was ever in any other camera's shot and no actor was ever blocking any other actor, all by the exact placement of each distinctly colored cue card—black for Kirk and a Santa face for *the best ever Christmas.*

I hope nobody else is color-blind, he thought. Then laughed at the irony, because that was the way he would've written this conflict. At least that was the way Paddy Chayefsky would've written it.

Paddy Chayefsky, the famed screenplay writer who wrote *Network*. Paddy Chayefsky, who'd died at the age of fifty-eight, only nine years older than J.T. was now. Paddy Chayefsky, who had a *funny* name . . . and knew it.

"Paddy Chayefsky," J.T. said aloud. Then, over and over again, "Paddy Chayefsky Paddy Chayefsky." He giggled, then laughed loudly. "I'm mad as hell and I'm not going to take it anymore!" he yelled. His favorite dead writer had suddenly become his muse. J.T. grabbed the colored pens, opened the Pooleys' script and began to copy "most" of the lines onto cue cards *almost* as written. *Thank you, Paddy Chayefsky, wherever you are.*

J.T. looked up to the rafters and paid tribute. Then got to work.

IT WAS 5:43 in the morning, according to the studio clock. J.T. had finished the last cue card with the last Santa face, hung it in the precise place for the actor, and marked up each camera operator's script with the corresponding moves, notes, and diagrams.

He'd also snuck in some rewrites. Not many, but enough.

J.T. went into the A.D.'s office and ran off a dozen copies of the newly marked-up scripts for the crew and crew only. The first copy to come off the $80,000 Xerox machine went into William's fax. J.T. keyed Kirk's number into the fax and watched as each page made it to North Hollywood. When J.T. closed his eyes, he could feel the surge of fear that would awaken Kirk on the other end of the fax line. So be it . . .

J.T. finally allowed himself to feel the exhaustion. It hit him as he put the brads into the holes of the final script for his crew. He curled up on the couch that had already made six young people millionaires, and dreamed.

He saw his slightly younger self in the mountains of Tennessee assistant-coaching for his son's basketball tournament. He strode like Paul Bunyan to Utah, where he hovered over a class of Mormon children he'd once taught. He skimmed the land back to the New York City of his childhood and his first acting gigs, then leapt kitty-corner to L.A., where he'd become famous and gotten blackballed.

In each location, there were televisions, front and center: in the home of an Appalachian dad who was eking out a living making moonshine for his family who had no indoor plumbing. In the classroom in the desert. In the airless Manhattan audition room. On the set of his breakout movie. And in each place, whether it was the child J.T., the children around him, or his own son with his face softly lit by the flicker from the TV, the children were watching the Best Christmas Ever. J.T. felt himself shrinking reluctantly from his Bunyan height above L.A. down, down, to where he was responsible for what those children knew, what those children wanted, what they visually and cerebrally absorbed, all because he was the one who decided what they saw. *The Best Ever,* his dream self said. Then he heard, *Pull it all down?*

Friday

THE LATE NIGHT set-mice had gone back into hiding, the rats were never completely gone, and the birds who'd been trapped in the rafters overnight flew back outside into the pinkish Los Angeles air as soon as the big elephant doors opened. Who knew where the stage ghosts went . . . maybe they hung around just for the mere awe of it all—the waste.

"D'ya think we should pull it all down?" The members of the painting crew were looking in puzzlement at all of the cue cards that were hanging out of the way of the lights.

J.T.'s guilt-inducing dream and the awareness of imminent disaster converged, and he bolted awake and came running in a panic.

"Please—no! Nobody pull down the cue cards! Please. Thank you very much. Just touch up the paint wherever you need to, but please, for God's sake, *please don't touch the cue cards!*"

J.T. made it just in time. What took about ten hours to strategize, plan, and position could have taken minutes to destroy.

William entered the cave limping, looking slightly ill, and smoking a cigarette. "Yeah, I'm smoking. Fuck it," he said before J.T. could comment. "You know how hard it is to finish a triathlon? Fuck! I was cramping after the swim. I was smoking after a mile on the bike. I gave up. Dumped my fucking bike in the bushes at the marina and hitched a ride home. Who in their fuckin' right mind would be a triathlete? Fuck, I hurt. After sex," William moaned, sincerely.

"Well, you missed . . . a lot. Yep. A whole lot. I'm getting fired, but you probably knew that," J.T. said.

"No!" William exclaimed, trying to be shocked and sincere. William was only capable of one falsehood at a time, so sincere was basically the only false emotion you got from William that was *almost* believable.

"Fuck you, William. You know I love you. You know we go back a million fucking years. But—shit, don't play me. I was history by at least Wednesday," J.T. said.

"Tuesday, after run-through," William said, sincerely.

"Yeah . . . I had a feeling."

"Where's Bling-Bling?" William asked.

"William, you are actually the one person here I could kill and somehow get away with it. Never call Ash 'Bling-Bling' again. Understand?"

"Sorry. I'm just grouchy. I'm in pain. I got fuckin' blisters everywhere. I mean, everywhere! I got blisters on my fuckin' balls! After sex."

J.T. had no time to listen to William complain. "William—quick long-story-shorter: we had no run-through, no blocking, not even a rehearsal. The actors, the Buddies, held out for more money and *don't want to be directed,* so I spent the night here putting up cue cards and synchronizing each cue with a specific camera move. So please—*no shit*—whatever you do—DO NOT LET ANYONE TOUCH THE CUE CARDS! I can't say it with enough emphasis. We've got *no show* tonight without those cue cards. Got it?!"

J.T. had to make sure William was a part of this campaign to let the cue cards remain hung. He needed William to be a watchdog, to bark at anyone who went near the cue cards—no matter what department they were from.

"And," J.T. continued, "if someone from the camera department wants to move a card because of light—COME TO ME FIRST!"

"You're the man! No one touches the cue cards. I got blisters under my armpits from the swim!" William tried to show J.T. "Oh, but anyway, how's my bro? All good in da hood?" he asked, sincerely. Then, without even thinking twice about it, he took out a bottle of liquid Vicodin and took a gulp.

J.T. tried to rub the sleep out of his eyes. "What is it with you people? What are you doing? Do you hate your job so much that you need to numb yourselves?"

William glowered sincerely at J.T. "Hey, don't gimme shit. I hate my job—don't you?"

"No. I hate certain things *about* my job, but I love ... other things," J.T. managed to say.

"Well, if you had to be an assistant director and everyone was chewing your ass out every second of every fuckin' day and everything was basically your fault, you'd hate your job. Plus—I think I got blisters inside my nose from breathin' so hard and I need to smoke and get numb till I die." It was the most sincerely sincere thing William had said all week.

"Well, it's good to know that my assistant is fucked up on drugs and half the cast is on liquid Vicodin, too," J.T. said sanctimoniously.

William got defensive. "Liquid 'V' is the drug of the month. Rocky Brook gets it by the fucking case. I think from a dentist. As soon as he gets bored with a drug or it doesn't give him the buzz he wants anymore, we'll be on to a different designer med. It's fun stuff, J.T. Makes the day go faster. You oughta try it. Sincerely. Want some? You won't mind bein' fired."

"I think I'll pass, William."

"Oxycontin?"

"If any P.A. is making a smoothie run, count me in. Narcotics? Count me out. Clear?"

"Cool. Clear," William said, sincerely on his way to being stoned.

"Shit, I got blisters on my asshole. After sex." William froze. He thought about that last comment. "Whoa, I certainly didn't mean I had blisters on my asshole after sex. You know that, right, J.T.?"

"Whatever." J.T. dismissed anything and everything that wasn't directly related to getting this show shot.

It was eleven o'clock and the camera personnel were coming in to get their equipment ready. J.T. ran to meet them and try to call a quick meeting with Mick McCoy there, as a source of strength.

"Guys, gals, aliens, and other insane and insecure creatures like me who choose sitcoms as a way to make a living: I have tried something out of desperation. As most of you know, I had no time to work with our beloved Buddies. So I wrote out all of their lines on cue cards that they cannot see *unless* they physically go to specific places where I want them to go. Hopefully, they won't think of it as direction. Maybe they'll think I did 'em some kind of favor or that it's part of my job description. I don't know. It doesn't matter because I've been unofficially fired by the Pooleys. Now, I have coordinated scripts for each camera that synchronize with the cue cards so you will know who to frame up on, and if it's a single, an over, or a master." J.T. began handing out the scripts to the department heads.

"It's all been documented and diagrammed for each individual camera. I know there will be confusion at first, but I think once each of you gets the hang of what I am trying to accomplish and we discuss any funky spots you may have, we might actually complete tonight's show."

"My God," Mick said, "this is . . . unreal. This is so above and beyond the call of duty. J.T., does anyone know what you're about to pull off?"

"Only you guys. To everyone else . . . who gives *an excuse-my-French*," J.T. said.

The crew members had their assignments and the cast had to be on their marks in order to read their lines, so, except for the performance, the show was shot and in the can.

Skip's way of showing his gratitude was typical of the crew's reaction. He held out his hand for J.T. to shake. "You're a real fuck, J.T."

"Is that a compliment, Skip?"

"Hey, my own mother's a real fuck."

"Like I said, 'Is that a compliment?'"

The two veterans exchanged a very brief, very genuine smile. Then it was back to cynicism as usual.

KIRK WAS LISTENING to an mp3 of his lines on his iPod through tiny earbuds. The crew thought he was listen-

> **The Hollywood Dictionary**
>
> **MASTER SHOT:** A shot that is wide enough to include all the action and that sets the visual geography.
>
> **OVER:** A shot that is framed to include the back of one actor's shoulder, focusing in the facial expressions of the other actor who is facing the camera; a.k.a. a "dirty single."
>
> **SINGLE SHOT:** A tight shot of an actor; a.k.a. a "floating head."

ing to music. It really didn't matter what anyone thought he was doing; Kirk was a *Buddy* on this hit show, and to the camera crew, there was no rhyme or even rap to what the actors did on the set. The crew members just continued their schmuck-work.

So did Kirk. He diligently followed the path of the cue cards for every scene, smiled every time he saw one of J.T.'s drawings of a Santa face, and when he was comfortable, came over to J.T. and spontaneously hugged him.

"Thank you."

J.T. blinked, and nodded in return. It was their secret, and he wanted to keep it that way.

"Kirk!" Lance's silhouette appeared in the doorway to the cave, the bright Hollywood light behind him piercing the surrealism of the cave. "Kirk, come on out here with your fellow thespians. The studio's got *a little something* for you."

Kirk kept the earbuds in place, but started to jog in the direction of his real boss.

Ash, looking rested, came up to J.T. and grinned. "Here's your five bucks," he said happily.

"How long have you been here?"

"Long enough to hear your speech. Listen, you might want to take a quick stroll out to the parking spots next to the stage." He wouldn't say more, just turned and fell in beside a curious J.T.

As they stepped outside into the oppressive heat, their eyes had to adjust to more than the sunlight. Rocky Brook, Devon Driver, Kirk Kelly, Betty Balz, Janice Hairston, and Helena (just Helena, thank you) were each standing next to a brand-new Porsche sports car. Mingling with them was a seven-foot red bird. Kalamazoo P. Kardinal, or rather the guy being paid scale to wear the suit, was hugging and mugging while a man from *People* magazine took their pictures.

"A whole bunch o' shiny, squeaky wheels getting oiled," J.T. muttered to Ash.

Lance was there to ensure that the newly crowned celebrities were *not abused* by the media. Standing to one side waiting their turn were the cameraman and reporter from *Entertainment Tonight,* followed by *Extra, E! News,* and some other crews that would have to grab "B" roll because they didn't weigh in as heavyweights.

The Hollywood Dictionary

"B" ROLL: Footage of stars doing something newsworthy, shot by second-tier entertainment shows to be shown on TV while the hosts of the shows read happy, clever quips as voice-overs, pretending they aren't seething because they didn't get an interview.

J.T. walked over to Lance, who looked strangely cheerful. "So, looks like you guys had to concede," J.T. said in an undertone, watching Deb manipulate each and every shot to include the big red bird.

"Quite the opposite! Just beat Deb and the network to the punch," Lance chirped in delight, forgetting who he was talking to.

"Make sure that, like, Kalamazoo P. Kardinal is in the foreground of every shot!" Debbie warned all the camera people, actually making eye contact to make sure that she was most certainly understood. "Do you, like, understand me? Tell me you, like, understand me!" The camera people all nodded. "Man, I'd *like*, like, to fuck her," the cameraman from A&E whispered, his sweaty eye stuck to the sweaty eyepiece of his Arriflex camera.

"I thought you were gonna say, 'like, fuck her *up*,'" the cameraman from Bravo whispered back, his sweaty eye stuck to his sweaty video eyepiece.

"Nah," the A&E cameraman said, "just fuck her."

Kalamazoo P. Kardinal began to negotiate his large bird costume toward the stacks of water bottles. "I'm dyin' in here. I gotta get a drink. Water. Please."

"Like, fuck the water, big bird." Debbie pushed Kalamazoo P. Kardinal deeper into the shots, making the poor, sweaty mascot-guy get into an automobile with the celebrities. "Like, get in the shot, you fuckin' bird. Whattaya think we pay you for? To drink? Can you, like, hear me under those fucking feathers?"

"Lady," a muffled, overheated sound came from inside the Kardinal costume, "I'm gonna hava fuckin' heatstroke in here."

"Do that and, like, forget about the other Kardinal gigs we've got lined up for you. I'll, like, find another guy to hop into the bird suit so fast you'll be able to drink water till you, like, drown. I'm talkin' replacing you faster than Disney character voices find sound-alikes! Now, like, get in the fucking shot!"

> **The Hollywood Dictionary**
>
> **SOUND-ALIKES:** When a studio refuses to pay an animated character voice actor his or her salary, it hires sound-alikes at scale, thereby saving the studio a few hundred bucks.

Lance leaned back against the warmth of the cave's exterior. It felt good on his back. Everything felt good to Lance now.

"We gave the kids a *slight* pay raise," he said to J.T., "and if the show remains the hit that it is, then they'll get a *significant* pay raise next year. We're even starting to negotiate the syndication fees. Piddly, but makes them feel appreciated. Second season and everyone smells the money on this one. Just a sec." He circled his hand in the air to signal to the Thing in charge of controlling the flow of the media crews to get *People* out and move *ET* in. "But we didn't get hit at all, actually," he continued in a more conspiratorial tone. "It's creative *product placement*. The studio got a sweet deal with the car manufacturer. I mean, it's great publicity for them. The six hottest, hippest young people in the country, the world maybe, are getting their pictures taken and their interviews done in front of *the only car they would ever want to drive*—at least, that's what the PR release says. And the network couldn't be more pleased. As you can see, Kalamazoo P. Kardinal is in every shot. The corporate iconograph that soon will compete with the Golden Arches for brand recognition."

J.T. wondered how this was any different from putting Saks Fifth Avenue on a shopping bag, but for once he kept his mouth shut. His eyes followed the *Entertainment Tonight* crew's camera, which was pointed at Devon Driver and Kalamazoo P. Kardinal. The *ET* interviewer was a trendy redhead who was noticeably taken with Devon.

"Devon, can you explain what is going on here, at the studio lot in front of soundstage number five where *I Love My Urban*

Buddies is shot?" the redhead asked seductively. Her cameraman snorted. The edgiest of the *ET* reporters was suddenly dripping with television-host affectation.

"Well, Sabrina," Devon said, the sun glinting off his slicked hair, "this is, like, a bittersweet day. I'd like all my fans to know we're here, like, to pay our last respects to Minnesota B. Moose and, like, welcome Kalamazoo P. Kardinal as the next network icon."

What is it with this "like" shit? J.T. grumped to himself.

Devon hugged the big red bird awkwardly, trying to keep his hair out of the way of its wing.

"Like, very, very good!" Deb nodded like a bobble-head network doll. "Everyone, like, get *that*? If you didn't, like, get it—like, *get it!*"

"And tell us about those magnificent cars that each one of you received today."

"The cars, like, represent the studio's and the network's appreciation for our hard work and their confidence in the fact that *I Love My Urban Buddies* is a number one show and will continue to be a number one show!"

"Like, very good!" Deb said in approval.

"I have to ditto that!" Lance dittoed.

J.T. felt himself being seduced by the media circus as if it were the Cirque du Soleil. He forced himself to turn away, and pulled Lance aside. "When do you think I'll get the six hottest young faces known to mankind this month for rehearsal? Will I get them in fifteen minutes? A half hour? Lance—no matter what the politics, your show that is going to make everyone rich and famous, and in your case add more *P* to your Vice Presidency of Current Comedy, has not been rehearsed for more than . . . I'd say an hour and forty-five minutes *all week*."

Lance's eyes kept straying to the sight of his perfect demographics getting far-reaching publicity. "Lance," J.T. protested, trying to keep his voice nonconfrontational, "we shoot tonight and then this pop-culture-phenomenon-in-the-making will air to millions of people, and you know what? It'll be pure shit. Pop goes the pop star. If I were you, I'd get them onto the stage as fast as you can, Lance. Just a suggestion. No matter how you plan to screw me out of my next two shows, on this episode, we're *teammates*."

Maybe he got a new car, too. Ah, who gives a fuck, J.T. thought. *The kids still aren't working.*

"'The future is literally in our hands to mold as we like. But we cannot wait until tomorrow. Tomorrow is now.' You know who said that, J.T.? Eleanor Roosevelt. A great woman. Would've made a great Executive. You know, for the Lifetime channel or some other female cabler."

"Are you comparing yourself to Eleanor Roosevelt, Lance?" The whole situation was deviant enough without that.

"You know, I'd have to think about that one," Lance said, and then continued without thinking, "I guess I am. I guess I am."

"You . . . are."

"I would've made a helluva first lady, if I may say so myself."

"Well, you just did."

"J.T.—*this* is what it's about. Not the show. It's them. Their charm and ability to get Americans to invite them on a weekly basis into their living rooms, bedrooms, what-have-you is a recipe that cannot be altered. They represent our complete annihilation of the other networks on Thursday nights. The red bird. The show? Ah . . . we'll get viewers, and the advertisers will get new buyers, and all will be good. Some sparkling moments, some great shows, and then a few turds like your show. So you just go back inside like a good little director and wait for our franchise to finish and then we'll knock out a show tonight—if not, we'll piece something together. It always gets done. You know that, J.T. Take a chill pill. I hear that the liquid Vicodin is flowing like tap water these days. Get yourself a bottle and just let it all happen. You can't fight it: television is the window to our souls," Lance finished in a philosophical non sequitur.

"May I suggest window coverings and blackout curtains?" J.T. countered.

"Hmm?" Lance may have been on Ecstasy.

There was nothing more that J.T. could do ... and no more bridges, canals, straits, tunnels, burrows, dens, lairs—you name it—for him to burn, vaporize, invade, or otherwise obliterate.

THE STRAGGLERS AMONG the media crews were being shooed off the lot. Janice stroked her Porsche and called to the others, "Hey, let's take these out and see how fast they go!"

"How many tourists you plan on mowing down, Janice?" Rocky snorted. He couldn't sneak any drugs while the media were watching, and now he was getting surly.

"Um, we do have a show to do, people?" Devon reminded them, suddenly the superior artist again. "I don't know about you guys, but I'm, you know, an artist? There's *work* to be done."

Slowly it dawned on the Buddies what that meant.

WHILE EVERYONE ELSE associated with *Buddies* was getting ready for the dinner break, the six actual Buddies came back inside the stage, still a little high from their triumph. Representing all of the Buddies, Devon Driver walked over and sat stiffly next to J.T., who was relaxing and playing mental Ping-Pong (right–wrong–right–wrong ...) on the famous TV couch. Devon addressed J.T. as if he were still in negotiations, very businesslike and distant, with a touch of bad acting-class stress patterns thrown in for credibility.

"So, like, we as a group want *to know,* like, how we are supposed *to shoot* tonight's episode," Devon announced.

J.T. couldn't resist a little sarcasm. "Well, if it is all right with you and the rest of the Buddies, I'd like, like, *to shoot* the show with four cameras and throw in a live audience just for fun," he said. "By the way, Devon—have you been, like, *seeing,* like, a lot of Debbie from the network?"

"Like . . . whattaya mean?"

"Like . . . nothing. What's on your—"

"What I'm getting at is," Devon said as if speaking to a very slow second grader, "are we *going* to, like, *go* . . . like, one line of dialogue at a time or something? Are we *going* to, like, have that script person *give* us the words *to say* and then, like, we *say* them and then, like, in postproduction you, like, *cut* out all the bad stuff?"

"Like, no. No, Devon, you can report back to the Buddies that we are, *like,* going to do a show tonight and it will be, *like,* one of the easiest hundred grand you guys, *like,* have ever made," J.T. said with the flattest of deliveries. "And what is it with the *like* shit? If you ever speak to me again, Devon, do not use *like* in a sentence. God only knows, when I think of you and the rest of the Buddies, the word *like* never comes to mind."

"Um," Devon said with a touch of panic, "we don't *know* our lines. We haven't *rehearsed* with cameras. How are we supposed *to act?*"

"Like professionals?" J.T. jabbed. Then he thought, *What's the use of being high and mighty now?*

"High and mighty?" Devon chortled.

"Devon," J.T. quickly covered, "after dinner, why don't you and the rest of the Buddies go through each scene and each set. What you will find is a color-coordinated series of cue cards, and if you follow them—like playing, um, Candy Land—you'll eventually come to the finish line, which in this case is page sixty-something and a whole bunch o' applause. Since I couldn't *learn your lines* for you, I took a giant leap of faith and hoped that all of you had decent eyesight and could recognize colors."

Devon looked up and finally noticed the cue cards that were printed in big friendly letters and color-coordinated for each character. "This is, like . . . demeaning," he pronounced.

J.T. half smiled and slapped his thighs. "I agree. It's, like, demeaning, like, shameful, like, disgraceful, like, fucking appalling, and, like, remarkably un-fucking-professional. You've hit the, like, *ignominy lottery*. But—you can always tell anyone who finds out that you were reading your lines from cue cards that *acting is an illusion*. What does it matter if you have a little help along the way? As long as you and the rest of the Buddies can find your cue cards, I think you're going to have a wonderful show." J.T. thought that was a perfect exit line, and started to get up off the couch. Before he could, though, Devon's big hand grabbed him on the shoulder.

"Like . . . what color am I?"

"You're green, Devon."

"Green. Like, what's up with the Santa faces? You tryin' to *fuck* with us?"

"Are the Santa faces in green, Devon?"

"No."

"Then Santa knows you're naughty."

Devon narrowed his eyes. "You know what I *think*?" he asked.

"No," J.T. sighed, slumping back into the couch. "No, that is beyond my talent. Pray tell: What do you think, Devon? I'd love to know. I'd pay to have cable installed so I could see your *E!* interview and hear, *like,* what you have to say."

"I *think* you're, like, jealous." Devon stared at J.T. with an air of arrogance that would get him killed on a New York playground.

J.T. sat up sharply. "Eat me. I *am* jealous, you little fuck. I am amazed that you and the rest of the Buddies are allowed to get away with the shit I witnessed this week. I am thankful that everyone hates my guts so that I can hopefully be officially fired, paid off, and get back to my family and to people who actually work for a living. Oh, and people who have pride in their work."

Devon pondered that for a nanosecond, just for effect. "You know something, J.T.," he remarked, "you are, like, very uptight.

You are a tense man. I don't know if you *know* this, but, like, you are, like, *working* on a COMEDY!"

J.T. waited long enough to reply for Devon to get uncomfortable. Then he said very slowly, jaw clenched, "Then make . . . me . . . *laugh.*"

Devon started to say something but J.T. cut him off with an upraised palm. "You told me what you think, now you're gonna listen to what I think. You, you all, are the ones who have to generate the funny. Right now, *there is none*. It's nonexistent. I'm sure, with or without direction, that all of you are capable of finding bits that are right for your characters. I think now might be a good time to start doing that. This may be, in the scheme of things in your life, your legacy: *Buddies.* Your work. Not your publicity. Your work will be on reruns ten to fifteen years from now, God willing, and you will want to be proud when you sit down and watch with your kids. And another thing I think: I think you ought to treat your fellow collaborators on the set—the camera crew, the grips, the electricians, the prop department, all of them—with a little dignity. Don't forget what it was like to be an out-of-work actor. You're in television. Sometimes the flavor of the month doesn't even last a month. Just beware. And that is all I have to say—except, if I were you and the rest of the Buddies, I'd get my ass onto the sets and figure out where my cue cards are and what color you've been assigned. Or else showtime could even, *like, ruin* your *wonderful* day."

And with that, J.T. got up from the *Buddies*' couch and vowed to himself that he would never put his ass on it again as long as he lived. He walked away from an openmouthed star and left the stage to find Ash and get his suit out of the trunk of Ash's car.

He changed in the men's room. Even though no one else seemed to respect the process of shooting a show, J.T. did. One of the ways he could show it was by wearing a suit and tie.

The Show

"*I Love My Urban Buddies*: 'The Best Ever Christmas.' Written by Marcus and Stephanie Pooley. Director, J.T. Baker. Take one."

"Action!"

The first thing you would have noticed if you were standing in the cave that night was that the show seemed secondary. It was treated as if it were a social event to drop in on, time permitting, by the bigwigs. Then—there was laughter. Honest-to-God laughter from the audience.

The first scene began and the actors walked and talked looking upward, making it appear as if they were characters dreaming or remembering a dream rather than actors who were simply reading their lines from cue cards hung above their heads. J.T. had anticipated this to such an extent that he took a page out of William's A.D. routine and, instead of adding "after sex" to every scripted line, added " . . . like in a dream" to nearly every line. Amazingly, it worked. J.T. had revised the show using the oldest TV trick in the book: the dream sequence. The script stayed the same but now the pure repetition of "like in a dream" became silly-funny. J.T. had learned that from watching *South Park* with Jeremy. If you say *shit* way too many times, it becomes funny. And when repetition becomes tiring, after a while it becomes funny again.

"And I was shopping—in a dream—" Janice read her cue cards

as her ditzy character (now blonde again, thanks to a wig), "and there were bombs and shattering glass and explosions—"

"Whoa. Where were you shopping? Somewhere in World War II?" Helena's character jabbed.

"In a dream!" Janice went on. "And I dunno where I was, but bombs and explosions were keeping me from the department store where all I wanted to do was buy you all great gifts . . . in a dream!" she read.

"There were . . . bombs and explosions?" Kirk said his line perfectly.

"I told you—*in a dream.*" Janice made her famous Janice-face and the audience responded with a reflexive laugh. They loved their Buddies, no matter what they were saying.

J.T. smiled to himself: he'd gambled that the actors would realize that if they didn't *act* as well as read, they'd be the ones looking like they weren't worth their Porsches. So far, it looked like he'd bet on the right horse.

"It was great. A car blew up right by the store . . . and I still went shopping—in a dream!"

Behind the lights, behind the cameras, Marcus grabbed Stephanie. "What the fuck? *In a dream?*" he whispered to his baffled wife. "Those aren't my lines. I didn't write any of that. Did you write that?"

"Cue and roll playback—*now!*" J.T. yelled. The scene they had shot that "wasn't on TV," the previous day's footage that Mick had had the lab process, was rolled into the feed to the audience.

"What the fuck is going on? What does he mean by 'roll playback'?" Stephanie growled.

And sure enough, the scene that wasn't on TV began to play on TV on all the monitors that the audience could see.

Lance and Debbie were watching the monitor next to the Pooleys. As the footage rolled, Lance kept glancing back to the audience, judging their reactions. Deb stood spellbound in front of the monitor. "Like, wow! It's like, so amazing! It looks so real, yet *just like a dream*. How'd you guys, like, do that?" she asked the Pooleys.

"Well . . . I didn't—" Marcus was about to add his own explosion to the pyrotechnics when Stephanie took control of the conversation and whispered, "We thought we needed to punch up the scene with visuals. See what we can do on a shoestring budget? It looks okay. I'm glad you like what we've done."

The audience loved it. *Luck*, J.T. thought. *Got lucky*.

When the playback ended, the actors had to wait to say their lines because the studio audience was honestly applauding without being prompted by an APPLAUD NOW sign.

"But," Janice said over the applause, "just like a dream, shopping means so much to me and, well, just like a dream, you guys mean a lot to me too, so—MERRY CHRISTMAS!"

Janice gave the bag of presents to the other characters.

"Man," Kirk said—

J.T. bit his lip hard, waiting, hoping—

"This is . . . like a dream. The *best ever* Christmas," Kirk said triumphantly, as the character and as a very proud actor looking at a Santa Face on a cue card.

"And . . . CUT!" J.T. yelled, pleased with himself. *It actually worked*, he thought. *Thank you, Paddy. Thank you*.

Marcus came running up to J.T. He pretended to smile because all the executives and the audience were loving the show, but his anger made his eyes even beadier. "What the fuck do you think you're doing?!"

"Marcus," J.T. said calmly, "I'm doing exactly what you asked me to do: I'm giving you a show that is worthy of being on the cover of *TV Guide* three times in two years. Oh," J.T. continued, "and about the scene that wasn't on TV? It worked . . . *like a dream*, huh?"

For a brief moment, J.T. thought Marcus was going to take a swing at him. J.T. didn't really know if he had made the decision to put the footage that "wasn't on TV" into the show because it was what was best for the show, or because, like a dream, it was so satisfyingly spiteful. At that point, it didn't matter to him. At all. "You don't have to pay me the hundred grand or whatever we bet," he said to Marcus. "The shot that wasn't on TV, I mean. It was a sucker's bet." He walked away from Marcus, who stood stunned in the middle of the *Buddies* home set.

Skip, Kevin, and Mick were howling.

"Great stuff, J.T.," Skip laughed.

"I guess it was *on TV*, huh, J.T.?" Kevin said, staring at Stephanie.

"I'm a 'real fuck,' huh, Skip?" J.T. stage-whispered loudly to Skip for the benefit of his entire camera crew. He just couldn't help his glee. *I must be a really bad winner*, he thought. Yet he couldn't stop smiling like the village idiot, the release of it all was so freeing, the rush of endorphins to his brain so orgasmic. J.T. was higher than the cast on liquid V.

"Thank you, Mick," J.T. said, shaking his hand. It was time to get ready for the next scene. "Shall we?" he smiled. And smiled.

Lance was scouring his script. "Why isn't all of this in my gold-enrod script?" he asked Stephanie.

"Oh, I apologize. We were working so late ... we ... didn't have time to get you the revisions. I think you'll like what we did with the rest of the show. But I won't *give it away*. I'll keep it a surprise."

"This is, like, actually good stuff," Deb agreed with Lance.

Devon turned to Rocky and placed his back to the audience. "You see that? They love us. We can do no wrong. We're just reading our lines. No rehearsal. Nuthin'. I say we hold out next week again."

"You may be onto somethin', buddy," Rocky nodded.

Kirk found J.T. going over the next scene's shots with Skip by the wing camera.

"Um, Mr. Baker?"

J.T. felt a small tap on his arm. When he turned and looked at Kirk, he could see Kirk's eyes were teary.

J.T. was still grinning like a fool. "Kirk, you did well. You better get ready for the next attack."

"Um, thank you—thank you." Kirk turned his head to the left twice, then backed up and came back. He backed up and came back again.

> **The Hollywood Dictionary**
>
> **WING CAMERA:** Of the four cameras, the wing cameras are the ones on the far left or the far right. On this show, ironically, the far-right camera was being operated by Skip, a man proudly on the far left.

"Hey, Kirk," J.T. said, literally putting his arms around the young man, "it's okay. Everything's okay."

"You did it."

"*We* did it. Except there's a lot more to do—so get in there and all of your hard work'll pay off. No surprises for you, my friend."

"What can I do to thank—"

"Knock the next scene out of the park, okay?"

"Okay."

Kirk managed to control his compulsions and went back under the lights.

"What was that all about, Kirk?" Janice asked, as if talking to the director were a sin. "What are you two scheming about?"

"Scheming?"

"We all know you're his favorite, you little Goody Two-shoes. What's up?"

Before Kirk could answer, William yelled, "Let's lock it up! Put us on a bell!" And the bell rang.

"Roll cameras. Waiting for speed . . ."

A voice yelled out from the sound booth, "Speed!"

"And it's all yours, J.T."

"Action!"

The Hollywood Dictionary

ON A BELL: Hollywood's version of Pavlov. When the bell rings, everyone quiets. (And wants pizza.)

* * *

THE REST OF THE evening went so smoothly that it played like a show that had been rehearsed out of town before Broadway.

As the night progressed, the Pooleys constantly walked past the director, going onto the set and giving camera notes and acting notes, perpetuating the illusion of their comedy brilliance.

There was only one anxious moment, and that was when Kevin, the vet with PTSD, had a delayed reaction to the explosions and had a Vietnam flashback in the middle of the "J" scene. Kevin tackled J.T., yelling "Incoming!" J.T. was very flattered that the one person Kevin went to save from the phantom incoming bomb was him. After a dose of smelling salts (kept on sets to induce tears for crying scenes), Kevin was fine and the audience laughed, thinking it was a rehearsed "bit" for their benefit.

"Cut!"

And it was over.

Spontaneously, the studio audience jumped to its feet and gave the show a standing ovation. J.T. looked at the actors soaking it all up, each taking a curtain call and trying to trump the others with designer humility and premeditated embarrassment. Then, as if scripted by Paddy Chayefsky, Stephanie and Marcus Pooley found their light, hugged each cast member, then turned in tandem toward the audience and took a long, macrodramatic bow.

Perfect, J.T. thought.

The actors called Lance and Deb onto the set to share the spotlight with the Pooleys, who shifted begrudgingly to make room. Marcus put his arm around Lance and air-kissed Debbie. Stephanie orchestrated one ensemble bow that included the cast, the stu-

dio executive, and the network executive. And, of course, the final
thank-you bow was reserved for the Pooleys.

End of show, and end of show.

"THAT'S A WRAP!" William bellowed, and patted Ash on the ass.
"Ash my bro, was that like the best Kwanza ever? Yo, K-gizzle,
yawanna toss my salad, homey?"

"William," Ash blushed, "do you know what you just asked me
to do to you?"

"Oh. Well, don't be up'n'up on the bye-bye wit' yer baad, maad
self, dotie?" William blurted, sincerely. "Gotta love dem bee-yotches,
eey'ight?"

"Um . . . ditto, bro," Ash said, trying to let William off the hook
and hoping this would cut off the Beverly Hills Ebonics for Eediots.
William let out a huge sigh, grabbed Ash's hand, and went through
a bizarre handshake that looked like palsied sign language.

Stephanie Pooley made a "B" line to the "A" camera where J.T.
was standing as soon as the show was over. She pulled him behind
the *Buddies* living room set, the only set standing for the half-hour
show.

"You think you're clever? Witty? Cute? Smart?"

"Well—"

"Let me tell you what you really are, J.T. Baker," Stephanie
snarled. "You are a nothing. A nobody."

"I appreciate the compliment and will remember it always,"
J.T. said, trying to back away from this crazed, power-mad showrunner who had bad breath from a night of dry mouth.

"I'm not finished with you," she growled, cornering J.T. "You're
the big loser here and let me spell it out for you."

"If that's what you're getting at, I don't think you have to spell
it out for me. Plus, you don't have spell check, so I wouldn't want
you to feel inadequate."

"If you *ever*"—she opened her purse—"let anyone, and I mean *anyone*, know what you did to my script, my show"—she moved her compact and revealed only to J.T. that her gun was sitting nice and comfy at the bottom of her bag—"I will destroy you. Physically. And legally, in every union and guild. And *then* I'll sue your ass and nail it to the La Brea tar pits, where you will disappear with the rest of the dinosaurs."

"You're getting really messy with your metaphors, Ms. Writer-slash-Showrunner-slash-Serial Killer."

Stephanie snarled, "You feel good about getting all those laughs from the studio audience? From the executives? Well, they are now *my* laughs. Because nobody knows! Only we know. And you can never tell."

"Ms. Pooley, I'm not proud of tonight's show. I am proud that I gave you a show with a beginning, a middle, and, thank God, an end—no matter how hard you tried to get in the way."

Stephanie's spittle sprayed J.T.'s face. "You feel good about making it *a better episode*? I'm no fool, it *was* a better episode—*my* better episode. That's what *everyone* thinks. The audience when I was introduced as the writer; the executives who believe I worked a miracle with this episode—everyone! Soon, America, when they read the written-by credit. So my advice to you, J.T. 'Squeal-Like-a-Pig' Baker, is you'd better go crawling back to that hole in the South you call home and fill your mouth with grits and collards and *barbeeeeeeque*, because it is now my goal in life to make sure you never, ever work in this town again as long as you live in this life, and be damn sure I'll find you in the after-life. And if by good fortune you fucking die and come back as a cockroach, it'll be me who flattens you on the bottom of my shoe, leaving behind nothing more than your smashed brown bug body covered with your fucking bug innards of white goo." She finally took a gulp of air.

J.T. waited the appropriate comic beats and then, as if he were the maestro at a symphony, dismissed the brass section with, "You're welcome." Baton down. Concert over.

AS THE TABLE of expensive desserts was brought out and placed in front of the couch on the set (for the cast and executives only), Deb held court. "So," she began, "like, what a week. Another one down. Funny! Funny! Funny show!"

"Food!" Dick Beaglebum appeared. "*Very* funny stuff!" he added, enthusiastically. "Those Pooleys! How 'bout 'em!"

"One word: *Funny!*" Lance said. "*Funny, funny, funny!*"

"That's, like, three words," Debbie said, and everyone enjoyed a big funny laugh.

"I'm speechless," Dick said to Marcus as Stephanie, sporting a big phony smile, walked to the table full of exotic desserts. "I don't know how you creative types do it, week in and week out. These cream puffs are to die for!" he mumbled with his mouth full.

"I agree!" Loretta Nady had also homed in on the dessert table. She took two cream puffs. Dick took two more; Loretta took three; Dick took three plus a couple of chocolate-dipped strawberries. Which agent could eat more? Which one could eat faster? Loretta stuffed a few gourmet brownies in her purse.

Lacking a purse, Dick conceded defeat. He put his chewed strawberry stems on the table. "Loretta Nady-o," he swallowed, "where'd you come from?"

"I'm never one to miss a celebration," she said, cramming a Mallomar into her mouth, celebrating gluttony as well. "Good show! Wonderful show! Funny show!"

"Yeah," Marcus Pooley said proudly, "this one came from our gonads. I mean, really, could we have been more taxed this week? An impossible budget, our dear director friend Jasper dead—what a tragedy—and the budget again . . . which, may I add, we not only met but came in under, quite substantially under. And a cast that refused to listen to an old has-been."

Stephanie joined them in time to add her two cents. "Maybe next time," she said, staring meaningfully at Dick's chocolate-drizzled tie, "somebody can pitch us a director who can actually direct."

"Just as long as we have a show," Lance interjected.

"You're welcome," Stephanie stole from J.T.

Lance needed to leave this set—this night—this week—with a sense of balance, of the status quo maintained; the show was still a hit. Tonight's show was adored by the studio audience. *Just don't rock the boat ... it's headed for* Xanadu, he thought. *Wait—that movie was a flop.* Paradise. *Yeah,* Paradise. *No*—Titanic! *The box office, not the boat.* "Well, *by God,* we have ourselves a tight, funny show!" he felt he had to add.

"Everyone is coming to my son's bar mitzvah tomorrow at the Staples Center, right?" Dick asked, enthusiastically.

The celebration came to a screeching halt. Lance gave Dick a withering look. "*Bar mitzvah?* Why'd you have to ruin the moment?" he asked.

The show was over. And the *show* was over.

As J.T. GATHERED his belongings, he watched the agents and the managers congratulating the *talent,* everyone now dive-bombing the dessert table. Debbie was all over Devon Driver. There was talk of feature films during hiatus and commercials in Japan for millions of dollars, but not a word or a look was aimed at J.T.

"I think I got the new Oliver Stone flick," Devon said with a sexy smirk.

"Like, no way!" Debbie responded lustfully.

"No way," Rocky repeated. "Veronica at Quad told me I was first on a small list to star in his film."

"Devon ..." Betty said, interjecting herself between Devon and Debbie, "I thought we were goin' out after the show."

"Uh," Devon thought fast. "Well, Betty, my girlfriend wants

me to come home and play Classic Rock to her tummy. Somethin' about, like, classic-music-programmin' the kid in the womb." He winked at Deb.

Ash walked onto the set and shook hands with Kirk. "You did a wonderful job, Kirk."

"Thank you. I really couldn't have done it without your help. And J.T.'s."

No shit, Ash thought.

"Yeah, I guess. No shit."

"Damn. I must be really tired. Did I say that out loud?" Ash mumbled.

"I guess you're spendin' too much time around J.T."

"Listen, Kirk—man to man, just between us: if you put in a good word with Deb and with Lance, you could probably save J.T.'s job. You didn't hear that from me, but it would be a . . . classy thing to do."

"Right," Kirk said, and twisted his head twice; then he walked forward, then back—then forward, then back.

Poor kid, Ash thought. And this time, he did just *think* it. Ash patted Kirk on the shoulder, then looked through the swarm of executives, agents, and managers on the floor for J.T.

Deb and Loretta Nady pretend-ran with itty-bitty baby steps to the approaching Kirk, with Lance following close behind. In triplicate, they opened their arms as if to say, *Come to our bosoms. We will care for you, nurture you, protect you.* And, of course, they threw in a smidgen of repentance. They hugged, they laughed, they air-kissed; and when Kirk opened his mouth and the words "J.T." came out, he had their attention.

"What about him?" Deb asked.

"Yes. I'd like your honest opinion," Lance chimed in.

"He's a shit," Loretta Nady groused.

"Um, J.T. . . ." Kirk said, and his eyes suddenly were in line with Ash's.

Ash nodded and mouthed, *This is your chance.*

Kirk pulled his eyes away, and looked at the three people who controlled his future. "Um, J.T.? Oh . . . nuthin'. So ya thought it was a good show?"

"Good?! You were *brilliant!*" Loretta slathered on the praise.

Ash tried to get Kirk's attention again, but Kirk refused to look back.

What a pity, Ash thought he thought.

"Say what-a-what?" J.T. asked.

"Oh . . . nuthin'."

As J.T. LEFT, the members of the camera crew gathered together. All the *schmucks* came over and quietly congratulated J.T. on a great job, and for the first time that week, J.T. knew it was all worth it.

Debbie looked across at the gathering around J.T. "What's, like, all *that* about?" she asked the Pooleys.

Stephanie was eating chocolate-covered cherries. A bit of liqueur goo dribbled out of the corner of her mouth when she opened it to say, "Oh, it's just the schmucks." She turned her back on the view of J.T. and the crew. "Now, about next week . . ."

Marcus took the baton and began to complain about the budget.

Ash stayed out of sight, listening.

J.T. AND THE rest of the crew were gathering outside of the elephant door, drinking beers off the prop truck.

"J.T.!" Ash called out.

"Sorry," J.T. said to his best friend, "I just had to get outta there. I can't breathe in the cave. I needed some air."

"J.T., listen, I just overheard a conversation."

"Yeah?" J.T. said.

"Yeah. The Pooleys, Lance, and Debbie—and get this, your wonderfully loyal agent—along with your new best friend, Loretta Nady, were scheming about how not to pay you for the two upcoming episodes that you were supposed to do. The episodes that you are *pay-or-play* on. They still believe you'll negotiate because you're so desperate for the cash for your kid."

"Thanks for telling me," J.T. said too quietly, and then turned and walked back into the cave.

"J.T.—" Ash started to protest.

"Asher, stay out of this one. Go home. Back to classes. Keep your cell on. You may be working next week or we both may be headed back to the real world. But for now, this may get ugly, and I've contaminated you enough."

"J.T.—"

"Not the time," J.T. said over his shoulder, walking with purpose toward the big shots back in the cave. He had been through this routine before: Ash was about to warn him about his temper. J.T. had had no sleep, and didn't want to hear it.

Ash ran and got in front of J.T., blocking his way.

"Ash—"

"Listen, man, you're my best friend—"

"I know, I know. Just lemme do what I've gotta do."

Ash stopped J.T. again. "And I wouldn't be much of a best friend if I didn't tell you that ... shit, J.T., you crossed the line. What you did with the cue cards—fucking brilliant. But changing dialogue? Putting the preshoot in and bypassing the executives, the showrunners, the producers—shit, you're one lucky mother that the audience dug this show. I don't think your stuff was funnier than theirs. I think it all sucked. People just love that cast. It's their time. Period. It's TV. And even though the preshoot was great stuff, you put that in to fuck with the Pooleys. I know you. You forgot about the show just to fuck with them. J.T., you got so *full* of yourself, and, and, so hell-bent on landing a sucker punch, you ended up just as bad as them. You got yourself one bad case of cave-madness, my friend."

J.T. blinked twice, trying to get moisture to his contacts. He wasn't sure that his vision was clear; he knew he heard the words, but they couldn't be coming from his best friend.

"Um, Ash? Is that . . . you?"

"You know it is. You know I'm right. And I know you know you were wrong."

"Morality? Is that where you're goin'?"

"It's the card you keep up your sleeve. It's not fair to use it as a trick. You either do what's right or you don't. Let's be real."

"And you're tellin' me this because . . . you're suddenly my conscience?"

Ash touched J.T. ever so gently, but it felt like the hand of a dad placing the paw of righteousness on his five-year-old boy's shoulder, and J.T. shrugged it off. Ash went on anyway, "Because you're gonna march in there the way you do, all holier-than-thou, and this time you're gonna set yourself up to lose everything you came here for: Jeremy. You fucked up. You crossed the line. Those are facts. They can use those facts against you. You won't see *three* paychecks. Shit, you'll be lucky to see *one*— if you're not fined, to begin with. Don't go back in there and make matters worse."

J.T. didn't really care if Ash was right, and he knew Ash was right. But J.T. was toxic with malice.

"You're a good man, Asher. I'm lucky to have you for a best friend."

Ash allowed himself to ease off when he heard J.T.'s kind words. Then J.T. began to move past him. "But get the fuck outta my way."

* * *

"Oh no," Dick whispered to the Pooleys, "he's *baaaack*."

J.T. stopped and stared at his enemas—one step past enemies. "Well, first off," he said, "I'd like to say, *Shame on you*."

"Shame? Really? That's the best you can do?" Marcus laughed. "Shame on . . . us? How 'bout shame on you, you fuck?"

"J.T., really, don't make things worse than they already are," Dick said, enthusiastically.

J.T. kept his voice carefully controlled. "You are my agent. I thought you were my friend. How can I ever trust you again?"

"Trust?!" Dick laughed. "Oh, grow up, J.T. Trust! That's a good one."

"I know all of you are trying to figure out how not to pay me for my other two episodes. I want you all to know that I will be here Monday morning, ready to work and ready to fulfill my contractual obligations and ready to be paid for my services," J.T. said.

"No!" Dick jumped in. "J.T., look, come to the bar mitzvah tomorrow at the Staples Center and we'll have everything worked out by then."

"Am I officially fired?" J.T. asked.

"No," Marcus Pooley said with hateful glee. "You're officially fucked!"

"By tomorrow at my son's Staples Center bar mitzvah, everything will be worked out," Dick said, with authoritative compassion. He gave the others a Significant Look, as if J.T. couldn't spot a conspiracy when he was the object of one. "Everything will be finalized. Trust me," he said reflexively. "Debbie, Lance, the Pooleys, everyone will be there. We will have discussed this little problem and we all will know what we can all look forward to for *the next two weeks of work*. Sound good?!"

Dick Beaglebum was actually enjoying—no, loving—all of the intrigue. *It must be like a gambler's high,* J.T. thought.

"You know, I'll be there tomorrow. It's been truly awful. Good night," J.T. said, never raising his voice, and turned his back on

> ### The Hollywood Dictionary
>
> **FIX IT IN POST:** The last stop on the Rationalize It train of false hopes. In film and on TV, when something isn't as good as it should be, the next phrase is usually, "We'll fix it in post." Postproduction, that is. (In music, the phrase is: "We'll fix it in the mix." In the real world, "I'll fix it tomorrow.")
>
> **DIRECTOR'S CUT:** The producers are obligated to give the director a day to do his or her cut. The producers are not obligated to ever view the director's cut.

people who, if it were wartime, would have shot him as he walked away. But it was just television, and since Stephanie had left her nuclear bomb in the office, all they could do was stab him in the back, hoping to see him slowly bleed to death.

The show was neither spectacular nor spectacularly awful. It just . . . existed. And J.T. knew that he had, under Directors Guild rules, one pass to edit the show and fix it in post. Just as a magician might use sleight of hand to give the impression that a lousy old trick was worth watching, J.T. would fix the show in editing. *Then again,* he thought, *if this is like most cases, the producers won't even view the director's cut.*

IN BED AT Oliver's that night, J.T. stared at the ceiling for hours, knowing his fate was in the hands of incompetents. He really did not know what his next step should be. *Ash was right,* he kept thinking. *Or was he? Shit. How would the show have been shot if I hadn't . . . Ash was right. Ash was right. Ash was right. Now what?* J.T. sat up in a panic. Virtue was no longer on his side. He had to play the game. He never played the game. He was a Go-Fish-Boob about to sit down at a table of Poker Champs. *Shit,* he thought, *what should I do? What's my first move?*

He remembered that at the table read, Debbie from the network had given J.T. her card . . . with her home phone number on the back.

"Hello?" J.T. was nervous. For a man who could lead over two hundred employees, he was exceedingly insecure when it came to matters that involved his own well-being.

"Who is this?" Debbie asked, clearly irritated.

J.T. hesitated, wondering if he should just hang up. Then he remembered *69. *Fuck!*

"I said, Who *is this*? What's going on? What do you want?"

J.T. finally spoke. "Debbie . . . I know it's late, um . . . this is J.T. Baker."

"Holy shit. Like, no way. Really?" There was a beat of what seemed to be orchestrated silence. Then J.T. heard, "Devon, like, get off me!"

"Um, yes. Listen, I'm very sorry to disturb you and call the personal number that you gave me, but if you don't mind, I need some off-the-record advice," J.T. said, sounding more like a high school geek than a director of twenty years.

"You wanna come over, J.T.? Wanna come over and *talk* about . . . things?"

There was a new inflection in Debbie's voice. *A purr*, J.T. thought. *Shit.*

"Devon," J.T. heard Deb whisper, "I said *get off of me*. I'm on the phone!" Then there was another awkward beat. "J.T., wanna come over?"

"No, Debbie, I really don't want to come over. I just want to ask your advice."

"Really?" Debbie was slightly amused and slightly perturbed by J.T.'s answer. He really only wanted advice? This from the man who'd just directed the sitcom she attended for her network? And she'd been all dolled up . . . wasn't she? Debbie tried to remember . . . *What was I wearing?* "Devon, get off of me! Now!"

J.T. plunged in. "I know, Debbie, that I am like a staph infection to the Pooleys, and Dick Beaglebum isn't fond of my presence on the planet, either. But I am ready to show up for work on Monday. I know how embarrassing that may be for many in the crew and even in the cast. Personally, I've been known to thrive on embarrassment, but I don't want to make it awkward for everybody else. That's why I'm calling you." As soon as he'd said it, J.T. thought, *What a stupid fucking thing to say!* "I need your help. I know I'm fired, but am I officially fired? And if I am, is anyone out there ready to honor my pay-or-play deal?"

"Well, J.T.," Debbie said, trying to sound very official and network-like, "like, you are putting me in a very awkward position. GODDAMMIT, DEVON—LIKE, OFF! DOWN! SIT!"

"Um, Debbie, I beg to differ. You *have* a job. *I'm* the one who is getting fired. *I'm* the one whose life is being altered by the whims of a few power-hungry no-talents. I think it is *I* who am in the awkward position," J.T. managed to say, still sounding very young and unsure of himself.

"Look—like, get a lawyer, J.T."

"I'm not getting into a financial war of attrition with the Pooleys, the studio, or the network. I have a sick son or else I wouldn't even have entered your sphere of reality. I'm trying to get my guild insurance and get paid what I'm owed." J.T. thought he just might be able to play the pity card with the knockout babe. It used to work in high school.

"Well—if you won't get a lawyer, then, like, call your guild. See if the union can help you. And, like, keep your family's sob story out of my sphere."

Who am I kidding? he thought. *This isn't high school.* "Sphere? You can't really mean that. Debbie? Please tell me you're not really that . . . cold."

"I have, like, a full slate of shows that I am responsible for and that the network believes will give us a ratings victory in the

November sweeps," the temptress unloaded. "My responsibilities do not include, like, babysitting unhappy sitcom directors with insurance problems. If you don't want a lawyer, then, like I said, call your fucking guild or union or whatever you call it. I'm, like, hanging up now, but if I were you? I'd renegotiate and let Beaglebum get you your salary for the episode you shot and then go home. Get out of our lives. Like, please. Good night."

The pity card hadn't worked. Maybe she would go for the loyalty card. "Debbie, I don't feel comfortable calling the union. I'm *not* a snitch."

Oh, I am so not a player, J.T. thought.

"Debbie, it's not my intention to hurt anyone or have the production company fined." He had, of course, just threatened the network executive—so he dug an even deeper hole. "Listen, if I was that kind of guy, I would've called the Screen Actors Guild when Marcus Pooley accused Kirk Kelly of being a drug addict. That was totally irresponsible and could've had an impact on the rest of that young actor's life, but I didn't . . . hello? Debbie?"

Debbie had hung up.

J.T. just stared up at the ceiling. *What have I done?*

For J.T. the control freak, everything was out of control. He didn't even feel satisfaction on the most personal level: Ash. J.T. jumped out of bed and paced, looking at his guilty face in the mirror every time he passed the bureau where only a few of his clothes had made it into drawers. His own image taunted him, scolded him. With every peek at his reflection, the mirror spoke to him: *You crossed the line. You made decisions out of spite, not for the good of the work. You suck as a friend. Maybe the Pooleys have been right all along; maybe you're impossible to deal with; maybe you're a horrible director. Maybe your wife thinks you have a small dick. And you still suck as a friend!*

J.T. stopped pacing and stared at his own haggard face. *I really need some sleep,* he thought. He picked up the phone and dialed quickly.

"Hello, Ash?"

J.T. heard the sound of the receiver hitting the floor, and another voice that was very familiar to him: "You want me to turn on the light?"

"Sure. Thanks, Kevin," J.T. heard Ash say. "Hello? J.T.?"

"Ash . . . um, I just wanted to say—I know it's late, I shouldn't be calling—is that Kevin? 'Incoming' Kevin?"

After a beat Ash whispered, "You said a mouthful."

"Oh. Cool."

"J.T., are you all right?"

"Well, I just wanted to make sure you—*we*—were all right, actually." There was an awkward beat.

"I love you, J.T. You know that. I only said the things I did because I wanted to protect you. I mean, shit, man—ow, Kevin—um, where was I—oh! I thought I had to give you a reality check. I didn't want to see you get . . . hurt. Maybe I was too—"

"You were right. It's cool," J.T. mumbled. "You're with *Kevin*?"

"Hey, don't ask, don't tell."

"No, I mean, I think Kevin's good for you. He's . . . really cool."

Ash tried to whisper as softly as he could into the phone, "If this works out, then this week wasn't a disaster after all."

"Yeah. Cool. I'm sayin' 'cool' a lot. I must be really tired. Um, well, I just wanted to . . . I just wanted to tell you how sorry I am for—"

"*Love means never having to say you're whorey.* You're my best friend. No harm, no foul. Now, get some sleep."

"Yeah. Cool. There I go again. Um, you two—I mean, you, too. 'Night."

J.T. hung up and flopped back into bed. *What if Kevin has a*

Vietnam flashback while they're having sex? J.T. thought. *Maybe it'll be fun. Maybe Kevin'll think Ash's a Vietcong enemy! Maybe I should call Ash back and warn him not to hide under the covers! Maybe I should go to sleep . . .*

Staring at the ceiling again, J.T. knew his next move. Even though he couldn't trust Dick Beaglebum, he had to go to that blasted bar mitzvah and deal with this, firsthand, first thing tomorrow.

J.T. turned off the light but never fell asleep. Instead he made an extensive shot list in his head and cut the show from memory. Then he got up and put all of his ideas down and e-mailed them to the editor of the show, asking him to send a copy to himself at his home address, and one copy each to Debbie, Lance, and the network president.

Saturday

THE BAR MITZVAH AT THE STAPLES CENTER

"Got two! I've got two. Who needs tickets?!" a scalper yelled out to the masses who were pouring into the Staples Center.

"You're scalping tickets to a bar mitzvah?" J.T. asked the scalper.

"You wanna T-shirt? I got *Take Me to a Bar . . . Mitzvah*, I got *David Gets Regal-Beagled*, I got *Take One in the Kishka, Go to Dave's Bar Mitzvah!* I got *Bring on the Shiksas, It's David's Bar Mitzvah!* I got *I'm No Bum, I'm a Beaglebum—*"

"I said," J.T. repeated, "you're scalping tickets to a bar mitz-vah?!"

"Hey, buddy, have you seen the Lakers this year? This bar mitzvah alone is worth a year's worth of scalping Lakers tickets. I'm making a friggin' fortune here. If you don't like it, go tell it to the mountain and get off my case. By the way, I've got a T-shirt here that says *Go Tell It to the Mountain and Get Off my Case. I'm at Dave's Bar Mitzvah, so Get Out o' My Face.* It's got Phat Azz's punim on it. Have you ever seen such a face? Really! Look at that punim! I feel for his mother. So—ya want this schmatta?"

J.T. took the ticket from his pocket and made his way through the masses to the proper entrance into the Staples Center. He-brew Nationals were selling like . . . latkes. And latkes were selling like . . . well, potato pancakes. J.T. found his section and finally his seat. All the executives and Beaglebum's *friends* and *Urban Buddies* were down on the floor. J.T. had nosebleed seats. J.T. looked at the empty seat beside him and wondered if Ash would show up. Then he remembered that sometime in the chaos of the last couple of days he'd made Ash swear that he wouldn't go to Dick's event. Now, J.T. was there and all he could think about was what Ash was missing. *Then again*, J.T. thought, *I don't want my best friend to be anti-Semitic. Maybe it's good that Ash didn't come, after all.*

The lights dimmed and a lot of the kids in the upper mezzanine were twirling their laser fiber-optic Yads that were meant to simulate the Yad that David would later use to read from the Torah.

"Tefillin! Get your frozen tefillin here!" a Hispanic guy yelled, selling a chocolate and vanilla frozen confection (nondairy) that fit into a little plastic tefillin holder, complete with straps so the kids wouldn't drop their desserts and make a mess.

"Lllllladies and gentlemen!" a loud voice boomed over the Staples speaker system, sounded exactly like the boxing guy who says "*Let's get ready to rrrrrumble!*"

J.T. listened hard.

"*Let's get ready to be hhhhhumbled!*"

It *was* the guy.

The light show was absolutely startling and impressive . . . for a Celine Dion-in-Vegas-style show.

"Will you please rise as tonight's special guest performer, Phat Azz, raps 'The Star-Spangled Banner' with the help of the new sensational recording artists, *Munch My Manhood*!"

Phat Azz and his posse came out, followed by MMM. The group was greeted by thousands of screaming white Jewish boys and girls who yelled out, "Munch it like it's rot!" almost in unison—a secret pop-culture code J.T. had been entirely unaware of.

Phat Azz did rap "The Star-Spangled Banner." J.T. looked

around to see if he was the only one who felt dirty ... or like he was in a John Waters movie. But everyone was having a blast and gettin' jiggy with it.

"For those of you over forty, we have a special treat," the loud voice boomed out over the PA system. "You can go into the home-team locker room for a mystical *Kabbalah for a Dollah*! You could win a car by interpreting the Zohar!"

Then the arena began to rumble with a thunderous, bottom-heavy, equalized bass and drums.

"Lllllladies and gentlemen—the Lllllllaker Girls!"

The Laker Girls came dancing out onto the floor of the arena wearing very risqué blue and white see-through outfits that were designed to look like the flag of Israel. They danced to a deafening klesmoric beat. Then came more Laker Girls dressed as Hasids, complete with black satin coats, long hats, beards, and curls (peyos) that hung down to their breasts. They launched into a very sexual dance with the see-through Israeli flag girls. It was erotic and hugely sensuous in all the most inappropriate ways.

J.T. was fascinated. He couldn't take his eyes off of this delicious car wreck of tasteless, offensive intemperance. Everyone in the audience was loopy with delight.

Phat Azz rapped to the dance, but the speaker system was so loud and muddy it was impossible to perceive specific sounds in what came across as nothing more than a sonic assault. But everyone was up on their feet, rockin' out. J.T. strained to hear what Phat Azz was rapping.

"Kadma munach zarka munach segol munach legarmeh munach revii maapach pashta munach zakef katon munach zakefgadol mercha tipcha munach etnachta mercha tipcha silluq pazer telisha ketana . . ."

How fitting is *this*, J.T. thought, giddy with embarrassment. But giddy nonetheless. He desperately wanted to film this. He closed one eye and panned the arena. *What a great documen-*

tary this would be. Shoot the bar mitzvah, then go to war-torn Israel and film the reactions of the battle-weary Jews watching this fiasco. Then maybe even find a Hezbollah spokesman and get his opinion. *What a documentary this would make,* J.T. kept thinking.

Phat Azz was actually rapping a prayer from the Haphtarah! It was so wonderfully tactless, so utterly insulting to the prayer's original intentions, that J.T. was in heaven. Now, this—*this* was *funny!* **Funny!** *Finally,* J.T. thought. *Somebody found the funny!*

"Okay, all you out there in my posse," Phat Azz said in rhythm. "Now, say 'Oy!' Say 'Oy!'"

The audience was really with him. The kids screamed, "Oy! Oy!"

"Now," Phat Azz instructed, "left to right, say 'Yo!' Say 'Yo!'"

And the entire Staples Center audience yelled, "Yo! Yo!"

"Oy! Oy! Yo! Yo!"

"Oy! Oy! Yo! Yo!"

J.T. got up to get a Hebrew National hot dog. Then, as things happen sometimes in unlikely places such as a concession stand at an overproduced bar mitzvah, J.T. ran into, of all people, Ron Copper. Ron was the man he'd told Debbie he would never snitch to. Ron was a union representative for the Directors Guild of America.

"J.T.! J.T., is that you?" Ron asked. They went back . . . *a long time.*

"Ron? Ron Copper, how the hell are you?!" J.T. said.

"Well, aside from my little nephews making me purchase two Phat Azz CDs, *Haphtarah and the Ashkenazim Bitch* and *Torah, Torah, Torah, Rap Me in My Sephardic Ass,* I think I'll plotz, then come out of shock . . . sometime next month. How about you?"

"This is funny," J.T. said. "Look, you can get your nephews *Peyos Pogo Sticks!*"

> **The Hollywood Dictionary**
>
> **PLOTZ:** Shit.
>
> **PEYOS:** Side curls worn by Hasidic Jews.
>
> **NOODNIK:** A pain in the butt (the person, not the pain).
>
> **YIDDISH:** Doesn't hurt to know some.

"I hear all the merchandising and ticket sales from the loge up are going to that noodnik Beaglebum. Brilliant. Throws the biggest bar mitzvah this year and is making his money back. Who could do such a thing, except Beaglebum?"

"Yeah."

"Speaking of which, I was walking your lot this week and noticed that you were slated to come back for two more episodes but you've been what— replaced?"

"I've been fired, Ron. But not officially. They won't say the actual words 'You're fired.' Really bad experience." J.T. just looked down.

"Well, you're pay-or-play, right?" Ron Copper said, suddenly changing his body language from a guy with his nephews to Union Representative.

"Yeah, I'm pay-or-play, but Beaglebum is negotiating with the Pooleys for partial payment. The Pooleys truly want me dead. Bad situation, Ron."

"My friend, *they cannot do that*. That's mishuggah and Beaglebum knows it. He can't do that," Ron repeated.

"Do what?" J.T. asked.

"J.T., you're being fucked—excuse my language: *shtooped*. It is against Directors Guild *precedent* for them to negotiate *anything* and they all know it! Just think what that would do to other directors. Suddenly pay-or-play would be meaningless, and the Guild fought long and hard for that. Beaglebum knows that better than anyone."

"You mean . . ." J.T. was astounded. He wasn't amazed by the fact that he was legally supposed to be paid, but he was sickened by the fact that his own agent was knowingly breaking DGA protocol, representing the Pooleys and not J.T. The Pooleys were millionaires. Beaglebum was a multimillionaire.

This even included Lance at the studio. Deb at the network. They all knew the DGA rules. Why didn't J.T. know the rules? After all these years? Because no matter how horrible a working relationship was, J.T. always *trusted* . . .

"I'm a fucking fool," J.T. said. "You can't believe . . . I need the money, Ron. My son . . . Look, I need to make the minimum so I can claim my insurance for the year. The insurance. My son . . . No sob stories. But . . ."

"Hey, genug es genug, my friend. Enough is enough! Have you got a BlackBerry on you?" Ron asked.

"I, um, got a cell phone—"

"Oy. Gimme the number." And J.T. did.

"Well, J.T., it's a small world and you didn't hear this from me, but I'm sitting with Beaglebum, the Pooleys, Phat Azz, and a minyan of famous clients and friends. Very soon I'm going to be called up to the Torah."

"Really? You're that close of a friend? I didn't know—"

"Beaglebum married my wife's sister. We're kind of related, I'm sorry to say. Brothers-in-law."

"Oh," was all J.T. could manage. *Did I just walk into another sucker-punch? How could this be? My Directors Guild representative is related to my thieving agent? How big of a schmuck am I?* J.T. thought.

"You're not a schmuck, J.T. I'm going down to the courtside seats now. I'll inform Lance, Beaglebum, Debbie, and those talentless Pooleys that they must tell you if you are officially fired. Then I'll inform all of them that not only have they broken several guild rules, but the guild is taking them down."

> **The Hollywood Dictionary**
>
> **SCHMUCK:** Schmuck.
>
> **SHUT THEM DOWN:** Retribution.

"What?" J.T. was suddenly sick. He didn't want any retribution—he only wanted what was owed to him.

"Who," Ron asked, "is going to direct the two episodes that you were supposed to direct?"

"I don't know. I think, Stephanie Pooley," J.T. said.

"Well, that's a violation as well. Enough of one that the Directors Guild can shut them down!" Ron was starting to feel his oats.

"That's wrong. I have to ask you, please don't do that," J.T. pleaded.

"Why?"

"Because, Ron, almost every single member of that crew, especially the camera crew, is my friend. This may be an ego move that I would secretly love—I mean, the Pooleys took years off of my life this past week—but the crew ... please, don't shut them down," J.T. begged.

"They wouldn't be out of work. Exactly the opposite. A producer of a show cannot direct an episode if the producers have fired a DGA director. They have to hire new blood. They have to hire another DGA director. *They all know this*, J.T. You're the only one left out of the loop. All I have to do is go down there to my seat, have a quick powwow with the Powers That Be, and give you a call on your cell phone, and then you, my friend, can go back to your wife and son, *paid in full*."

"You must really dislike Beaglebum," J.T. found himself saying.

"Dislike? Yeah. He's a putz! And to think he thought he could pull the wool over your eyes on my watch? Pfft!" It was the strongest reaction J.T. had seen all week, and that was really saying something.

"Thank you so damn much, Ron. Thank you."

"You just hang right up here by the silent auction. Can you believe Beaglebum is auctioning off a chance to help Kobe Bryant take the Torah to the Arc?" Ron said in disbelief.

"You mean, take the Torah *from* the Ark, right?" J.T. asked.

"No, my naïve friend. Ten-thousand-dollar opening bid to accompany Kobe Bryant and the Torah as he walks *to* the *arc*, just above the foul line. The arc. The three-point arc."

"Ten thousand bucks?" J.T. managed to say.

"J.T., that's Beaglebum. And that's why I'm goin' down there right now to get you your money. Wait here. You'll get a phone call in about two minutes." Ron turned, then came back to J.T.

"Hey, you bring your swim trunks?" Ron asked J.T.

"My swim trunks?" J.T. asked, not sure if he'd heard Ron correctly.

"Yeah," Ron said, "you could go out to the parking lot. There's a Mikvah Pool. They got a water slide set up and everything."

"Oh . . . no. I didn't bring my swim trunks."

"By the way, J.T. Whattaya think about the bar mitzvah?"

"Well, Ron . . . seeing that you are related—"

"It's a crime, isn't it? To allow a few wackos to give an entire religion, a heritage, such a bad name. You wanna know why people hate us? Because of the man my wife's sister married, the fuck! I'll go get your money!"

Ron gave J.T. a giant bear hug and then disappeared into the insanity inside the arena. J.T. took out his cell phone and just stared at it. As he paced back and forth, he began to fight back tears. He felt ten years old, very much alone—yet finally saved.

Just then, the famous public-address announcer rattled the entire arena.

"*Lllladies and gentlemen*, the *Rabbi to the Stars* and also one of the top literary agents at William Morris, *Ggggoooooordy Guffelman!*"

J.T. checked out the sweet-'n'-sour dreidel candy wondering if his son would like a souvenir. Then he did a quick systems check on his own common sense and realized only a complete idiot would buy a dreidel full of sweet-'n'-sour candied powder.

"Can I have a sweet-'n'-sour dreidel, please," a grown man beside J.T. said. "Oh, and two yarmulke Frisbees."

J.T.'s cell phone rang. Surprised that it was so fast, J.T. thought, *Maybe things actually do work out. Maybe it's not such a horrific business after all.* He opened his cell phone and looked silly trying to remember how to answer the darn thing; what tiny buttons you had to press!

One time, J.T. thought, as if his life were moving in slow motion (about 120 frames per second), *one time, let it be good.*

J.T. remembered the cell phone call when he was first told that something was very wrong with Jeremy. It was ten minutes before a show on a Friday shoot night. J.T. hung up the phone and ran toward his car, never looking back except to tell the assistant director that she was in charge. He fought Friday night Los Angeles traffic and drove like Steve McQueen, arriving at the airport just in time to catch the last plane home. He was at the hospital before Jeremy was put under anesthesia. He was able to kiss him, hold him, reassure him, love him. And then once they rolled his son into the operating room, J.T. began to tremble and broke down and sobbed in Tasha's arms.

"Hello?" J.T. said.

"J.T. Ron Copper here. I've just had a little chat with the momzer—yeah, you, Beaglebum, you putz you! Anyway, this negotiating bullshit is over, I spoke with the network, the studio, and the Pooleys. Congratulations. *You are officially fired.* You are *pay-or-play*, so get your butt to the airport, stop living in limbo, and know that when you get home to your family, you will be paid for three episodes and, more importantly, you will have made the

DGA minimum, which makes you eligible for an entire year of in-surance, buddy. Mazel tov!"

"Ron . . . I don't know what to say," J.T. said as he watched a kid purchase a Peyos Pogo Stick and go bouncing down the cement corridor of the Staples Center.

"There's no need to say anything. Hey—they're calling me up to the Talmud. I've gotta go. Be safe my friend, and feel good."

"Thank you . . ." But Ron had already hung up.

PICKIN' BLUEBERRIES . . .

J.T. LOOKED AROUND at the cultural mess and could not get out of there fast enough. First he called Natasha and Jeremy to tell them the good news: Daddy was on his way home. Then he called Ash.

After he flipped his cell phone shut, J.T. took great pleasure in dropping the electronic device on the cement in front of the Staples Center and stomping it to death. With every stomp, J.T. was reminded of all the bad movies he'd seen where the protago-nist finally shoots the antagonist and kills the evildoer with the first shot, but keeps shooting for melodramatic and stale enter-tainment value—continuing to pull the trigger even after all the bullets are used up. *I'm so pathetic,* he thought, stomping on the cell phone even after it was mostly shards of metal and plastic. *A one-man Cell Phone Riot.* The phone bleeped a last, pathetic ring-tone, then was silent. He finally stopped stomping.

He looked up and noticed he had a small audience of onlook-ers, cheering him on—the same way onlookers cheered on O.J. in the white Bronco.

"Step away from the phone," J.T. said comically, his tension re-lieved. "There is nothing to see here."

And then the battered cell phone rang. "Raindrops keep fallin' on my—" The onlookers laughed. *Now, that's funny,* J.T. thought. And gave the cell phone its death stomp.

J.T. high-tailed it on his bike back to Oliver's, threw his few clothes together, thanked Oliver for agreeing to return his bicycle in the morning, hugged Oliver, called an L.A. cab, waited impatiently for the L.A. cab, rode impatiently in the L.A. cab to the airport, and got himself on a flight that would get him home in time to drive up the mountain to his Natasha and Jeremy before they went to bed. In theory.

Before J.T. was able to get onto his flight, he heard his name being paged over the airport loudspeaker system.

Oh my God! Why did I stomp my cell phone to death? It's Jeremy, isn't it? Jeremy's sick and I didn't even get a chance to say—no! It's Tasha! She's been hit by a car and pinned to a tree. Oh my God, she's been torn in two and the lower half of her body is attached to her upper half only by the car, just like in that stupid M. Night Shyamalan movie, keeping her torso together so that I can give her last rites even though I'm not an Episcopal priest! Noooo! J.T. thought he thought. He was actually howling "No!" at the top of his lungs, obviously not mentally stable from the past week of work in the sitcom world.

The passengers waiting for their flight to Pensacola, Florida, watched J.T. as he lunged for the hollow, carpeted cylinder that helped keep the ceiling the ceiling—and also housed the white airport phones.

"Hello?! Please don't tell me this is Tasha! Is anything wrong with my wife?! My son?!"

"Is this J.T. Baker?" a nasally voice asked.

"Yes! Of course it is! Why else would I pick up th—"

"Hold for your party, please."

"Party? My wife could be dead and you're making party referen—"

"Dick Beaglebum's office, *please* hold," an emotionally disconnected voice demanded sternly.

J.T. might as well have been slapped in the face by the wet, arctic-cold tail of a walrus.

"Huh?" J.T. appropriately mumbled. *Dick? Why here? Why now? Oh crap,* he thought, and began to pace, continuing to mumble to himself.

A few of the tense passengers waiting to go to Pensacola, Florida, began to come to the conclusion that J.T. wasn't a hijacker-to-be who had lost his nerve but just another nutcase in L.A.

"Mommy, is that man crazy?" a little girl asked her concerned mother.

"He could be, Amy, so just stay by Mommy," J.T. overheard as he tried to gather himself and focus.

"Y'hello?" J.T. tried to cover his worst fears. *What are my worst fears?* he thought. *Didn't I just have them? Why do I have to have them again?*

"J.T. Baker?" a female voice asked.

"Yes. Yes! YES!"

"Please hold for Dick Beaglebum."

Dick Beaglebum, J.T. thought. Now, every showbiz scenario about being cut in half crossed J.T.'s mind, except for the one that was about to take place.

"You fucking bastard!" Dick said, still managing enthusiasm.

"Beaglebum," J.T. said, "let me see if I understand what just happened. I was paged at an airport, I picked up the phone, was asked to hold so that my agent could call me a fucking bastard? Phone calls don't work that way outside of Hollywood, Dick. I'm in Inglewood. 'Ingle,' not 'Holly.' I'm not in *your* world now. I'M LEAVING. On a jet plane. Going far, far away."

"You fuck. You snitch. You betrayed me!" Dick Beaglebum was in a fury.

"I beg your pardon?" J.T. looked out the huge airport picture window, watching the ballet of jets coming and going, passing one another on different strata. *If I ever shoot airplanes flying from left to right of frame simultaneously, I've got to remember to do it on at least a two-hundred-millimeter lens,* J.T. thought.

"A two-hundred-millimeter lens? You rat-pig! I wouldn't fuck your mother with a two-hundred-millimeter lens!"

"Whoa . . . Dick, um—"

"You fucking did the absolute worst thing you could've ever done. You went to the Directors Guild! You snitched! ON ME!"

"Now, um, hold on there. Aside from Deb at the network advising me to go to the DGA, Dick, your very own—what is it, brother-in-law?—came up to me at David's bar mitzvah and asked why he had heard I wasn't directing the next two episodes," J.T. said honestly.

"Yeah! And you fucking *told him the truth*! You snitched! By the way, what did you think of the bar mitzvah? I woulda asked you then, but it was a fuckin' bar mitzvah for fuck's sake! So what did you think of the bar mitzvah? Stellar production, huh?"

J.T. watched a young boy draw airplanes, reminding him so much of his son. *Why am I talking to this fool? I've got to get home to my family,* he thought.

"Well, Dick, to be quite honest, the bar mitzvah was garish and embarrassing. And, on top of that, you turned a religious ceremony into a moneymaking proposition. Only *you*," he couldn't resist adding.

"I knew you would be ungrateful. I comped you for nothing, you snitch!"

"Will you stop calling me a snitch? Shit, you're the one who told me to get a lawyer," J.T. began to defend himself and take the phone call seriously.

"That's right. And do you know why? Because I knew after a few weeks you would give up on the whole thing because the studio and the network can beat a guy like you in a lawsuit. I've seen those wars of attrition, and believe me, they were made for schmucks like you. You would've crumbled under the paperwork and bills. But no! You had to go to Daddy. You had to go to the Directors Guild of America!"

J.T. looked at the little girl who was holding her mother tight as they waited to go to Pensacola. "Mommy? Is that man going to blow up the airplane, Mommy?"

J.T. tried to shake his head no and calm the child, but first he had to wipe the froth from his mouth. He decided to just deal with Beaglebum. His voice lowered and got gravelly, like a cross between Mercedes McCambridge in *The Exorcist* and Harvey Fierstein in *Hairspray*. "Okay—so what? *You* made a deal for me that was for three episodes, pay-or-play. I found out from your brother-in-law that you *knew* the rules and still, as *my* representative, told me I should negotiate. That's . . . that's *immoral*, Dick! *Grrrrr!*"

The Pensacola-bound little girl screamed. J.T. tried to shake his head, mouthing, *It's okay, it's okay,* but the mother pulled her child away and said, "You ought to be ashamed of yourself!"

I should, J.T. thought. *I am. How did I end up feeling such shame?*

"That's showbiz," Dick fumed. "Grow up. But it's personal now, J.T. You fucked me. ME! So now you'll never get your money for the other two pay-or-play episodes. Never. Do you hear me? You will never get your fucking money!"

"Well, that's not what Ron Copper told me," J.T. said defensively.

"Ron Copper? My brother-in-law, Ron Copper?"

"Yup! *That* Ron Copper!"

"Let me spell it out for you, J.T. According to the deal memo *I now happen to have,* you were supposed to work *one week and one week only*. You will be paid for one week and one week only."

"Dick! You fucking dick!" J.T. blurted. "Beaglebum, that's a bald-faced lie! How can you do that to me? I'm your *client*."

"Not anymore, you fuck."

"Dick, why are you being such an asshole? Is it because you know I'm at the airport and want to get home so badly I wouldn't take the time to come to your office and—"

"Fuck fuck fuck you! You really fucked this one up, J.T. I coulda got you one and a half episodes of pay. But *noooooo*—you wanted *pay-or-play* for all three episodes. Well, like I said, this deal memo *now* reads you were only set to direct *one fucking episode*. You had to make it personal. You had to be a snitch, didn't ya?"

"Dick, I wasn't a *snitch*. I was *honest*. And this isn't the playground. This is my life!"

"Whatever! You fucking betrayed *me*! Betrayed! You fucking turncoat! You Eggs Benedict Arnold! You Jewy Judah!" Dick screamed, enthusiastically.

"I did what was right. How can you and the Pooleys and the studio and the network suddenly be the victims here? I was the one who got *fucked*."

Dick Beaglebum's voice was distorting out of the receiver. "You think you got fucked? Not only are you *not* getting your money, but let's see how many times the production company can lose the check for your one episode. This oughta be fun."

"With all the money you make, Dick, with all of the success you have, how can you be taking so much petty pleasure in screwing me out of my paychecks? My DGA minimum? My *insurance*. The insurance *you know I need*?"

"What have I been saying all this time? BECAUSE IT'S PERSONAL! We all knew that negotiating with you was against your DGA contract. Everyone knew *but you*, you dumb fuck. You were more interested in the fucking *camera angles* and some *retard actor* than knowing the ropes of the business. By turning us in, you could've really fucked up a lot of people's careers. Mine included. ME! So good luck with your life in Bum-fuck Wherever, and never call me again. I'm making a special mark on my calendar to call you every three weeks to piss all over you! Every three weeks to remind you you're not getting a fucking penny! Every three weeks just to make sure your piddly little check got lost again! And again! *I win. You lose,* you schmuck."

And Dick hung up, leaving J.T. with the warm sickness of an iodine flush.

Another Phone Call

When J.T. finally arrived home, he was greeted by a family three-way hug that lasted a lot longer than the usual three-way hugs because no one wanted to let go. Tasha whispered the same question she always asked J.T., the one she'd asked the day they married: "So, you love me or what?" The same words in the same order, over two decades old, yet the delivery was never stale, and the intent always honest and loving. By now Jeremy knew the husband-wife script so he answered back in sync with his dad, "If you were a vegetable, I'd become a vegetarian."

About three weeks passed and the weather in the Smoky Mountains became fickle. One day snow and a wicked wind; then a day of fog, followed by a taunting day of almost springlike headiness; then snow again, settling in for good.

Jeremy loved the snow. Snow meant snow days, which meant no school. Whenever a public school bus couldn't get to every single stop on its route, school was called off, and Jeremy was ecstatic. They never had anything like that in New York when J.T. was a kid.

J.T. took lots of walks with Tasha and talked about . . . anything and everything. J.T. was mesmerized by Tasha's startling silver-gray hair; he wondered why he hadn't noticed it as much before he went to L.A.

"Gray is the new blonde," Tasha said proudly, happy to just be the woman she was. Definitely not Hollywood material.

Sometimes the discussion would veer toward the sitcom work. J.T. had been afraid to tell Tasha what a fool he was for adding the "... *in a dream*" lines in the script, but of course he had. He never kept anything from Tasha. "I've left myself open to scrutiny," he told her, hashing over the same ground yet again as they took a walk in the snow. "I'm supposed to be on higher ground. Now I'm a few feet below sea level."

"Look, J.T.," Tasha said, her breath fogging as she spoke, "you fixed their show. You shot a show that was unshootable. Stop beating yourself up."

"I committed the cardinal sin: I fucked with the words. It's not my job to ever fuck with the words. I was just trying to take care of—"

"Darling, it's your job to take care of you. Take care of us. Stop whining about how it's your job to take care of those frigging, spoiled strangers."

She walked ahead and soon disappeared in the darkness of white.

J.T HAD FIXED, by himself, the tractor-thingamajiggy with a drink holder. Actually, he now knew that it was a seven-year-old used L3400 gear-driven Kubota tractor with 37.5 PTO (power takeoff) horsepower that made for a good clean cut with his old Bush Hog mower. (*I hate dilettantes! From now on, I'm doin' this right. Oh man, I do love this ol' tractor. I think I'll try and paint it a shiny orange. Maybe red. No, blue!*)

Here they were in their own paradise, yet that phone call lingered. Beaglebum's words—*I win. You lose*—kept J.T. from taking a step back and realizing he wasn't on a snow set in Burbank with a fake family. He was still toxic. He knew he'd be that way until the money came. If the money came.

While J.T. was in L.A., Jeremy had bonded with the new calf. He'd named her Fugeddaboudit. (When it came to farming, Jeremy had inherited his father's city genes.) Fugeddaboudit wouldn't take milk from her mother, so Tasha had to go out in every kind of weather to milk Lola so her udders wouldn't get infected. Natasha would refrigerate the excess milk and Jeremy would take a giant baby bottle and feed little Fug. They became fast friends. So much so that little Fug would go on walks with Jeremy, as if she were a pet dog.

Every single day, three times a day, J.T. turned up his collar and headed out to the mailbox, hoping, praying that the check Ron Copper had promised him (all three episodes of his pay-or-play deal) would be in there. The irony of being so far away physically yet so close to the business wasn't lost on J.T. as his boots crunched and compressed the wet snow. *One time,* he thought on every trip, *one time, couldn't the showbiz gods look down upon me and grant me this one wish?*

The Hollywood Dictionary

GRANT ME ONE WISH: An old Hollywood joke with many variations. The variation J.T. would tell goes something like this:

A genie comes out of a bottle. A TV director looks at the genie and asks, "Can you grant me a wish?"

The genie says, "Only one, because I'm a real genie and you Hollywood types have ruined everything telling the world that I can grant three wishes. Only one!"

"Okay, my one wish is that there be peace in the Middle East. Here's a map."

"Forget it," the genie, says. "I've been trying to grant that wish for over five thousand years. Gimme something I can handle."

"Well," asked the TV director, "how about a funny sitcom?"

The genie looked at the director and then said, "Gimme back the map."

Jeremy's doctors were becoming more and more certain about how soon Jeremy would need a kidney transplant. *Please,* he begged—to whom, he didn't know or care—*please let there be a check in there for all three episodes.*

On the second of what would turn out to be four snow days in a row, J.T. trudged out to the mailbox once again, past the barn where Jeremy was feeding Fugeddaboudit. This time there was a stiff white postcard with maroon lettering sitting on top of the junk mail. It was addressed to T.J. Berker. J.T. turned it over. His cold lips didn't work that well when he was reading the postcard out loud to himself: "'It is our pleasure to inform you that your household has been chosen to be a Nielsen Family for a one-week survey!' You've got to be shittin' me."

"What?" Tasha yelled back. She was in the barn with Jeremy, holding Fug's head while he fed the calf.

"We're a Nielsen Family," J.T. called out, looking at his *new name* on the postcard.

"What?" Jeremy hollered. "We can't hear you, Dad!"

"J.T.? Are you okay?" Tasha tried to ask.

"We're a Nielsen—oh, never mind."

Underneath the junk mail and a small stack of bills was an envelope—an envelope from the *I Love My Urban Buddies* production office.

J.T. began to sweat, even in the twenty-degree cold, with "winds whipping out of the west with velocities of up to sixty miles an hour," according to the weather report that morning. J.T. took the check in his bare, chapped hands. Before he opened it, he looked toward the warm barn where Jeremy and Natasha were caring for the beasts. He turned his back to them and sheltered himself from the wind and from the world. He opened the envelope.

It was . . . there. It was *all* there! All three weeks' worth. A miracle. "Thank you!" he yelled. Ron Copper had come through. J.T. had never, ever, been on the good side of an ugly equation. *What luck. What a gift.* Tears froze on his cheeks. He knew what he had to do next. Immediately. Without waiting a beat.

"Who wants to go to Pappy's?!!" J.T. yelled, trying to raise his voice above the decibels of the wind laughing through the trees.

A blizzard was threatening, but they drove to Pappy's, Jeremy's favorite barbecue joint. He couldn't eat much on the menu, but he loved it there.

"Hey, Dad?"

"Hey, Jeremy?"

"Are we going to Pappy's 'cause it's next to the Bank of America?"

"Will you be my business partner, Jeremy? Because the answer is, yup!"

"That's really cool," Jeremy said.

The Bakers made a quick stop at the Bank of America, where J.T. had friends in high places who cleared the check on the spot. Then they went to Pappy's and celebrated. All was good in the world. No matter what the cost of hell was at the time, J.T. knew it was a pittance compared to the reward.

FULL AND CONTENT, the Bakers made it back from Pappy's just before the storm worsened. J.T. had just started a fire when the phone rang. Against all of his natural instincts, he actually answered it.

"Y'hello?" J.T. said.

"J.T. Baker?" a nasty, familiar, dispassionate voice asked.

"Yes."

"Hold for Dick Beaglebum."

Dick Beaglebum calling, J.T. thought, and pulled the bank deposit from his pocket and stared at it. *This isn't a prop, is it?*

"You fucking bastard!" Dick said, still managing enthusiasm.

J.T. mentally counted the weeks since he'd left L.A. Three. The fucker hadn't been joking.

"Hey, you fuck snitch bastard," Beaglebum laughed. "I just saw the weather report and it looks like you're freezin' your titties off in Deliveranceland. Got enough money to pay the oil bill?"

"We use propane, Dick," J.T. heard himself say. *Why is this guy calling me? He must have better things to do. There's always an agenda with Beaglebum.*

"Just saw the blizzard conditions on CNN as I was enjoying the sun here, and speaking of sons—how's yours?"

"Why are you doing this, Dick?"

"Fun. Just for fun," Beaglebum said. "I wasn't having enough of it today, so I thought I'd call J.T. Snitcharooni-to-the DGA-palooza and have some good ol'-fashioned funny-fun-fun. I have it on my fucking calendar to call you every three weeks and see how many times you've gone to your country fart-house mail-box and found no checkaroonies from the Buddy-palookas!" he snorted. "Guess they lost your check again! Could it be?! Ha! I'm lovin' this! You'll never get your money. Never. Do you hear me? You will never get your fucking money!"

J.T. suddenly was awash with calm. He couldn't believe it. He had beaten Dick Beaglebum to the punch. How great was it that the Hollyweirdos were posturing, yet the little guys were doing their work and cutting J.T.'s check on time!

"Wow, Dick, you're killing me." J.T. tried not to betray his grin with his voice. "I mean, ouch." Then, staring at the deposit slip, he faltered, starting to doubt the system. *Could a deposit slip not really be a deposit slip? Is there a dual universe where at this precise mo-ment in time I'm not actually getting paid?* he thought.

"Nope. Only one universe, and you ain't EVER getting paid if I have anything to do with it, you fuck!" And with that, Beaglebum ended the conversation. No matter how far technology has come, the insult of a sudden dial tone has yet to be improved upon.

There was a bucolic, ever-changing masterpiece right outside his living room window; his loving wife was typing a letter to the editor of the local paper (something about the pesticides used on all of the Christmas tree farms in the area and the runoff into the streams that fed the well waters); and his sick little boy was feeling well for the moment and working the fire in the fireplace. But J.T.'s head was right back in the cave. *Fuck,* he thought.

For about a minute, J.T. was too stunned to do anything. Should he make sure the check cleared again? Nah, he had his money. The check *had* cleared. Was it a dream? Was it a dream sequence? How could the check clear and Beaglebum not even know he'd been paid in full? How could J.T. suddenly feel so filthy again? Finally, common sense told him to go to his address book and look up the number for the Directors Guild of America and call Ron Copper, the man who despised and vowed to go after Dick Beaglebum and his illicit ways. After hearing Dick's joyful, four-lettered rant, J.T. felt a moral obligation to call and thank Ron Copper for coming through for his *family.*

When he went to dial the number, J.T. suddenly felt numb. Flashbacks. All the old symptoms were returning in full force. *Why?* he thought. The more he thought, the more he began to tremble. He forced himself to dial.

"Directors Guild of America. How can I *direct* your call?" The young receptionist chortled at his own play on words.

"Yes ... Please ... I'm trying to reach Ron Copper. Ron C-O-P-P-E-R," J.T. spelled it out, thinking nothing should be left to chance any longer.

J.T. was put on hold only for a moment before the obnoxious voice returned. "I'm sorry. Ron C-O-P-P-E-R does not work here anymore."

Only in Los Angeles would someone make fun of someone else so quickly and brazenly, J.T. thought. "Yeah?" he said, trying to control his temper. "He doesn't work there?"

"Oh, I see we have a clear connection!" the young man sneered.

Am I talking to Lily Tomlin? "Can you tell me if he left a forwarding number? A referral number? A way to get in touch with him?"

Tasha looked up from her typing. Her intention had been to let this moment of fear and paranoia pass because she knew the check had cleared. But from the tone of J.T.'s voice, she could tell the check no longer mattered. She got up and went to stand by his side.

"Yes, a referral number, please," J.T. asked again.

"A referral number *is* a way to get in touch with him. You are being redundant."

"Why do I have the feeling that if I were standing directly in front of you, you wouldn't be such an asshole?" J.T. had to say. He *had* to. *What is* wrong *with these people?*

"Why don't you try it?" Mr. Obnoxious responded.

"I'm calling from a cell phone and I am just outside the building. Unless you give me Ron Copper's new number, I will come into the building, find you, and make it impossible for you to ever physically answer a phone again."

"Jeez," the voice changed, "no need to get all huffy. Ron Copper's new number is 818–555–0148. Happy?"

"No," J.T. said, "I'm coming in after you anyway, you little shit," and hung up the phone. *Maybe, just maybe, that little arrogant ass will be nice to the next caller.*

"Good one, Dad," Jeremy said.

"You weren't supposed to hear that . . ." J.T. mumbled.

"I'm *in the room,* Dad."

Natasha patted J.T.'s arm. "I'm here, sweetheart. Do your thing. But I'm here."

"No. No, I'm okay. We're okay, I mean. Let me just find out some information . . . I can do this. Don't worry, Tasha."

"Worry? Me worry?"

J.T. stared at the number as he was dialing it. He wondered why it looked so damn familiar to him. "Hello?" he said as soon as he heard someone pick up at the other end.

"*I Love My Urban Buddies* production office," a female Thing answered.

J.T. found himself sitting down. On the floor. He knew he had been standing but didn't know how he actually ended up on the floor.

"Hello? Hello?" Thing Umpteen was about to hang up.

" . . . Yes . . . I'd like to speak with Ron Copper, please," J.T. almost whispered.

"Ron Copper. Who should I say is calling?" Thing Umpteen asked.

"Um, tell him it's . . . Tell him it's *Dick Beaglebum*. Dick Beaglebum is calling."

The next thing J.T. heard was the theme song to *I Love My Urban Buddies* playing as hold music.

"Yeah, hello—?! Hello? Whattya want now, Dick, you chazzer?"

"Ron? Ron Copper, formerly a member in good standing with the Directors Guild of America?"

"Who the fuck is this? This isn't—? Beaglebum, this isn't you, is it?"

"Ron . . . This is J.T. Baker."

Silence. Actually, J.T. could hear Marcus Pooley screaming at some poor Schmuck-Thing in the background. Finally J.T. heard Ron clear his throat.

"J.T., bubbalah. I saw your director's cut. Everyone who's seen it has loved it. The next two episodes were all crap; a pure schlock-fest. The Pooleys are pissed. They're so angry that your episode looks great that they're actually trying to recut it to make it look like shit! But Lance, Deb, and the president of the network have already seen your cut. And they love it. They know you're the real thing. Can you imagine sabotaging your own show just for spite? But, zug gornisht, the network's going with your cut. You did a helluva job for us," Ron said.

"*Us*? You saw my cut? I did a helluva job for . . . *us*? Does that mean . . . *you*, Ron?"

"Look, J.T., I got this offer to quit my honorable but pays-like-shit job at the DGA and I was offered an executive producer credit and some major action on *I Love My Urban Buddies*. Come on. What happened to you was a shondah. But J.T., how 'bout a little rachmonis for your ol' pal. Really. How could I turn that down?" Ron Copper protested, a little too much. "Listen, my friend, you may have made a decision not to work out here, but don't gimme tsooris. I actually like the process and think I can do some good work."

"Oh," was all J.T. could say.

"Hang on, J.T.," Ron said. J.T. could hear him close his door. "Did you get your check?" he asked in a whisper.

"Yes. Yes, I did, Ron. I was calling the guild to thank you."

"Hey, man, you don't need to thank me. You earned it. I've heard everything that happened here; the entire spiel, and man, I'm amazed you didn't go postal and run around like wild animals at feeding time. I'm gonna make sure that doesn't happen here ever again."

> ### The Hollywood Dictionary
>
> **I DON'T SPEAK YIDDISH:** I'm a bad Jew.
> **"OH . . .":** "Are you friends with Mel Gibson?"

Ron sounded like an excited teen on his first job. "*Biz hundert un Bvantsik!*"

"Um, Ron? I don't speak Yiddish."

"Oh . . ."

"Listen, you've gotta cash that check. I mean pronto, man," Ron said in a hush.

"I did."

"That's my J.T.! See? You kick ass, my friend. And I wasn't kidding. Your director's cut looks far better than anyone could've dreamed for that god-awful week. Good going."

"Thanks."

"I gotta run. I hear screaming down the hall. Talk at ya soon, my friend."

"Ron?"

"Yeah?"

"Thank you. Thank you so damn much."

"Hey, man, it was my pleasure. As we say in Yiddish, 'You give me such nachas, knowing you and what you accomplished, I can only kvell like a peacock.' Even if you don't understand it, you get my drift. Now—go give your boy a hug for me."

And with that, Ron went toward the lunacy and J.T. went toward the sanity.

"Hey, Jeremy. Come here. Daddy needs to hug you."

Jeremy came over to J.T. and sat in his lap. J.T. hugged his son and the two stared out into the blizzard. J.T. tried to savor it, knowing Jeremy would soon become too self-conscious to cuddle with his dad. He tried even harder not to think, *If he lives that long*. Which made him try not to think about the fact that he didn't know where next year's insurance would come from after this hard-won year's worth ran out.

Natasha came over to be with her men. "J.T., are you okay?"

"You know what, honey? I don't think I have ever been better." He and Natasha kissed deeply, passionately—

"Um, Mom? Dad? Child present. Kid here." The little family looked out the window at the astounding power of the storm.

The phone rang. They let it ring. The answering machine finally picked up. "You've reached us. We'll get back to you as soon as we can. Thanks for calling. *Beep*."

"Um . . . J.T.? J.T., pick up if you're there. It's me. Dick. Dick

Beaglebum. Dicky-baby. Your agent. J.T., listen, I was out of line before. I was . . . stoned. On this new painkiller patch that I smoked instead of sticking it to my arm. It made me do and say some stupid things. I called you, didn't I? About five minutes ago? I can't remember. See? I was fucked up. Whatever I said, it was the drug talking. It wasn't me. Hey, come on. Pick up. I'm really sorry. Really. Sorry. And to show you how sorry I am, I'm going to make it up to you *big-time*! I'd talk to Oprah if she'd listen. I'd go to Betty Ford if they'd take me. Don't make me beg, big guy. You know I love you!"

Beep.

Ring.

J.T. lifted his left leg and jabbed his right fist into the air with a hockey-like victory dance.

"Dad . . . ? Should I get it?"

Natasha stared at the phone and then shifted her look toward J.T. He responded with a gentle kiss.

"Who feels like some popcorn?" Natasha asked.

"I wonder what it's like to really feel like some popcorn," Jeremy commented.

"One day I'll tell you," J.T. said.

"*J.T.- goin'-to-Carolina-in-my-mind,* the president of the network saw your cut and was so impressed with your work that he wants you back for six more episodes! He's actually demanding that you come back. Can you believe it? Not only that but the show tested through the roof! Highest numbers since the pilot! You! J.-Tee-Time-Eight-A.-M.! You did that, my main man, J.-T.-for-Two! And here's the kicker! I can get you ten grand more! Okay, twenty. See? No hard feelings on this end. I'll let you have fun at my expense? Have fun, call me names every three weeks. You can put it on your calendar: Make Fun of Beaglebum Day. It can be a showbiz holiday. So whattya say? J.T.? Pick up. Come on. Please. I know you're there. What am I gonna tell these guys? This is the

president of the fucking network for crap's sakes. He likes your episode better than the pilot episode! Remember the dead guy? You
did better than him, too. The pilot director, the dead guy, wow,
J.T.—you're *the man*! Come on, J.T., pick up the phone! What do
I have to do, beg? I won't beg. All right, I'll beg. I'm begging you!
Okay, twenty-five grand more. J.T., the Pooleys are sending you an
apology basket of lemon muffins from Mrs. Field's Bakery—shit,
I mean Mrs. Beasley's! Beasley's Bakery. And they know you love
chocolate. They're sending Godiva! J.T., do you realize what shit
we're all in if—J.T., the Pooleys are very sorry. Everyone's going to
conference-call you in a minute to say—"

J.T. stared at the phone the way a recovering addict eyes
heroin.

"Should I get it, Dad?" Jeremy asked again.

"Dad . . . ?"